WOODWORKING

LONGLISTED FOR THE CENTER FOR FICTION FIRST NOVEL PRIZE 2025

Named A Best Book of 2025 by *Vox, Elle*, NPR, *Bustle, Marie Claire*, Chicago Review of Books, Chicago Public Library, Brooklyn Public Library, *Them*, Xtra, and Autostraddle • Matty Maggiacomo's March Book Club Pick

"A charming, sparkling, and very human novel that packs a heavy punch . . . This book is a hoot and a ride." —*Vox*
(A Best Book of the Year)

"Writing a funny book is hard. Writing a convincing takedown of one of America's most popular prejudices is harder still. Writing a funny novel in which complex, imperfect characters make a compelling case for one of our culture's most maligned groups—that takes smarts *and* heart. Fortunately for her readers, St. James is in full possession of both." —Meredith Maran, *Washington Post*

"I flew through *Woodworking*, cheering for Abigail and Erica and their against-the-odds friendship all the way. Only Emily St. James could write a book so big-hearted and hilarious, an ode to authenticity and a must-read in our current times." —Shelby Van Pelt, *New York Times* bestselling author of *Remarkably Bright Creatures*

"A stunning, heartbreaking, hopeful book . . . It speaks to the challenges and gifts of visibility and the importance of community, no matter what that looks like." —Chicago Review of Books
(A Best Book of the Year)

"*Woodworking* doesn't offer easy lessons. Ugliness and hate rub shoulders with glimpses of freedom, growth, and transformation. Like St. James, I believe in the magic of television, films, and books to transform hearts, and I hope that for readers, her authentic, though fictional, stories might create a little space to counter the lies of those currently in power." —*LA Review of Books*

"St. James deserves a spot on the Mount Rushmore of transfeminine authors of our current moment." —Xtra
(A Best Book of the Year)

"Pristinely characterized, this debut novel is by turns funny and heartrending." —*Kirkus*
(starred review)

"A testament to the power of intergenerational trans stories . . . dazzling." —*VOGUE*

"One of the most heartfelt, funny, and moving portraits of transition I've ever come across." —Imogen Binnie,
author of *Nevada*

"Delightfully rendered . . . full of friendship, romance and chosen family." —NPR

"St. James enthralls with her depiction of what it's like to be trans in a conservative and insular community, and the courage it takes for people to openly be themselves. This engrossing drama is a must-read." —*Publishers Weekly*
(starred review)

"In *Woodworking*, St. James demolishes the simplistic closet concept, revealing lives that are marked by many transitions, and that pass through any number of gradations within the continuum of showing up, hiding, slipping under the radar, or openly demanding respect." —*The Atlantic*

"A wonder of unexpected characters in complex relationships in a more-than-meets-the-eye small town in an unusual coming-of-age story . . . St. James's debut is complicated in the best ways and straightforward in the best ways too, empowering, important, and even heartwarming in its insistence on that which is true for all of us, in spite as well as because of our differences."

—Laurie Frankel,
New York Times bestselling author of *This Is How It Always Is*

"The trans-and-life- affirming story readers need."

—*Booklist*
(starred review)

"Emily St. James is one of our most cherished writers whose work carries the kind of compassion, humanity, and braver world-building we need now more than ever."

—Amber Tamblyn,
author of *Listening in the Dark: Women Reclaiming the Power of Intuition*

"With propulsive wit and unshakeable honesty, St. James debuts a novel unquestionably deserving of its place in the transfeminine literary canon."

—PEN America

"One of the funniest and most humane novels of the year . . . St. James integrates questions of identity, red-state politics, school culture, romance, and belonging with heart and heft."

—*Columbia Tribune*

"A moving and big-hearted novel about people finding community as they find themselves . . . This is a tender, funny, page-turning story about trans women finding their way, in a world that needs all the softness and humor it can get."

—Lydia Kiesling,
bestselling author of *Mobility*

"Delightful and sharply told . . . a literary debut that deserves to reach as wide an audience as possible." —*Paste* magazine

"A new milestone in trans letters, *Woodworking* proves Emily St. James can craft stories just as brilliant as the ones she has written so beautifully about for over a decade. Sparkling, intimate, and life-affirming, this debut novel lands with all the quiet force of a secret spoken in a parked car. Not to be missed."

—Samantha Allen,
author of *Real Queer America* and *Patricia Wants to Cuddle*

"With undeniable wit and a wealth of empathy, St. James tells a story about not only finding oneself, but what comes next."

—*Electric Lit*

"Heartfelt and winning." —Autostraddle
(A Best Book of the Year)

"Emily's prose is masterfully mimetic and deeply grounded . . . *Woodworking* has a big heart, and an incredibly important point to make." —*The Transfeminine Review*

"This story of a trans woman coming out in small town South Dakota in 2016 isn't just earnest and moving, but surprisingly funny and joyful—all without pulling any punches about the struggle to be yourself in a world that may not want you to be."

—Crooked Media Reads

WOODWORKING

Emily St. James

Crooked Media Reads
A zando IMPRINT

Crooked
Media
Reads

Crooked Media Reads is an imprint of Zando.
zandoprojects.com

Originally published in hardcover by Crooked Media Reads, March 2025
First trade paperback edition: May 2026

Design by Neuwirth & Associates, Inc.
Cover design by Grace Han

Library of Congress Control Number: 2024946679

978-1-63893-147-8 (Hardcover)
978-1-63893-417-2 (Paperback)
978-1-63893-148-5 (ebook)

10 9 8 7 6 5 4 3 2 1
Printed in Canada
MARL

FOR ROBERTA

Whatever she might become

she would never be static.

—*Main Street*, Sinclair Lewis

September

Erica

Monday,

September 12

Erica didn't know any other trans women. So when she learned Abigail Hawkes had called everyone in her current events class "a bunch of fascist cunts," Erica switched detention duty slots with Hank DeWaard to be able to talk to Abigail one-on-one.

"Whatever, ████," Hank said. Since she had chosen the name Erica for herself in a frenzy on a baby-name website, Erica's old name had come to sound like it was enveloped in fog. It was very far away from her now, somewhere out at sea. Hank dumped three packets of salt into his steaming Lean Cuisine. "Go ahead! Take all my slots as far as I'm concerned."

"I wouldn't go that far!" Erica laughed collegially, trying to seem like she was the kind of man Hank could clap on the back and call "a real good guy" while they were out having a drink after work. Hank would never see her hiding in plain sight. In a town like Mitchell, South Dakota, she had to disappear before she was spotted.

Erica realized she had been laughing a second too long, at something that wasn't even funny at all, something *she* had said, no less. She had the uneasy feeling lately that she was watching herself on a thirty-second delay. Everything moved so much more slowly now that she was aware she was trying to escape herself.

She had lost so much time already.

She managed to stop laughing. Hank ran a plastic fork through his beige tortellini, eyebrow raised in amusement. "This stuff tastes like crap, but the wife makes me eat it. Do you want some of it? All of it?" Hank's face tilted toward concern. "Oh, buddy, are you okay?"

Erica had lost track of her facial expressions. She replayed the last few seconds and found she was staring into the middle distance, an empty expression in her eyes. If she didn't fix this immediately, she was sure Hank would realize the truth. He would say, "You're looking awfully weird there, bud. Wait. Abigail Hawkes has detention today. Do you want to talk to Abigail Hawkes? Are you . . . a transgender . . . like Abigail Hawkes?" As soon as Erica had become incredibly, constantly aware of her own gender, she had also become convinced everybody around her had a full CSI team dedicated solely to figuring out what was up with Erica's gender. So dedicated was she to keeping anyone from examining her too closely that she missed everything else she was feeling. Her emotions were occurring in another room somewhere.

Hank's hand was now on Erica's shoulder. When had he stood up? "Hey, buddy, it's okay. You want to pray about it?" Erica only realized she was crying after Hank pulled her into a hug and her tears stained the shoulder of his shirt. "God sees your pain, ████. He knows how hard it is to wake up alone every morning."

Right. Hank thought Erica's crying jag was all about the divorce. Well, great! She could salvage this situation yet!

"I guess I'm sadder than I thought I would be," Erica said, remembering to put a hitch in her voice in *just* the right place. "I miss Constance so much, and she's auditioning for *Our Town* tonight. I haven't seen her since we—"

"Oh, buddy," Hank said. "Feeling sad's only natural. Do you *have* to do the play?"

Erica nodded overzealously. "I promised Brooke I would."

The lounge was empty but for the two of them. Hank continued to hug her. She knew he would see this as just good, caring,

Christian male bonding, so she dutifully played the part of The Man. She was so good at playing him. "I just need to have strength. A prayer might be nice."

Hank beamed, taking Erica's hands firmly in his. She didn't even hear his prayer. She looked, instead, at her nails and wondered what they might look like painted pink.

Abigail wasn't the only student in detention that day, but she had by far the longest stint. Three girls in trouble for mocking a classmate were dismissed after a half hour, then a handful of boys in trouble for a variety of offenses at the hour mark, then someone else (Erica hardly knew who) at ninety minutes, and then there was Abigail, with a full hour left on her sentence, staring straight ahead. Abigail had transferred to Mitchell High from the nearby tiny town of Corsica a year prior, at the start of her junior year, and Erica had known Abigail was trans before she had known Abigail's name. Erica had heard via Mitchell's rumor mill that there was a sister Abigail lived with after her parents had kicked her out. Every time that same rumor mill coughed up the name Abigail had been given at birth, Erica's brain simply refused to retain the information, which should have been Erica's first clue something was up with herself.

"You can read a book or something," Erica said.

Abigail startled at the sound of Erica's voice. "Isn't that against the rules?"

Erica shrugged. "It's just us. You've got another hour, and I have papers to grade. I won't say anything."

Abigail leaned forward, and Erica briefly became terrified that trans people had a secret radar she didn't yet know about, and that Abigail *knew everything*. But she only dipped down to her bag and withdrew a copy of Howard Zinn's *A People's History of the United States*, then did her best to make reading look effortful.

Erica had often imagined what she might say if she ever talked to another trans woman. She always assumed she would be personable, smooth. She would find a way to be, like, "Hey, we're all trans here, right?!" then laugh blithely. Instead, she abruptly realized how little Abigail probably wanted her own teacher—her fucking *teacher*—telling her that, actually, she wasn't *Mr.* Skyberg at all but was, instead—

Abigail cleared her throat and turned a page, furrowing her brow with great intensity. She wore, as always, the too-big army jacket that followed her like a ghost, and both of her shoes were untied. Her shoulder-length hair was dyed shock-white blonde, and her T-shirt advertised some band Erica had never heard of. Abigail looked to Erica like a series of conscious choices designed to irritate and confuse specific demographics, rather than a person with a coherent center. Erica decided she loved this about her.

"So I was thinking . . . ," Erica said. Abigail looked up, and Erica regretted saying anything at all.

Abigail folded the corner of the page she was reading, deliberately, as if the act required ten to fifteen separate motions. She leaned forward into Erica's long silence. "You were thinking . . . ?"

"Forget it."

"No, go ahead. Ask. You're in a classroom with a political dissident. What else is there to do except ask her embarrassing fucking questions?"

"But I don't want to ask you—"

"Yes, you do! Everyone does! Pervert."

"No! I— No!" Erica's breath caught in her throat, and she stared down at her polish-less hands. They grew watery as her vision blurred, and she found herself imagining them as empty fuel gauges. She had run out of *man* to expend, and now she needed to refuel with something that would burn cleaner. She chased the metaphor around in circles, growing ever tearier, when she looked up at Abigail and saw the girl staring at her, clearly trying to figure out what Erica wanted from her. Erica winced, every thought in her head suddenly flapping away at once. "Okay. I have one question. What do I do now?"

"Huh?" Abigail said. "I don't fucking care, do whatever you want. God."

"No, what do I do . . . now that I *know*?"

Something thawed inside Abigail's expression. Erica could *feel* her realize the link between them. "Oh," she said, and then, her voice filled with a seventeen-year-old's approximation of compassion, "*Oh*."

The five-minute timer on Erica's phone had gone off three times already and was headed for a fourth when Abigail finally slouched out of the Super Walmart's sliding doors. She hovered in the glow of the store's front doors for a few moments, before disappearing into the gloom of the parking lot as she made her way to the farthest corner, where Erica waited in her car.

Erica blinked at the sudden incursion of light as Abigail opened the passenger door, a crooked smile spreading across her face. "So you sat here in the dark like a spy but forgot the interior lights would come on the second I opened the door?"

"Get in the car," Erica said, but Abigail was too overcome with laughter to do anything but let out great gulps of it. Erica was sure the entire world had turned its eyes toward the teenager and her teacher, who still had a mustache (oh God, why did she still have a mustache?), leaning across the center console and attempting to drag the girl inside.

Abigail plopped herself down in the car and closed the door. "Relax," she said. "Like *nobody* is here."

"People are here," Erica said, gesturing to the half-full parking lot. "*People are here*."

Abigail sighed and withdrew a tiny bottle of nail polish from her jacket pocket, depositing it in Erica's palm, along with a nickel and a handful of pennies. "It was more expensive than I thought, but this is a good brand."

Erica turned the nail polish over in her hand, imagining being the kind of person who might wear it. "Okay . . ."

"It's going to be okay." Abigail looked at her with a soft, even kind, expression. "If they haul me in for questioning, I'll tell them everything was aboveboard, and I was buying you nail polish because you're questioning your gender." Abigail smiled, then looked out the back window to where fast-food restaurants lit up the night. "Ooh, can we get Culver's?"

"What do you think this is?"

"You asked me to buy you nail polish, and I did. Also, I'm hungry."

Erica looked again at the nail polish. "Everything's Rosy," the label read, to delineate the infinitesimal differences between it and the other pink shades on the shelf. She had wanted this for as long as she had been alive, and she was just now realizing how much. Or, rather, she had been alive for thirty-five years, and she felt like she had only *existed* for about three weeks.

"Hey. Heeeeeey. Mr.—Ms.—Erica? I promise it's okay! Nobody saw me walk across the parking lot. Nobody *cares*. They think they hate us, but they don't even see us half the time."

"That's easy for you to say," Erica said, gulping back a sob.

"I guess it is," Abigail said.

"I was watching TV one day, and I thought, *That girl's dress is really cute*. I looked her up, and she was born two days before me. It was like I was seeing who I might have been. I caught myself off guard or something, because the next thing I knew, it wasn't who I might have been but who I could be. Even with my . . ." Erica gestured to her unruly lint ball of a body.

The words kept coming. She realized she had been waiting three weeks to talk about this with someone. "She was inside of me. I don't know another way to put it. And she was pissed as hell. I kept—" Erica contorted her fingers, like their commands were being overridden by an unearthly force—"I would just be driving along, or teaching a class, and I would be twitching my fingers because I could feel her in my brain. Mad at what I had done with my life. With her life." She noticed the clock with a sudden panic. "Oh my God, I need to get to auditions."

"Nobody noticed." Abigail sounded like she choked back a snort to let her most compassionate self out. "We think the rest of the world spends all its time noticing these tiny little signals we're giving off, but they don't think about this stuff. The cis are oblivious. Even I didn't notice you doing the weird spider-finger thing."

"I didn't think anybody did," Erica said automatically, almost before she realized she had said it. Lying to yourself made you very good at lying to everyone. Abigail started to speak again but Erica cut her off, concluding her shift away from herself, back into Mr. Skyberg. "Let's get you your Culver's, then take you home. I'm late as it is."

Erica agreed to let Abigail out a few blocks from the house she shared with her sister, less because Abigail was worried and more because Erica knew that if anybody saw her alone with Abigail, even in a professional context, it would create gossip. A gust of wind slammed into a "TRUMP/PENCE 2016" sign in a nearby yard, causing it to bend, then snap back. Its presence did little to allay Erica's anxiety.

"Look," Abigail said, holding up her phone so Erica could see. "I saved you in my contacts as 'Erica.' Absolutely nobody is going to think that's you. Text away."

"What if someone gets curious and tracks my phone number back to me?" Erica knew she was being paranoid, but she also knew she would lose everything if her secret were exposed. Oh fuck, she had a secret that could be exposed.

"Do you want to pick a specific rock we can leave notes for each other under? That won't be suspicious at all!" Abigail opened the passenger door, and the car flooded with light again. Erica instinctively dipped her head to hide from anyone who might be watching (almost certainly the entirety of the Central time zone). "Nobody is going to guess you're trans unless you tell them. So fucking text me, okay?"

Erica swallowed but nodded. "I'll text. If I need advice."

Abigail nodded and started to close the door. Erica felt a stabbing loneliness. For a little under two hours, she had been a person, without caveats or qualifications, without having to add up all the hashmarks in her brain to find the answers to questions. She hadn't had to perform. She had just been Erica Skyberg. And the second Abigail shut the door, the light would turn off, and Erica wasn't sure if it would ever turn on again.

"Wait!" she said.

Abigail placed a single arm atop the car and leaned down to stare inside. She sighed heavily. "Look: I'm not your friend. I know who you are, but that doesn't make me your friend."

"I didn't say it did."

"I know baby trans girls, Erica. You're going to go home and write in your fucking diary about how you made a friend today. You didn't. We're on the same team. That's all. Friends, no. Teammates, sure."

"Go, team." Erica smiled, and Abigail rolled her eyes. "Seriously, what do I do next? I have no idea."

"I'm not your *coach*, either," Abigail said. "But fine, sport. Find some other woman to bother about girl stuff because I don't think you can pull *this* off." She gestured to the chaotic assemblage that was her own outward presentation. "Oh, and put on your nail polish and see how it feels. After auditions. Wait. Are you doing one of *Brooke Daniels's* plays?"

"Yeah. Why?"

Abigail made a disgusted face. "Good luck with that, *Erica*." She swung the door closed, and the light shut off.

Erica barreled into the theater, door slamming behind her. Her armpits were drenched with sweat. Some poor old man onstage, mouth half open, hand raised to gesticulate, turned his eyes toward her. "Excuse me!" he said.

Brooke sat in the center of the front row. She turned her shoulders and neck to look at Erica. She moved jerkily, like a stop-motion figurine, some of her movements lost between frames. "Mr. Skyberg. You're late." She faced the stage again. "Very hard to hold auditions without my assistant director."

Erica squeezed past a few hopeful auditioners on her way to Brooke. "Sorry. Lost track of time."

"Can I continue?" the old man said.

Brooke waved her hand. "Why don't you start over, Paul? Since we're all here now." She looked at Erica, then shook her head before returning her attention to the stage.

Erica knew why Abigail thought working with Brooke was a bad idea. Brooke was part of one of Mitchell's most powerful families—vastly rich, incredibly Christian, deeply conservative. Yet she and Erica had worked together in the community theater for years now, and Erica didn't think she was *evil* (probably). They were friends. Maybe. At least something beyond a shared interest kept them working together.

As Paul rambled (badly), Brooke scrawled something on paper with a black Sharpie, then handed it to Erica. In large, block letters, she had written: "CONSTANCE IS PLAYING EMILY. IS THAT A PROBLEM?"

Erica gave Brooke a smile so confident that Brooke let out a skeptical laugh, cutting Paul off. Erica's eyes blurred with tears as she folded Brooke's message over once, twice, three, four times. She couldn't understand if she was crying because she would be seeing a lot of Constance or because she had missed Constance's audition and, thus, her one chance to see her that night.

When Erica left, it was nearly midnight. She and Brooke had spent almost an hour arguing over who to cast as the Stage Manager, when Erica knew Brooke would ultimately get her way and cast Lance Michaels, the large-animal vet who looked a little like Paul

Newman if you had five beers and squinted. She always got her way. Shadows of clouds scuttered across the street. It was cold for September, which meant the cold bore a hint of worse to come.

Someone was leaning against the theater's back wall, illuminated by the orange glow of a cigarette dangling from fingers, only lifting to lips after considerable pauses. Erica knew that arm. Constance stared at her.

"Oh good," she said. "It's you." She had the creamy white coat Erica had bought her on their honeymoon draped around her shoulders. "Did I get the part?" Her long, curly black hair framed electric pale skin, smudged red lipstick, and emerald-green glasses. She dropped the cigarette and crushed it beneath her heel.

"You always get the part, Constance. As you know, rehearsals are Mondays, Tuesdays, and Thursdays, so . . . see you next Monday. Looking forward to it." Erica *was* looking forward to it. She missed Constance terribly. But her smile died before it even started when she saw the expression on Constance's face, one she knew too well. "Did you want to talk about something?"

"No," Constance said, but she immediately shook her head. "Keep a secret for me? I haven't told anyone, not even John." The specter of Constance's boyfriend, all corn-fed six feet of him, stepped into the darkness between them.

"Should I know this?" Erica said.

"No," Constance said. "You're right. Bad idea."

Erica cleared her throat, then waved goodbye. As she got in her car, her eyes fell over the nail polish bottle sitting in her cup holder. What if she told Constance? What if she let her know the end of their marriage wasn't entirely Constance's fault?

When she looked up, Constance was standing just a few feet away. She sucked in her breath. "Fuck it. Do you remember that first Christmas we spent together? When your family insisted I spend the entire night watching your three-year-old second cousin? Because I exuded maternal energy? And on the way home, I said, 'I'm *never* having children,' and you said that was fine by you?"

Erica leaned against the car door, lest she fall over. Swallowing her desire to have children had been part of the bargain she made with herself to be married to Constance, cloaked in the guise of nonthreatening heterosexuality. But now . . .

"You're pregnant," Erica said. She couldn't see straight, so she looked away, her eyes finding the nail polish again. "You're pregnant."

"I'm pregnant."

Abigail

Monday,

September 19

Everybody always asks me the same three questions, so I'm going to answer those questions right now and pretend you're not fucking rude for fucking asking, even though you are.

"Abigail, how did you know you were trans?" One day, I just did. Maybe one day, you'll just know too. *Scary.*

"Abigail, how did you pick your name?" Why would I have picked a name *other* than Abigail?

"Abigail, are you having 'the surgery'?" Which one? Facial feminization surgery? Vocal feminization surgery? Breast augmentation? Something I read about on Reddit called "teeth reassignment surgery"? Or are you actually asking, "Are you going to have 'the sex change'?" like you think I'll be super validated by shoving my dick into a lawn mower?

(For what it's worth, it's called bottom surgery. See? You learned something!)

I would like the world to forget I'm trans for five seconds. I could pull it off. I look in the mirror sometimes, and I see a super-hot, super-cool teenage girl. If nobody knew I was trans, I could sleep with so many guys. Just left and right.

But everybody here knows "my secret," and they're going to know until I leave Mitchell and go to Minneapolis or Chicago or somewhere. I'll get my surgeries and change my name and never, ever tell anybody else again. I'll be like any other girl you pass on the street. You'd never know. Yeah, my hands are a little big, but do you go around measuring the hands of every woman you meet? God, I hope not. Pervert.

From the second I got to Mitchell High, all anybody knew about me was that I was trans. Somebody found the last school picture I took in boy mode, printed it out with my dead name, and taped it up on my locker in my first week. I knew then that nobody was ever going to want to be seen with me, and even now, the people who are kinda nice to me want to know everything there is to know about being trans, like I'm not just some dumb girl who read a bunch of Reddit threads and half-assed her way to a life that made sense. (Actually, if I tell them that, they'll think the internet transed me.)

That's why I'm disappearing the second I can. I read about that on Reddit too. This old bitch made this post called "A Warning," and she talked about how she grew up in Brazil but got her hands on hormones when she was sixteen (like I did!) and ran away to New York and completely fucking disappeared. Back then, in the 1980s or whenever, they called it "woodworking," because you disappear into the woodwork. And she said, "It destroys you. You can't pretend you're not who you are."

But just let me try, lady. I'll run so far and so fast that you'll never see me again. I'll be hiding in the walls, trying to be any other girl, like in that one story with the yellow wallpaper Ms. Skyberg made us all read last year.

Yes, *Ms.* Skyberg. As you can imagine, my *English teacher coming out to me* has been hugely inconvenient, given my overall mood.

A couple months before he kicked me out, my dad took me fishing because his pastor said I "lacked positive male role models." I think the idea was that I would hold a slowly suffocating fish and be like, "Okay! Manhood! I get it!"

My dad was excited when I kinda got super into fishing. We just sat there, and he wouldn't talk, and I could keep planning out how to get feminizing hormones shipped in from Bolivia. Then, sometimes, I would catch a fish, and who wouldn't feel a sense of accomplishment at that? During the four-hour drive back to Corsica (the shit-ass town I grew up in), my dad was so pleased that he let me listen to Mitski's "Townie" on endless repeat. I don't think he even noticed how often she sings, "I'm not gonna be what my daddy wants me to be." Okay, I know he didn't, because he slept most of the way.

My plan to get hormones from Bolivia worked, and when my mom found them, it was a whole thing. My dad was all, "No son of mine!" and I couldn't stop laughing, because it was all so ridiculous. He said, "You laugh one more time, and you don't have a bed to sleep in tonight, mister," so I laughed one more time because Jennifer had already said she would take me in. He stood up and cocked his fist to take a swing at me, and my mom screamed, and I said, "I'm going, I'm going," and I ran all the way to the quick stop, and I called Jennifer, and she came to get me.

Anyway, that's why I live in Mitchell with Jennifer and not where I grew up.

Right, right, the fascist-cunts thing.

The class is called "current events," so you can probably draw your own conclusions. But Mrs. King wanted to talk about the upcoming election, and who we would vote for *if we could*. It was just this endless lineup of dumbasses who were like, "Trump" or "Make America great again" or whatever, and when Megan

Osborne said, "I like Hillary," like a human bumper sticker, they laughed at her.

So I called them a bunch of fascist cunts, because I'm a lady, which means I get to say "cunt."

Mrs. King didn't like that. She said we needed to be respectful of each other's differences and that I didn't get to say that word, because I guess she didn't hear about me being a lady. (I can tell when a teacher is only calling me Abigail because the school board said they had to. Mrs. King is on that very long list.) She sent me to the principal's office. On the way out, I turned back and said, "I wouldn't vote! Neither of them give *a shit* about people like *me*!" Mrs. King added on an extra half hour of detention.

The worst thing was that when I turned back, I looked to see if Caleb Daniels was looking at me, but he was looking at everything *but* me, so that he wouldn't lock eyes with me and reveal his true feelings in front of everyone. I felt like I had to do something to overcompensate, really let him know what he was missing. What I'm saying is I got an extra half hour of detention for that piece of shit, and his mom is an *actual* fascist cunt.

If half the people in this town heard me calling Brooke Daniels a fascist cunt, they would drop me into Lake Mitchell or set me on fire or (worse) make me apologize to her. There are fifteen thousand people in this town, and, I guarantee you, they all know who Brooke Daniels is. She's involved in everything. She directs the plays and does bake sales and goes to all the football games. She's always there, front and center. Like a big zit.

I get it. She has money. Her husband owns that big farm out on the edge of town, and he lives in that big farmhouse on top of that hill, and when he and Mrs. Daniels couldn't have kids, he basically just bought some. He basically bought her the theater, too, because they were going to tear it down otherwise, so he donated a shit ton of money so the city would build a "performing arts center." Must be nice.

But she's Satan, and all up on Isaiah Rose's dick. He's this pastor, and he's also in whatever the version of Congress is that's in Pierre and not Washington. Earlier this year, he tried to make it harder for trans people to use the fucking bathroom, and even though I can't prove it, I *know* it was because I started going to school in Mitchell, and people got all upset about that, and he saw an opportunity. Good for him too, I guess.

Mrs. Daniels loves that guy. Goes to his church. Helps with his campaign. Has his fucking sign in her fucking yard.

The worst thing about her is that she's nice all the time, in that way that's a lie. When I first came to Mitchell, I was minding my own business at some pep rally, and I looked up and saw her *staring* at me. I stared right back, and she looked away. Afterward, she came up and said, "I'm Brooke Daniels. I'm Caleb's mom," and I said, "Okay?" and she looked so sad that she couldn't hand deliver my soul to Jesus Christ.

I don't think Brooke is everywhere because she wants to be seen. I think she's everywhere because she wants to see *you*. And that's basically the definition of a fascist cunt.

Anyway, because I got detention, I met Erica. She's the first other trans girl I've ever met in the flesh, and she's my teacher. Which is *great*.

Turns out Erica and Caleb are both embarrassed to be seen with me, and they both want to hang out with me all the time, so long as nobody ever finds out we've so much as breathed the same oxygen.

Erica gets more of a pass. When you figure out who you are, you want to tell everyone, and you want to tell no one, so you settle for telling the first trans person you can think of, and then you assume they're going to be your personal advisor in the mysteries of our ways. I mean Erica and I have nothing in common but this. But I guess *this* is a big fucking thing to have in common. You never know who's going to want us dead, so we've gotta look out for each other. I'd rather Erica have me than some rando on the internet.

Erica came out to me a week ago, and now she thinks we're best friends, which I don't need. She's my teacher, yeah, but also, all she ever does is talk about herself and being trans and how she's going to lose her job and how she already lost her wife and how her ex-wife is pregnant and how I shouldn't know that and how I had better not tell anyone, please, Abigail, no, don't. Then at the end of her whole whatever, she'll realize she said everything to a literal teenager and panic. And then I smile, because I'm fucking charming.

Every time we have a conversation, Erica swears it's the last time we'll ever talk, but then she'll text me an extremely basic question ("What's an informed consent clinic?" was the latest) that she could have googled if she didn't just miss me. Then she gets embarrassed about hanging out with a student again and cuts off contact for half a day or so, before she needs to know what HRT stands for or something. Maybe she's lonely.

I don't know. She's been talking for a while now. We should probably see what's up, huh?

"You must get that, right?" she says. "I've been talking your ear off about this for a week, so you *have* to get it."

I don't know what I'm supposed to get, but I probably *would* get it if I'd been paying attention. My mouth is conveniently full of fries, so I nod, then look out the windshield. We're sitting up where we can look out over Lake Mitchell and watch the water trickle over the spillway. It's pretty if you like concrete.

"You weren't listening, were you?"

"No. But was it about your ex again?"

She sighs. "I'm a burden to you. I know I'm a burden to you."

"Maybe you should talk to somebody else about this stuff? My number of failed marriages is very small. And I've only been a part of one pregnancy, but I had to claw my way out of that one."

She laughs. "I don't have friends," she says suddenly.

I almost say, "So? I don't either," but that might make her think *we* should be friends, when I've been quite clear on that point. Instead, I go with, "There's a trans support group over in Sioux

Falls. I've never gone, but they probably have some other people there who are not, you know, teenagers."

"I don't want . . ." Her voice trails off. Shit. She really thinks that if she tries hard enough, her skull will split open and the teenage-girl version of herself will step out, and I'll suddenly think she's cool. God, how annoying would that be? Teenage girls are the worst. (I'm an authority.)

"I'll go with you," I say, because I'll find a way to get out of it.

A list of facts about Caleb Daniels, who I have sex with sometimes:

- He's very hot. These are his best features: his eyes, his laugh, the way he chews on his lip, the way he'll lock eyes with you when you've almost given up on him remembering you're there, that little divot in his back that looks like you should be able to put a quarter in it, the way that his body seems to exist for the perfect amount of space and then just *stops*.
- He's adopted from China, a thing he calls a "miracle" in a tone of voice that makes me think he has concerns he's not sharing. His parents adopted him from some orphanage. This is probably a good thing for him, because if Mr. and Mrs. Daniels could have had babies, they would have given birth to a bunch of unblinking hawks, and, as mentioned, Caleb is really fucking hot.
- When he cums, he turns his face away. There's a picture of him and some blonde girl at prom sitting on his dresser, and I think he would tell you he's looking at that, but I would tell you, more accurately, that he's just not looking at me.
- After we're done, he usually cries and talks about how he's an awful person, and I have to say he's not awful, even though I'm feeling terrible myself. Then he looks at me and says, "I'm not gay." One time I said, "Fellas, is it

gay to like girls?" but he didn't entirely take it in stride. I should have stopped hooking up with him after that, but he's really fucking hot.

- I would tell you how we met, but that's the kind of thing a girlfriend tells you about her boyfriend, and Caleb Daniels has made it very clear that he doesn't see me as girlfriend material. In the end, Caleb Daniels can only ever see my penis.

Those are some facts about Caleb Daniels, who I have sex with sometimes.

There was one good time. Almost.

In July, Caleb's parents went out of town, and his sister was away at camp. He texted to ask if I wanted to hang out, so I told Jennifer I was going off to have sex with a boy. She laughed and told me to have fun. (If she really thought I was going off to have sex with a boy, she probably would have said something serious. She's a very good legal guardian; she just doesn't entirely understand that boys do sometimes find me attractive. I want to be clear on this point.)

I put on a dress for him, something I never do. It had this flowy skirt and a cinched waist, and it was covered in sunflowers. When he saw me, he smiled, and I realized how bad he had it for me. We got pizza and watched a movie. He didn't look *at* me when he came, but he kind of looked *near* me, which I counted as a win. And he let me sleep next to him.

I woke up in the middle of the night to pee. I tugged on the shirt he had been wearing, because it smelled like him, and I went to use his parents' bathroom, because why not. They have a big walk-in shower, and Mrs. Daniels has a whole lineup of skin-care products. I looked at myself in the enormous mirror for a long time, and I thought about this dream I had when I was a little kid, where I would be looking in the mirror, and I'd see a girl there, and then she would fade away, and I would be a person without a reflection. I don't think that can actually happen, but I thought it might that night.

I didn't want to go back to sleep, so I got my phone and headphones, and I put on Mitski's "My Body's Made of Crushed Little Stars," and I explored the house, all three stories of it. Right above the grand piano in the living room, they had hung a big family portrait, and I could feel Mrs. Daniels *watching* me again from it, so I flipped her off.

I walked over to the big picture window and opened the curtains to look down the big, grassy hill their farmhouse sits at the top of and imagined I was the kind of girl no one would be surprised to see standing there. It felt like I could see everything and everyone, just like Mrs. Daniels.

Then Caleb found me. He put his arms around my waist from behind. For a couple seconds, I imagined it was because he wanted to kiss my neck, but he was just trying to drag me back to the bedroom where he could hide me more efficiently.

Like, Caleb, you live in the middle of the fucking country. Who's going to see me? The dog?

Wednesday morning at school, there's a little basket of cookies in my locker. Chocolate chip. That's my favorite, though if you're going to take a stab at picking somebody's favorite cookie, chocolate chip is a good guess.

I think it's a prank, but when I turn around, Megan Osborne is standing there, grinning. She seems pleased with herself. "Your sister told me you like chocolate chip." I take a bite. The cookie has salt on top, a really cool idea. Megan grins even more. "I got the recipe from the *New York Times*. They say it's the best chocolate chip recipe ever."

"Why'd you make me cookies?" I say, mouth full.

"Because last week you helped me in current events class! We liberals have to stick together!" She sticks her fist out for a fist bump. The look on my face makes her hand shrink back. "Well. I hope you like them." She just sort of peters out, which is a reaction I'm used to. When she turns to go, I'm surprised to find I wish she wouldn't.

I suppose you got there ahead of me. For whatever reason, Megan Osborne is trying to be my friend. Megan's not super popular, but people seem to like her okay, and people *don't* seem to like me okay, so it doesn't make a lot of sense for her to be friends with me. Her loss, I guess.

"These cookies are really good," I say. She turns back around and smiles.

Anyway, we're going to hang out tomorrow after school.

It just goes to show: If you want to make more people like you, call everybody in your class a bunch of fascist cunts.

Erica

Thursday,

September 22

For the whole week after she learned of Constance's pregnancy, Erica kept asking herself: Why now?

Constance had never wanted children. Though Erica thought she could someday possibly (maybe) want children, thought she could hack being a dad (even with manhood feeling so alien), she was happy to live within their childless reality so long as it kept Constance nearby, a signal to the rest of the world that Erica was a normal, married, heterosexual man. Nothing to see here, gender-wise!

Constance held the secrets of her past so tightly that she seemed to be suffocating them and only ever told Erica the slightest details about her childhood in the context of the children they would never have. She said her parents had been cruel and favored her brother. As she talked, she would run a thumb over the knee that turned slightly outward, the knee that gave her a hitch in her step. The one time Erica asked Constance about that knee (five years into their marriage), she said her dad used to make fun of how she walked, said she did not want to visit that cruelty upon a theoretical child. She'd thanked Erica not to mention it again, then changed the subject.

So why had Constance reversed course? Was John just that persuasive? Or had Constance's "no children" stance stemmed less from her past and more from *Erica*, from a subconscious understanding that even if Erica fathered a child, she could never be a dad?

At Tuesday's *Our Town* rehearsal, Erica had realized with a jolt that Constance no longer walked with the hitch in her step. She moved in straight lines now. *Did you have surgery on your knee?* Erica texted Thursday morning between classes. *It doesn't turn outward anymore.* She felt the faux pas almost instantly and added, *Sorry. Rude.*

I was going to say, Constance replied. *No surgery. I woke up one day and decided to be normal lol. // Found some videos on YouTube.*

Well, good for you! Erica put her phone back in the messenger bag she had purchased in a futile effort to convince the woman in her brain it was a purse. *She's erasing herself*, Erica thought.

Her phone buzzed just as she began a sad attempt to get her students excited about Nathaniel Hawthorne. *Going to tell John I'm pregnant tonight! Wish me luck!*

It had been ten days since Constance had told Erica of her pregnancy. Why was she only just getting around to telling her boyfriend?

In the sixteen years Constance and Erica had been together before the divorce, the two of them had shared everything (as far as Constance knew). Even when their marriage was at its worst, Erica and Constance had tried to dispassionately split the pieces of themselves that were best friends off from the parts that were failed spouses. They dissected everything they hated about each other as if describing other people who weren't there. It was a fucked-up way to slow-walk yourself into a divorce, Erica now realized.

At the time, however, Erica didn't want to fight for her marriage. Had she wanted to, she could have simply opened her mouth and *actually* shared everything with her wife, could have told her the way her growing certainty that something had gone very wrong with her gender had become so all-consuming that it was all she could think about. Instead, she just kept letting Constance outline all the wrong reasons she *should* leave Erica and agreeing with her because none of them were the real reason, the secret Erica had at that time intended to die with.

She didn't even fight for her marriage as it ended. Constance had begun that conversation casually. "I need to talk to you as a friend more than a spouse."

Erica sighed. "What did your damn husband do this time?"

Constance smiled faintly. "It's not my husband. It's me." She took a long moment to stare out the window into the backyard. "I'm in love with someone else."

Erica had to remember how to talk. "We can fix it," she said, as if reading from a "how to save your marriage" script. "Counseling or a marriage retreat or . . ." She had built herself into the shape of Constance Ward's husband for so long that she didn't know what would happen to her if that were no longer true.

"You stopped loving me," Constance said. "You went somewhere, and I couldn't find you. And then I found . . . him. I'm sorry. I fucked up. Terribly. But you disappeared."

"Where did I go, Constance? I've been right here!"

"I don't blame you," Constance said quietly. "Sorry to imply that."

Erica looked at Constance and saw the tears she barely held in, how little she had slept recently, the mark on her finger where her wedding ring had once been. Erica had missed all of it. She *had* worked so hard at performing the man she thought Constance wanted that she had forgotten to be Constance's husband. Or maybe she had never known how to be him to begin with.

So she gave up, already trying to convince herself the marriage's end had been inevitable.

Erica helped Constance find a few boxes to put her stuff into. They put a cheery sitcom on TV and talked here and there but mostly avoided looking at each other as Constance packed. Erica felt numb, but numb was a familiar feeling to her. Numb, she knew how to treat.

Erica logged onto a chat room as Constance worked. She knew Constance was right. She had disappeared these last several years. She'd been online, role-playing stories where she transformed into a woman. She'd never felt more alive. She needed to interrogate that. She didn't want to interrogate that.

One of her regular partners had logged on, one of the rare chat room members whose understanding of womanhood extended beyond inaccurate descriptions of cup sizes. He and Erica had formed a vague understanding of each other's lives over the near-decade they had spent talking to each other, both seeing womanhood not as an escape but a reprieve. It had been so hard not to be women. In the stories they coauthored while chatting together, something in the world went soft and let them tumble through to their other selves.

Erica enlisted him into one of her preferred scenarios: Via a medical accident, she was transformed into a teenage girl, and her wife had to adopt her as a daughter. As she pitched the idea, Erica realized that every time she fantasized about being transformed into a woman, she also fantasized, obliquely, about Constance. She fantasized about becoming her daughter, her sister, her best friend. Never her wife. Some part of Erica's brain thought that the likelihood of proprietary gender-changing technology turning Erica into a confused teenage girl who *needed a mother* was somehow greater than Constance loving Erica if she really knew her.

The thing was, Constance had also stopped loving the Erica she thought she knew. That Erica had closed herself off inside a shell where no one could reach her. Constance had kept trying to get inside, and Erica had been unwilling to let her. So Constance had given up. Anyone would.

Erica stood from the computer, mouth open, trying to find words. Constance paused in her packing. "I understand, now," Erica said. "I've been gone. Somewhere. Inside a box. But . . ." She gulped, aware how alarming the words sounded even as she said them. "But coffins aren't built for two."

Constance carefully set a folded shirt in her box. "That's a terrifying thing to say. Are you okay?"

Erica had to tell Constance the truth. She had to come out. If ever there were a time to explain everything, if only to hang on to her best friend, it was now. Erica didn't know how long they stared at each other, either thirty seconds or several hours. "No," she finally said. "I'll be fine."

Constance returned to folding her clothes. "Sure you will, ▒▒▒▒."

Maybe the question she should be asking herself, Erica thought, wasn't "Why does Constance want a baby now?" Maybe she should be asking herself, "Did I love Constance? Or did I love that she let me hide who I was?"

John came to rehearsal with Constance. They walked down the aisle together, hands entwined. Brooke only paused her explanation of a too-complicated plan to have the blocking across the show precisely mirror itself to say, "You're here early."

"I have good news," Constance said.

"*Great* news," John said. He beamed. The slight pudge of his belly hung over his jeans, and he wore a Pioneer seed-corn jacket over a Minnesota Vikings T-shirt that Erica had seen both him and a black Lab wearing in a photo on Constance's Instagram. (Erica did not stalk Constance's Instagram. That much.) He had hair on the back of his hand so thick it gave Erica secondhand dysphoria. Like everything else about him, the hair fit him with terrifying precision. Of course Constance was having a baby with him. This man would be incomplete without several.

As Constance told Brooke her news, John wrapped an arm around her shoulder, kissing the top of her head. He looked off to the side, then blinked twice, as if banishing his tears to some other dimension. When he saw Erica watching him, he grinned.

Brooke waited a moment too long to say, "Well, that's wonderful news!" Erica wondered if she had forgotten her line.

John gave Constance another squeeze. "Better take it easy on her!" He laughed.

"Fortunately, *Our Town* doesn't have many stunts," Brooke said.

"Oh, gosh, I know that!" John said, blushing. "It takes place in a small town in New England, right, Connie?" Erica mouthed, "Connie?" at Constance, but she was smiling at John. "Hey, I've got a bunch of lumber out in my shop. My friends and I could probably build a set for you. Would that be a help?"

"That sounds like a great idea!" Brooke said. "Please sketch something out."

John beamed again, and Erica could feel his happiness at having something to contribute in some small way, and she hated him passionately. He was everything she never was (namely, a man), and Constance deserved the best. The thought gutted her. John gave Constance another kiss before the two of them parted ways, her to the stage and him to the back of the theater, where he would watch and be supportive, the fucking asshole.

"Well, good for them," Brooke said. "They're a nice couple." She seemed to abruptly realize Erica was there. "Sorry."

"Whatever. It's fine." Just as quickly as her all-consuming hatred had swept over her, it began to dissipate. Once you got used to never feeling things, it was hard to reboot your emotions. Erica merely catalogued them as they passed by on their way to wherever they went.

"He's a very nice man," Brooke continued, before stopping herself again. Erica gestured for her to go on. "I shouldn't be ungrateful, but I wonder if he even knows that *Our Town* is representational and shouldn't have a set at all?"

Somewhere in the second hour of rehearsal, Brooke, disappointed in the actors, had them break to list the times they felt most let down by their community. Erica excused herself, saying she had to pee. Really, she didn't want to answer the question.

The theater's lobby had a large glass atrium. It had once been a hot-air balloon museum before the city repossessed it, and the balloons had hung in such a way that they seemed to hover beneath the glass, trapped within an illusion of sky. Now, the enormous windows dwarfed anyone who might enter, like John, who sat on a bench, making a phone call.

"I'm at Connie's thing. If he wants it fixed right now, he'll have to be fine with Tom heading out there. And if he wants me to fix it, he can wait until the morning." Erica thought about offering to give "Connie" a ride home, but John gave her a too-big wave. She had lingered too long. She entered the men's room.

When she emerged, John beckoned her over. "This doesn't have to be awkward, ████," he said.

"Of course not," Erica said, ignoring the peach-fuzz mold surrounding her old name.

"It's cool she told you first. It really is. You two have known each other so long. That must be quite the bond. I know she misses you a lot," he said. "I'm sure it's hard for you too."

"I'm fine," Erica said. "It's fine."

"We should get a drink sometime. I live way out in the middle of nowhere, and I don't have a lot of other guys my age around. Any friend of Constance's . . ."

"I was married to her," Erica said.

"And now you're not," John replied. He clearly believed that at some point, the door marked "Erica" had closed in Constance's heart and one marked "John" had opened.

Already, Erica's hate was wearing away to dislike. Who could truly hate a man with such an earnestly doglike demeanor? "Maybe a drink, yeah, maybe," Erica said.

"You're a good man, ████. She worries about you, and I hate when she worries."

"I didn't know she thought about me at all."

"Oh, buddy, does she ever." For the first time since her marriage had ended, Erica wondered if Constance was similarly sad about it, at least in her own way.

"Again, my number of failed marriages is very small," Abigail said, "but I'm gonna guess that becoming friends with the father of your ex's future child in the hopes of getting back together with her is a terrible idea."

Erica forced herself to pay attention to Interstate 90 and the drive over to Sioux Falls for the support group she had been sure Abigail would bail on attending. "We're just having drinks," she said. "And I don't want to get back together with Constance."

"Uhhhh, she's all you talk about?"

"I don't think that's true," Erica said. "On this car trip, yes, but only because it's on my mind. And anyway, he's right. So is she. I don't have a lot of friends. I could use a few more, and I could probably use a few guy friends."

"*Why*? Aren't you a lesbian or whatever?"

"I don't think I get to call myself a—"

"Oh my God, Erica, you get to call yourself a lesbian. You're going to hang out with your ex's new lover, all while you pretend you're not still hung up on her. You're maybe the *most* lesbian."

"Maybe." Erica quieted. They neared an enormous metal sculpture of a bull's head rising against the graying sky. They were about halfway there. She and Constance had made this drive to Sioux Falls many times when seeking to simply get out of their house, to escape their lives, to maybe escape each other. "Constance was my wife, sure. But I tried to make her everything else too. She was my . . ." Erica thought for a long moment. "My access to femininity. She could wear a dress and look pretty in it, and it wasn't like *I* was wearing the dress, but it was like I could feel it secondhand. She was my wife and my best friend and my mom and my sister and my daughter, and that was maybe unfair to her." She thought again. "I should apologize."

"But then you'd have to come out to her." Abigail turned to look at the bull's head as they passed. "I get it, though. I was like that with my mom when I was little. She loved to get dressed up all fancy, and after she did, I would go into her bathroom and smell the perfume and imagine I could get all dressed up too."

In the handful of times Erica had talked to her the last two weeks, Abigail had not once mentioned the events that led up to her living with her sister, so Erica remained silent and hoped Abigail would fill that silence. Abigail didn't want a friend, obviously, but perhaps she needed a confidante.

"God, gross!" Abigail said. "What a cliché! Little trans girl wanted to be her mommy, boo hoo hoo."

"I thought that was quite moving. I'm sorry you had to be a secret. I'm sorry *we* had to be secrets."

Abigail rolled her eyes. "I want to be clear: I'm *your* trans mom. So don't try to be my real mom. And as your trans mom, here is my advice: Apologize to your ex. Then go find literally any other woman to hang out with because, God, you need *female* friends." She fidgeted slightly in her seat. "And don't be weird about it. Don't make them your . . . excess of femininity or whatever you called it. Be that yourself." She leaned over the center console. "And that friend is *not me* either."

"I'd never do that to you." It took Erica several miles to become aware she was performing the mental equivalent of holding two fingers crossed behind her back.

Abigail

Thursday,
September 22

When I wake up, Jennifer is yelling outside. She keeps saying, "Abigail! Her name is Abigail! Call her Abigail!" So I look out the window, and, shit, my mom is there. It's half-dark, and the headlights on my mom's car turn them both into shadow puppets.

My mom goes for the front door like four times, but Jennifer blocks her. My mom calls Jennifer a whore and finally stomps back to her car like she came here to cross "call oldest daughter a whore" off her chore list.

My mom drives this big Ford Explorer. She got it used, and when she bought it, it had a "NO BLOOD FOR OIL" bumper sticker on it, which clashed with her "CHOOSE LIFE" license plates, so she made me try to peel it off. It was super stuck on there, so I had to leave "D FOR OIL" behind, which you've gotta admit is pretty funny.

Jennifer stands on the lawn, watching Mom drive off, then bends over at the waist and starts crying.

The thing is, I could almost imagine myself sleepwalking out of the house and down the front lawn and getting into the back seat. Mom would pat my head and drive me away with her. I could just *go home*, and I could see her again.

But she'd never call me Abigail, and that's a nonstarter.

When I go out to the main room to talk to Jennifer, her boyfriend Ron's up too. He's standing, holding a cereal box with both hands, watching the front door like he's waiting for it to explode. Jennifer comes back in, wiping her eyes with her sleeve.

"You gotta let me handle her, babe," Ron says.

"No, it's fine. She's not—" Jennifer sees me and sucks something back up inside herself. "I'm sorry you had to see that."

"Mom's a total bitch," I say like it doesn't bother me, because that's how you get it to stop bothering you. "And she's gone now, so whatever."

There's a weird silence before Ron says, "Babe, you should tell her."

"Tell me what?"

Jennifer sighs. "She comes here every few weeks in the early morning. She thinks I won't be here, and that she can convince you to go home with her. But I told her this is my house. *My* house."

Jennifer used to work overnights at the truck stop because she liked being up late. She'd get home at 7:30 a.m., say bye as I went to school, then collapse. But then Ron pulled some strings with his dad so she could work the day shift. She said it was because she wanted to be around when I wasn't at school, so she could take better care of me, but you already know I take good care of myself.

"It's my house too. I'm staying right here," I say, because if you tell Jennifer you love her, she doesn't believe it. The best way to let her know you love her is to sleep in her guest room every night until she figures out you'll still be there when she wakes up and when she goes to sleep.

She comes over and hugs me before taking the cereal box from Ron and making herself breakfast. "I'm worried she's going to take you away from me."

"I'm almost eighteen," I say, because it's September and January 28 counts as "almost," I think. "Isn't that a get-out-of-jail-free card, Ron?"

Ron's brother is a lawyer, so he nods enthusiastically and points at me as though I've just made a great point, but his mouth is full of cereal so he can't say just how great my point is.

"She's Mom," Jennifer says, pouring out the last of the cereal, then crushing the empty box between her hands. Her voice sounds far away. "She's Mom."

I have five siblings, because my parents liked having kids. They had two sons, then two daughters, then two more kids they thought were sons, except one of them was me. You'd think my transition would've made them happy I'd evened out the ranks for guys-versus-gals family game nights, but no such luck. (Also, like we ever had a "family game night"!)

I'm the baby, and my mom used to say she had to be done having kids because I was so perfect. This is probably not a thing she tells people anymore. After my parents kicked me out, I didn't want them to worry about how to explain why I wasn't around anymore, so I took out an ad in the local newspaper (seriously, it was twenty-five dollars) announcing my transition. I threw some "It's a girl!" clip art on there and everything. I'm sure they appreciated my thoughtfulness.

My dad runs the grocery store in my hometown, and my mom works there. They made all us kids work there too. They're probably a little angry at me because if I'd stuck around long enough, having a trans girl working the register would've started rumors, even *if* they could've paid her/me basically nothing.

Jennifer is my oldest sister. She's twenty-three and worked her way through college at USD to get a degree in journalism. She wanted to be a writer and that degree seemed "writing adjacent," as she puts it. Except now she works at a truck stop, and she's fucking Ron. Ron is the son of the guy who owns the truck stop, and he's at least thirty-five. (I've never asked.) He has two kids in Chicago he sometimes talks to on Skype. After he hangs up, he cries in the bathroom. I'm pretty sure Jennifer moved in with Ron mainly because it solved the problem of how to afford a place big enough for both me and her. But Jennifer's had some real shit-ass boyfriends, and Ron isn't one of them. It's cute how he thinks he could take on my mom when his response to hearing her yelling is to turn a cereal box into a stress ball.

Jennifer was the first person I came out to. I was a fucking mess, and she ran her hand over my back. We were both three wine coolers deep ("You've got me drinking like a college girl again!" is a thing Jennifer says, like she's not fucking twenty-three), and I opened my mouth, and I said it, the thing I had never been able to say to anybody but could say to her.

I think maybe I told her because, deep down, she was the one I knew wouldn't run screaming into the street when I said it. Our two oldest brothers sided with Mom and Dad. The sister between us says she's supportive but also lives in San Diego (Navy), so she hasn't had to put that support into action. The next brother up from me says he approves but also always says, "Whatever makes you happy, bro," so I don't think he gets it. Anyway, most of us don't talk to each other anymore. Which is my fault.

I don't remember what I said to Jennifer when I told her. Only that she asked me what my name was, and I said Abigail, because I literally thought of it in that moment, with her hand on my back and the sticky taste of bad wine cooler coating my mouth and snot running down my face. It sounded good, and it sounded right, and it sounded like me.

She smiled and said, "Okay, Abigail. My sister, Abigail." She gave me a big hug and whispered in my ear, "Thank you for trusting me with you."

I know I said I was going to hang out with Megan Osborne, but the more I thought about it, the more I realized she could only be disappointed by the experience, so I've been trying to get out of it. But every day, she would ask if I could come over after school. And she always seemed sad when I couldn't. I eventually caved and said I would go today because, all evidence to the contrary, I hate making people sad.

I can hear you being, like, "Aw, Abigail's going to make a friend!" but people like Megan Osborne only want to have a trans friend so they can tell people they have a trans friend. Last year, for example, I hung out with a girl who wanted to talk to me constantly about "queering everything." She introduced me to her parents as "Abigail, my trans friend I was telling you about." I asked her to stop doing that, and by "asked," I mean I stopped talking to her. Point is: People only hang out with me because they think I make them seem cooler and more accepting, or because they pity me and want to "help me out."

Let's find out which one Megan is.

Megan's house is huge. The backyard ice rink her dad built for her two brothers dominates the view from her bedroom window. The Osbornes are the kind of people who say they're middle-class as they skate around on their private rink.

"It's so my brothers can work on their sprints in winter," she says. "They're very serious about hockey."

Megan's whole family is very serious about everything. I think her dad's a lawyer? Her mom seems like she really listens to what her kids are saying to her, because when I walked in, she came out from the kitchen to ask Megan how her day had gone, then to ask me how I liked the cookies from the other day. Then she said, "Now you girls have fun," and she winked at me. I have no fucking clue what that was supposed to mean.

The handful of times I'd talked with Megan Osborne before today had me convinced that she was trying to turn being the student body vice president into a personality, and her bedroom confirms my suspicions. It's covered in pictures of normie politicians, like Obama and Hillary. "Notice anything?" she says.

"You like politicians a lot?" I say.

"There's nooooo Republicans!" she says, like she's being a badass, and for Mitchell, she kind of is. (There are maybe six Democrats in this town, and Megan's family is five of them.) She plugs some speakers into her MacBook and starts playing Taylor Swift. "Do you like Taylor?" she says over the music. I don't bear Taylor Swift any specific ill will, so I nod. "I got to meet her in Chicago last year before her concert. It was my birthday present."

I should say something, but I'm distracted again by her enormous room and the picture on her dresser of her and Taylor making hearts with their hands together. I know money can't buy you happiness, but it evidently can buy you a chance to meet Taylor Swift and the confidence to keep pestering the weird girl in your current events class until she hangs out with you.

"What kind of music do you like?" she says. I'm clearly frozen in place (I do that sometimes, bad habit), and she sags a little. "I know it's too much."

"No, it's nice," I say. It *is* nice. "And I like Mitski."

"Oh, I don't know them!" Within about ten seconds, she's playing "Your Best American Girl," nodding her head along. "Yeah. *Yeah*. I *like* this."

"Why do you want to hang out with me?" I say. "You don't have to."

Megan shrugs. "You seem cool and fun?" I don't know what to say, so the song fills the quiet. "And you stuck up for me. I appreciate that."

I don't know that I stuck up for her so much as I wanted those guys to stop being such fuckwads, but those things live next door to each other, huh?

"I don't like fascists, and I don't like assholes. It wasn't, like, a calculated attempt to make you like me. I guess I figured you have other friends to hang out with."

"I can't have one more?" She turns up the music and shouts, "This is really good, Abigail!" over it.

The more I look around the room, the more I realize there aren't any pictures of anyone who isn't a world-famous politician or pop star. No pictures of friends or family or a prom picture or anything. I realize that even though I always see Megan around other people, I don't really see them around her. She's always off to the side, cheering everybody else's friendships on. Her brothers are super popular, because they're rich jocks, but Megan is sort of popularity-adjacent, which is maybe lonelier than nobody liking you at all, because you're always right next to what you're missing.

Shit. Now *I* have to pity *her*.

The song ends, and Megan starts it again. If nothing else, I've gotten her into Mitski's most popular song.

"So I'm fucking Caleb Daniels. He'd never admit it in a million years, but I am." We might as well get into the deep end. Why not?

Megan stares at me. Maybe I should have worked up to that revelation? But after a second, she giggles. "Oh shit! I thought he was super Christian."

"A Christian boy having sex? Before marriage? That's never happened before." This makes her laugh even harder. I expect her to ask if having sex with me makes Caleb gay, but she doesn't. I should have had more faith in ol' Megan Osborne. She's the kind of person who probably googled "things you should never ask a trans person" before deciding to invite me over.

But then she says, "Speaking of Caleb Daniels, I did have another reason I wanted to hang out with you. I need your help." She stops. "Or we can help each other. Or something."

I sigh. I guess "pity" won in the end. Like I said: Nobody ever wants to be my friend to be my friend.

"Well, if anybody can stop Isaiah Rose, it's you and Megan," Erica says.

We're almost at Sioux Falls, and I already regret going to this support group with her. I know I said I was going to get out of it, but then I thought it might be funny to see who turns up at the Sioux Falls, South Dakota, trans support group.

Instead, I'm already super annoyed. Erica started talking about her ex-wife soap opera the second we got on the interstate, and when I said one tiny thing about my mom, she turned into Detective Erica, trying to get me to give up my secrets. So then I brought up Megan's idea to get out of talking about *that*, and now I'm stuck. Erica thinks Megan's idea is great. She thinks Megan and I should absolutely rally the people of Mitchell to vote against a beloved local minister in favor of a lady nobody (including me) has ever heard of.

"The other queer students at our school would appreciate having someone standing up for them," Erica says. (As a new queer, Erica loves using the word "queer." We all like having something to call ourselves.)

I want to tell her that I don't *want* to do things and that I resent being asked. Instead, I say, "He's going to win though. Why do something if it's just going to fail?"

"Maybe you can convince people. Maybe you can help them see we're not weirdo perverts," Erica says. (Good luck convincing half of Mitchell of *that*.) "And it would look good on college applications!"

I laugh because fuck you, Erica. College applications?

"Am I wrong? Wouldn't it look good on college applications?"

"I have no idea what would look good on college applications because I'm not fucking going to college. My parents disowned me. I believe it's come up." I fold my arms and look away and feel like a dumb baby. "I just don't want Megan to fucking pity me."

"I doubt she pities you."

"Everybody pities me."

Erica lets that one sit for a little while. Out the window, combines run in the fields lining the road, scooping up corn stalks and sending kernels shooting up through a nozzle and out into a wagon. It's a little early for harvest. Caleb tried to explain it all to me once, but I didn't really care.

"I don't think that's true. People are seeing you be yourself. All we can do is live as ourselves. That's the most radical act of all, right?" She's been reading a lot of trans shit online. She likes to quote it back to me like I haven't heard it all already.

"Says the woman who's now best bros with a fucking tractor man. This isn't a way to help anybody. It's a way to help Megan feel better about herself. Nobody *cares* about people like us, Erica. I *believe* it's *come up*." I bite my lip because I'm thinking about my shadow puppet mom in front of her headlights. Fucking hell.

"Are you okay?" she says. I turn away again, hunching up my shoulders to keep my tears in. She continues. "I'm glad you're here with me. I'm glad we're going tonight. Together. We can do *anything* together, right?"

I'm not talking to her. I'll let her think she won that argument. But she doesn't know fucking shit. Erica has come out to exactly one person, and she doesn't dare wear her nail polish to school, and she thinks she can tell me what will be good for queer people in Mitchell? Erica sees being herself as a series of progressively difficult challenges in a video game. Yeah, transition is a series of tiny things you do that add up to one big thing. But it's also the way you get to the rest of your life, and then you've gotta fucking live it.

I'm in a tiny room at the Sioux Falls Public Library with Erica and six other people. The old trans woman in charge, who looks like she's seen some shit, says it's a good turnout. I wonder if she would have said that if Erica and I hadn't shown up and it had just been her and three other people who've barely said a goddamn thing all night.

The lady tells a story about how she recently got to meet her grandson for the first time ever. One of her kids didn't want to talk to her for a long time, but things are softening slowly. Erica has tears in her eyes. When the old lady finishes, everybody applauds, because if nothing else, she told the story well.

Erica talks about how she realized she was a trans woman. We've all heard this plotline before, so let's look around at the other people in the room. Why not? Erica is the person closest in age to me, which is incredibly depressing. Most of the people here are *old*, and they're only just getting a chance to live. One guy is in overalls and a seed-corn cap, both of which are way too big for him. Another lady is dressed like she's going to prom in 1955. She tries to sound dainty when she clears her throat. Sitting across the room from me is a lady in a shabby wig and ripped-up clothes, coughing into her hand. I sometimes have thoughts of coming home to Jennifer's house and finding out that she and Ron are dead, or that my mom is inside, or worse, my dad, and they'll tell me it's all over, and I'll have to go with them, and then someday, I'll be that lady, trying to find my way back into myself.

Everybody claps as Erica finishes. The old lady asks if anybody else has anything to say. She looks at me. I haven't talked yet. Why should I? We're five minutes from the end, and Erica could easily fill those minutes with thoughts on the irony of her first nail polish being called "Everything's Rosy." But oh my God, that would be so fucking annoying.

"*Fine*," somebody who sounds a lot like me says. "My name is Abigail. I came out to myself two years ago, and I've been on hormones for fourteen months. DIY. I order the pills from Bolivia because there's a whole deal where I'm still on my parents' medical insurance, and they don't want me going to a doctor to actually do it safely. The only way I know it's working is that one of my boobs is bigger than the other. By a lot. Doesn't matter. I'm still hot."

"One breast being larger than the other is common," the old lady says. I wait to see if she has more to say about boob size, but she doesn't.

"I don't know why I did this. I really don't. Nobody likes me, my parents don't want me around if I'm not cosplaying as their son, my sister has lost *everything* trying to take care of me, and I don't have any friends." I can tell Erica wants to correct me, but she doesn't. Thank God.

There are two minutes left. I could just wait this out.

"The night I figured all of this out, it was 3:00 a.m." (I'm still talking for some reason. Let me know your best theories.) "I was on the family computer in the living room. I felt like I was sitting on a bomb. I closed all the browser tabs, and I erased the history, and I was still so scared my mom would catch me and . . . figure me out? I guess?

"But I knew I was a girl. I knew it as much as I'd known anything. And I was never going to get to *be* a girl." (Yep, *still* talking.) "So I got up, and I went out back to my dad's toolshed. I was going to grab the box cutter, and . . . well, I wasn't going to use it to cut boxes, if you catch my drift." Nobody laughs. "But the family cat is lying there, on my dad's workbench, and to get the box cutter, I'm going to have to move her. And she's a mean old piece of shit, so I don't want to do that. I face off with her, and I think, *If she goes, I'll just end it all, and if she stays . . .*" I swallow. Something got to me in that. "She didn't move, so I turned around, and I went back inside. And my parents still have their cat, but they don't have me, which I'm sure they prefer.

"I wish that cat had gotten up and left sometimes. Yes, I'm really nailing this whole skater-punk thing I'm going for, but I don't have a future. And even if I did, even if everything magically gets better after high school, the whole planet is doomed. A fascist might be president, and nobody fucking cares. The whole world is going to burn itself to death, and nobody fucking cares. So what? I lived that night, so I can die in a broken pile in my twenties or thirties? The world hates us. It doesn't want us around, and it doesn't want me specifically around." I fold my arms. "I'm done."

"Thank you, Abigail," says the old lady. "We want you here."

What does she fucking know?

We park a block from my house. Erica gives me an awkward hug. I go stiff, and she pulls back to pat me on the shoulder. "My life is better because you're in it. I'm proud of you for saying all that stuff." Ugh. "And I'm really glad you didn't . . . do the other thing that night in the shed. I'm happy you've been here to show me the way."

"It's all online. You would have figured it out."

"Yeah. But you were here, so I didn't have to." She gets almost as serious as Megan for a second. "Having you in my life—"

"Shut up!" I rub my face. "We're not friends, Erica. You keep forgetting that. You just drive me around sometimes."

Her smile fades back into itself. "I didn't say we were friends. I'm aware this is an emotionally complicated—"

"You *wish* we were friends, and don't fucking deny it."

"Don't lash out at me because you're mad at someone else," she says. Her voice trembles.

"Welcome to womanhood, bitch." I get out before she can say anything else. Then I realize I should let her know this has all been in good fun and turn around to flip her off. I see her wiping her eyes, but she waves. Was I too hard on her? Let me know in the comments.

I walk up the road toward my house. When I get there, Jennifer sits on the curb. She stands up when she sees me and hugs me when I get close. We go back inside together.

Erica

Monday,

September 26

AT SOME POINT IN THE LAST MONTH, Erica had begun to have the creeping suspicion that she had a body.

She had been so used to ignoring her physical form over the years that when she realized how poorly she had treated it, it felt overwhelming. She focused on how she huffed and puffed climbing a flight of stairs, on how clothes Constance had bought her a year earlier barely fit, on how ugly her toes were (like little packing peanuts). It was exposure therapy but for herself.

Her body had always seemed a minor inconvenience, a vessel to tote around her brain. If her body died someday, so be it. She would detach from it and float around looking for a new host.

But now? She longed for everything about her to be different.

She'd started walking in the mornings before school, making her way down toward Dry Run Creek, passing a long-closed western-wear store, the little five-screen movie theater, a half dozen churches. Few people woke up that early, and she felt in communion with the lone skater on the half-pipe, the garbage collectors, the bored woman watching her dog lope through the park.

This morning, though, when she rounded the corner to turn back home, she saw someone new: a tall, thin woman with hair dyed dark red, grappling with a yard sign larger than herself. It read "SWEE FOR STATE SENATE" in black and gold (a transparent attempt to draft off the high school's colors), and it was too large to be supported by such thin metal sticks. Signs for other Democratic candidates dotted the yard around her. The woman sank one of the sign's stakes into the ground, only to have the wind catch the other side and rip it out.

By the time she arrived on the sidewalk by the woman's house, Erica was huffing and puffing so loudly that the woman turned to look. Erica apologetically smiled and held up a hand to indicate all was well. Conversations among women happened before the conversations even started, Erica was realizing. She was also realizing, with gratitude, that she already knew how to perform these rituals.

"Sorry if I surprised you. Just out for my morning walk, and I couldn't help but see you fighting with your sign . . . I'm so sorry," Erica said. "Can I help you?"

When she talked to other women now (*other* women—the thrill!), Erica practically prostrated herself before them, hoping they would accept her endless apologies as a precursor to letting her enter their world, a place she still feared she was not welcome. She had always apologized endlessly, probably because her mother had made such a habit of it, but women had never trusted those apologies. They would freeze, weigh her very being, then rebuild the walls Erica had briefly attempted to dismantle.

But this woman smiled. "You're fine," she said. The sign fell over again. "But yes, I might need help."

As they positioned the sign together, Erica learned the woman's name (Helen Swee), her occupation (campaign consultant, now the state senate candidate running against Isaiah Rose), and where Erica could vote for Helen come November (Gertie Belle Rogers Elementary). At no point did Helen seem to have flipped some inner switch into campaign mode, even though Erica knew Helen must be acting so nicely to her because she wanted Erica's vote. And throughout, a tattoo on Helen's arm—a figure huddled in a small boat, their line of vision blocked by a wall of swords—kept catching Erica's eye. She wanted to ask what the tattoo represented but worried the question would seem too forward.

"I think we did it," Helen said eventually. The sign bent but didn't collapse. "And I never got your name."

Erica opened her mouth to say the old name, the wrong name, then had the sensation of her real name flooding into the front of her skull, as if trying to capsize her sense of self. She laughed, and Helen looked at her curiously. "Sorry. Brain fart. Forgot my name."

"God, I have to say my name so many times when I'm talking to voters or trying to convince donors I'm not some kook, and every time, I panic a little bit. *Really?! That's my name?! That's a stupid name!* Then I say, 'I'm Helen Swee,' and they all think it's weird that I just spent ten seconds trying to remember who I am."

Erica laughed, the floodwaters of her new self swamping everything in her cerebral cortex, except for the lone hand sticking above those waters, holding up a yard sign that reminded her she was still in hiding. Maybe she could compromise. "█████," she said. "But everybody just calls me Mr. Skyberg."

Yes, Helen seemed cool and cosmopolitan, like top-notch "I just made a friend in my thirties!" material. But like a dog trained with a shock collar to stop chasing cars, Erica had long ago learned to stop pursuing even the slightest hint of female friendship.

It hadn't always been that way. She had spent a drunken night junior year riding in the back seat of a car driven by a girl named Lindsey, as three other girls in Erica's class grilled her about what boys liked. During college, she had occasionally found herself at house parties sitting silently in a circle of women sharing their darkest memories as they passed a joint around. In her professional life, there had been woman after woman she ate lunch with, settling into the teacher's lounge and watching them stab at cold bits of egg in homemade Cobb salads as they talked about problem students in their classes.

But something always went wrong. Lindsey, fearing that her crush would think she was dating Erica, made Erica lie down in the back seat so no one could see her. In those college sharing circles, inevitably, some girl would start to say something too horrible, then clam up, saying she didn't want to talk about that right now, her eyes holding Erica's. Especially in Mitchell, where many still held that the only woman a man should be at all close to was his wife, she could feel a bubble of smoky glass form around her the second she tried to turn a cool woman she had met into a friend. She could look, and she could observe, but something about her would always raise their suspicion if she got too close. Erica had been holding a shoe her entire life, and many of the women around her had always been waiting for her to drop it.

The more Erica thought about it, the more she realized she had hoped Constance would act as a female proxy in this regard too. Perhaps if Constance had gathered a diverse and multifaceted female friend group, Erica could have hovered at its edges. But Constance never particularly cared about having friends, leaving Erica starved and frustrated in a way she had not been able to define the whole time they were married and would not be able to put words to now without coming out.

She pondered all this at rehearsal the night after she met Helen. (A whole day had evidently passed without her quite noticing . . . she *had* to stop getting lost in her thoughts like this.) Beside her, Brooke, who had been examining the set-design sketches John dropped off, cleared her throat. "What are you looking at?"

Erica realized she had been staring thoughtfully in Constance's general direction and jerked her gaze away. "Nothing. Sorry." She pretended to focus intently on the sketches.

Brooke clucked her disapproval. "Oh, ████. Don't *yearn*."

When she and Constance were still together, Erica had hoped they might make couple friends. At the end of every play's run, Brooke would invariably suggest to Erica and Constance that the three of them, plus Brooke's husband Victor, all grab dinner sometime. The event would be agreed to in the hypothetical, and then Constance would find six different reasons not to go on a double date with "Brooke fucking Daniels and her fucking husband." (Erica, as per usual in those days, didn't know how to ask herself what she wanted—or how to want much of anything at all.)

Two Christmases ago, however, Brooke had been particularly insistent on them gathering and finally wore Constance down. The four had gathered at the Sioux Falls branch of Johnny Carino's, a chain Italian restaurant. Constance had drunk too much red wine before the appetizers even arrived and seemed compelled to fill all conversational voids. Erica knew she was supposed to bond with Victor, who was taciturn but pleasant enough, but she simply could not force herself to care about the Minnesota Vikings, and she knew very little about agriculture, which removed most of Victor's conversational topics and left him smiling blankly.

She had a much better time talking to Brooke. The two had worked together on seven different productions over the last five years, whether for the community theater or at the high school, and they made a good team. But at dinner, Brooke was *fun*. With her hair let down to the tune of a gin and tonic, Brooke made Erica laugh. Brooke had seen so many shows in New York—she treated herself to a trip there every year—and she had so many opinions, and so many of them were catty. The little voice in Erica's head said: *You two have a lot in common. Maybe she'd even invite you along to New York sometime*. In Johnny Carino's, anything was possible.

"How about you, ?" Brooke had said. Erica must have looked confused—she had checked out of the conversation briefly—so Brooke smiled more warmly than Erica had believed her capable of. “Any dream productions?”

“I’ve always wanted to do *Our Town*,” Erica said. “I love that third act so much. Realizing how much of every moment you’re missing just by being alive? Gives me chills.”

Constance flagged a waiter, holding up her empty glass of wine. On the table, her phone buzzed.

“Oh, I love that play too,” Brooke said. “It’s a little cliché for a small-town theater troupe to put on, but we should anyway. It’s like you said, [illegible]. The distance between a life as it’s lived and a life as it’s remembered is so vast. And then sometimes we get just the shortest glimpse of what’s behind it all. Hallelujah, right?”

Erica, who wasn’t sure if she was having the most profound conversation of her life or being proselytized to (probably both), nodded generously.

“Well, I think it’s hokey bullshit,” Constance said, looking down at her phone. The waiter reappeared to fill her wine glass, and she gestured for him to keep pouring.

“Do you two have a church?” Brooke said, changing the topic.

“We’re not really . . . ,” Erica said.

“We had an ulterior motive for inviting you out,” Victor said, his first words virtually all evening.

Constance bark-laughed. “*Great*.”

“Victor! Don’t make them think they’re being preached to,” Brooke said. She turned back to Erica. “I need some help with the Living Waters Christmas pageant this year. I want it to be more elaborate than the usual, and I need a Joseph and Mary, so I thought . . .”

“To be clear, it’s *then* that we’ll be preached to, right?” Constance said. She gave Erica a “Can you believe this shit?” look. “Also, wasn’t Mary a teenager or something?”

“We don’t know that that’s true,” Victor said.

“Ah.”

“If the answer’s no, then the answer’s no.” Brooke looked calm.

"We're not really into church . . . Christianity . . . so on," Erica said, completing her thought at long last.

"I got dragged there three times a week until I was in college," Constance said. "I've heard enough to know it's all . . . well, like I said, it's hokey bullshit." Her phone buzzed again, and she instantly picked it up.

"Do you have someone you'd rather be talking to?" Brooke said.

Constance slammed her phone on the table. "No. I'm enjoying this conversation."

"Constance," Erica said. She hated the way she said it, like a disappointed husband.

"It's bullshit!" Constance said. "It's all made-up bullshit that's actively making the world a worse place."

Victor hailed the waiter for the check.

Constance continued. "None of you care about helping people. You care about speeding toward the end of the world, so if Jesus comes back, you can gloat about it." Erica squeezed Constance's leg under the table, trying to find a space between "Reel this back in" and "I'm here for you" and probably skirting too close to the former. "Three times a week. And when . . ." She trailed off, skirting around the edges of her past. "Nobody ever tried to help me. Is what I'm saying."

"I'm so sorry," Brooke said. She looked directly across the table at Constance until Constance locked eyes with her. "That should not have happened."

"Yeah, well, it fucking did."

"You're not wrong. The church can be a cruel place. But it doesn't have to be." Brooke took one more sip of her gin and tonic, now almost surely mostly water. "When I was seventeen, my parents died in a car accident. I was an only child, so then I had no one. I inherited some money, and I sold off their house, so I had a little nest egg. But I was seventeen and grieving. I blew it all." Victor ran a hand over her back.

"I met Victor a few years later, and he brought me home to his family, to his church. I grew up Catholic, so, like you, I grew up being dragged to a place I didn't want to be. But at Living Waters . . ." She took another sip. "I know Isaiah is a firebrand, but come and just look around. There are people helping each other and holding each other up. I love it like I love the theater. We make things bigger than ourselves there. We build a place where people can find a home. Or peace. Or maybe even whatever we call God."

Victor had tears in his eyes. "Amen."

"Sorry," Constance said, too forcefully. "I'm . . . a little drunk."

"I had surmised," Brooke said. She smiled, and Erica realized the tiniest of doors into Brooke's soul had opened the tiniest of slivers. Erica wanted to see more, to know more. Maybe she *should* ask Brooke to coffee. Maybe she *should*—

"Do you mind if I lead us in a prayer?" Victor said. Brooke immediately bowed her head. Erica obligingly closed her eyes and half paid attention.

On the table, Constance's phone buzzed again. She snatched it up to reply as Victor prayed.

The memory of that dinner stuck with Erica. The polite South Dakotan decorum of not going out for coffee with someone else's wife if you appeared to be a man had held firm, but some part of her had always imagined she and Brooke might be able to turn one of their many blocking meetings into a blocking meeting over coffee. She had not yet been bold enough to ask. Unsure of how to pull *that* off, she instead asked Abigail what to do.

The two ate lunch in an empty classroom, under the guise of working on a special project to help boost Abigail's grades and make college a possibility for her. Abigail continued to avow that college "sucked ass" and was "for rich dumbasses like you" (as though she'd never heard about teachers' salaries), but she was happy to have lunch somewhere other than the lunchroom because "everybody else is gross."

"Your 'potential BFFs' list needs to have more people on it than just *me* and *Brooke*," Abigail said. "Other people exist, right? I'm not making that up?"

"In theory, yes. I just don't know several billion of them. And I want to hang out with other *women*."

"Should I list women who aren't me or Brooke? I'll have to dig deep, but I'll try." Abigail thought for a second. "Mrs. King? Hates political dissidents but also seems like she'd put up with a three-hour movie in French or whatever you think is fun."

"She's in her seventies! You should assume I've thought of everyone I work with and found them wanting."

"You're so picky!" Abigail shook her head. "What about the old lady who runs the support group? She's probably in her sixties, which is absolutely not her seventies."

"Bernadette?" Erica's sandwich somersaulted in her stomach. "I don't think I could do that."

"There has to be someone in that support group young enough to be your friend."

"It's not that," Erica said. "It's . . ." She didn't want to say it.

"What? She's too obviously trans for you to hang out with?"

Erica didn't say anything, instead taking the last bite of her sandwich and gathering her trash.

"You're such a fucking hypocrite! What about when you don't pass yet? When you're six foot whatever, barely squeezing into some dress you found in the very back of a Macy's, struggling to cover your beard shadow with foundation? Will you still want me to hang out with you then? Give you advice on how to get the other girls to like you?"

"That's different," Erica said. Abigail glared at her, and Erica fumbled for *how* it was different. "Because . . . we're not friends. You made that clear. You give me advice, and I help you do college prep."

"The fucking college thing again! Do you even *listen* to me?"

Erica listened to everything Abigail said but, if she was honest with herself, dismissed most of it. The girl didn't understand how lucky she was. She had thrown herself a rope from shore before she washed away to sea. And now she got to simply live her life. Erica, meanwhile, had been swimming against the riptide her whole life and had gotten too good at it.

"I listen. You said 'when you don't pass yet,' and the 'yet' implies I will someday."

"I can't believe you're bringing up *grammar*. I'm starting to wish one of my math teachers was trans instead." Abigail ran a hand through her hair (now an electric red). "Most of this is getting people to see you the way you want them to see you. After you've been transitioning for a while, you'll figure it out. I mean, just look at me."

"You're young."

"Shut up. When I look at myself, I don't see what you do. All I see is the stuff that's still *boy*." Abigail did a full-body shiver. "For instance, I have enormous hands, and my voice dropped when I was, like, ten, and if I think about that for too long, I decide I must be fucked. I'll forever and always be known as a tranny."

"Don't say that word!"

"I get to say that word." Abigail pointed at Erica with a carrot stick. "*You* get to say that word too. Lucky you. You have a slur to play around with at home."

"I will *never* say that word."

"You're missing the point. Because we're trans, because we pay way too much attention to this stuff, you and I see the things about Bernadette that mark her as trans, but I guarantee you that no cis person looks at Bernadette when she's in Hy-Vee and says, 'Look at that transgender person.' To them, she looks like a normal-ass old lady. You will someday too."

"*If* I ever transition—"

"*If*? Bitch?"

"—I will never pass. I just won't."

"If you look hard enough, you'll realize *nobody* passes, Erica." Abigail took a bite out of her carrot stick.

"I'm so comforted. Once again, I'm glad I asked you for advice. Look how I'm making friends left and right."

Abigail ignored her, plowing ahead. "I was where you were once. I thought, 'Oh, shit, it's too late for me, I'm a hideous troll, fuck, fuck, fuck.' Then one day, I looked at my mom, and I realized she had a hairline that almost made it seem like she was balding. My dad couldn't grow a beard, like, at all. I started looking at other people, really looking at them, and saw that *nobody* passes." She started counting off on her fingers. "Your bestie Brooke Daniels's voice is almost as deep as mine. Megan Osborne? *Enormous* Adam's apple. And Caleb has tiny little hands."

"How do you know how big Caleb's hands are?"

"C'mon. You've seen his hands!" (Erica didn't think she had ever noticed Caleb's hands, even when he shot a basketball. Maybe she just didn't pay the same freakish amount of attention to people's bodies that Abigail evidently did.) "Show me your ex again." Erica handed over her phone, open to a picture of Constance, and Abigail studied it. "Look at those broad-ass shoulders. Yikes."

"Constance has amazing shoulders."

"Constance has *man* shoulders."

"Constance is *pregnant*!"

"A famously assigned-female-at-birth thing to do."

"She's not a . . ." Erica stopped herself before she said "man."

Abigail folded her arms. "My point: Cis people don't think about this stuff because they've never *had* to. So stop worrying and just, like, enjoy yourself. Try on your stupid fingernail polish or whatever. And, yes, I stole this whole speech from Reddit, but it's good advice, okay?"

Erica smirked. The bell rang, and the hall began to fill with students. "We should go before anybody spots us together."

"Nobody cares, Erica," Abigail said. "You wanna be friends with another lady? Don't think about them figuring *your* secret out. Think about how you've figured *their* secret out. You wanna be friends with Brooke Daniels? Then walk up to her, look her dead in the eye, and say, 'I know you're a fucking tranny.'" Abigail grinned malevolently.

"Go," Erica said. "Go *anywhere* else."

After school, Erica drove past the "SWEE FOR STATE SENATE" sign. Wind buffeted it, but it held firm. Her hand fell across her phone. She imagined texting the number Helen had given her to ask if she'd want to get coffee sometime. Then she thought about how she would have to qualify that it wasn't a date, and she was just looking for some new friends, and she had only *just* gotten divorced, and . . .

She put her hand back on the wheel.

Tuesday night, Brooke and Erica met at the theater. Brooke had canceled rehearsal in favor of an emergency directorial summit to rework the show's blocking to account for John's monstrosity of a set.

And so, without even trying, Erica had found herself alone in a friend-adjacent situation with a person she might possibly want to be friends with. Erica stared at Brooke, trying to figure out how to broach the topic of "friendship." Erica knew she was being too paranoid, but she also didn't know how to stop being paranoid. Abigail's "imagine the person you're talking to is a t-slur" strategy had come up wanting. It was actually incredibly obvious that the overwhelming majority of people were not, in fact, t-slurs.

"We're friends, right, Brooke?" Erica said. The direct approach!

Brooke looked up from her notes. "Yes, I suppose. I think these ladders will be too tall for the people in back to be able to see the actors when they're on them."

Erica hopped offstage, walked halfway back into the theater, then turned. Brooke's instincts were right, as always. The actors' heads would be lost at that height. "You could bring them down to stage front and work around them?"

"That will be more trouble than it's worth."

"You don't have to fit what you want around what John wants."

"It's not a problem," Brooke said. She extended her hand out to help Erica back onstage. "I already told him the set was fine. It's easier for you and me to deal with it."

Brooke walked the length of the stage, counting each footstep to get a rough estimate of the space she would have to work with once John's set was in. She cringed.

"Won't do?" Erica said.

"We have to fit fourteen people on this stage." Brooke put her hands on her hips and sucked on her teeth. "Why did you ask me if we were friends?"

Shit. "Uh, well, since Constance left, you're one of the people I spend most of my time with. It's fine if that just makes us colleagues. But I have friendly feelings toward you."

Brooke's eyebrow raised a half inch, and Erica knew she had gone too far. Before Brooke could say anything in response, though, Erica gestured toward the back of the stage. "He's left us space over there. What if we put all the actors who aren't in the scene here?"

Brooke took several strides toward the back of the stage and nodded. "I suppose I feel friendly toward you as well."

"Oh. Good." Now, Erica found herself in a conversation that felt like the beginning of an illicit extramarital friendship, but at least she was headed in the right direction. She should talk about something else Brooke cared about. "I met Isaiah's opponent. She lives in my neighborhood."

"Ms. Swee? She's a sweet girl." Brooke took big steps along the back of the stage.

"Are you worried about her at all?"

Brooke gave Erica a confused look. "I'm not Isaiah."

"Yes. I know, but . . ." Erica gestured futilely.

"I have friendly feelings toward him?" Brooke smiled, and Erica laughed.

"Aren't you running his campaign?"

"Isaiah doesn't have to *campaign*. People know what he stands for, and they agree with it." Brooke walked, counting out loud.

The old Erica, 2014 Johnny Carino's Erica, would have let things be at that point, content with having different politics and not wanting to let those politics intrude on a good friendship (or series of friendly feelings). The Erica having this conversation, however, couldn't quite ignore the waters that flooded her cerebral cortex again, the ones that wanted her to know she now, unfortunately, had skin in the game. When Brooke reached a triumphant, "Fourteen!" Erica said, "You think people agree with him trying to ban trans students from using the bathrooms at school?"

Brooke snorted. "Isaiah thinks people should be allowed to use the bathroom."

"You know what I mean. It was a cruel bill."

"It was vetoed."

"Who knows what the next governor will do? Or a legislature with enough Isaiah clones to override a veto?" Erica's brain kept pushing. "There's only one trans person at Mitchell High School. Who was that bill meant to protect?"

Brooke turned to look at Erica, excruciatingly slowly. "Is this because you're close with Abigail Hawkes now?"

Erica took a step backward, the back of her shoe hovering over the edge of the stage. She wobbled before righting herself. "She's in my American Literature class, but—"

"Caleb says he's seen you giving her a ride a couple of times."

"Caleb?!" Erica laughed shrilly. "Your son?!" Her pulse was racing. Some genie had screamed its way out of a bottle. If anyone was going to figure out Erica was trans or accuse her of corrupting a poor student's soul, it would *so obviously* be Brooke.

"He is the Caleb I talk to most often, yes. We do live in the same house."

Erica laughed again. Even to her ears, she sounded unhinged. *Brooke knows*, her paranoia insisted. *You stupid motherfucker.* "I gave her a ride after detention one day. They gave her two and a half hours! It was cruel and unusual."

Brooke looked over Erica again, this time with something like renewed appreciation. "That was nice of you. You're a good man, █████."

Erica made herself hop down from the stage, excusing herself to the bathroom. As she raced out of the room, she texted Abigail, *ABORT, ABORT, ABORT!*

Within a few seconds, Abigail replied, *Did you mean to send this to your ex?* But Erica didn't even register it. She was huddled on a toilet in the men's room, willing herself to breathe.

Abigail

Wednesday,

September 28

When I was twelve, my grandpa died. My dad never got along with my mom's family, so I'd only met Grandpa maybe ten times total in my life. A couple of those were when I was a baby and don't really count.

Dad had waited until after the store closed at 8:00 p.m. the day before the funeral to drive to eastern Montana where Mom grew up. They crammed four of us kids into the car, then traded off who was driving when one of them needed to sleep. We stumbled into my aunt's house at six in the morning, and she gave us all hugs. I slept on the couch until noon, then I went to the funeral, and then Dad drove us home without Mom, who wanted to spend a few more days with her family. I think they fought about her doing that. I'm fuzzy on the details, but I do remember her saying, "I'm sorry my father picked such an inconvenient time to die," and then she laughed like a balloon leaking air.

As you picture this, you're probably imagining me wearing a sad little black dress, but twist: Everybody at that funeral thought I was a boy. I even wore a tie that my aunt's roommate (girlfriend) Claire called "snazzy." I didn't cry, and I didn't get in the way, and I was a perfect little gentleman. My mom used to say I was such a sweet little boy until I started "acting up" (being myself), but the joke was on her. She loved a figment of her imagination.

On our way home, Jennifer told Dad we needed to eat *something*. He said, "Okay," in that drawn-out way he did when he was really fucking mad, then found a random pizza place. As I ate my pizza, hoping he would stay angry at Jen and not pay any attention to me, another family walked into the restaurant. Dad, mom, three girls, probably ten, eight, six. The littlest girl swung her mom's arm back and forth. They were laughing.

I just *knew* that if I sat down with them, the world would start making sense. I would stop being my parents' youngest son and become those people's oldest daughter. I would even fit into their "let's have a baby every two years" pattern. All I had to do was stand up and go over there, and my real mom would look at me and smile and say, "There you are. How did I forget you?" All I had to do was stand up and go over there, and Dad would forget me. All I had to do was stand up and go over there. All I had to do.

Jennifer said, "Hey, are you all right?" She smiled sadly. "Hard day, isn't it?" I nodded. The other family laughed together. I ate the rest of my pizza.

I try not to think about my life before I was Abigail, but I do think about that night a lot.

I find Caleb rummaging through his locker while his jock friends all hang around. He's got this thing where he stands like he hasn't ever thought about how to escape attention. He likes being seen, the fucker.

He and his friends laugh at something, and he takes a step back. I have an opening, so I walk up to him quickly and slam his locker shut. "You spying on me?"

His eyes cycle through several variations of terrified. The last thing he wants is people knowing he knows me, much less fucked me.

"I don't know what you're talking about," he says, faking an easy smile.

"Then why is your fucking mom asking our English teacher about giving me a ride home from detention a couple of weeks ago?" (Finding ways not to misgender Erica in casual conversation is fun. You should see if you can do it too!)

"My mom and Mr. Skyberg are friends. I thought she'd want to know?" Caleb swallows as a couple of his friends drift toward class. "I was worried. I don't want anybody taking advantage of you."

"Pretty fucking ironic of you to say that, huh?"

His friends turn back to listen. Caleb's face goes green. "I don't know what you're talking about."

His dumbass best friend Kyle glares at me. "You want me to get rid of her?"

"It's fine." Caleb leans in close, like he's about to kiss me or punch me or both. "It wasn't just after detention though. I saw you and Mr. Skyberg having lunch together the other day."

"For fuck's sake, Caleb. Our teacher is helping me get into college." Fuck. It *is* a pretty good lie. "Stop spreading rumors about the trans girl, or I'll start spreading rumors about you." His eyes flinch, and his throat makes a noise I'm not sure he realized it would. "And stop. Watching. Me." He immediately falls back into the huddle of his friends, who collapse around him to protect him with their laughter. It goes from unnerved to jeering quickly, and he joins in. The fucker.

Megan is waiting at my locker for some reason. "Are you okay?"

"I'm fine. You can go to class."

"I can be late."

"You? Can be *late*?" She grins, and I can see she's leaning down the hall, so she can bolt for it. But she's still standing here and looking at me. Weird. "Seriously, I'm fine."

She nods like she's about to deliver an important speech. "That guy is a total fucking asshole."

"You're so bad at swearing," I say, but I laugh.

After that, everything goes back to normal for, like, thirty-six hours. Erica doesn't text me or talk to me outside of class, and Caleb ignores me so hard I know he'll jerk off to me before bed. Jennifer has a tense phone call that must be with Mom, and Ron restarts *Breaking Bad* for the five hundredth time.

Except Megan keeps bugging me. She wants me to come along Thursday when she goes to see Helen Swee, the poor bitch running against Isaiah Rose and someone with a name that sounds like she's trying to cover a swear word by pretending to sneeze. Megan's theory is if I'm there, Helen will let Megan take over her campaign, because "people instinctively trust you, Abigail!"

I do not think this is true, but Megan has a nice car, and she always lets me pick what we listen to, so I go along.

Helen is running her own campaign, though there aren't any billboards featuring her face or anything yet. (Who am I kidding? She's a Democrat in Mitchell. She'll never raise enough money to get a billboard.) She's probably thirty-two or thirty-three, with short red hair (dyed) and clothes spattered with fresh paint. There are photos of her rock climbing everywhere and one of her with Bernie Sanders. I'm starting to see why Megan wanted me here. If Megan has the brains, I have the vibe. You can imagine me living in this house at thirty, right? I'd get a cat, but that would be the only difference.

"Want a snack, girls?" Helen says, then tosses us a pack of Oreos. "I don't bake. Never ends well. What can I help you with?"

Megan sets down her binder. (I didn't tell you Megan had a binder before this, but I 100 percent guarantee you that when you were picturing her meeting with a local politician, you pictured her with a binder.) "Okay," Megan says. "So—"

"I'm not putting a high schooler in charge of my campaign," Helen says. "But I have plenty of buttons if you want to hand them out at school." (Oh, damn, she raised enough money to make buttons? She's really going places! She might lose by less than thirty points.)

Megan's face falls, like she's ready to give up already. I can't have that. I'm hoping to snag a couple more Oreos for the road. "Megan knows more about politics than anybody in this town," I say.

Helen's eyes shift toward me. She probably just realized I'm not a holographic projection Megan brought along to make it seem like she knew people her own age. "I graduated with a poli-sci degree from Georgetown."

"Who graduates from Georgetown and moves to Mitchell?" I say.

"My mom's here. Don't know how many years I have left with her. Besides. Should we write off places like this just because they've traditionally voted for Republicans in large numbers? Why not try giving a shit?" Okay, *fine*, I'll wear this woman's button.

"So, Dakota Wesleyan University," Megan says. She must have been giving her presentation mentally this whole time. "A tiny school. Past campaigns have largely ignored it. There's an untapped pool of voters there. Mitchell High has over one hundred students who've turned eighteen already or will turn eighteen before election day. *And* Mitchell has a huge population of service-industry workers who don't tend to vote. Abigail and I think these are potential Swee voters." (I do?!)

Helen laughs at Megan's Megan-ness. "I've thought of all of this, you realize. The problem is money. The state party has no money. The local party *really* has no money. My mom lent me $123 to make buttons. Meanwhile, Isaiah Rose is backed by Victor and Brooke Daniels, and they'll outspend you every time." Fucking Caleb's family. Now I want Helen to win so he cries.

"Oh, Megan's dad is loaded," I say. Megan winces.

"I know," Helen says. "Your dad already told me he supports me but doesn't want to give me any money. I'm a lost cause, he says."

"He might donate if I was on your campaign!" This is, like, fifteen pages in her binder past where Megan left off. Good for her for rolling with the punches. "We could get some of our friends to help us campaign. We'd call it Students for Democracy."

"What about Principal DeWaard? I'm sure he'd be *thrilled* to have someone start a Democratic student organization. He just *loved* me when I went to school there."

"He's an ass, yeah," Megan says. "But the members of Students for Democracy wouldn't support you specifically. We'd support democracy."

Helen full-on laughs at that. "Fuck." Then she sizes me up, trying to figure out my deal. "Why are you here? Other than because she asked you to come?"

Sometimes I don't let myself know the answer to a question until somebody else asks it. "Because I'm trans. And Isaiah Rose doesn't want me to be."

Helen doesn't hire us as her campaign managers because we're teenagers. (If you really thought we were going to take over the campaign from someone who graduated from Georgetown, what are you even doing here?) But she does give us a bunch of buttons and promises to speak to "Students for Democracy" whenever we want.

We put the box in the back of Megan's car, and she gestures for me to follow her down the block. "Now we need a faculty advisor, and Mr. Skyberg lives right around here, so I thought we could ask him. You two are close, right?"

"Just because Caleb—"

"He was trying to start shit. I don't buy it. But I've seen you and Mr. Skyberg talking a lot. It's cool. I have teachers who really inspire me too."

Before I can come up with a good reason why we *shouldn't* do this, Megan walks up to the house, then rings the doorbell. She rings it again, and then she knocks, and then she rings it some more, and then, finally, out of breath, Erica throws open the door, and from the desperate look she gives me, I can tell she was doing some sort of girl something and is now completely freaked out to see me like this. Oh, one of her nails is smeared pink. It's cute!

"Mr. Skyberg, we have a proposition for you," Megan says. Erica quickly waves the two of us in, and as I enter, she glares. I try to silently communicate that this was *not* my idea, and it works because all trans people are telepathic.

No, it doesn't work. Erica shuts the door and leans against it, hand plastered flat out against the door. "What's up?"

Megan launches into her pitch. It's basically the same one she gave Helen but tailored for Erica's ears—important to help students understand their role in democracy, help work to effect positive change right here in Mitchell, etc., etc., etc.

I, naturally, take the chance to look around because I've never been to Erica's house before. (Yes, if anybody caught me there, it would be a Big Problem, but there's never a problem being anywhere when Megan is around because her entire personality is a piece of paper saying you have permission to be where you are.) It's a little rundown and a little empty, and there's barely any furniture.

I must have wandered too far away because Erica, who has been doing a great impression of someone who finds Megan fascinating, clears her throat.

I'm at the entrance to the hall that leads to the rest of the house. I should probably stop seeming like I want to check out my teacher's stuff, but I also want to check out Erica's stuff. I make my best innocent face and say, "Bathroom?"

Erica sighs. "Second door on the right."

When I leave the bathroom (always take the chance to pee!), Megan is saying, "Representative Rose has sponsored horrible anti-trans legislation, which my colleague, Abigail, can speak about when she returns," and I hear Erica say, "Uh-huh, uh-huh," like she's much more worried about what I'm doing. And she's right to be because before I know it, I'm in her bedroom.

On a card table lined with paper towels, the bottle of nail polish I bought her lies on its side, pink oozing from it. From the big pink smears on the paper towels, I can see where she tried to wipe off the polish before answering the door and made things worse. I turn the bottle right side up, so she doesn't lose any more.

I turn to leave and see a picture on the wall. Erica wears a tuxedo at her wedding. She's got her arms around her ex, whose boobs look amazing in her dress. (She was evidently kind of hot before she decided to live among the Pinterest moms.) I look at Erica in her tux again. Her mouth smiles appropriately, like she's assuring everyone this is the happiest fucking day of her life. But her eyes have this look of sad isolation in them. She didn't realize it when she took the picture, but she was trying to contact me, Abigail, who just happened to live over a decade into the future. I have that look in my old pictures too. I found her, and she found me. That's something, at least.

When I get back to the living room, Megan is still talking, and Erica looks like she's going to jackhammer herself into the floor. She's doing the weird thing where she stretches out and collapses her hands, and I realize she's trying to hide her nail polish. She's just making it more obvious. Fortunately, Megan is not known for picking up on minute details. "So how many magazines can we interest you in?" I say, and they both stare at me.

"No magazines," Erica says, "but I'd be happy to help out with your little club."

"Thank you! Thank you, thank you, thank you," Megan says. "We won't let you down!"

"Technically, I won't let you down, but I appreciate the sentiment."

I'm already at the door. "C'mon, Megan. Let's let . . . Skyberg . . . have a nice evening." (Shut up. You're so much worse at not misgendering her, and I fucking know it.)

Megan talks the whole way back to my house, and I think about texting Erica again. I know it's annoying when she does it to me, but I kind of want her to know everything's okay. I'm not a *total* monster.

Finally, when I'm back alone in my room, I decide to. *Thank you for helping us save democracy*, I text. *PS: Your singular pink nail looks cute.* She starts to type something, then stops, but after a couple minutes, she gives that last text a little heart.

Unfortunately, Erica really is the first trans woman I've met in real life who isn't me. Yeah, I've met other trans people online, but they all either bummed me out or made me want to stab them because their parents let them get on hormones in the womb. Erica is different. She annoys the shit out of me, but she's *real*.

Megan has been studying statistics to combat Isaiah Rose's shitty arguments. The other night, she said, out of nowhere, that "trans youths" (hello!) are much less likely to commit suicide if they have the support and affirmation of a parent or other authority figure like a teacher. I laughed and said, "Imagine a teacher at our school treating me like anything other than a mess somebody else was supposed to clean up!" She made a sad face and changed the subject.

I think maybe now I get what she means, though. I've felt a little bit less like dying these last few weeks. When Erica came out to me, I hated it, but it was also the first time anybody had ever *recognized* me. I *felt* it before she said anything. She didn't see the trans part of me or the girl part of me or even the trans girl part of me. She just saw *me*. She didn't even have to *try* to see me. And I could see her, too, the second she said her name. Even with her dopey mustache and her slightly too-small coffee-stained shirt, I saw *her*. It's a thing we transes can do. The second we learn who somebody is, we can make them snap into place. "There you are," we say, because there you are.

Erica's not my friend, but she's not just my teammate either. She's some secret other thing. Maybe I have to figure out what that is.

This is all really complicated, and I can admit I'm in over my head here, so let's ask an adult authority figure who supports and affirms me. Let's ask Ron. He's washing the dishes. He's probably not thinking about anything too important.

"Ron, have you ever known someone who you had one big thing in common with, but then almost nothing else?"

He frowns. "Tyson at the shop and I don't have much in common, but we're both Bears fans, so we bond over that."

Jesus fucking Christ, Ron. "It's a little more than that."

He sets down a plate and turns toward me, trying to look authoritative. "*Oh*. Is there another trans girl at your school?"

"You could put it that way."

"Good for you! That must feel like a relief! When I was the only Bears fan at—" I laugh, and he laughs too. "Sorry. Not the same thing."

He gives me a hug, which is a new thing we're trying out, and then, somebody knocks at the door. "Who the fuck is that?" he says. It's weird when he swears too.

I answer the door. Caleb stands there, hands in his pockets. His enormous truck has a wheel up over the curb, mushing the grass. He takes a deep, wavering breath. "Hi," he says.

"This better be good," I say. He steps inside and wobbles, grabbing the doorframe. "Are you drunk?"

"Not drunk." He notices Ron, who's drying his hands on a towel. "Who's that?"

"Hi. I'm Ron." He waves. "I can give you kids some—"

"Stay, Ron," I say. "Whatever Caleb has to say to me—"

"I'm here, okay? My truck is parked outside where everybody can see it. Is that enough for you?" Caleb takes a step toward me, backing me against the wall. "Abigail," he says. He puts a hand on the side of my face. "Abigail."

Ron starts to say something, so I say, "It's okay, Ron!" I put a hand on Caleb's elbow. "I don't want to be a secret anymore. It really fucking sucks."

"Okay. No more secrets. Okay." He cradles my face between his hands, then leans in. "My mom," he says just before he kisses me, "is going to shit a brick."

October

Erica

Sunday,

October 2

Erica spent Sunday afternoon painting and repainting her nails. Keeping the soft, sunset-pink color from spreading everywhere proved frustrating, but by her third attempt, if you ignored the hair sprouting from the backs of her thick, blotchy fingers, her nails looked lovely.

She doused a cotton ball in nail polish remover then paused. She wanted to show someone other than herself. And the only person she could show was Abigail.

She hesitated. Yes, last Wednesday, for the first time ever, Abigail had sent Erica a text unbidden after she and Megan visited. But Erica had been right to draw a hard line and not reply. If too many people started asking questions, they would assume something untoward was happening.

Fuck it. It was one text. She sent the picture captioned: *Sunday afternoon.*

Almost immediately, Abigail replied, *better than I can do???*

Thanks. I googled "how to paint fingernails." // Felt like a dumb asshole.

It's hard!!!!!!!!!! // painting the nail and not your entire finger??? // this is why I gave up on being femme and went for broke on my cheerfulness convincing everyone I'm a lady

Erica could feel herself getting sucked back in. Talking to Abigail often felt like trying to convince a dog whose back legs had been replaced by a cart to trust you, but Abigail also *knew* Erica. No one else did. Still, Erica had sworn off most intoxicants years ago—they made the gender feelings too potent. She could swear off this one too.

Until another text floated in: *WEAR THEM TO SCHOOL TOMORROW*

What?! No!

oh I'm Erica and if I do something nice for myself everybody will notice I'm not a miserable piece of shit and ask me what's up sob sob sob // JUST DO IT // NOBODY WILL NOTICE // GUARANTEED

Everyone will notice, Abigail. Everyone.

Less than five // FOR REAL // and zero is less than five

Erica knew Abigail was wrong. Everyone around Erica watched for any sign of queerness like a hawk. She hadn't survived boys' locker rooms in the 1990s to *not* learn that lesson.

She scrolled back up to the picture. Her nails *did* look cute . . .

Fuck it.

In all, five people noticed Erica's nails. The first was Abigail.

She arrived for American Lit early, not so subtly let her eyes drop to Erica's nails, then nodded. "Happy Monday!" she said, in the manner of a body snatcher, before sitting at her desk and pulling out her phone. After a second, Erica's phone buzzed with a *NICE NAILS, BITCH.*

When the bell rang at the end of class, Abigail lingered, seeming like she might say something, before she gave a thumbs up and turned to go.

At the door, she turned back. "I don't count. You're still at zero."

Erica set her internal counter to one.

The second was Megan Osborne.

She waited outside Erica's last class of the day, clutching two Tupperware containers of cookies, rolled-up posterboard, and a box full of markers and Helen Swee campaign swag. A Crock-Pot sitting at her feet sent tendrils of steam into the air. She wore a light blue T-shirt reading "Students for DEMOCRACY!!" in black, bubbly letters.

"Are you ready? It's our first meeting!"

Erica laughed. "Seeing you, I'm starting to think I'm not." Erica picked up the Crock-Pot and was greeted with the scent of cinnamon, cloves, and apple cider. "Principal DeWaard said all I have to do is watch to make sure you don't do anything too partisan."

"Partisanship is an important part of democracy, so I won't tell if you won't tell."

Megan's eyes drifted across Erica's fingers. She said nothing but almost dropped her box of markers, only catching it at the last second. At the door to the classroom where Students for Democracy would meet, Megan smiled. "Your nails look rad, Mr. Skyberg."

Erica had the lie preloaded. "My eight-year-old niece painted them. I haven't had time to remove the polish." She didn't have a niece at all, much less one interested in helping her confront the vagaries of gender in the form of pink nail polish. But Megan wasn't going to fact-check this conversation. Most likely.

"Tell your niece I think she's amazing at painting nails."

Inside the classroom, Abigail perched atop a desk, while Caleb Daniels straddled a chair backward, gazing up at her. They smiled indulgently at each other. If Erica didn't know better, she would swear they were dating.

"Are *you* joining the club?" Megan said to Caleb, her voice brittle.

"I care about democracy," Caleb said, eyes fixed on Abigail, who slid her gaze over to Megan. The two carried out a silent conversation over the top of Caleb's head before Erica cleared her throat and made everybody set up for the meeting.

A handful of other students trickled in, and Megan stepped to the front of the classroom, looking to Erica. "Should I start?" Erica waved for her to begin, and Megan's gaze briefly snagged on Erica's nails again before tearing free to look back at the others. Abigail still sat on her desk, legs dangling. Caleb leaned back against her. Megan clapped her hands and said, “Democracy!”

Erica set her mental counter to two, even though she was sure Abigail would say Megan didn’t count either for reasons Abigail would make up on the spot.

The third—and Erica was quite sure even Abigail would admit this person counted—was Helen Swee.

Erica and Helen had bumped into each other a few more times after the yard-sign encounter. The experience had always been pleasant. Across that handful of meetings, Erica had realized that Helen was aware of who people were on some deep, subterranean level. It was probably why she got into politics.

Helen showed up halfway through the Students for Democracy meeting, a computer bag and purse slung over her shoulder. She balanced two cups of coffee atop a pile of boxes.

Megan, still standing, turned toward the door with such excitement that she took a tiny step to keep her balance. “Here’s one of our local candidates now!” She went to Helen’s side to help, gingerly lifting the two coffee cups and carefully setting them down on Erica’s desk.

“Megan, they’re not filled with *acid*,” Abigail said, laughing.

Helen grimaced. “I see we already have cookies.” She opened one of her boxes to reveal store-bought cookies with smiling jack-o’-lantern faces. Caleb plucked one out and bit off an eye. Helen’s other box held a large collection of “SWEE!” buttons. Her face fell farther when she saw Megan had brought those too. “I see we’ve got it all covered.”

“Sorry,” Megan said. “I should have brought *Halloween* cookies instead of these. My mistake.” She looked like she might cry. Megan clearly had an enormous crush on Helen, but she and everyone except Erica hadn’t realized it yet.

Helen picked up the coffee cups, turning both in every direction until spotting the word “PUMP” on one. “This one is yours if you want, Mr. Skyberg. They gave me a pumpkin spice latte when I wanted a cappuccino. No, I don't know how they got from A to B."

"I love pumpkin spice season, thanks," Erica said.

Helen grinned. "I'd make a joke about you being a basic white girl, but—" she nodded to Megan, who already had her mouth open to say something "—that would be sexist."

Erica didn't think the moment counted as the first time she'd been properly gendered by someone who didn't know she was trans, but she would count it as a win all the same.

Also, she was terrified. She tucked her nails up into the meat of her hand, where they couldn't be seen. Helen's eyes caught the movement. She seemed like she might say something, but she launched instead into her presentation, which was mostly an opportunity for Megan to ask questions about the importance of state government and why Helen thought *she* should be the senator for South Dakota Legislative District Twenty. (Megan evidently knew more about what legislative district they lived in than Erica did.)

Megan and Abigail had lured eight students from across the school's various cliques to the meeting, and the kids listened surprisingly closely. Caleb even took notes. Only Abigail seemed distracted, staring out the window, even when Helen directly invoked her.

Helen lingered at the meeting's end, until only she and Erica were left in the classroom. "I like your nails," Helen said. "That's a good color on you."

"Thanks," Erica said. "My eight-year-old niece . . . you know how it is."

"Sure." Helen seemed unconvinced. "Whoever painted them, they look great. Fuck anybody who tells you otherwise."

Erica tucked her nails back into her hand again. "Thanks." She couldn't think of anything else to say. Well, one other thing, but— "Would you want to have a drink sometime? Or coffee?" She had evidently just said it.

Helen's face fell by a millimeter. You would only notice if you were a careful observer of the many microexpressions of disappointment, which Erica was. "I'm busy right now. I have a boyfriend," Helen said in a way that made the two thoughts seem unrelated, separate excuses arrived at independently.

Erica flailed. "Oh, God! No! I'm sorry! I have play rehearsal tonight, and I have . . . an ex-wife? Which, obviously, I will probably start dating again someday, but not right now and probably not with you."

The slenderest of threads tugged one corner of Helen's mouth upward. "So you're saying you need a wingwoman? I'm down for that. Let's get coffee. Soon."

Relief filled Erica so swiftly she almost missed that a real human woman within plus or minus five years of her age had agreed to do a friend-like activity with her. She held the door for Helen as she carried her precariously balanced items out of the room. "I'll text you?"

"Please! I will absolutely forget we had this conversation in five seconds." Helen took several steps down the hall, then took smaller steps to turn in place to face Erica, looking at her over the top of the items in her hands. "Remember: Fuck anybody who tells you otherwise."

Erica, mentally setting her counter to three, gave her a thumbs-up.

The fourth, to Erica's horror, was Brooke Daniels.

John and some friends accompanied Constance to rehearsal that night to start building the set, and the clamor left Brooke perturbed. She would begin telling Erica what to do, only to be interrupted by the sound of a power drill or the clatter of something falling over above the stage, followed by a muffled "Sorry!" Brooke would look above her head, grimace, wait a five count, and resume, only to be interrupted again a minute or two later.

Finally, Brooke shook her head and angled a thumb toward the exit. "Let's go talk out in the lobby. That might be easier."

Brooke sat down on one of the lobby's benches, then stood again a moment later after another clatter from inside the theater. "They're so *loud*," she said. "How can they be so loud?"

"Power tools. Loud." Erica gestured broadly for emphasis.

Brooke's eyes fell across Erica's fingers like a spotlight. Erica immediately closed them back into her hand, and Brooke walked toward the opposite end of the lobby, tucking her hands in her jean back pockets. "We need to get started." She looked back, eyes flickering to where Erica's fingers made imploding fists.

"I could work the act-three stuff with Constance. Maybe?"

"Yes. I don't buy it right now. She's not desperate enough, not sad enough. I know she has it in her. As an actor, I mean."

Erica stared through the enormous glass walls of the lobby at the cars passing the theater. She tucked her fingers even more tightly in on themselves, so none of the people in those cars could see her nails either.

"I think my son might be dating Abigail Hawkes." Brooke sounded like she was calling to Erica from the bottom of a well. When she turned, she saw Brooke had her back to her, voice just loud enough to be heard. "Have you heard anything?"

"No. But they're in a club I supervise. They seemed pretty . . . close."

Brooke snorted. "No wonder he cares about politics now."

"Megan Osborne could be blackmailing him, but I think it's more likely he's into Abigail."

"I can't have them dating." Brooke waved her hand in the air. "Isaiah."

"Is it only Isaiah?" Erica found herself saying, "Abigail is a good kid. She'd make a great girlfriend. If that's what's happening."

"You can find fingernail polish remover at most stores," Brooke said. "It's very cheap."

Erica sagged against the glass, imagining it splintering. "My niece painted them."

"I didn't know you had a niece," Brooke said. "I get it. When Ruth was little, she liked to paint Victor's nails. It was cute. But he always made sure to wipe it off before he left the house."

"I didn't have the time," Erica said. "I will tonight."

The door to the theater burst open, John and company pushing through. He waved to Brooke, then offered a salute to Erica. "Theater's all yours," he said.

"Thank you, John!" Brooke said. After the men had left, she shook her head. "And only fifteen minutes late!" She disappeared into the theater without another word.

A nauseated whimper escaped Erica's throat. "That's four," she said.

Brooke was right. Constance didn't sound desperate or sad enough.

In the third act of *Our Town*, Emily, whom the first two acts follow through youth and eventual marriage, discovers she has died. The Stage Manager—a character equal parts dramaturg, narrator, and god—offers her the chance to revisit any day from her life, though he recommends against it. Emily doesn't listen and chooses to relive her twelfth birthday. The third act had long been one of Erica's favorites, for reasons she now found laughably on the nose. (A woman realizing how much of life has passed her by only after it is too late? Please.)

When Brooke cast Constance in the role, Erica had been certain that Constance would capture the aching feeling of someone reaching out to grasp a life they could see but not touch. Yet so far, Constance's performance felt distant and lost inside herself.

"It's not working," Constance said. She and Erica had gone back into the lobby to run the monologue over and over again. Erica had asked Constance to stand on a bench and perform to the handful of cars still out as the hour crept past 9:00 p.m. She had hoped that Constance delivering the monologue to the town she had lived in for so long would unlock something good, but it had just made things even stiffer. "Why isn't it working?"

Erica tried the direct approach. “What was your twelfth birthday like?”

“If I have to relive my twelfth birthday, I’ll murder someone,” Constance said.

Erica sighed. She should have known her question would smack into the iron walls Constance placed around her past. “Never mind that. How long did you live here in Mitchell?”

Constance narrowed her gaze, like she had been asked a trick question. “Nine years. And Stickney’s not far away. I’m still here all the time.” She hopped off the bench.

“I never see you.”

“I make a point of not visiting Mitchell High or our former house, so it’s not that hard to avoid you.” She winced. “That was meaner than I wanted it to be.”

“How mean did you want it to be?”

“Only a little.” Constance took a step toward Erica, bouncing on the balls of her feet. “I know you’re trying to get me to build a personal attachment to the material, but I don’t love Mitchell like you do.”

“I don’t love Mitchell either! You just implied I only leave my house to go to work.”

“Maybe you don’t love Mitchell.” Constance took another two steps closer to Erica. She was close enough to touch now, and to stop herself from doing so, Erica reached up to run a hand through the long hair that didn’t exist yet. Constance’s eyes watched Erica’s hand move. A spark of recognition flickered in them, but Constance didn’t say anything. “But you do love knowing what to expect.”

“That’s not fair.”

“[redacted], you’ve wanted to direct this play for as long as I’ve known you, and it’s about a town where a man can literally tell you who’s doing what at any given time of day.” Constance was so close to Erica that she had to look up, her lower lip disappearing beneath her teeth. “The asinine blocking scheme mirrors itself, so nothing is ever out of place. I feel trapped.”

"By the blocking?"

Constance abruptly turned on her heel and walked back to the bench. Erica suddenly, painfully felt her absence. "When I die, nobody is dragging me back here for anything. But if I *had* to pick a day to relive, it would be pet-store day."

Her face fell at Erica's blank expression. "Tell me you remember pet-store day? █████!" Constance rolled her eyes and plunged ahead. "There was a rumor that Isaiah Rose and the Living Waters crew were snake handlers, so you and I went to Pet World to see how many snakes we could buy. The lady got this albino boa out and handed it to you. You stretched your arm *all* the way out, and the snake wrapped itself around your hand, and you made a noise like a baby spotting himself in a mirror. I asked the woman if I could order a dozen poisonous snakes, and she said, 'Ma'am, we don't deal reptiles in bulk.' You gave the snake back, and we ran out of there, laughing, like dumbass kids." She sat down on the bench, smiling a little. "But when I die, I won't need to revisit that day. I remember it pretty well."

"I had forgotten," Erica said. Like too much of her past, that day had slipped beneath the waves of her dysphoria. "You'd go back to that day? Not one with . . ."

"I love John, but he's scared of snakes."

Erica laughed, and the open joy of the sound startled her. Constance beckoned her to sit down beside her, and when Erica did, Constance pulled out her phone, searching for something. Constance leaned forward, her curly hair falling so it obscured her face, and as she shifted her weight, her thigh pressed more fully against Erica's, leaving Erica tongue-tied.

"You wanna see this stupid baby's heartbeat?" Constance handed her phone to Erica. Onscreen, white outlines haunted the edges of a fuzzy black image. Erica realized it was a video and pressed play.

Erica felt Constance's eyes take in her pink fingernails. Once again, she said nothing. Onscreen, something fluttered, a firefly blinking on and off. The heartbeat's thrum echoed softly, and then John, off camera, said, "Oh my God, Connie, look—"

The video cut out, and Constance leaned over Erica's shoulder, her hair falling across Erica's arm in soft tendrils as she took her phone back. "I can't believe you let him call you Connie."

"Unlike you, I like trying new things."

"Like having a baby?"

Constance's smile faltered. A memory from another life, one where she and Constance decided to have a child and Erica was the one showing this video to everyone she knew, pierced her. (*Had* she wanted to have a baby all those years? The question was worth exploring once she could take a break from the full-scale renovation of her gender.)

Erica took the phone to watch again. "That's beautiful." Constance looked away.

The lobby door opened, admitting John and his friends once again. One (Erica thought his name was Ollie) sipped on a soda from Taco John's. Constance slid a millimeter away from Erica as John approached. He put a big, meaty hand on Erica's shoulder, then looked down to see the heartbeat thrumming on the phone screen. "Isn't that great?" he said.

"What's great?" Potentially Ollie crowded in to watch. "Oh, awesome! That's your kid!" John preened, and Erica's stomach lurched. She realized all John's friends could clearly see her pink nails holding Constance's phone. Erica had just started to hope they hadn't noticed, when Potentially Ollie took a slurp from his soda and said, "I see why things didn't work out with Connie! Look at this guy's nails!"

John, who seemed to have missed the pink polish before, patted Erica on the back. "Don't be a dick, dude. ▒▒▒'s just a theater person. Makeup and costumes. All that. It doesn't mean anything. Right, ▒▒▒?"

Erica opened her mouth to say something, then shut it again. She was aware, somehow, that Constance was looking right at her, gaze focused. Her lie swooped into the middle of her distress and escaped her lips before she could catch it. "My eight-year-old niece painted them, and I haven't had a chance to wash it off."

Fuck. Constance knew she didn't have a niece. She met Constance's gaze, psychically pleading with her not to blow her cover. For a millisecond, something ran wild in Constance's eyes, and she was no longer a thirty-five-year-old sometime actress. She was the girl Erica first met and fell in love with. Just as quickly, the moment disappeared.

"Kids!" John said. "If we have a girl, she'll probably wanna do my makeup too, right, babe?"

"Right," Constance said, looking up at John with a forced smile.

"Shelly did my makeup once," another guy said. "I told her she'd made me look like a fucking fag."

The others laughed, and Erica fumbled Constance's phone, dropping it. John stuck out his shoe, so it didn't land directly on the cement floor. Erica stooped to grab it, her breath short. "Relax, ████. We're just giving you a hard time," John said. Erica could hear the "It's just us guys!" behind his words. He was trying to be a good man. He was trying to make everything okay. He was only making things worse.

Erica handed the phone back to Constance, whose eyes still fixed on her. Something blossomed between them. "How is my best niece Ellie anyway?" she said. "I miss seeing her."

Erica diverted the tears that almost fell into a boisterous laugh. "You know Ellie. She's always a little bit too much."

"Tell her," Constance said, "she picked a very good shade for you."

So that was five.

And six and seven and eight and nine and ten if you thought about it.

Which Erica couldn't stop doing.

In the mirror on the back of her closet door, Erica looked at herself.

Her fingers were red from how hard she had scrubbed to get the nail polish off. She could still smell the scent of acetone from the open bottle on the counter in the bathroom. She touched each finger on her right hand to her thumb in turn. These were not fingers that deserved nail polish. They looked so stupid with it on.

She held her phone to her ear. Abigail had initially been annoyed that Erica had *called her* on the *phone*, which was something *only psychopaths* did, but when she heard how distressed Erica was, she immediately tried to help. She was a good kid. Everybody was wrong about her.

"Guys are dicks, Erica. Especially to non-guys," Abigail said. "But they were dicks to you when you thought you were another guy too."

"It hurts less," Erica said. Her belly hung over the waistband of her boxers like a berg about to calve off a glacier. Her navel was so large Constance had once said you could fit a little jewel in there.

"It doesn't hurt less. You're numb. You notice it less," Abigail said.

Erica's rib cage was so large that even if she were able to grow breasts, she imagined them pointing in different directions. Thick hair covered her chest, but it was unable to hide her ridiculous, tiny pink nipples. Her arms were thick and flabby. Her neck looked like a tree stump. Her shoulders—oh, God, her shoulders—spread out and out and out, like they didn't know when to stop. How had she not noticed this before?

"Erica?" Abigail said. "Erica, I promise you can do this." After another long silence, she sighed. "I'm not *only* saying that as your teammate. I'm saying that as someone who cares about you. A lot. I want you to succeed. Go, Erica!"

That ridiculous mustache, the one she once joked she had grown because people in disguises have mustaches; her hollow, sunken eyes, dark circles under them from all those nights staying up until 3:00 a.m. imagining some other self; her rapidly receding hairline; all six feet two inches of her height—how was she *fooling* anyone? "That's easy for you to say, Abigail. You don't have to be me."

"You think I haven't been where you are?"

Erica pulled back her boxers' waistband and looked down at her penis. It was small but obvious, and the second the doctor had pulled her out of her mother, he had taken one look at it and set the entire course of her life in motion, a life full of thwarted attempts to fit in and awkward male bonding that felt like trying to pass a test she hadn't studied for. "It's a boy" wasn't a statement of fact. It was a prophecy, and people hate when prophecies don't come true.

"Erica?" Abigail said Erica's name as though she was trying to remind Erica of something she had forgotten.

"You don't understand, Abigail. At a certain point, you've invested too much in your life. It becomes a sunk-cost fallacy. Millions and millions of men across human history have *wanted* to be women. Maybe now we can be a little bit, sure, but—"

"Don't lump me in to your 'actually a man' business. I am a *lady*, as we know."

Erica wanted to laugh. She couldn't. "Why should I get to transition? Because of the accident of when I live? Because I *want* to? Lots of people want things they can't have, Abigail. You're lucky. You're young. You didn't have a life to screw up."

"I live with my sister because my parents disowned me. Why do you keep forgetting that?" Abigail was pissed off, which was good. Erica needed her to forget she existed if any of this was going to work.

"You can still disappear," Erica said. "Do your woodworking thing."

"Okay, well, that's *different*."

"It's just easier to keep being a guy. There's less painful bullshit. When you're my age, you already know how to hide inside your own life. So I can keep doing that. Wouldn't that be woodworking too? Kind of?"

"Fuck you if you're doing what I think you're doing, Erica."

Erica looked at herself in the mirror again. She had given it a try, and it had gone poorly, and now she was going to give up. There was power in knowing the obvious and choosing to ignore it.

"Thank you for everything, Abigail, but I don't know how to be Erica, if I even ever was her." She smiled to herself, letting the "she" burn up in the atmosphere of her decision. "I know how to be ▒▒▒▒. And that's who I'm going to be."

"Erica, wait, you stupid bi—"

▒▒▒▒ took a deep breath and hung up before Abigail could get him to change his mind.

Abigail

Monday,

October 3

you HUNG UP ON ME??? AFTER ALL I'VE DONE FOR YOU??

you are such a DUMB SLUT, ERICA!!

I squeeze my phone in my hand so hard I worry I might crush it. I really want to throw it through the window.

Fine. One last text.

You'll come crawling back

I block her number, a thing I'm an expert at thanks to how many times I've blocked Mom. I used to have a bad habit of texting her when I felt like shit, until Jennifer told me if I wanted Mom to understand I wasn't ever going to be her brave little man again, I needed to stop encouraging her.

Focus, Abigail. Erica's the piece of shit here. She's bluffing. She wouldn't give up. You've seen the goofy way she smiles when you call her Erica. No way is she giving that back. If—when—*she wants back into my good graces, you'll make her beg. The dumb bitch.*

I crank "Nobody Dies" by Thao & the Get Down Stay Down, put my phone on top of my dresser, then pancake myself on my bed. It's 11:54 p.m., so some would consider playing loud music inconsiderate, but sometimes, the only other trans girl you know a little bit tries to take everything back before hanging up on you.

Also, Jennifer and Ron are watching *The Office* in their room. I'm not waking them up. I'm not a *total* bitch. Not like Erica.

Or Mom. I *could* text Mom, you know? Call her a dumb bitch too. Really light up her Monday night. I lift my head up to look at my phone on the dresser, a few steps away. Still. It's over there, and I'm right here. If I text Mom, Jennifer will get pissy. I lay my head back down.

Focus, Abigail. It's hard to think about one thing sometimes. My brain finds five different thoughts and chases them all at once. I get caught in the middle. But okay. If I thought about texting Mom, something's got me all fucked-up.

Obviously, it's fucking Erica. She wouldn't do it. She *couldn't* do it.

The song starts over. About thirty seconds in, someone pounds on the door. "Abigail, it is *midnight*," Jennifer says

I get up and open the door. "So? Aren't you and Ron trying to watch TV until you think I've fallen asleep, so you can have sex?"

Jennifer takes a deep breath and lets it out slowly, trying to seem like I didn't just piss her off. "You think you understand everything." She looks more closely at me and frowns. "Have you been crying?" (Have I been? Maybe? Like I said—hard to focus.) "Did you and Megan have a fight?"

It briefly throws me that Jennifer knows Megan exists, but I guess I talk about her often enough. "It's nothing." Jennifer folds her arms. She's not letting this go. Cool. "My . . . friend . . . Erica—I know her through support group—we had a fight. About trans stuff."

I'm betting no cis person (especially Jennifer) wants to get into the middle of a fight trans people are having about trans stuff. And I'm right! Jennifer shakes her head. "I can see why that would upset you. If you want to talk . . ."

"I don't."

"Sure. Well, ten more minutes of music? Then *you* should get to bed. School tomorrow. Jesus, listen to me."

"Fifteen more minutes."

"Fine." Her eyes flicker across my evidently-cry-adjacent face, the phone on my dresser. "Talk to your friend tomorrow. When you've both had time to get out of the blast radius of your fight.

And whatever you're upset about, come get me before you text Mom, okay? Please?"

Fucking Jennifer. "You think you understand everything," I say, a pitch-perfect imitation.

She smiles. "Love you, Abigail."

Despite Jennifer's advice, I decide not to talk to Erica again until she begs. It doesn't take long. The next day, after American Lit, she asks me to come up and talk to her, probably because she wants to apologize and tell me how much she misses me.

When she says my name, though, it's like she thinks I'm the same as any other student. She doesn't look up from the paper she's reading when I wait by her desk. Only after all the other students have gone does she finally look at me.

"I said some things yesterday that I'm not proud of. I wanted to apologize."

A good-enough start! "You were stressed. It happens."

"When you talk to me in class, I would appreciate if you don't call me 'Skyberg.' 'Mr. Skyberg' will do." She straightens her pile of papers by knocking them against the desk. "I'm not kidding."

"I'm amazed you found a way to be even more annoying."

She gets up and closes the door to the classroom. (*So* much more suspicious, Erica!) "I know that when I was thinking I might be trans—"

"Erica, you're trans."

"I'm not. But even if I was, don't I get to decide if I transition or not?" The bitch *smirks* at me. "I read about it on Reddit."

"If you were *anybody else*, yes. But you're you, and you are being extremely irritating, and I, Abigail, get to decide that you, Erica, are trans and should start taking hormones so you become less irritating."

"Mr. Skyberg. Please."

"Jesus Christ." I pick up my books to leave. If she wants to lie to herself for the rest of her life, I'm not going to play along with it. Yesterday afternoon, she was ready to face paint a trans flag on herself. Now she backs out? Fine by me.

"You act like this is easy. You act like I'm not literally endangering my life if I go out some night and happen upon the wrong group of people. I'm too old, Abigail." Her voice cracks. "Not all of us get to live our lives. There's nothing wrong with that."

"You're so scared of losing your life you don't even have one."

Her eyes get a little glassy and distant. She looks out the window in the door to the hallway, where we can both see Megan standing just off to the side. She thinks we can't see her, but she's looking into the room, watching everything closely. Also annoying. "Megan's waiting for you."

"She does that. She's dumb enough to want to hang out with me." Erica opens her mouth, but I cut her off. "You don't get to tell me not to be mean to myself, because if you're going to spend the rest of your life lying to yourself, then we're *really* not friends."

"I'm not lying to myself. I'm being selective about which parts of myself I acknowledge."

I don't even know what to say to that, so I laugh and start to leave.

"It's not *easy*, Abigail. Please stop acting like it is just because things turned out okay for you."

I have a billion things to say back to that, but something in me says she's trying to keep me arguing, so I don't. I walk away and leave her alone with herself. I'm not going to give her the satisfaction. "Fuck you, *Mr.* Skyberg." She mumbles something that doesn't sound like words. "What? I thought you wanted me to call you that."

She swallows hard. "Are you sure dating Caleb is a good idea, given who his mother is?" I fold my arms and glare at her. "She hates people like . . . you." It's obvious not saying "people like us" made her feel like she was stabbing herself.

"Fuck you again. I don't need your advice. We're not friends. Remember?"

She grips the papers in her hand so tight her knuckles turn white. I could swear she's trembling. She swallows again and motions toward the door.

I should leave, but some part of me refuses to. "You are a ridiculous person, but if you decide to be you again . . . you can tell me. Until then, leave me the fuck alone."

Megan's expression makes it clear that she heard how I ended that conversation. "You'd tell me if anything was wrong, right? You and Mr. Skyberg *do* spend a lot of time together, and if you're telling him to leave you the fuck alone . . ."

What the hell *is* this? Stop giving a shit about me, Megan! "It's not a problem. Just a persistent teacher who thinks I can be convinced to go to college. Which I'm not doing."

"Why not?" Her face crumples. Did she think we were gonna be roomies or something?

"I'm not you. I didn't clear out an entire bedroom wall so I could make an upper-middle-class vision board to make sure I never do anything interesting." Okay, that was too much. Fucking Erica. Getting me all off my game.

Megan balls up her fists and takes a deep breath, disguising a sob as a hiccup. "I didn't deserve that," she says. She spins on her heel and walks away.

Follow her, Abigail, you dumb bitch.

I turn back to my locker because I have current events with Caleb next, and I want to do my makeup in my mirror. (I'm embarrassed too.) But as I'm staring at myself, I can see my face is red, like I'm really mad, which is maybe true? Megan obviously just went to the bathroom. If I go in there, maybe I can still—

At some point, Megan Osborne stopped being "Megan Osborne" and just became Megan. In fact, part of me thinks maybe the stupid club is a way to spend more time with me. Otherwise, why would I even be the vice president?

I thought she was trying to get me to be her friend for political reasons, but maybe she's using politics to get me to be her friend? That doesn't sound all that different, but it is. And, *yes*, Megan is annoying, but she also occasionally makes me laugh, and she has gotten even more into Mitski than I am in the past few weeks.

God, *are* we friends? Maybe you're way ahead of me here. Here are some other friend-like qualities Megan has:

1. When you tell her something, she leans forward and crinkles up her forehead. I know she's imitating Hillary Clinton, but it's nice to feel like she's paying attention.
2. If she needs to, she asks follow-up questions.
3. She doesn't bug me to tell her about my life. Even Caleb has barely come up again, even though she obviously wants to hear more about that whole situation.
4. Her brothers have a "hockey room" in her basement. It's padded on three sides and has a mirror on the other, so they can watch their form, then do quick little one-on-one face-offs to make goals. (I don't know hockey, sorry.) When she showed it to me, Megan said, "I've had sex in here," then provided no further details. (I am not particularly good at follow-up questions.) (Also, she was definitely lying.)
5. She has not yet once mentioned that I'm trans. She either doesn't care, or she is super intent on making me feel comfortable, and those are kind of the same thing.
6. She's great at debate, even though I cannot follow debate. (Yes, I went to a debate game for her, which I'm aware sounds like *I'm* trying to be *her* friend.)
7. She's not my dumb-bitch English teacher.

And she's in the bathroom right now. Probably crying her eyes out. If I don't go in there . . .

Fine. Fuck it.

Megan didn't even close the stall door. She sits on the toilet seat, knees drawn up to her chest, and she swallows all her tears the second I walk in. "You're mean sometimes, Abigail. *Really* mean."

"I know. It's kind of central to my whole appeal."

She lifts her face, the crisscross of denim imprinted in her skin. "No, it's not. You don't have to hang out with me anymore. Promise."

Ugh. Ugh, ugh, ugh. "I'm sorry." Even I can hear how much I sound like my mom is making me say it. "You just annoyed me. I overreacted."

"I'm *worried* about you. That's annoying?"

"Yeah, kinda!" Megan worries about me like she's checking election polling numbers. I guess that's how she shows she cares? Still. "You don't have to worry about me. I'm fine."

"Okay." She looks at me for so long I need to look away. There are tiny windows with frosted glass at the tops of the walls. I can see the silhouette of a bird through them. It looks like maybe it's feeding some baby birds. Good for the baby birds, except it's almost winter. Can't imagine they'll survive that. "You'll tell me if you're not fine?"

I get so sad, and I don't know why. Sometimes, I feel like I'm chasing something inside myself, trying to keep it from getting out, but I don't know its name or what it's trying to do to me. I chase and chase and chase, and I usually keep it from getting out, except when it attacks some poor person who gets in its way. Like Megan. "I am really sorry."

She gets up and hugs me. I don't cry, but there's a version of myself who does. "I miss you," she says.

Ugh. I'll just say it. "Look: This sounds suspiciously similar to something I would say to an actual friend instead of a colleague in democracy saving, but . . . what if we just hung out sometime? *Without* having to save democracy?" She narrows her gaze, and I'm terrified I fucked up. "You don't have to. I don't really have friends. Maybe I'm *horrible* at it. Like I just made you run away to the bathroom and cry. You never know when that might happen!" I laugh, and I think I might vomit.

"I would like that," she says, and she's doing her patented lean-in-and-listen-intently thing, and I realize she's waiting for me to take it back. "I would like that a lot."

"Find some time in your calendar," I say, "and shoot me over some dates."

She laughs. "Asshole. Wait. I don't talk like that, do I? Oh my God, I talk like that."

"A little bit," I say, grinning. The bell rings, so she eeps and scurries off to current events. I still have to check my makeup, but I'm absolutely crushing that class, as we've established. (I haven't called anyone a fascist cunt in weeks! Go, me!) It's only when I'm walking into class late that I realize I was making fun of Megan for something that maybe only a close friend would have noticed. Weird.

My best shot at passing current events is to hope Helen wins her election with my help, then argue that I *am* current events and deserve at least a B on that basis. Caleb has other ideas. When Mrs. King announces our class project, he suggests we do it together. She loves him almost as much as she hates me, so maybe she'll average out her emotions and give us a C. The assignment is to make a presentation on the most important issue in this election. I suggested "the end of the world," but Caleb bargained me down to "the climate." He's sneaky that way.

When we go to his house after school, I can hear that people other than him are home, so I hope he isn't already wondering how hard it would be to dig a tunnel to sneak me out. He drops his truck keys in a bowl by the back door. "Mom, do we have posterboard?" he yells into the depths of the house.

"You don't have to yell." Mrs. Daniels steps out of the laundry room, smiling as if I've stumbled into the middle of *The Caleb Show*, where she's the always-smiling mom who patiently puts up with his bullshit. When she sees me, she stops. Her eyes dart between him and me and then me and him. She finds a way to re-smile, but like she had to remember how. "Abigail!" she says. "It's Abigail, right?"

We lock eyes, and I would swear she's more scared of me than I am of her. "Abigail. Yeah."

"We're working on a school project," Caleb says. "We need posterboard."

"It's not a great time. Isaiah's coming over," she says, breaking eye contact with me. Oh shit, bathroom guy. How fun for me.

"And we need to work on our project. So we can leave you alone."

"Are you sure that's wise?" Before Caleb can say anything else, she says, "Actually, Caleb, can I speak to you in the other room?" She looks over at me again, but this time she doesn't quite look *at* me. "It's nice to have you here, Abigail. There's some fruit in the kitchen off to the left if you'd like a snack."

Sometimes, when adults around town know who I am, I can tell they're forcing themselves to call me Abigail, either with an invisible sneer or with extra emphasis that shows me they want a gold star. Not Mrs. Daniels. What's interesting is that she calls me Abigail like it's no big deal.

She leads Caleb down the hall, and I go grab a banana, then go to the living room. There's a binder with "ROSE CAMPAIGN" on the cover. I pick it up and leaf through it. It's full of potential signs that Mrs. Daniels appears to have drawn by hand. They say things like "THIS IS ROSE COUNTRY" and "ROSE: NO MORE THORNS" (that one makes no sense) and "ROSE: PROTECTING OUR CHILDREN."

"Am I not a child?" I say in my best Megan voice before I realize I'm all alone and must sound stupid as shit.

The door down the hall opens, and I drop the binder. Mrs. Daniels and Caleb step into the room. "Oh, I'm sorry you had to see this mess, Abigail," Mrs. Daniels says of a room that seems like it's already been fully cleaned five times today.

Caleb puts a hand on my shoulder and squeezes. "We're going to go work in the screw-around room." And before I can process that his family has a room named the "screw-around room," where we're going to go "work" "on" "our" "project," he grabs my hand and tugs me out of the room. No, he's just holding my hand. Okay.

"Hope you two do good work!" Mrs. Daniels says. There's a long pause, and then she adds, "And maybe don't come upstairs while Isaiah is here." For once, we're on the same page.

After Isaiah leaves, we head back upstairs. Mrs. Daniels invites me to stay for dinner, because she's a Midwestern mom and there are rules. I say no. The last fucking thing I want to do is spend one more minute with her. I want to go home and have cold pizza and watch Ron watch *Breaking Bad*. Caleb says he'll give me a ride home after he uses the bathroom.

While I wait, I go into the room where he and Mrs. Daniels had their quick chat. Two desks sit against opposite walls. The one closest to the door (probably Caleb's dad's) has a computer with an enormous flat-screen monitor and a roller chair so huge it looks like it should be able to launch missiles.

The other desk is a saggy table. A computer from before I was born sits on it. Paperwork is stacked so high I imagine it smothering the desk, but when I look closer, I see there are pictures lining the desk behind the paperwork. They're mostly of Caleb and his sister, Ruth, but a few have Mrs. Daniels in them. In the best one, she has baby Ruth in her arms, and a tiny Caleb hugs her legs from behind, his face peeking around her hip. She smiles like she can't believe how lucky she is.

There's an old landline phone on the desk. I pick it up and zone out to the dial tone for a second, and then I dial home. I just want to hear her voice, I think. I don't know. She won't recognize the number, after all. (This is what I tell myself when I realize what I've done.)

"Hawkes residence," my mom says. I hear our janky dishwasher grinding away in the background. I used to hear it as I fell asleep and dream it would wash me away. "Hello?"

"We should get going," Caleb says from the doorway. "Abigail, what are you—"

My mom says the wrong name on the other end, so I hang up and turn to him. "Just making a phone call." I smile, like duh. That's what the phone is for.

I can see him wonder what to say, and then the phone rings. The caller ID shows my parents' number. I lift the phone up and slam it right back down.

"We should go, so you don't miss dinner," I say. He looks back into the office, but he lets me lead him by the hand into the hall.

On our way out, the phone rings again, and this time, Mrs. Daniels answers it. She sounds confused, then says, "Oh, do you mean Abigail? Yes, she's here." She stops me and holds out the phone. "Abigail, it's for you."

"It's not for me. I promise." I drag Caleb outside, where it's just starting to get dark.

Wednesday, October 5

HADN'T TRIED *NOT* BEING TRANS. So he decided to do just that. And it was easy to be . The easiest thing in the world. He had been doing it for years. What were another few decades? He was closing in on forty-eight hours since he had told Abigail he was tapping out of the whole trans thing, and he felt *great*.

Not being trans came easily to most men, even those who had to work at it. When was a little *boy* (he added emphasis to *boy* to remind himself) growing up in Chamberlain, his father had had a friend named Carl. Carl put up a reasonable facade of being just one of the guys. He talked about football and laughed at dirty jokes. People knew him as a good dad, a good husband, and the one mechanic in town who could fix nearly any problem with your car. He wasn't just good. He was *solid*.

Then, after a night of heavy drinking, Carl let slip something that nearly instantly worked its way through the Chamberlain rumor mill: Sometimes, when he and his wife wanted to spice it up, Carl would put on her lingerie during sex. Now, people knew Carl was a good dad, a good husband, a brilliant mechanic—and a cross-dresser. Suddenly, he was less solid.

The jokes at Carl's expense were good-natured; they were also relentless. Eventually, Carl joined in, gently mocking himself to indicate that he knew his habit was weird, but, hey, the things you gotta do for The Wife sometimes, am I right?

The last time ███ had seen Carl, ███ had come home from attending a high school football game to find his dad and his friends laughing. One slapped Carl, who laughed hardest of all, on the back. "We don't mean it, Carl," the friend said. "We're just giving you a hard time."

Some part of ███ wanted to start singing "I Feel Pretty" mockingly, but his eyes locked on to Carl's. Behind the face red with laughter and the "happy" tears glistening in his eyes, ███ could see Carl was bleeding deep inside. ███ felt suddenly dizzy. He walked to his room as quickly as he dared, wiping his hands on his jeans.

A few days later, Carl headed the wrong way down the interstate while incredibly drunk. He smashed into another car and died almost instantly. He was barely sixty, and at his funeral, one of the men who eulogized him made a joke about how he had loved "the finer things." Everybody laughed.

Later, at the reception, Carl's buddies wondered why he had decided to drive when he was that hammered, but even as a teenager, ███ had known that going the wrong way on the interstate, drunk as a skunk, was suicide with plausible deniability. Carl hadn't *wanted* to die, but he also wouldn't be upset that he *did*.

Had Carl been trans? Maybe. He and ███ had shared a look that night, one that stopped ███ from making his joke. But did it matter if Carl was trans or "just" a cross-dresser? The important thing was that he had died as Carl. If he had carried another name in his heart, that name died with him. He had died a man, albeit one with an embarrassing habit, but he had *died* a *man*.

He had won.

███ could win too. Practice made perfect, and ███ had so much practice being this person. He had learned meticulously from watching men (correction: *other* men), and if he seemed a little awkward and stilted in most social interactions with "the guys," well, they wrote it off as someone who didn't fit in but always tried hard. He was safe here. He knew how to do this.

Today, he'd felt like he was living in second person, calling out instructions to himself from some other corner of his brain, making sure his legs lifted to take steps and his arms swung just so. *You are going to school today*, he thought, as he drove to his job. *You remember how much you love* Hamlet, he thought as he taught. *You got through another day*, he thought when he got home. (The days just fly by in second person.) *You will have a nice time imagining being a woman, a thing you can never be, because you are so clearly a big, bulky man*, he thought as he logged into his favorite IRC role-playing server.

"Hey!" his friend said in the chat. "I thought you decided to transition?"

"Wasn't for me," █████ typed.

"Cool." See? Other guys could handle this longing by pretending to be other selves too.

"Had a new idea for an RP," █████ wrote. "I'm a high school teacher, and one of my students decides I would be better as her best friend. She's a witch, and she transforms me into that girl."

"Great," said the other man. As their chat continued, █████ managed to ignore the thrumming chorus in the back of his brain: *You're doing it wrong you're doing it wrong you're doing it wrong you're doing it wrong you're doing it wrong you're doing it wrong*.

█████ had to tear himself away from the computer when the time came to head down to The Depot for drinks with John and his friends. Social interaction with other men would help █████ seem normal. He could camouflage himself there, changing into the color of tree bark and holding very still. Still, as he stared down at an IPA he told himself to enjoy, some part of him was back home, staring at the screen, waiting for his online friend to tell him what happened after Holly, the teen witch, finished transforming him into her new best friend Anna.

"You get it, right, ████?"

("John said something to you," the part of ████ that had been half paying attention thought. "Respond. Generic advice, if possible.")

"Relationships are hard," ████ said. "It's important to listen and try to find ways to support your partner, to make room for their bullshit."

"Well, yeah," John said. "I guess that's true."

████ went pale. He had misjudged the tone of this conversation. He could still save this by pretending to be a man in a TV commercial. "But fuck that, right?" Everybody laughed, and Ollie even clapped him on the back a little too hard. He could be friends with these men. He could.

"████?" a woman said. He turned to see Helen Swee, smiling tightly. She held a glass of red wine. "Nice to see you not in a shitty tie. No offense to your ties." Her eyes considered the other guys at the table, who had all turned their gazes toward her, waiting to pounce. ████ did this too. Why not?

"Ha," ████ said. "Just out with some friends. Guys, this is Helen. She spoke to my students last week. We hit it off."

"Is that all you hit?" Ollie said. Helen's smile fell a half millimeter.

"Ollie, shut the fuck up. You're not even making any fucking sense." John was a good man. ████ could count on John, which made it awkward that John was with the woman Erica had always loved. (But also, Erica wasn't real, so it didn't matter.)

"████ here is a fantastic guy," John said. "I'm with his ex-wife, and we're still buds."

Helen's eyes flickered as though staring directly into a supernova. She let out a little puff of air, a laugh strangled before it could escape.

(*Jesus fucking Christ, Erica*, said a voice that sounded like Abigail in ████'s brain. *What the fuck are you doing?*)

Erica downed the rest of her beer.

(*Ugh. Must I do everything for you? Go have a drink with Helen. After you apologize to her for these guys making it weird. Look at her. You* understand *her. You don't understand them. Because you. Are. Not. A. Guy. I'm the authority on this. You know I am.*)

"Are you with anyone, Helen? Because if you're not . . ." John patted twice on the shoulder, displaying just how great a guy was.

"I have a boyfriend," Helen said, ice hardening over the surface of her voice.

"She has a boyfriend," said, a few seconds behind Helen.

"Two years," Helen said, holding up two fingers. "*He's* a great guy too." She sipped her wine, and her gaze returned to . "See you around, Mr. Skyberg." She returned to a booth where she sat alone, studying an array of papers that recognized as those dictating her campaign strategy.

(*Well?* said almost-Abigail. But Erica——couldn't make his feet move.)

"Two years?" said a man also named Jon (without an *h*), just loudly enough that Helen could surely still hear him. "Her boyfriend better lock her down. I sure fucking would."

"Tough break," John said. "But she'll see what she's missing soon enough. And you'll be ready."

 watched Helen a moment or two longer than strictly necessary, but she leaned over her papers and never once turned to look back at him.

 wasn't sure why he agreed to drive a slightly-too-drunk John home to Stickney, since lived a half hour away in Mitchell and would rather be pretending to be a girl online. He headed west on I-90 anyway.

John flipped through the radio presets to find a song he liked, settling on an oldies station playing Steely Dan. He drummed along on his legs for a moment, before stopping, seemingly embarrassed. "Can you believe I was in marching band in high school?"

John gestured to himself as if he didn't look precisely like a guy who would have been a drummer in marching band.

"Constance always wished I could play an instrument," ████ said.

"Well, maybe that explains it." John slurred his words. Maybe he was drunker than ████ realized. "Connie's a good woman."

Some part of ████ was furious, so he said nothing. *Why*, that part of him asked, was he trying to befriend his ex-wife's new boyfriend, the father of her child? Was he that desperate to fit in? (Yes. Probably.)

████'s phone buzzed with a text in the cup holder, and John picked it up. "Who's Abigail?"

████ felt blind panic race through him. First, Abigail wasn't supposed to be contacting him. (He needed to block her number.) Plus, if John opened their conversation and saw what they usually talked about, he would think ████ was something he wasn't. John would know that—

"Can you please put that down?" ████ said, forcing his voice to sound level.

John immediately looked chagrined and dropped the phone. It fell in between the seat and the console. "So you *do* have a girlfriend. Don't worry. I won't tell Connie."

████ scoffed. "Trust me. Abigail is not my girlfriend."

John shrugged, then resumed drumming on his knee. He nodded toward something outside in the darkness. "Scott—my best friend when I was a kid—moved to California but he used to live right over . . . there. Now he lives in . . . Oakland? I think? He posts on Facebook about the election a lot. *Lectures* a lot. Thinks he's better than us. But he's a good guy deep down. I know."

"A lot of people are worked up about the election," ████ said.

"Connie worries about it all the time. All she can talk about some days. She really likes Hillary. I try to tell her it'll all work itself out, but she . . ." He trailed off. "You two lived in California, right? Los Angeles?"

"Close enough. Long Beach."

John leaned his forehead against the passenger window, staring in the general direction of wherever Scott had lived. Bright pinpricks of yard lights dotted the night. He sat up suddenly. "Turn here!" slammed on the brakes to avoid passing the dirt road John had indicated. "Sorry. Should have told you about my shortcut."

slowed as his car juddered over deep and heavy ruts. The "check engine" light blinked on, but knew it would likely turn off once he was back on the highway.

"Take a left at the stop sign," John said, even though no stop sign was evident yet. He started flipping through the radio presets again. "Hey, why didn't you and Connie ever try to have kids?"

"The timing wasn't right," said instinctively.

He diligently checked left and right when he reached the stop sign, even though no one else was out this late. John settled back on the oldies station, now playing Bob Seger. "Connie got all pissed at me when I insisted we tell Brooke and everyone about the baby. 'It's so early,' she said. 'Let's not get ahead of ourselves.' I just figured everybody could use a little more good news. Especially me and her." He let out a deep sigh. "I just hope the baby makes her happy."

wanted to ask if John meant he hoped Constance would be happy to have a baby, or if he hoped the baby would fill the hole in her that had always been there, but when turned the question over in his head, he realized John hoped that the answer was both.

turned onto a long dirt path at the back of the tractor implement's parking lot, then crept past the looming hulks of rusting farm machinery. He braked as cats burst from the tall grass, suddenly appearing in his headlights.

"I set out food for strays in the garage," John said. "Then they all pay me a visit. Especially as it gets colder. They know I'm soft." He laughed ruefully.

At the end of the path, John's house, tall and narrower than ████ expected it to be, rose out of the prairie. It looked like a rowhouse transplanted from the East Coast, albeit one with a sharply triangular roof. ████'s headlights fell across the "TRUMP/PENCE 2016" and "THIS IS ROSE COUNTRY" signs in the middle of the yard. There was no way passing cars could see either, but ████ doubted John cared.

Beyond a small deck painted brick red, a tongue stretching outward from the house to meet the path, the front door yawned open. Constance stood, silhouetted. The wind caught her hair and the robe she clutched around her, and she shielded her eyes against the headlights. After a moment, she went back inside.

"I'm in for it now," John said. ████ had the sense John performed the version of masculinity he assumed everyone found most comfortable. *The old lady's always getting in the way of my fun*, he seemed to say. Yet all night long, John had spoken of Constance with reverence, even when he complained about her. Erica would have been frustrated by how good of a guy John seemed to be, but ████ was happy for John and Constance. He couldn't let himself feel any other way. John had to lean heavily against ████ to get inside, and he realized just how drunk the man (reminder: *other* man) was.

Inside, the small kitchen was the fading yellow of plaque-covered teeth, complementing the tonguelike deck. Constance poured coffee into a mug that featured Calvin peeing on the John Deere logo. "There's my guy," she said. John slouched into a chair at the small table, then rubbed his face. "How many did he have?" Constance said to ████.

"I didn't think too many," ████ said. "Two? Maybe three?" John held up three fingers guiltily.

"Two is too many for Johnny. He's a lightweight." She set his coffee on the table and dipped down to hug him from behind. "Let's sober you up a little."

(*Johnny?!* said almost-Abigail in ████'s head. *Johnny and Connie? That's it. You* have *to break them up*. Have *to.*)

John took two hearty slurps of coffee. "We met the girl [redacted]'s going to marry tonight."

"*Did* you?" Constance turned away to put the coffee pot back in place, as if remembering her stage blocking. When she turned back around, she was smiling a little too broadly.

"Her name's Helen," John said. "Nice gal. Working on some project at The Depot, if you can imagine."

"The election's a month away," [redacted] said. "She's running against Isaiah Rose for state senate."

"Poor girl's gonna get slaughtered," John said. Constance's smile grew tight. "Anyway, the bar's not where I'd choose to work. Maybe she wants to meet a guy."

"She has a boyfriend," [redacted] said, giving Constance an apologetic look.

She smiled. "Well, the course of true love never did run smooth."

John raised his now-empty mug to Constance. "Well said, hon." He stumbled to the pot to pour more coffee. He gulped it down then yawned. "Think I might get up to bed. Thanks for the ride, [redacted]."

"I'll be along soon. I want to crack this monologue."

"She's such a hard worker. Means she'll be a good mom," John said. Constance's mouth puckered for a millisecond as he leaned over to kiss her. He disappeared into the darkness beyond the kitchen, into the gullet of the house.

[redacted] couldn't make his feet move. "So," he said.

"You shouldn't have let him drink that much." Constance stopped herself. "He shouldn't have let himself drink that much. You had no idea. Sorry."

"You're good at this." [redacted] waved his hand around to encompass the kitchen, the house. "Being there with what he needs."

Constance laughed. "It is rarely hard to anticipate what John needs. I like that about him."

"Unlike . . . ," [redacted] said.

Constance poured the dregs from the coffeepot into the sink, then wiped down the spills on the counter. She focused on her rag.

"John likes you. Believe me, it wasn't my idea for him to hang out with you. You must admit it's a little weird."

"It's very weird," said. He looked back at his car through a small window and suddenly remembered the text from Abigail he hadn't read. He should probably delete that. Or respond to it?

Above them, floorboards exhaled as John made his way across the upstairs. heard the shower turn on, and a wash of white noise filled the room. There was the faint sound of music, John singing along.

"I should probably go," said. Constance ran her eyes over him, as if trying to make his pieces fit together. He looked away. "I should thank you for covering for me, for telling the guys I have a niece. 'Ellie' thanks you too."

"So you *are* seeing someone, then? If she's painting your nails?"

blinked. What made her think that? "No?"

"Oh. Sorry. I was remembering . . . Never mind."

Above them, there was a clatter. heard John's muffled swears through the ceiling. Constance took a few steps away from the counter and toward , wringing her rag between her hands. He dug in his pocket and pulled out his keys.

"When I painted your nails in college, they were that same shade of pink. I thought you looked cute, but you freaked out and made me wipe it off." She shrugged. "Twenty-year-old me was right. You *do* look cute in that shade."

realized Constance had never called him "sexy" or "handsome." She always used "cute" or another word you applied to a person you loved but weren't sure how to sort. Constance had always seen the parts of himself he kept hidden from her, even if she didn't know quite what she had spotted.

"I don't remember you painting my nails," said. "At all."

"Sophomore year. My dorm room. You made me wipe it off right away. Like you were embarrassed?" Above them, the shower shut off, and John's heavy footsteps crossed the floor again. Constance looked upward, then tossed the rag back on the counter. "Do you wanna get out of here?"

He swallowed. "Where?"

"Outside? We're surrounded by dead farm machinery. That doesn't entice you in the slightest?"

████ laughed. "So we're going to go look at broken-down tractors and . . . what, exactly?"

"I run lines out there sometimes. We could work on that. Or you could tell me what the fuck is going on with you." Constance walked back toward him, then veered away to grab a coat. He could have taken hold of her, and—

"Nothing's going on with me," ████ said. He let out his breath and willed his heart to slow. It had been racing.

"Bullshit. You went away again."

"I'm right here." He jingled his keys. "And I should go."

"No, you're not here, ████. You were, but you went away again." She held his gaze for a long moment, but before he could clarify where he was meant to have gone when he was literally standing right here, Constance stepped outside. "*Fuck*, it's cold. Are you coming or what?"

████ followed her, shutting the door quietly behind himself. Constance moved down the long dirt path into the darkness beyond the house's glow. She slipped her phone out of her pocket and turned on its flashlight, the beam catching the tall grass and casting its shadow onto the path. She disappeared behind the wall of dead tractors.

████ unlocked his car, but he couldn't make himself get in. He did want to be here. He wanted to be *with her*. (Or someone in his brain did.) He reached under the passenger seat to fish out his phone to use as another flashlight, then saw he had missed six messages from Abigail. First, *you there?*, and then, *something really fucked-up happened to me*, and then *can we talk it was really fucked-up*, and then, *Erica?*, and then, *Erica?*, and finally, *Mr. Skyberg?*

Sorry, I was busy, ████ wrote back. *Can I call later? I know it's late.* ████ stared at the screen, then added, *I'm out with Constance. Bad idea, I know.* After another moment, ████ added, *Apparently she painted my nails in college, and I totally forgot about it. Seems weird! I don't like it!* Then, finally, *We can talk at school.*

████ put the phone down again. ████ felt nauseated, dangerously close to failure. ████ wanted to drive back to Mitchell and make sure Abigail was okay. ████ wanted to go home and see if his friend was still in the chat room. ████ wanted to run down the path to where he could just see the light of Constance's phone in the dark. ████ wanted to be someone else, and when ████ was chatting online, or when ████ was talking to Abigail, or when ████ could feel Constance *seeing* him, he felt dangerously close to becoming that other person.

To becoming Erica. If ████ thought about it for five fucking seconds.

A car whisked by on the nearby highway, far too fast for city limits.

████ thought about Carl, smashing into someone else. Did he regret who he had not become in that moment? ████ thought about dying, about people finding his chat logs, about them finally seeing the moments when he had always been the most unguarded and the most honest. The image of someone lifting his corpse into the air and violently shaking his secrets out of him like crumbs from a keyboard pierced his thoughts. ████ had to stop online chatting, to delete all evidence of it. ████ would fail. ████ had tried this before, and ████ always came back. ████ only felt like himself when he was pretending to be someone else.

Or, maybe ████ had been pretending his whole life, forcing himself into a shape others found more convenient for him. He had been his parents' son, his sisters' brother, Constance's husband, the much-loved Mr. Skyberg. But he had been coasting. The person those people loved wasn't real. He had always been someone else. ████ hadn't tried not being trans? That was a fucking lie.

His whole life had been spent running from himself to the point of exhaustion.

"You're doing it wrong," ████ said out loud. He laughed, then realized he was crying.

Yes, someday ████ would die. And to keep coasting until then didn't mean winning the victory over himself. It meant losing.

Fuck that, ████ thought. Fuck that.

Something reawakened in her then, and she sobbed with relief. She wanted to tell someone, anyone, and there, just down the path, was Constance, who—

Erica

—KNEW WAS THE ONE PERSON who had understood before even Erica had.

Constance sat sideways in the door that led to the cab of a tractor, her legs dangling out over the top step, flashlight trained on the pages of her script. She smiled at Erica. “Took you long enough!” she said.

“I’m transgender,” Erica said, breathless. “I’m a woman.”

Abigail

Thursday,

October 6

My mom came by last night. Jennifer had a late shift, and it was like Mom knew I was unprotected. Yeah, Ron was there, but we all know my mom would stone-cold murder Ron if she thought it would help her force me to be her happy little fella again.

Here's how it happened: Caleb came over after school to watch Netflix and stuff. Jennifer and Ron have *no* idea what to do when Caleb's around. Jennifer tried to have a conversation with me about safe sex that she obviously threw together in about five minutes when she realized that, oh, Caleb and I actually *were* dating.

I could tell it was a rush job because she mentioned birth control, then immediately shut up when I stared at her. Evidently, she forgot I was trans for fifteen minutes, which is nice.

"I can try taking birth control," I said. "Just to see what happens."

"No, no, no. That's fine." She pulled out a condom and held it out to me.

"Are you going to have me put a condom on a banana?"

She laughed. "A cucumber actually."

"Trust me, I've had plenty of practice. No fruits or vegetables required."

That was the end of Jennifer and Ron trying to talk to me about sex. They still seem like they're observing Caleb and me for a science experiment. They want to give us space, but it's a tiny little house, so Caleb and I spend most of our time watching *Breaking Bad* with Ron as he says stuff like, "You'll love this part, Caleb!" (Now *this* is male bonding.)

Then I'll look up at Caleb and smile as he tells Ron how good this hugely acclaimed TV show he's never seen before (because he's too Christian) is. I can't help it. I turn into a gooey mess. I hate the person I am around him sometimes, but I need him to keep looking at me because I'm worried he might stop. Every second I'm with him I'm imagining how it's all going to fall apart. There's no future here. Like, is he going to take me to prom and ask his mom to take photos of us together like she's not internally vomiting at the thought of me and her son touching each other?

Back to my mom "dropping by" last night.

Ron ordered Chinese food because he wanted to keep watching TV instead of cooking. The episode they were up to is super tense, and Caleb was *really* into it, so when the knock at the door came, I went to get the food. And then I opened the door, and my mom was there.

I hadn't seen her in over a year. Just her silhouette that one day when I woke up and saw her and Jennifer arguing. But last night, I could see her, all of her. I tried to run away. Well, my brain *wanted* me to run away, but it couldn't make my stupid frozen body move. She said my old name, and then she said, "Look at what you've done to yourself," in a sad voice.

Someone else came up the walk, and I had just enough time to realize it was my brother Josh—he must be home from the Marines for the first time in a while, and nobody had told Jennifer or me that he was—before he hugged me without me saying he could and said, "Love you, little brother. Don't you think it's time to come home?"

Mom's voice trembled. "Or we'll get the police involved."

My brain suddenly got control back. I pushed myself away from Josh and stumbled back into the house to see Ron slide between me and the door (and my mother in it) holding up his hand, a cop blocking off a parade route. "All right, now. This isn't your house, Mrs. Hawkes. Please leave." Caleb stared at us all, slack-jawed.

Mom started yelling, so I ran to the bathroom and locked the door. I saw myself in the mirror and realized how much I'm starting to look like Mom. I think I knew on some level that I was dyeing my hair a million different colors so I wouldn't have the exact same shade as her. But I can't hide it, not really. My mom kicked me out, yeah, but the joke was on her, because I turned into her anyway.

I stayed in the bathroom a long time, sitting on the floor, leaning against the tub. But I didn't cry. I'm not weak. I texted with Megan, but all her solutions involved her dad preparing a restraining order. Every so often, Ron would come to the door and tell me I was safe, but I didn't want to leave the bathroom until Jennifer got home.

I assumed Caleb had gone, but after about an hour, I was surprised to hear his voice after a quiet knock. "Abigail? It's safe, I promise. You can come out."

"No," I said.

He paused. "Then can I come in?"

I opened the door. He looked tired, and his clothes were rumpled. I guess I had been in the bathroom longer than I thought. I lose time sometimes. Something gets to be too much, and I kinda slip outside myself and have to piece together what happened later, like I'm doing now.

He gave me a hug. "I'm sorry. I'm so fucking sorry."

"Shut up." He kissed the top of my head, and my breath got shaky. "It's fine. Don't be annoying."

He didn't say anything, just hugged me even harder. My mouth was tight against his shoulder, so I started screaming into it until I ran out of screams. He held me up while I let it all out.

We sat against the tub, and he told me a dumb story about going pheasant hunting with his dad, and how he didn't hit a single bird, but his dad didn't mind because that meant he got to shoot more than the limit. It wasn't a very good story, but I listened to every second of it. But eventually, it was over.

"I wish she hadn't called you that," he said. "That's not your name."

I traced an *A* into the fluffy bathmat, so you could just see it if you knew what you were looking for. It didn't look right, so I used my hand to wipe it away. I tried it again, wiped it away again, tried it again. Caleb ran a hand over my back.

"My mom can be a real bitch too," he said. He paused for a long time, waiting for me to say something, probably. "I don't know if you know this, but I'm adopted." I cracked up because I just needed to laugh about *something*. He smiled because he was joking (probably). Like, obviously, he's Asian and his parents are white. Maybe he has feelings about that that a girlfriend would want to ask about. I'll think on it and let you know. "Sometimes, I think about finding out about my birth family. Mostly who they were. I want to look at somebody and *know* I was related to them. Maybe."

"I hate how much I look like my mom."

"I like the way you look."

It really wasn't the point. I smiled anyway. "So *did* you find your family?"

"Not yet. It's a complicated process, and there's no guarantee it'll happen. The records are a mess. I don't know what's true and what people have told me to get me to stop calling."

I put my hand on the back of his neck. His skin was warm, and I ran my thumb over a freckle I found there. I thought I'd seen every inch of Caleb, but I'd missed this one freckle. So I kissed it. Stupid. I know.

He put a hand on the side of my face. I thought we were going to start making out, but he kissed my forehead again and pulled back. "Even if I found my birth parents, they might not want to talk. And there's a lot of paperwork. I asked for my mom's help. But talking to her about it was a huge mistake." He shook his head. "Sorry. I know this is a lot."

I put my head on his shoulder. "I told my mom I was a girl first, because I was too scared of my dad. But she turned around and told him for me. I used to think she told him because she didn't know what else to do, but now I think she told him because she didn't want him finding out from me. Like it might get her in trouble."

He stroked my hair softly, like he's in love with me or something, which he's obviously not. "I think my parents are scared that Ruth and I will realize we're not really their kids. Which we are. I love them! So much! But I think they worry we might find other people who feel more like home." I kissed his freckle again. It's cute. Sue me. "A few weeks ago, Ruth was out past curfew, and my dad drove around with the floodlight he uses when he's deer hunting, lighting up the countryside. Yeah, she should have been home, but he acted like she maybe disappeared entirely. Mom kept pacing and praying and . . .

"I think Mom is scared Ruth and me will figure out our story doesn't begin and end with her. But as far as either of us know, Mom doesn't have a past. Like I don't even know where she grew up. Her parents died in a car accident, apparently."

"Maybe she's a space alien," I said.

He laughed. "A couple years back, she got a card in the mail, addressed only to her, which basically never happens. I was mad at her, so I opened it. It said, 'I love you, and I miss you. Danielle.' Fuck if I know who that is."

Holy shit, Brooke Daniels had a lesbian lover. "Do you think she's—"

"Do I think she had a girlfriend? Probably. Or she's a spy and that's her handler. Ruth and I have gone over every single possibility, and we keep coming back to: She doesn't want us knowing about our pasts because hers must have been super fucked-up. But I mean . . . I hope not. I hope she's just a spy."

"Does she even want you to find your birth parents?"

"She says she wants me to find them. But she also keeps saying that nothing will change her being my mother. Like she's helping me just so she can remind me how much I need her help. I don't know. She's a good mom. I just . . . You remember last year when we had to write personal essays?" I nodded. "I wrote about my parents adopting me. How much they loved me. How I was the blessing they'd been praying for. When I was done, you raised your hand and asked, 'Does it ever suck?' We'd maybe said three words to each other before that. And I thought to myself: *I don't know. Does it?* I couldn't stop thinking about it. And then I couldn't stop thinking about you. Obviously."

"I don't remember that," I said.

"Well, I do."

"God, I'm a bitch." I laughed, and then we were quiet a long time. "My mom . . . ," I started saying to myself. "My mom . . ." He kissed my forehead, and it felt warm. "Thank you for being here."

"Where else would I be?"

"Not with me." I didn't know how to say what I wanted to. "Since you started dating me, it's been better. People don't make fun of me anymore."

"Yeah, because now they make fun of me. The second you're not there, it's 'Caleb's gay' this and 'Caleb's gay' that."

"But you're not. I'm not a *guy*. Like . . ."

"You're not. And I'm not dating you as a favor either. I tried to stop thinking about you, and I tried to stop wanting you, and I tried to stop . . ." He swallowed.

I squeezed his hand tightly. "Okay. I believe you. And I really like you." It escaped my mouth before I could pull it back in. (This is happening a lot lately. Let's keep an eye on it together. It's getting me in trouble more and more.)

"I really like you too," he said. Nobody has *ever* smiled at me like he did then.

I leaned my head against his shoulder until I heard the front door open and Jennifer yelling, "Abigail?!" She wouldn't stop shouting until she could see I was safe.

Jennifer fussed over me so much that I considered detransitioning. But it was nice? I guess? It was fine.

She and Ron went to their room to have a serious chat, and Caleb stepped outside to call his parents and tell them he was staying over here, which he *really* didn't have to do, but I guess that was nice too.

I realized the person I really wanted to talk to was Erica. (Don't tell her I didn't call her Mr. Skyberg, huge eye roll.) Fuck her, but she would get how much it hurt to have my mom call me *that name*, like she was trying to erase me and draw something else in my place.

I unblocked her—shut up, I made it almost forty-eight hours—and texted her. She didn't text back. Maybe she was busy. Ugh. I know her job isn't to be there whenever I need her, but it *should* be. I'm always there when she needs me. (Usually.)

Caleb came back in. "My mom said she understands having a bad mom, which is literally the most she's ever said about her parents, so."

"Can you sleep with me?" I said. "Just . . . sleep? Jennifer wouldn't like it if we . . ."

He gave me a hug, and I took him to my ratty-ass bedroom. We laid down on the bed, and he wrapped his arms around me, and I stopped thinking about the look on my mom's face.

My phone buzzed with some texts as I was falling asleep. I woke up just enough to see they were from Erica, but I didn't feel like reading them. See if I'm there for her the next time her ex-wife does something.

(I will be there, because I'm a sucker. We know that already.)

I wake up just before six in the morning. Caleb's mouth presses against my shoulder, and he's snoring. I regret to inform you that I think it's cute.

I slide out from under his arm, and he whimpers. In the main room, Jennifer sits at the table, drinking coffee in her bathrobe. She looks like absolute shit, but she gets up to give me a big hug. "That's some boyfriend you have," she says.

"Stop. It's so weird that he spent the night."

"I don't think it's weird." She looks at me for so long I turn away. "Can I make you something? Or do you just want cereal?"

I nod when she says "cereal," and she gets me a bowl. "You talked to Mom?"

Jennifer focuses on opening the cereal box. "She's serious about getting you back this time. Did you call her again?"

I go to the refrigerator to get some milk. Not saying anything is like saying something in this case.

"Goddammit, Abigail."

"I called her from Caleb's house. And I didn't *say* anything. She just guessed it was me."

"Every time you do that, she thinks you're making a cry for help. That you want her to save you from the people who have corrupted and perverted you. To save you from me!"

"I could take out another ad in the newspaper? Just to be, like, 'By the way: I'm serious about this. Here's a recent photo and some clip art of a baby girl.'"

She laughs. "Won't work this time. I think we need to have dinner with her. And with Dad."

It's like my body stops working again. I can't even make myself put the milk back. The refrigerator door hangs open, five feet away, and I just stare at it like a dumbass. "Why Dad?" This is when my brain unhelpfully fills in that after he raised his fist to hit me that night I told him that no, seriously, I was a girl, I ducked out of the way, but he grabbed my arm and—

Jennifer takes the milk from me and squeezes my hand. "Abigail, breathe. I will *not* let anything happen to you. Okay? I will murder him before he takes you back."

She's close enough for me to really look at her. She has dark circles under her eyes, and her bathrobe has a hole under her left boob. Her hair is tangled. I'm pretty sure she didn't sleep. I realize I look like Jennifer too. Maybe even more than I look like Mom. That's when I finally start crying, and she hugs me.

"Hey, it's gonna be fine, okay? I got Mom to agree to you having anybody you want at the dinner. If you want to invite Megan or Caleb or your teacher—"

My blood goes a little cold. "Which teacher?"

"Mr. Skyberg? He's given you some rides home. I figured you were close to him." I must look terrified because she looks almost more scared. "Abigail. If he's making you do things you don't want to do . . ."

"No! God, Jennifer! Nothing like that. Just, Jesus Christ, you think I'd be friends with a teacher?"

"Maybe you trust him? I had teachers like that."

"Skyberg's a good teacher, sure. But I wouldn't inflict our parents on anyone." I fake laugh, trying to get her to stop thinking about how often Erica and I have hung out. "I could have the president at dinner, and they still wouldn't call me Abigail, and that's rule one." My voice cracks. "I wish Mom would call me Abigail. I don't know why she won't."

"I know. It's the bare fucking minimum." Jennifer picks up my cereal bowl and carries it to the table, like I'm her little baby, and she needs to make sure I don't spill the milk everywhere. I don't mind, though. I even give her another hug.

When I get to school, Megan launches herself at me. She hugs me and keeps saying, "I'm sorry I wasn't there." I know I make fun of her for being a human hall pass (I just did it again), but nobody else would hug me like that. And since everything Megan does becomes the most boring, normie thing imaginable, a few of the other girls in Students for Democracy hug me and ask me how I'm doing too. They don't even know what happened! Weird.

""""Erica"""" rounds the corner. She's whistling. Shit. I never texted her back. Maybe I should have let her know I was okay, at least. The annoying, shitty shithead.

She stops when she sees Megan with her arm around me. She walks toward us slowly and starts to raise her arm, like she's going to put a hand on my shoulder and ask me what's wrong. The fucked-up thing is I would like to hear what she'd say if I told her. She's annoying, but she gives good advice.

Erica drops her arm. "Everything okay, girls?"

"Just a rough night," I say. Megan squeezes me more tightly.

"I'm sorry to hear that," Erica says. "I'm here to talk if you need it. You too, Megan."

"We're fine," I say. "But I might need to skip first period."

"Sure. That's fine. Whatever you need." Erica clearly wants to say more, but she doesn't.

Megan and I leave through the double doors at the end of the hall. (Is this the first time she's skipped class in her life? Probably.) Erica watches us the whole way. I realize she must have given up on her plan to stop being trans, because I could see her again. *Welcome back!* I text her. She sends me the emoji of the lady raising her hand, like she's dying to be called on. So I guess she not only gained a spine but also some self-awareness. Good for her.

Megan and I get in her car, and she immediately says, "Oh God, I'm *so* bad," but she pulls out of the parking lot anyway. I wonder what would happen if Erica was just another girl here, if she could run out and get in the car with us and blow off school for the morning. It might be nice.

Forget I just said that. It would be *so* annoying.

Erica

Thursday, October 6

On some level, Erica had been building toward confessing her womanhood to Constance from the moment they had met.

In the twelve years they were married, Erica had been aware of her gender lurking in the background of every interaction they had. Every once in a while, she would be so distressed that Constance would sense that something deeper was desperately wrong and ask if Erica was okay. Erica would tiptoe right up to telling her, but she always chickened out. To tell Constance was to lose the only person she could not lose.

In retrospect, the time to have had a frank conversation with Constance would have been in their first year of marriage. They got married right after college, largely because everyone else they knew was doing so. Most of those couples were divorced now, too, but few had made it more than a handful of years. Erica and Constance gutted it out for as long as they could through sheer force of codependency.

A few weeks after their wedding, they had moved to Los Angeles, so Constance could try being an actress. Erica got a job at a school in Long Beach, and Constance responded to Craigslist ads for parts in student films and lost fifty pounds. They sniped at each other and went long stretches of time without talking, not out of malice but out of the isolation Southern California seemed to impose on them as they both got into their separate cars and drove in different directions each day.

Their marriage entered a doldrums, mostly thanks to Erica. She spent long hours crowding out everything in her life that wasn't her online role-playing, getting lousy performance reviews at work, and barely making time for her wife. Constance knew something was wrong but didn't know the questions to ask. They settled into a spiral of slow-building resentment. Neither of them wanted to say their marriage was over, even if it took another ten years to officially die.

If Erica were honest with herself, she might have admitted that relocating to California, a place ever so slightly kinder to "LGBTQ+" people than South Dakota, had made her start more pointedly wondering why she so often fantasized about becoming a girl. She still refused to look at that idea directly, but she could at least admit "I might like being a woman" existed somewhere in her brain, if only behind the frosted-glass plausible deniability of fantasy.

After a few days teaching at her new school, Erica met Crystal, a Cuban American lesbian whose sense of style could perhaps best be described as "futch Elvis." (The Erica of 2007, unaware of the term "futch," would have stammered and said Crystal had cool hair.) Crystal taught English too, and she once teased Erica for crafting a syllabus entirely composed of dead white men. Erica immediately added Isabel Allende to the curriculum.

From that, something almost like a friendship was born. And okay, if Erica had a little crush on Crystal, what was the harm? Every so often, however, Erica would smack into the same plexiglass barrier that always kept her from the women she longed to befriend. Crystal, tearing the leaves in her salad into tiny pieces at lunch, would grin and say, "I just don't understand you, Skyberg." (Years later, Erica would realize she had no memories of Crystal using her old first name.)

Constance got a job at an Old Navy and watched herself get older than her teenaged coworkers at an alarming speed. She prickled when Erica told Crystal stories. Erica would come home later than she had promised, bearing dinner, and Constance would ask, in a tone of voice meant to suggest she really wasn't bothered, "Where did you go?" She repeated the question so often in those days that Erica came to realize Constance was never wondering where she had gone geographically.

The intrusive thoughts, ones she had never invited in but was stuck with anyway, were with Erica constantly, deeply destabilizing her. She couldn't even go grocery shopping. While in line, she would find herself looking at the women on the covers of fashion magazines. She imagined having long blonde hair and a tiny waist and not a care in the world. She imagined being that beautiful. Deep down, everyone wanted to be a beautiful woman. Didn't they?

When you were surrounded by attractive women, eventually you would see one who looked enough like you to feel like a funhouse mirror. Erica would find herself fixating on *her* dirty-blonde hair, or *her* broad shoulders, or *her* slightly too-large stomach, or *her* off-kilter smile. All women were beautiful if you could see yourself in them, she used to think. (She stopped herself before she thought, *And* I *have dirty-blonde hair and broad shoulders and . . . and . . . and . . .*)

She could no longer fantasize about being with a woman without simultaneously fantasizing about *being* her, the two thoughts intrinsically bound up in each other. She longed to dissolve into a diaspora of herself, her molecules a part of every woman she had seen on the sidewalk or in the store or on a magazine cover, every woman she had longed to understand on some level she felt frustrated in her inability to articulate. She wanted to tell them how lucky they were. She knew they wouldn't get it.

One night over drinks to celebrate the impending end of the school year, Crystal asked her, "Dude, what's up with you? I'm trying to talk to you, but you're somewhere else."

Erica smiled sickly. "Constance always says that. You should compare notes and try to find me."

Crystal's eyes filled with concern. Erica was just drunk enough to try explaining to Crystal where she went, how she just wanted the thoughts, the fantasies, the dreams to *stop*.

Crystal's face tilted from amused to concerned to tender. "Sweetheart," she said, "have you ever thought you might be transgender?"

It was like her life smash-cut from that moment to the parking lot, where she vomited while leaning on her car, dimly aware she had shoved two twenty-dollar bills into Crystal's hand and run from the bar. She had let someone into her box, and they had *said the words* Erica must not say. That must not happen again.

And yet . . .

As Erica drove home, Crystal's words played in a loop in her brain. She imagined, for the first time, that her body was not a tomb to die in but a foundation to build upon.

When she arrived home, she found Constance curled up on the couch under a blanket, watching TV. She knew, in an instant, that if she told Constance the truth, Constance would at the very least not be cruel. She would try to understand. They would stay in California as wives or friends or occasional lovers, and they would *figure it out*. What if there was room for more people in the box than just Erica? What if there didn't need to be a box at all?

Then the old fear rose again. What if Constance didn't understand? What if she laughed in Erica's face? Worse, what if she *left*? Erica loved Constance, yes, but she feared losing her more, and those were two different things, she realized. One required honesty, and the other required swallowing yourself.

Constance looked up at Erica, soft smile bathed in the TV glow. "Everything okay?"

"Do you want to move back to South Dakota?" Erica said.

Constance sighed with relief. "God, yes. Fuck this fucking state."

And that was that.

Almost a decade passed in a blur. The moments when Erica rose to the surface of her consciousness became fewer and further between, and she self-medicated her Gender Thing online every night. When Constance would ask what was wrong, Erica would say, "Nothing."

She thought about telling Constance. She did. Yet she could not take the risk until one night when she did, just after midnight, surrounded by dead, rusted-out farm machinery, behind the tractor implement owned by the father of Constance's child.

Constance didn't speak after Erica completed her wild, disorganized coming-out monologue. (Felt this way my whole life, sorry I didn't tell you sooner, name's Erica, don't know about hormones, support group's Friday, friends-and-family night if you want to come. God, she just kept *talking*.) Erica was sure she had broken everything.

"Please don't tell John, okay? I can't have this getting out, not until I'm ready." Erica smiled sickly, realizing how much she had trusted to a woman she no longer had reason to implicitly trust.

Constance tilted her head to the side, her eyebrow raising into a parenthesis. Erica had always loved her like this, the face that preceded a barrage of questions.

"Sorry . . . " Erica said to break the silence.

Constance's critical gaze broke just long enough for her to snort. "Did you just *apologize*?"

"Yes," Erica said. "Sorry."

"*Again*? God, you *are* a woman." She stared at Erica, like she was trying to see through her.

"You just keep *looking* at me. Like you're about to thumbs-down me. You can tell me you hate me. I deserve it."

"Sorry." Constance immediately laughed. "See? Apologies! Such a bad habit. We all do it. Fucking Midwest." (Erica imagined for a moment that the "we" also encompassed both women present but also didn't dare hope it did.) Constance sighed, then laughed, then reached up to wipe tears from her eyes. "Do you know what a *relief* this is? The whole time we were married, it was clear there was *something* you weren't telling me." She repeated, "The whole time . . . ," so quietly Erica could barely hear it.

Constance stood, wobbling on the narrow stair. She opened the tractor's door, interior light spilling outward. She gripped the handrail and leaned her whole body out over the grass.

"I don't know if it was the *whole* time. I only figured it out a few months ago." Erica took a few steps forward into the light. She had to look up at Constance from this angle.

"Uh-huh. And when you said that thing about the coffins the night I left? Did you know then?" Erica looked away, caught. Constance straightened. "How about the night of auditions?"

"Yeah."

"Thought so," Constance said. "When I got home that night, I told John there was something different about you." Wind caught hold of Constance's hair, and she wrapped her arms around herself. "That night in bed, I realized: It was like you'd come back to me."

Erica stepped to the bottom of the tractor, putting her own hands on the rails.

"I'd taken a pregnancy test that morning, and I didn't know what to do, who to talk to, what to say. And then there you were. My oldest friend. The guy—" she cleared her throat "—*girl* I met that first week in college. Who drifted away until I couldn't see her anymore. And then . . ." She smiled. Erica thought about making a joke, both to puncture the moment and extend it. "And then there you were."

The realization slammed into Erica all at once. She was in love with Constance. Desperately. Had been since that pale girl, somehow overconfident and shy all at once, sat down beside her on day one of Intro to Theater at South Dakota State and said, "I'm Constance, like the virtue. Don't worry. I'm actually really lazy."

Erica had fallen in love then and there, except that emotion had been horribly delayed and was just reaching her now. The fucking timing.

Erica swallowed. She had been looking up at Constance for several seconds now, and her gaze hadn't wavered. "I'm a lot more than *just* your oldest friend." She put her foot on the bottom step.

Constance slowly took a step down, one foot, then the other, her eyes locked on Erica's. A dog barked nearby, and she snapped her gaze away. She gestured to the edges of the light. "Go. Turn around for me. Let me relearn you." She made a spinning motion with her finger.

Erica laughed. "Okay. Prepare for the gracefulness." She stepped out into the grass and turned slowly. At the end, she extended her hands and bowed. "Beautiful, no?"

Constance smiled. "Yes." The wind caught hold of her again. Erica almost didn't hear Constance add, "You are," over the sound of it.

Erica's freshman class had reached the witch Circe and her powers of transformation in *The Odyssey*. Erica found this an auspicious sign, so she wrote "CHANGE" on the board in enormous letters. She immediately regretted the decision. For one, she felt like a teacher in a TV show who wrote the week's theme on the board. For another, she spent the entire class with the word looming behind her, like it could alert a bunch of pimply teenagers to the realities of her heart.

Now that Erica had told someone other than Abigail, the "secret" of her transness had begun to escape her. Soon, she would have to tell more people. Someday, she would have to tell *everyone*. The confidence that had built since coming out to Constance caught in Erica's throat. *I am going to lose my job*, she thought.

Even though Erica had taught so many of Mitchell's children and would teach so many more, she would have to be dealt with.

Men like her boss wanted anybody who looked at Abigail or Erica and thought they had seen a better way of life to know that they had not found a window but a wall they would crash into.

The moment class was over, she erased the blackboard, stretching to reach where she had overzealously written an enormous *C*.

"ANGE?" Abigail said. She stood in the doorway, wearing a Students for Democracy T-shirt. She looked embarrassed when Erica noticed it.

"It used to say 'change.' For Circe."

"Oink, oink, right?" Abigail read something in Erica's expression. "Oh, fuck you! I know *The Odyssey*! I've heard of books!"

Erica smiled. "For a second, I thought, *What an appropriate lesson to be teaching right now!*"

Abigail stepped into the classroom and mostly shut the door. "Because you're transforming and metamorphosizing and stuff?"

"I told Constance. It went well, and we're going shopping on Sunday. And I thought briefly this wouldn't be so bad after all. And, yes, I'm transforming and metamorphosing and stuff."

"I don't know if 'men turn into pigs' is great trans representation."

"I felt like things might be okay after I told Constance, but today, all I'm doing is looking at people and imagining them knowing the truth. It's like everybody around me is a bomb. Or I am." She swallowed. "I'm going to lose everything."

"It fucking sucks, huh?" Abigail seemed hollower than she normally did. "Listen, Megan sent me to get you for Students for Democracy. We can't start without you. But, yeah, the terror of everybody else in the entire fucking world never *really* goes away."

Erica suddenly remembered the texts Abigail had sent the night before and winced. She'd meant to apologize. She had. But another day had slipped away from her. "I'm sorry. You have shit too. I'm such a bad friend."

"We're not friends. So it's all right." It did not sound all right. "My mom's being a fucking cunt again." Abigail pointed at Erica.

"I get to say that word. *You* get to say that word. Don't give me detention."

Erica set down her eraser and gathered her things. "You want to talk about it?"

"Not really." Abigail picked at a fraying thread on her jacket. "Maybe Friday. On the way to Sioux Falls." She turned and opened the door to go.

"Oh, Constance is going to come. For friends-and-family night?"

"What?!" Abigail tried to laugh, but it came out in a strangled squawk. "No! Fuck you! I mean, that's supposed to be our . . . I mean . . . that's when we talk. You drive. You annoy me. Then we go see even more people who annoy me. Then I'm hungry and we get Culver's."

Erica was slightly baffled. Abigail had gone with her to the last two support group meetings, and Erica would have sworn she hated the experience. "We can go to Sioux Falls one time without—"

"What's in Sioux Falls?" Helen Swee waited in the doorway. "We can't start the club without you, Mr. Skyberg, and I . . ." She looked at the two of them, and Erica could see her realize how emotional they both had gotten. "What's in Sioux Falls?"

"Tutoring," Abigail said, too hastily. "College things are happening, and I need to do them, so Skyberg is taking me to Sioux Falls for tutoring. I don't have a car."

Helen's eyes locked in on Erica. Erica should just come out to her, she thought, before Helen reached any terrible conclusions.

Her mouth remained glued shut.

"Nothing's happening," Abigail said. "We're just . . . nothing's happening."

Erica felt the lie slide into her mouth. "I believe in Abigail's intelligence and abilities, but her grades aren't quite there for college purposes. Her sister can't always drive her to Sioux Falls for ACT prep sessions, so I offered to help out."

"You promise?" Helen said.

Abigail nodded her head ferociously. "I promise. Nothing . . . weird is happening. Skyberg is the best teacher I've ever had." She scrunched up her face like that had been painful to say.

Helen sagged. "Well. We need to get started. So . . ."

Helen had decided to buy the lie. Most people are looking for an excuse to ignore the truth, even Helen, and Erica was still really good at lying when she put her mind to it. Staying closeted would do that to a girl.

When Erica arrived at rehearsal, Isaiah Rose was in her usual seat next to Brooke. The two's heads were bowed together, and they talked in hushed tones. For such a commanding presence in Mitchell—the third in a family line of ministers who had long translated their pulpit power into political power—Isaiah was shorter than Erica always expected him to be. Perhaps she had gotten too used to seeing him on billboards, towering over the interstate, next to the words "COME HOME TO LIVING WATERS." His visage had been such a presence in Erica's life since moving to Mitchell eight years ago that she had forgotten he was a real person who wanted to hurt people she knew. (Also, possibly, people like her, though Erica could not yet let herself go that far outside of a mental note to self.)

The stage door opened, and a handful of the actors entered, stretching out. Isaiah took note of them, of Erica, and unwedged himself from her seat. "We'll talk later," he said to Brooke. He greeted Erica with a smile as he passed her in the aisle. "A pleasure to see you, ████." He said Erica's old name like he knew he was getting away with saying a dirty word.

Inside, Erica's paranoia roiled. Yes, the events of the day, the near miss with Helen, yes, yes, yes. And Constance, who was usually at least a half hour early, had texted to say she was running late. What if Erica had somehow overstepped and Constance had decided to drop out of the play altogether? What if John had found out that Erica was a woman, still in love with her ex-wife? What if *Brooke* knew?

"I'll need you to take Monday's session," Brooke said. Erica nearly jumped at the sound of her voice. When had she sat down? "[illegible]? Can you do that for me?"

"Sorry. Distracted. Why do you need to be out? Is everything okay?"

Brooke scowled. "Isaiah saw two yard signs for Helen Swee and has decided we need a 'full-court press.' It's not like he has *anything* to worry about, but he needs distractions to feel like things are okay. Actually, could he come and speak to your little club?" Brooke's brow furrowed. "What, exactly, is that club even meant to promote?"

"Democracy," Erica said. "Of course, Isaiah can come and speak to us. *Absolutely*, he can. I made Megan send him a letter to that effect."

"Which was clearly written under duress," Brooke said. "So far as I can tell, this group isn't presenting a nonpartisan message that voting is one of our most important civic responsibilities. No, it exists to get Helen Swee elected. You've had four official meetings, and Helen Swee has been at five of them."

"I'm not going to tell the kids not to support the candidates they support. If someone in the group wants to make a speech supporting Isaiah Rose, I'm not going to stop them either."

"Caleb says the girls won't let him speak up for his Christian values."

"Caleb is welcome to say anything he wants. He just evidently chooses not to."

"He's a very shy boy. You need to coax things out of him."

Before Erica could respond, Constance hurried into the theater, followed by John. John grinned ear to ear, and Constance raced forward with a "Sorry!" before vaulting onto the stage.

Brooke opened her script, the prior conversation immediately forgotten. Then she looked more closely at Constance and smiled. "Good for her."

Erica looked more closely too. When Constance saw Erica's gaze falling across the enormous diamond ring on her finger, she slid her hand in her back pocket.

"Great news!" John said, and Erica got up to leave before she heard the rest.

Abigail

Friday,

October 7

Sometimes, you *feel* Megan waiting for you to notice her. You'll be standing there, and you'll feel a little tickle at the back of your neck and spontaneously start thinking about polling data, and you'll know she's there. The trick is to talk to her before she talks to you, so she knows it's creepy to hover nearby.

"Abigail," she says as I dig in my locker between classes. (I guess I lost this round, but I'm distracted thinking about going to support group with Erica's ex tonight, which is going to *suck*.)

"You can just text me," I say. She's standing way too close, leaning forward on her toes, bouncing. Uh-oh. Her anxiety only gets this bad when things take a turn for the worse. "Everything okay?"

"I've been asked to see the principal. Come with me. Wait. How do I look?"

She's wearing a gray sweater over a white shirt and a pencil skirt, so she looks like she was spontaneously generated by a bank, but she doesn't need to hear that right now, so I say, "You look fine." She closes her eyes and takes a deep breath through her nose, then leads the way.

Principal DeWaard's face sours when he sees me, but he forces a smile and turns to Megan. "Thanks for coming, Megan. You brought a friend!"

"I brought *Abigail*, our vice president. Now, as to why you wanted to see me: Mr. Rose may speak to Students for Democracy whenever he wants. I sent him a letter saying exactly that."

Mr. DeWaard folds his hands together. "Megan, do you think I'm stupid?"

Megan doesn't say anything, because she's terrible at lying, so I hop in there. "She thinks you're incredibly smart. She's told me that dozens of times. 'Mr. DeWaard and I only agree on one thing: He's a gosh-darn genius.'"

Megan looks at me like a little kid who's terrified because her mom stopped holding on to her bike. But she says, "Yes. I did say that. More or less." I gesture to her. See? Megan thinks you're a *gosh-darn* genius!

Mr. DeWaard laughs. He's obviously not going to admit he's dumb as shit in front of God and Megan. "Thanks for the compliment, kids." (Technically, I didn't compliment him. Instead, I repeated a compliment I made up. But let's not get in the weeds here.) "What are your plans for your little club after the election?"

"We're going to have local political leaders in to talk to us about being responsible citizens," Megan says, reading off mental cue cards. "We'll also help students register to vote when they turn eighteen, since voting is our most important right."

"Voting is a privilege, not a right."

"Still," Megan says.

Something about this feels gross. "Why are you talking to *us* about this? We have an advisor. If Megan and I aren't in trouble, then why are we here?"

"Your advisor Mr. Skyberg?" He laughs. "When he first told me about this . . . " he waves his hand around like he smells a fart, ". . . *organization*, I was assured it would be fair and bipartisan. But it's become clear that you're using valuable school property to get Helen Swee elected."

"Again: Mr. Rose is free to speak to us at any time," Megan says. "He just hasn't wanted to, which is odd, given how often he addresses the Fellowship of Christian Athletes—"

"That's different. He's a minister."

"I wasn't finished." (I don't know if you forgot, but Megan's dad's a lawyer.) "And even *if* this group *were* meant to elect Helen, which it's not, that wouldn't be *illegal* or even a violation of school policy as I read it."

"What if I wanted to start a group to elect Isaiah Rose?" I say.

Mr. DeWaard looks like he forgot I was there. "Why on earth would *you* do that?"

"I don't know. I hate myself?"

He laughs again, but he looks pissed off. "If you wanted to start a group to elect Isaiah Rose, kiddo, I would praise God that you found the light, but I would still say you couldn't. You forget, Ms. Osborne, that 'school policy' only matters insofar as I interpret it. Got it?"

"Unless the school board says otherwise," I say. (I have got to stop chiming in.) Megan nods loudly. "You tried to keep me from going to school as Abigail, and the school board said you had to let me, and you're still a little bitch about it every time you're forced to interact with me."

"Do you want detention?" Something bulges in his neck.

"How else am I going to make friends?" I give him a sweet little smile.

Now Megan hops in to keep him from saying anything too bad. "We're finalizing the details with Mrs. Daniels, but it seems that we're having Mr. Rose in a week from Monday. Caleb and Abigail helped us set it up. We would have told you sooner, but it's not locked down yet. You should attend! Anyone at Mitchell High can." She's lying, but I guess she's counting on Mrs. Daniels liking me way more than she actually does so I can call in a favor. We'll worry about that later. "See? Bipartisanship!"

"Fine. But Ms. Swee can't join you again. That's over. She's not in your club. Got it?"

"What if we organized a debate?" Megan says. "For right before the election? We could hold it in the community theater! Mr. Skyberg and Mrs. Daniels could help us get access! And we could invite local media to cover it." God, I bet she's been mentally organizing this debate all along. I'm weirded out *and* impressed, which is hard to do.

"Why would Isaiah waste time debating Ms. Swee? He's going to win."

"Then I guess I'll just look like an idiot. And even if we don't make the debate happen . . ." Megan swallows. "Please don't kill this club, okay? We're just trying to do a good thing. We'll recalibrate."

He waves to the door. "Fine. Set up your debate. Maybe Mrs. King will give you extra credit or something." He looks at me. "And if you use language like that with me again . . ."

"I don't know what came over me, sir. It won't happen again," I say, even though it absolutely will.

Class is back in session, so the hallway is quiet. The sound of the jazz band tuning up drifts toward us from far away. Megan puts her hands on her hips and paces the length of the lockers.

"Are we really going to host a *debate*?" I say, because while I keep getting myself into weird situations, I don't think I'll be much help with this one.

She slams her fist against one of the lockers, then does it again. She puts her arm against her mouth, and she screams into it three times. Blood drips from her hand onto the floor, spattering against the white tile. (I'm as surprised as you are!)

"You're bleeding," I say. I ball up my jacket, so she can put it over her cut. But she just lets her hand hang by her side.

She looks up at me, eyes red, and shakes her head. "They don't get to win, Abigail. They win all the time, but this time . . ." She stops breathing, then looks up at the ceiling, blinking a bunch. When she looks back at me, her eyes aren't red anymore. "Don't worry about the debate. That's another fucking mess I fucking made and will have to fucking clean up."

Her being angry at herself is a little too Abigail-adjacent, and I don't find it all that flattering. "I'll ask Mrs. Daniels about Isaiah, okay? I don't know if she'll say yes, but—"

"Aren't you dating Caleb?"

"Doesn't mean she likes me. And look: I'll help you set up this debate. It's just been a while since I took the lead on Obama/Romney 2012, so I'm understandably a little rusty." I grin.

She laughs so loudly a nearby door opens, and the teacher comes out to stare at us. Just before we part to go to our separate classes, she says, "Abigail, thank you," then gives me the biggest hug I think I've had in my life. She lets go and heads off to class, leaving me standing in the middle of the hall like a dumbass.

I have Caleb give me a ride over to his house at lunch, so I can talk to his mom about Isaiah. When I ask, Mrs. Daniels smiles and puts a hand on my shoulder and squeezes.

"I'm sure we can make that work," she says. "He'd be honored to speak to you."

She holds my shoulder like that for maybe a second too long. Then she squeezes again and smiles again and removes her hand, almost in perfect reverse, like she's a GIF of herself.

"Where are my shoes?" Erica says from down the hall. Weirdly, she asked me to come to her house before we drive to group, like she didn't just almost get busted. (I *think* Helen bought it, though.)

"If I know you, they're under the bed," Erica's ex says. (I'm still mad that Connie—I get to call her that if I want, I checked—is going with us, but Erica needs this, so I'll shut up about it.)

Constance is pretty, in that way where nobody she's not sleeping with has ever told her she's pretty. She wears a baggy Case IH sweatshirt that somehow still shows off her boobs, and she keeps sniffing, like she's being haunted by a cold. She coughs into her hand, and I see the enormous engagement ring she's been hiding beneath her sweatshirt sleeve. "This baby is giving me a runny nose. Which hopefully stops after trimester one."

"My mom said that I gave her heartburn when she was pregnant with me. When I came out, I'm sure I just made it worse, ha ha."

Constance doesn't laugh. "Erica told me your mom sucks. I'm so sorry. Fuck moms, right?"

"What about you? You're, like, a quarter of a mom."

"Fuck me too then." She rubs her nose with a single finger, like she's trying to chase a sneeze out of it. "Imagine having to be my kid!"

"I'd take my chances."

That she smiles at, and then Erica practically skips into the room, showing off a pair of pale lavender Chucks, one of the laces undone. She's beaming. "They were under the bed, Constance. You were right. What do you think?"

"Cute!" I say and mean it.

"Gosh, those are *great*," Constance says.

Erica looks like she might explode. "I've wanted shoes like this my whole life. I've wanted . . ." She shakes her head and pinches her nose. "I'm really happy about them."

"I'm happy you're happy," Constance says. She squeezes Erica's hand lightly, and then they *look* at each other, until Constance finally clears her throat. "We should get going."

I am saying this right now, before this goes any further: If they sleep together, I'm not responsible in any way. It's a terrible idea, and we all know it. But then they smile at each other again, and ugh. They *are* cute together.

Just don't say I didn't warn you.

At group, Bernadette, the leader lady, invites everybody's friends and family to introduce themselves. Brothers and daughters and best pals and moms. In case it isn't obvious, nobody is there for me.

Constance tells the story of Erica coming out to her, and every so often, Erica makes fun of herself, and everybody laughs. (I'm happy for Erica, but Constance's instant acceptance is weird, right? I'm going to keep monitoring the situation.) A mom who's here with her sixty-five-year-old son (so she must be, like, 150) dabs at her eyes with a handkerchief.

Even though I know the story is 100 percent true, I feel like they're lying, removing everything about it that sucks to make a better story. They're performing the most entertaining version of themselves, and I hate it. So I go to the snack table.

I pick up a cookie shaped like a ghost and break it into pieces, popping one in my mouth and waiting for it to soften. Constance finally says, "Thank you!" and everybody applauds her courage or sense of humor or something. I fill a glass with hot cocoa, then pick up another cookie. When I turn back, Bernadette is looking at me.

"What?" I say, mouth full.

"We have a larger crowd than usual tonight, Abigail. Please only take one cookie." She gestures to the only other person here without a friend or family, an old, heavyset trans woman with a patchy wig. "Florence worked really hard on them." Florence clasps her hands together and beams. I'm guessing she bought them at Hy-Vee, but sure. We can humor her. I set my second cookie back down.

Bernadette drapes her arm over the back of the chair next to hers, where her child Bex sits. They're maybe a couple years older than me. Bex leans forward at an angle, like a knife sticking out of a body. They're jittering their leg. They cast me a sidelong glance and smile. Fuck, they're hot.

"Who wants to speak next?" Bernadette says, but she's still looking at me, and she must see that I'm looking at her child.

I shake my head. "I don't want to say anything."

Bernadette shrugs. "You don't have to say anything."

Bex gets up from their chair then and heads out of the room toward the bathroom. I very obviously follow them with my eyes, and now everybody is looking at me, especially Erica, who has that "Abigail, what are you *doing*?" expression on her face.

"In case you haven't noticed," I say, "I don't have any friends or family here, so I don't have anything to contribute."

"I wouldn't say you have *no* friends or family here, Abigail. Erica's here." Anybody else want to punch Bernadette?

"Erica really doesn't count, given our . . ." I gesture back and forth between us. You know. The big, obvious thing we have in common? The one I don't even have to say?

"Does Bex not count, because they're also trans? They're still my child."

"That's different," I say.

"Okay," Bernadette says.

"What about your sister?" Erica says. "She could've come."

Fucking Erica. "We can't have Jennifer here, can we? Because she'd take one look at you and know your secret, and we can't have *that*." I glare at Erica, and she looks away. "I could bring my friend Megan or my boyfriend or . . . I don't know . . . a candidate for the South Dakota state senate who's randomly become quite important to my life, and I could say, 'Look! My family or friend!' But I *can't*, can I? Because I have to make sure nobody knows Erica's big, stupid secret." I break another cookie in two and shove part of it in my mouth. "Sorry, Florence."

The door swings open, readmitting Bex who just . . . leans. I should stop talking and stare, but I'm on a roll. "And anyway, why would I bring anybody even if I could? Megan doesn't care that I'm trans. Caleb doesn't care that I'm trans. Why make a big deal out of it? A year from now, I'm going to be so far away from here, and I'm never going to tell anyone my deep, dark secret. I'll be just another girl on the street."

"That sounds like a hard life," Bernadette says. I don't look at her. She shouldn't get to interrupt me.

"No, it would be an easy life. When nobody knows you, you can do whatever you want."

From the corner of my eye, I see Bex shake their head, side to side. And, like, it's fine for Bex to be so aggressively themselves all the time. Good for them. Seriously. But that doesn't mean I have to have that life too. Especially after I leave Mitchell.

"I want everyone to forget I'm trans. *I* want to forget I'm trans. I want to go to a club and get blackout drunk and sleep with some random guy. I want to have to drag myself out of bed to go to brunch the next morning. I want to get home from work and eat frozen dinners and pass out on the couch with my boyfriend in front of Netflix. I want to push a fucking child out of the fucking vagina I don't fucking have. I don't want to be an *accident*. I should get to have that. Okay? I know it's embarrassing and maybe, like, anti-queer or something, but *I should get to have that*."

"You're right. You should," Bernadette says, and she sounds like she's right next to me and very far away all at once. "Erica, grab Abigail some Kleenex, please?" (Great. I'm crying again.) "Now, Abigail. Do you dream?"

Bex laughs, a sharp bark. "Mom, oh my God," they say in a perfect, scratchy voice.

Erica stands up and hands me a Kleenex, then puts her hand on my shoulder. I pull away to wipe my eyes and blow my nose. "Of course, I *dream*," I say. "Do *you*?"

She laughs at that, and it's genuine. She seems so *glad* to be laughing. Ugh. "I came out to myself when I was fifty-six years old. My whole life before that, I dreamed in third person, like I was a movie camera, planted in the corner of every scene, watching someone who I knew was meant to be me. I would see this little man named Martin—yes, I was another Lutheran boy named Martin—scurry around and try to survive another day. I thought that was just how people dreamed.

"One night, about a year after I came out, after I'd been on hormones a while, after my wife had kicked me out, after I didn't know where I was going to land, after I'd lost nearly everything, I had a dream where I was standing on the porch of the farmhouse in Mankato where I grew up. A flood crashed toward me, tearing apart the cornfields. I knew even if I went back inside, the house itself would be torn to matchsticks. No matter what I did, the flood was coming.

"But then I had a revelation: *I* was seeing the flood. I was looking through my own eyes, watching my death come for me. I was dreaming in first person. I didn't even know you could do that. I really didn't! I had been so disconnected from myself that I hadn't allowed myself to be a person even in my dreams. I planted myself then and watched the flood come for me, and I woke up before it got there.

"If you asked most people, they would say my journey was from Martin to Bernadette, but that's not true. My journey was from 'Martin' to 'Bernadette' to me. For so long, I had only understood myself as a figure on the edges of my peripheral vision. Then, suddenly, bam! I could see through my own eyes."

The room is so quiet that I need to make it stop being quiet. "So?"

"So, I look at you, and I think you are *lucky*, Abigail. You found your way to 'you' much more quickly than just about anybody here. You don't see it that way, and I don't even *want* you to see it that way because in some ways, it's still a terrible curse. It always is, no matter how old you are. You *have* lost a lot, more than a girl your age should have to face. And it's natural to want to lose less, to pretend your past isn't your past. But that's also a good way to forget who you are. I know you want to run from the flood. I do. But one way or another, it's coming, and at least if you stand firm, you can see it for what it is and call it by its name."

Everybody looks at her. Nobody looks at me. Even Bex wipes tears from their eyes. I never want anybody to be looking at me, but right now, it feels weird and lonely, like I'm on a mountain while everybody else is being sucked out to sea.

Bernadette looks at the clock and sees we're at time. She raises her hands like she's a conductor and brushes them against the air once, releasing both herself and us.

"Thus endeth the lesson," she says, and the room fills with the sounds of people exhaling, released from whatever spell she had us under. I run outside into the chilly October air. I want to keep running, but I only get as far as Constance's car. For now, I don't have anywhere else to go.

Erica

Sunday,

October 16

The night before Constance took her shopping, Erica shaved off her mustache in the shower. It took longer than she expected, yet after an hour of Lake Mitchell's water running down the drain and a handful of cuts along her upper lip, her face was hairless for the first time since college.

She swiped away the steam on the bathroom mirror. For a moment, she could imagine that she was the person she was. The real version of her didn't have a mustache, so now she didn't either. Seeing her lip so bare sent tingles through her, like a foot that had fallen asleep slowly waking up but for one's entire identity.

This confidence lasted all of a second before it was replaced again by nagging doubt. Every epiphany she had came with a chaser of regret. Erica had been trying to accept that she was in the right body, but she kept getting hung up on all the ways someone had altered it without consulting her.

The clear patch in the mirror slowly fogged over and hid her from herself again.

Constance picked Erica up at 8:00 a.m., coffee in hand. She smiled at Erica's mustache-free face. "I like it!" They talked about *Our*

Town the whole way to Sioux Falls, safe ground that didn't risk upsetting the precarious balance of their current "friendship."

This early on a Sunday, the mall was mostly empty. That emptiness should have relieved Erica, but she was still sure everyone was looking right at her. Even the security cameras, she imagined, closely tracked her movements, seeing an enormous pervert and his tiny ex-wife. She kept wiping sweaty palms against her jeans.

Constance yawned as she riffled through maternity clothes at JCPenney, the only store open so early. "Sorry," she said. "I'm not sleeping."

"Nausea or something else?" Erica said.

"Nah. I'm just not sleeping. It's harvest season, so John doesn't get in until three or so. I'm hopeless sleeping without him. And then, of course, I have to pee a million times, so I end up getting two, maybe three hours of sleep."

Right. John. Every time Constance reached up to cover her yawning mouth, her engagement ring twinkled. They still hadn't talked about it. Erica's eyes scanned over the racks of clothing for anything that might fit someone shaped like a bulky pencil. Erica briefly locked eyes with a grandmotherly type, who smiled, and she nearly bolted.

Why had she even agreed to do this? Since Erica had come out to Constance, they had only been able to talk in rehearsal. Thus, the shopping trip—a Constance suggestion she eagerly agreed to. But was she going to try on anything? Even her subatomic particles rebelled at the very notion.

For as grateful as she was to be with Constance, she also felt unexpectedly betrayed by her. Constance was trying so hard that Erica suspected her of playing a game of femininity chicken with her. If Erica didn't follow her every step of the way, Constance would reveal her true purpose: To expose Erica's ruse and reveal her for the man she so clearly was in front of everyone, and then John would emerge from a nearby dressing room, carrying a camera, and—

She swallowed. Constance had given her no reason to be paranoid (lately). Better to try being a good, supportive girl friend (space intended).

"How did John propose?" she said.

"Matter-of-factly. Like everything he does." Constance moved through the racks, fingers playing along each item of clothing. She grabbed a polka-dot knee-length dress off one of the maternity racks. "This would look *cute* on you! Maaaaaybe with a brightly colored belt? And darker tights? It might be more of a summer look, but you could make it work!" She grabbed a few other items and pushed them into Erica's hands.

This was the moment, the test. Erica clutched the dress. It was lovely, and its starchy fabric had a surprisingly welcoming quality. She wanted so desperately to put it on and wanted desperately to throw it in the nearby trash can and walk out of the store and out of the mall and drive home. It was hard enough seeing herself without a mustache. Now that she was here, wearing a dress felt like a test of object permanence that her brain would fail every time. It would see her and say, "We really fucked this up!" and cease to recognize her. Everything had gone too far, and she was a big, fat, faking faker. She had failed the test before she even took it.

She made herself say, "What are you doing?! I can't wear this!" then dropped the dress. It fell to the floor as though a phantom had been animating it.

"Erica," Constance said. Her hand reached up to touch Erica's shoulder. Erica saw how she towered—*fuck* how was she *so tall*?—over not just Constance but the grandmotherly woman hovering nearby, now pointedly ignoring the nearby mutant man having a full-on meltdown and trembling. "We don't have to do this. I thought—"

"*What? What did you think?*" Erica said, far too loudly.

Constance took a step away, then stooped to pick up the dress and return it to its hanger. "Maybe this was too rushed. I'm sorry. I wanted to give you a fun shopping trip. I wanted to help, but maybe that was a bad idea."

Now that she wasn't holding the dress, Erica badly wanted to be holding the dress again. Her whole life, someone (usually just herself) had taken the dress away from her. She had hoped that she might be ready, finally, to try, but maybe, she realized, she was always going to be holding the dress and wanting to wear the dress and keenly aware of just how horrible she would look in it, belly bulging, shoulders tearing, height skewing. She would only ever look like a man in a dress, which was what she was, after all. Also, *did she even like dresses*? She could be a woman and wear a T-shirt, right? Women wore T-shirts! She didn't have to do *any of this*.

She didn't know how to explain any of this to Constance, so she didn't. She sprinted out of the store.

She found a bench in a branch of the mall filled with mostly empty storefronts and sat.

What had she wanted out of this trip? The more she thought about it, the more she knew she hadn't wanted the trip at all. She had just wanted to be near Constance. She had wanted to believe they could be just friends, gal pals, besties.

No, that wasn't quite right either. She had wanted Constance to *see her*, properly, but what Constance had seen was what she thought a trans woman should be. She was trying, yes, but she was trying to help an idea of transness more than she was trying to help Erica. Erica realized she felt vaguely insulted.

She stood, wobbly. She had miscalculated everything, and maybe she had irreparably destroyed everything, and she had no ride home, and—

Her stomach growled. At least she knew how to fix that.

Erica alarmed the poor teenagers opening the Dairy Queen for the day by ordering a Blizzard in a sweaty, out-of-breath wheeze. After her blood sugar had regained equilibrium, she felt mournful. She and Constance had almost redefined their relationship, but now, they'd upended it all over again, Constance in her haste to push Erica further than she wanted to go and Erica in her inability to just fucking deal with the circumstances of her newly gendered life already.

As she chased the last few globs of candy-studded vanilla ice cream around the bottom of her cup, Erica looked up and saw Constance at the other end of the food court. After a moment, their eyes met, and Constance wavered, body angled to go back into the mall, eyes still on Erica. Her shoulders hunched in the way they did when she was furious. Constance had a bad habit of assuming that all emotions happening in her vicinity had her as their target. Erica could only imagine how she had interpreted a dysphoria spiral.

Then Constance shook her head. She approached, hesitated, and ultimately sat down. She got out her phone. Erica slid the cup to Constance, but she didn't take it.

A minute later, Erica cleared her throat.

"Let's go home. I should help Megan and Abigail get ready for Isaiah's speech tomorrow. I should read over Megan's introduction again, at least."

Constance didn't look up from her phone.

"Thank you for coming here with me," Erica said. "I'm sorry I let you down." She knocked on the table and stood.

Constance set her phone face down on the table and looked up. Erica could finally see just how angry she was. Erica sat back down, as if commanded.

"No, let's go," Constance said, voice flat. "You need to help your teenage friends solve all their problems. Please let's not talk about whatever the fuck that just was."

Erica had been planning a short presentation on the effects of gender dysphoria, but it fell away. "I got scared."

"Of other people seeing you?"

"Of me seeing me."

Constance laughed darkly, then braced her hands against the table, pushing away with fully extended arms. She dropped her head to look at the floor, her hair falling around her face. "Welcome to the club."

"That's a cliché. Welcome to womanhood? I'm not picking out a new gender at Lowe's."

"I didn't say, 'Welcome to womanhood.' I said, 'Welcome to the club.' Of people who don't like what they see in the mirror. Which includes people of every gender."

"This is different."

Constance looked up from the floor, and the curly strand of hair that fell in front of her eyes was deeply sexy. (Erica was annoyed to have noticed.) "*Is it?*" Constance said. "You left me there with some random woman staring at me, and you didn't bother to say what was going on."

"It was too much. I got freaked out."

Constance huffed. The gravity of the argument Erica had put off having for their entire marriage dragged her toward it.

"This was your idea," Erica said. "I didn't want to come. I certainly didn't want to *put on* a dress. I'm not ready for that. Did you want to help me? Really? Or did you feel guilty? Did you want to retrofit . . . whatever we had into something new? So that you can say you did your best? So you can win the divorce?" Constance shot Erica a warning glare. "I see I'm onto something. Well, I'm sorry, but turns out we can't just be . . . BFFs because you want us to be."

"No, we cannot." Constance laughed again, or maybe she sobbed. "I loved you. I *loved you*." The words hissed out like they were escaping her.

"I loved you too," Erica said.

"No. Some *other person* loved me. Or pretended to at least." Erica didn't know what to reply to something that was simultaneously completely correct and completely wrong. "I wanted all of you. I was owed that. And I tried *so hard*, Erica. But all I ever got was half, at best. And then that fucking night after auditions, I saw you, and you were *there*, like the second I left, you decided to come back to life."

"You think I should have told you earlier I was trans? Like it was just that easy?"

"What's the worst that would have happened? I would have left you?"

Erica let out a single bitter laugh. "Right."

"I don't know what I would have done. The point is: You didn't want me enough to tell me the truth. You wanted a safe harbor, so you could hide from the storm. And I loved you. *I loved you*, but I got stuck with him." Constance slammed her hand down on the table. The Blizzard cup fell to the floor, spattering ice cream.

Erica picked it up and stared at her too-big hands. She massaged the place where her wedding ring used to be. "It wasn't like I chose to lie to you. I just didn't know what to say. I didn't want to hurt you."

Constance winced, holding back tears. "No, you didn't want to hurt *you*. It never had anything to do with me."

The mall's doors swung open to admit a wave of high schoolers in rumpled church clothes. They looked so young, Erica thought, before she realized they were Abigail's age.

"You're being very cruel," Erica finally said. "I don't think we can be friends."

Constance shook her head, took a deep breath. "Fine. Fine. I didn't ask *you* what you wanted today, and I should have. I'm still fucking furious about the rest."

Erica looked back down the long hallway of the mall. "It was a nice dress."

"It's still there. I could buy it and hang on to it until you're ready to try it on." She met Erica's gaze for a moment. "Besides, John's rolling in that tractor money. He'd never notice."

Erica's eyes fell across two students seated on the other side of the food court. A taller girl locked her arm around the neck of a shorter girl, who swatted it away and burst with loud laughter. "That night I came out to you?"

"Yes?"

"I guess I thought . . ."

"Erica," Constance said sadly. Their eyes locked again, for what felt like the last time. "Please don't."

A single tear spattered the table between them, and Erica blinked when she realized it was hers. Her phone, long since forgotten, buzzed to life with a call from Abigail.

Constance smiled, her own eyes red. "You should talk to your friend."

"I'm sure you're, like, 'Abigail is calling *me*? We really *are* friends!' but I promise this is a call where I need you as a teacher first, an advisor second, and a friend a distant five thousandth," Abigail said before Erica could even say hello. A car whisked by on its way out of the parking lot. "Are you on a street corner or something?"

"I'm in a parking lot. So sort of?"

"Oh." Abigail was silent a long time. "Are you okay? You don't sound great."

"Not especially, but I'll get over it." What she wanted to say felt too heavy for Abigail to carry. "The same story you're sick of. Erica still loves her ex. Wah, wah, wah."

"Fuck. That sucks." It was maybe the first time Abigail hadn't immediately leapt into rolling her eyes at Erica's poor life choices, which was how Erica knew the girl must really need help. "I can call back later. It sounds like this is maybe not a great time."

"Please say your thing. It might take my mind off . . ." Another car whisked by.

"Basically, Megan's freaking the fuck out about tomorrow. She thinks giving Isaiah Rose a platform is suggesting she agrees with him and supports his desire to destroy trans people." There was a pause. "I *may* have given her that idea." She paused again. "Okay, so, ugh, I said that him talking to us was a good way to let him say anything he wanted to about people like me and have most people believe him, you know?" Another pause. "Like, Erica, c'mon! Most people think we're lunatics! If someone like Isaiah Rose says, 'Look at those lunatics!' too many people will see how normal he looks and how weird I look—with *intent*, but who cares about that—and they're not going to care what I have to say. You get it, right?"

"And you told Megan all of that?"

"More or less. But I was funny and charming about it. Or I thought I was."

"Tell Megan you're sorry and that it'll be fine. Then go see a movie with her or something."

"It *won't* be fine, Erica. He's a fucking piece-of-shit prick."

"It'll be fine for the next twelve hours. I promise."

"Ugh! *Fine*. This better work. Megan's not supposed to be the one who's overemotional and fucked-up. She's undercutting our working relationship. As always, fuck you, and bye."

Erica slid the phone into her pocket. She rubbed her fingers, raw from a chill wind her light jacket was no match for. She stood on a low, grass-covered rise overlooking the street and a man twirling a sign on the corner. A few ice-cold raindrops spattered on her shoulder, the top of her head.

"How was Abigail?" Constance said, coming up behind her.

Erica turned to her, infinitely grateful to see her. "Fine. Teen-girl friendship problems. They'll work it out."

Constance looked up at the sky. "What were you going to say to me? Before I stopped you, I mean."

"I hadn't figured it out yet."

Constance stretched her arms out wide, then let them fall to her sides.

"But you're right," Erica said. "I wasn't there. I was a terrible husband, for the obvious reasons, and I wasn't even a very good friend. You deserved better. I'm sorry."

She knew she should leave it there, but the memory of Constance hovering above her the other night in the open door of the tractor had its hooks in her.

"But I'm here now and having you back in my life is . . ." She shook her head. Whatever she was saying felt too small. "I still love you. I always will."

Constance squeezed Erica's frozen hands.

"I'm not sure you're happy," Erica said. "Maybe you are, and that's good, and I'm sorry. But I don't think you are. And I know I'm not. I'm really, really sad. All the time."

Constance leaned against Erica in something that was either akin to a hug or two dominos frozen in the moment where one has begun to knock the other over. "I'm sad too. Constantly."

She pulled back and looked up at Erica. Erica knew that when she tilted her head at that angle, looked with that expression, it meant one thing. "I'm going to kiss you," Erica said.

"Okay."

She did before she lost her nerve.

Abigail

Sunday,

October 16

Caleb gets out of bed, still naked, the last light trickling in through the window. He throws a blanket around himself like a cape. "Please don't laugh, okay?"

"At you looking like Dracula?" I laugh so loudly that it must fill the whole house, but all he does is smile. His dad is out hunting, and his mom and sister are at church. It's just us, and I can almost pretend we're just any other couple. I like being with Caleb when he's not flinching at every single noise or convinced every shadow is his mom bursting into the room to catch us in the act of me not getting pregnant.

"No, I have something to show you. It's very important to me. Don't laugh." He opens his closet, then stretches up on his toes to reach to the top shelf. He pulls down a notebook, colorful tabs sticking out of the side, and tucks it against himself like he's handling old dynamite. He sits next to me on the bed, then places the notebook between us and runs his hand over the cover. "So. This is my novel."

"I didn't know you wrote things." (The paper he wrote for our current events class was good, but that's a low bar to clear.)

"I don't talk about it. I once told my mom I wanted to be a writer, and she asked if I wouldn't rather do something, anything, else."

"Do you want me to read it?"

"I mostly want you to know it *exists*, so somebody else does." He presses down on the notebook so hard it makes an indentation in the mattress, but then he releases it and looks away.

I pick it up slowly, like I've realized it's old dynamite too. He doesn't stop me, but when I look up, he's tense, his lip sucked into his mouth. "I don't have to read it. It already makes me feel special that you shared it with me."

"You can read it." He gets out of bed and slides into his pants, looking away from me.

The first page is dedicated to an unfinished table of contents. The next two pages are taken up by a map he's drawn, one filled with imaginary cities and roads and empty places, all underneath a banner reading "AURORA." It's amazing. It feels like now I'm *actually* seeing him naked.

"I named her that before I knew how I felt about you," he says as he puts on some socks. I don't know what he means.

"I'm looking at the map. It's really cool."

"Oh," he says. "Turn the page."

The first sentence of chapter 1 reads, "Havock remembered his sixteenth nameday less for the festival that greeted it than for the arrival of Abigail from the West Marshlands."

My head swims. I try to read more, but all I can see is the name. "Is she based on me?"

"I didn't think she was. But maybe a little."

"What does she . . . do?" I look for other mentions of "Abigail." There are so many.

"She's a powerful mage from the sun-blighted lands."

"It says she's from the West Marshlands?" Like, at least keep my character consistent, Caleb.

"Those *are* the sun-blighted lands."

"Oh." I keep going. I find a scene that starts, "Havock, having succumbed to his desire for the maiden, took it upon himself to go on sabbatical." I close the notebook. "I don't think you know what sabbatical means."

"I'm not really looking for *notes*," Caleb says, trying not to be angry. "I shouldn't have shown you." He takes the book from me, clutching it against his chest again.

"I'm sorry. It seems really cool. But I literally just found out this exists *and* that I apparently inspired a major character."

"You didn't. Not really."

"She sounds pretty badass, at least."

"She is." He nods excitedly. "Super badass. Havock has never met anyone like her, and when he starts to fall for her, he thinks she's enchanted him. He'd never fall for someone like her otherwise."

"Uh-huh." Yeah, Caleb. This character *clearly* isn't based on me.

"She's the love of his life *and* the only one who can help him navigate the Lost Caverns. She was born with secret knowledge that will allow him—both of them—to escape the land of Aurora." He smiles and looks away. "When I starting writing, I realized I had it bad for you. I could hear Abigail so clearly with your voice. I didn't think she was going to be an important character, but I kept wanting to spend time with her. I wanted to . . ."

The garage door downstairs growls as it opens, and Caleb thrusts the notebook at me, like he's trying to cover me in his words. "Get dressed!"

I've just finished when Ruth throws the door open and says, "You'd better not be having sex up here." When she sees me, her eyes go wide. "I'm telling Mom."

"We're studying." Caleb's voice wobbles. I hold up the notebook as evidence.

"Studying what? Each other's *bodies*?"

"This is beneath you, Ruth." Caleb folds his arms across his chest.

"Sounds like *Abigail* was beneath *you*." Ruth makes what's supposed to be a sex face. It looks like the final expression of an animal hit by a car. You'd think she'd have seen sex in a movie at least once.

"Kids, don't fight. I have a headache," Caleb's mom calls from the hallway. She steps into the room to give Caleb a hug. I try not to move, because maybe her tyrannosaurus eyes can't see me if I stay still. Doesn't work. She gives me a little nod and says, "Hi, Abigail."

"Caleb's not supposed to have girls here when nobody else is home," Ruth says.

"We were studying," Caleb says.

I hold up the notebook again. "Study buddies."

His mom looks me up and down. "Abigail's different," she says. "Abigail's special."

She disappears back down the hall, and Ruth follows her, trying to catch her in some minor hypocrisy she can turn into a winning argument. (Best of luck, Ruth! Younger-sister solidarity!) Caleb smiles and shakes his head. "You're special. Evidently."

"Evidently?" I laugh. He grabs my arm and pulls me into a kiss.

As I leave for school the next morning, I'm trying not to think about roughly fifty things, not limited to but including Isaiah's speech to the club later on, being in a room with both him *and* Caleb's mom, and how I told Megan I had homework to do last night before I went to have sex with Caleb instead. Also, his novel? That's weird, right? And I'm special? *How*, exactly?

Jennifer stops me at the door. "We need to have dinner with Mom and Dad before they get any angrier. Can we please talk about this without you blowing me off?"

"I'm trying not to think about it." (It's one of the fifty things.)

"Do you have plans Saturday?"

"I have a very rich social life, so I can't say."

"Right. Well, because you've been avoiding this conversation, I'm going to just tell them Saturday. It'll be fine." She puts a hand on my arm and squeezes. Hard. She must be scared. "Okay?"

I want to tell her I believe her, but I don't. Outside, Caleb honks his horn. "I should go to school."

She releases me, and I can feel her watch me all the way down the walk and into his truck.

Isaiah Rose grins like a shithead kid who got all the cereal dirty when he fished the prize out of the box. He greets everybody who walks into the Students for Democracy meeting with a big handshake, even Megan. (She seems confused he can pretend to not be a shitbag.) When he sees Caleb, he gives him a huge hug, and they clap each other on the back.

He wears a pale-blue button-up shirt that's a little too small for his campaign gut, the sleeves rolled up. The shirt's tucked into blue jeans, and his shoes have one of the laces undone. I find myself thinking that's a strategic choice, like he's wearing a costume that's supposed to make us like him, which is something I know a lot about.

I try to steer clear of him, but Caleb's mom guides him to me and says, "This is Abigail Hawkes, the group's vice president." It sounds impressive when she says it.

He grips my hand so tightly I think I'm going to have a seizure. "It's nice to meet you, Abigail. Brooke won't shut up about what a great kid you are." He doesn't say my name with an invisible sneer. Instead, he greets me as just one of the guys, which is much worse.

Unlike the usual crew of eight, twenty-six people show up to the meeting today. Half the cheerleading squad is here, and so are the quarterback and his friends. Erica raises her voice over the commotion to say, "Let's get started!" Most of the newcomers clap, only to sag when they realize Megan's going to introduce Isaiah. Caleb sits next to his mom at the front.

"Isaiah Rose is a local political icon," Megan reads from a note card she had to run by Caleb's mom. (She's not allowed to ad-lib.) "His father also represented Davison County in the state legislature, and according to the *Argus Leader*, Mr. Rose is a likely candidate for the governorship in 2018."

Isaiah holds his hands up. "Don't commit me to anything!" He's wedged himself into one of the desks, his belly bulging over top of it. Caleb's mom looks over at him and smiles, and then she looks to the back of the room and finds me and smiles at me too. Okay.

I stare at her hand as she runs it up and down Caleb's back. I try to send him little telepathic beams that remind him I'm here. It maybe works. A little wave passes through his shoulders, and he shakes his mom's hand off. She hesitates, then sets it in her lap. He hunches forward. I wish I was running my hand over his back.

"And with that, let's welcome Representative Isaiah Rose!" Megan says. We all clap.

"I remember when I was your age, I thought the world was going to keep getting better and better!" he says. "How many of you think that now?" The quarterback thrusts his hand straight up in the air, and a few other popular kids join him, with less enthusiasm. Caleb's mom raises her hand and nudges Caleb until he does as well. "I see a lot of hands! That gives me faith in the future." He crosses to loom over Megan, who sits with her arms folded across her chest. "What about you, Meg? You're a smart kid. What do you think?"

She sits up in her seat. "The planet's getting hotter, and we're still bound to medieval ideas about womanhood that hold an entire half of the species back, so I'll be very surprised if we maintain the status quo." She gives him a sweet smile. Why do fascist cunts always think they can pick on Megan?

"Gosh, if I felt that way about the future, I wouldn't raise my hand either." He chuckles. A few people laugh along. "I get it. It's a big, scary world. But are you worrying about the right things? Because I don't stay awake at night worried about the planet or anything so big as that. I worry about what's happening here in Mitchell."

"Do you worry about me?" Shit. That was me. I opened my mouth, and something fell out. "I'm the only person in this room you tried to pass a law against. I'll bet everybody else feels left out."

He locks in on me and smiles. "I wondered if you'd speak up, Abigail. Brooke warned me about you." Everybody laughs again, even Caleb. "You have some distorted ideas about my beliefs. But tell me: What gets you excited about the future?"

I'll play along. "You know me. I'm an optimist. I'm young enough that when I'm an adult, I might be able to get a uterus transplant, so I can experience the miracle of childbirth." Everybody's looking at me, except for Caleb's mom, who digs around in her purse. Caleb smiles faintly, clearly sick to his stomach. My heart starts to pound. Megan thought if I just spoke up, Isaiah might realize I'm a human being or whatever, but then everybody started *looking* at me. I hate that because I know what they're thinking.

"Motherhood is a sacred gift from God—"

"I don't know if I wanna have babies, but if it would make motherfuckers like you leave me alone, sure, I'll have some babies." The air goes out of the room when I say "motherfuckers," but Isaiah holds my gaze.

"I'm aware you're one of those . . . transgendered people," he says, frowning seriously.

"I'm Abigail Hawkes. Students for Democracy vice president. You tried to make it illegal for me to use the bathroom. You gave an interview where you said kids like me are just confused and need better therapy. Or to go to church."

"An overenthusiastic reporter took me out of context—"

"You're an asshole who thinks he knows what's best for everybody." My brain sounds like the janky grinding of my mom's dishwasher. I imagine her here, running her hand over my back. I want to run away. "Why do you think I started this fucking club?"

"*We* started this club," Erica says (and I've never been so glad to hear her voice), "to teach everyone about the importance of democracy. And isn't speaking your mind part of democracy, Representative Rose?"

"Of course!" That smile returns. "Though a little civility is always appreciated."

"Abigail is one of our most passionate students," Erica says. "She cares deeply about these issues. As she's reminded me a million times, what our trans students need is support and affirmation. That's the best way to give them a chance to thrive and survive."

Isaiah looks at her like she's an alien. I know how big this is. She's admitting she knows one tiny thing about being trans, which, granted, she would probably know from being a caring teacher. But in admitting it, she's taking a tiny risk to protect me. She's letting the room stop spinning. She's trying to give me space to sit down and shut up, to let everybody think Isaiah and I have a little difference of opinion. Totally fine and normal.

But that's just what she doesn't get. What not enough people realize. Things *aren't* normal. Isaiah Rose wants people like us to go away or die.

"What do you care, Mr. Rose?" I stand up, except my jacket gets caught, so I look awkward. "I'm sorry I swore at you, but can you just tell me why you care so much about how I live my life? You don't fucking know me at all. So why?"

"I only want to make sure you understand the gravity of these decisions. Do I believe you're on a godly path? No. God gave us a clear set of instructions for how to live our lives, and you disobey many of them. But this is a free society, and when you're an adult, you can make the decision for yourself. But those are the key words. 'When you're an adult.'"

Everybody listens to him, even Megan. He's saying the things you say when you want everybody to pretend you're not a snake, even if they disagree with you. The second I came out, I saw how easily people like him say anything they can to seem smart and reasonable while they push you out of a plane without a parachute.

"You are so *fucking boring*. Somebody told you how to live your life when you were five, and you never tried anything else. Which means I know myself better than you ever fucking will," I say. My jacket is still caught on the desk, and as I yank it away, it tears. It's a big hole, and even if this jacket is on its last legs, it feels like the last shitty thing of a pretty shitty ten minutes.

I have to go. I have to leave. I have to be *anywhere else*.

"Abigail—" Erica says, but I'm already gone.

I sit on a flight of stairs down the hall, and Megan approaches me carefully like she's one of those bomb-disposal guys. She sits with me for a little bit, until I lie and tell her I'm fine. I want her to make sure I didn't just blow up the stupid club, which I don't even care about anymore, but she does, and I care about her. This is why you should never have friends.

So she goes back inside, and I get to think about what a disaster I am for a few minutes. Somebody's shadow falls over me, and I look up to see Caleb. "That was pretty rad what you did in there."

"No. Now everybody thinks I'm an unstable piece of shit."

"Do you know how many times I've wanted to tell that hypocritical piece of shit what I think of him?" he says. "You didn't hesitate, you just did it."

"I do have impulse-control problems."

He laughs. "You're my hero. Do you know that?"

"Fuck you, Caleb."

"I mean it! My therapist says I pretend to be the person I think people want me to be all the time. I go along to get along. You never do that. I don't think you even know *how* to do that."

I probably should have taken more away from that than *Caleb has a therapist??* but I'm me, so I just stare at him until he stretches out his hand and pulls me up into a kiss.

He doesn't let go of my hand all the way back into the classroom. Isaiah stops talking to gawk at us. "I want everybody here to know that I love Abigail Hawkes," Caleb says. He squeezes my hand. "You can make fun of me for that. Say I'm gay. Whatever. I can take it. My life is better with her in it, and you—" he points at Isaiah "—owe her an apology."

Isaiah half laughs. "Brooke?" he says. She tilts her head to the side and says nothing. "Fine. Sorry, Abigail." I can tell he wants to fill in the ways I was a jerk to him, but he knows I'm a literal teenager and he's a grown-ass man.

Accepting the apology means being okay with everything Isaiah said, if not the way he said it. Accepting the apology means being okay with Isaiah getting to make me a political chew toy. Accepting the apology means being okay with how he spoke to Megan. But Caleb's arm is around my shoulder.

"Apology accepted," I say. Caleb kisses the top of my head.

The applause carries Isaiah into the hallway after he eventually finishes. I dig around in my bag while everybody leaves, and when I look up, Erica is there. "I'm proud of you," she says.

"Don't be *proud* of me. I just don't like when assholes are assholes to Megan."

"I'm still proud of you." Fucking Erica.

Caleb meets me in the hallway. He winces. "I need you to know this wasn't my idea. Just tell her you're busy Saturday."

Shit. Remember my stupid fucking parents and their stupid fucking plans? "I actually am busy Saturday. Why?"

The women's room door opens, and Caleb's mom emerges. "Abigail's busy on Saturday," Caleb says. He winks at me.

"Oh, that's too bad," she says. "If my son's in love with you, I should have you over for dinner. Maybe some other week?"

Fuck. I maybe liked it better when Caleb hated himself for secretly fucking me. At some point, I lost control of this thing. At some point, I wanted to lose control of it.

Still. Caleb's mom won't make the cops drag me back to Corsica. Which my parents might do.

"I can get out of the other thing." I dig my fingernails into my palm and smile.

Erica

Thursday,

October 20

The wait for three photos of Abigail to resolve into actual images instead of blurry blobs agonized Erica. She clutched her phone close to her chest, so no one else in this coffee shop with terrible Wi-Fi would see what she was looking at. If anybody did ask what she was doing, she planned to say she was looking at porn, instead of helping her teenage best friend choose which dress to wear to dinner with her boyfriend's family. That answer felt less embarrassing.

When Erica asked why Abigail was entrusting her with this decision rather than Megan, Abigail had said, *have you seen how she dresses???* and left it at that. Erica suspected the increasing amount of time Abigail spent with Caleb was a sore spot in her friendship with Megan and didn't want to press.

Finally, the images loaded. *The orange one. For sure*, Erica wrote.

yeah makes my boobs look great

Not acknowledging that in case these text logs are subpoenaed.

haha what are you doing??

Helen Swee entered the coffee shop then, carrying both her purse and a reusable shopping bag full of "SWEE!" buttons ("I sound fun, don't I?" Helen had said at the first Students for Democracy meeting. "I *am* fun," she'd added, nodding with grim determination.) She dropped the bags on Erica's table, threw her hands in the air, and said, "College students!" before going to order.

Meeting Helen for coffee. Need Constance advice.

what mine sucks???????????????

As you love pointing out, you have zero ex-wives.

SO DOES HELEN!!!!!!!!!!!!!!!!!!!

Erica was searching for an emoji to respond with when Helen settled opposite her, shaking out her hand. "Every time I dig around in that bag, I stab myself. There's gotta be a better way." Erica set the phone face down on the table between them.

"A better way than letting a bunch of buttons with sharp, metal sticks live free-range in a shopping bag?"

Helen rolled her eyes but laughed. "So, what's the deal with the ex?" The phone on the table between them buzzed.

Erica had worried that Helen had permanently slotted her into a box marked "sketchy men" after seeing her with John and his friends. She wasn't sure what she thought her friendship with Helen should be, but she knew it *should be*. Texting Helen *Can we get drinks? I need advice about my ex and have nowhere to turn* did the trick. Evidently, Helen Swee loved a train wreck.

"We kissed." Erica smiled bashfully. "A *bunch* of times." Erica knew she was understating things a bit. Since the kiss during the shopping trip, they had furtively made out every time they were supposed to be running lines, constantly terrified someone else at rehearsal would catch them (which only made the making out better, Erica supposed).

"Oh, Jesus Christ. Bad idea! Didn't she leave you for your friend?" The phone buzzed twice.

"It's different now." Erica thought about explaining how what she had with Constance now was something new and worth nurturing. However, to say that would require telling Helen about her gender, and Erica wouldn't risk that yet. "I wouldn't really describe John as a 'friend.' I tried hanging out with him that one time, and . . . Sorry. I know they were assholes, but to be fair to me, *I* wasn't."

The phone buzzed again. Helen's eyes floated to it, then snapped back to Erica. "That isn't as foolproof a defense as you'd think. Look: This woman left you for another guy, I assume after an affair. Now she's cheating on him with you? She sounds like a real piece of work."

"It's different now!" Erica heard how whiny she sounded.

Helen laughed. "Awww. Girl."

Panic rose in Erica's throat. (And, admittedly, a small electric thrill.) Helen had seen her nail polish, after all. There was a door marked "womanhood" out there somewhere. Who better to guard it than Helen Swee? But, also, maybe someone like Helen would leave it open a crack.

The expression on Erica's face caused Helen to look panicked herself. "I hope that was okay! At Georgetown, I called all my guy friends 'girl.' I don't know why. I was nineteen and lonely and surrounded by East Coast privilege and trying to get over the death of my dad. Maybe I thought I was proving something."

Erica smiled and summoned a tiny scrap of fortitude. "I let my niece paint my nails, then wore them to school. I'm fine with gender exploration."

"Yeah!" Helen said. "I knew you were cool. By the way, I have this fundraiser on the twenty-ninth. I need money for 'get out the vote' stuff. Megan's dad is hooking me up with all his rich friends, blah, blah, blah. Can you come and just . . . stand around? Be a pillar of the community? After all, half the people there have had you teach their kids. You have a nice, steady, nonthreatening vibe." Erica must have made a face because Helen winced. "I mean that as a compliment. You're just . . . chill. You're a chill dude."

"Right." Erica ran her thumb over her coffee lid. "My dad died too," she said suddenly. She wasn't sure when she'd last told anyone about the death, an event that felt like it should define her more. She hadn't even mentioned it to Abigail. "When I was twenty-four. Heart attack."

"Sixteen for me. Leukemia. Fucking sucks, doesn't it?"

"My dad and I weren't close, even if we weren't estranged or anything. He didn't try to understand me, so I didn't try to understand him. Which also sucks." Erica thought for a moment. "I have a family. I almost never think about them, and I suspect the feeling's mutual. Which is probably not how it should be, but . . . my sisters both have enormous houses and solid marriages and perfect toddler sons. I have none of that, which makes me the family fuckup. No fun."

Erica closed her mouth before she revealed how hard it was to deal with the expectations that came with being "the son," a truth she only now realized her brain had been beavering away at since she self-accepted. She had almost just *said* that to Helen. Out of nowhere! What was with her?

Fortunately, Helen filled the sudden silence. "So you want your ex back to better fit in with them? Probably a bad idea, but I understand. Intellectually." She pointed to herself. "*I'm* an only child. My mom miscarried three times, then I was born a month early." Helen blinked twice, as if surprised to have said something so intimate. "I don't usually talk about it."

"You don't have to." The phone buzzed.

"My therapist says half the reason I'm running this obviously doomed campaign is for him. He was a New Deal Democrat in Mitchell, South Dakota. He thought the game was rigged against him. Because it is. Somebody like Isaiah Rose says an obviously dumbass sweetheart like Abigail is a deviant, and so many people just believe him. But my dad also thought the NFL was rigged, so maybe he was wrong about other things too."

"The NFL's not rigged?"

"Ha. Look: Just don't keep making the same mistakes because you want someplace—or someone—to suddenly become who you hope they could be."

"People can change." The phone buzzed another three times.

"Who the fuck keeps *texting* you? It better not be the ex!" She picked up the phone before Erica could, and Erica had a millisecond of recognition that Helen really *was* treating her like a good friend before the openness in Helen's eyes slammed shut. She threw the phone back at Erica, who clumsily caught it and saw the stream of texts she'd missed from Abigail. Helen stood, grabbing her bags. "So much for just tutoring her, huh? If the choice is between fucking your ex-wife and fucking a literal teenager, *please* pick your ex-wife. At least she'll know her life's being ruined."

Coffee shop patrons looked over at the commotion. "It's not what you think," Erica said. She knew she should explain everything to Helen, but all that emerged was, "I'm helping her."

"She's funny and chaotic and a very sweet person," Helen said. "But you are an *adult*, and she is a *kid*, and unless you're her dad, then no kid on the planet needs that much help from you. I *really* didn't think you were capable of that, █████."

By the time Erica had thought of how to respond, Helen had left.

Erica spent the two hours before rehearsal in a paranoid stew. She texted Abigail to tell her Helen knew something was up, and Abigail wrote back, *she knows you annoy me??* which didn't help. It should have been so easy to tell Helen the truth, but it felt like a mountain Erica couldn't climb. Helen was yet another woman who misread her intentions, disastrously so. She wrote back to Abigail, *we just need to be more careful*, and Abigail didn't respond.

When Erica eventually arrived at the theater, she heard a power drill whir overhead. The outline of a Main Street lined the back of the stage, looming over Erica. John descended a nearby ladder and clapped Erica on the back. "What do you think?"

"It's definitely a town," Erica said.

"That's the idea. Connie said it might be too much, but I said you and Brooke thought it was good. So what does she know?" He stooped to put his drill in its case. "We should get drinks again."

"Yeah, I don't know . . ." Disappointment flickered over John's face, and Erica cursed herself for wanting to smooth it over. "Maybe after the play's done."

He brightened and gave her a thumbs-up, then retreated to the back of the theater. He now watched every rehearsal and enthusiastically applauded everything, which only made Erica want to murder him even more.

Erica made her way to Brooke, who paged through her script. "Our production sure will put the 'town' in *Our Town*. Anyway, I asked Constance to work with you again out in the lobby. She's still not getting it." Brooke looked up at Erica and frowned. "Are you all right? You look like you've been through it."

"You know me. Multiple crises at once."

She nodded. "Right, I want to run Act Three after the break tonight. So have her ready by eight thirty."

The theater door opened, and Constance stepped inside, softly backlit by the lights outside. Even though Erica couldn't see Constance's eyes, she still felt them land on her. "You wanna do this?" she said.

"Please," Erica said. Constance turned to go before she could catch up.

Erica reread the text Constance had sent her: *I'm in the women's room.*

Erica could imagine wearing women's clothing and changing her name and having a vagina installed before she could imagine putting a toe over the threshold of a women's room.

She spent several long moments in the men's room, dutifully washing her hands while staring at herself in the mirror and trying to work up the nerve to step the handful of feet between her and Constance. Her foot wobbled slightly as she eased the women's door open, its movement causing the lights to flicker on. She braced her hand against the doorframe, leaning forward, feet still outside the threshold. "Hello?"

"It's so hot. I'm dying in here," Constance said from the back stall.

"The door doesn't lock," Erica said. She looked for something to block it with. "This is a terrible idea. Someone will find us."

"No one is finding us in here. And even if someone comes in, we'll be quiet until they leave. Nobody thinks about you as much as you do. I promise."

Erica held her breath and walked as quickly as she dared to the very last stall. Constance sat on the toilet, knees a few teasing inches apart, a couple buttons undone on her blouse. "Hi, Erica. Took you long enough."

Oh. Now she understood. Constance wanted to have sex. In the women's room at the theater. With her fiancé somewhere nearby. Did she think Erica's paranoia would *enhance* the mood?

"Oh, you want to have sex," Erica said.

"Feels like we've been heading in that direction, yeah."

Erica swallowed. She had always been unable to perform sexually when still pretending (badly) to be a man. Yet seeing Constance's obvious desire for her—for *Erica*, not an Erica-shaped facsimile—caused Erica to become immediately, painfully aroused. That arousal made every sensor in her body, especially those that had become aware nothing about her body made sense, go completely fucking nuts.

Erica turned, stumbling, to close and lock the stall door, sliding a hand down to cover the bulge in her pants. "Fuck," she finally said.

Constance laughed gently. "What's wrong?"

Erica felt Constance's eyes slide down her body to where her hand cupped her crotch. She blinked back tears. "Evidently the trick is for you to call me Erica. We probably should have tried that five years ago."

Constance stood up and placed her hand over the one Erica used to block her crotch, gently squeezing. When Erica whimpered, Constance removed her hand. "Does it hurt? We can just kiss. I promise it will be okay. You've always been the best at kissing."

"I don't *want* to just kiss." Erica felt trapped between two monsters, one warning her of the dire consequences she would face if she had an orgasm, and the other warning her of the dire consequences if she didn't. "But I also don't want to feel like when I get horny, some other person is running my body into a wall."

"Wait. I googled this," Constance said with the tenderness of a kindergarten teacher. "Your body is a woman's body, Erica. It has a penis, a woman's penis."

"That's easy for you to say. It sure doesn't *feel* like a 'woman's penis.'"

"Fuck!" Constance said. "I always screw this up."

"No, you're just *going* too fast, again," Erica said. She pressed her hand to her eye. "I want you, but I don't know how to want you the right way. Not in this body. I'm sorry."

"Don't apologize," Constance said. She touched Erica's arm softly, waiting the handful of moments it took for Erica to relax, before putting her arms around Erica's neck. "Is this okay?" Erica nodded against the top of her head. "I'm not here because I want to fuck you, although I do. I'm here because I love *you*, Erica. I always have. Not the guy you pretended to be, not John. Nobody but you."

Erica hugged Constance so tightly her erection rubbed slightly against Constance's pelvis. Constance ground back against it, bracing herself against the wall, and Erica tilted Constance's head back, running a hand through her curly hair, feeling its tangles drip through her fingers. She covered Constance's mouth with her own, then softly reached beneath Constance's blouse to cover her breast with her hand, thumb rubbing against the lace of Constance's bra.

Constance gasped. "Erica," she said. When Erica whimpered and gave a gentle squeeze, Constance added an "Erica, Erica" for good measure. Constance slid her hand down the front of Erica's jeans, gently cupping her—

Erica bolted backward, colliding with the metal door of the stall. The feeling of intense wrongness was back, like everything could tilt from pleasurable to painful at the slightest touch.

Constance smiled sadly and sat back down on the toilet. "It's okay."

Erica tried to imagine that she looked like a woman, which was to say that she looked nothing like herself. "No. You should be able to *touch* me there without—"

"We have time."

"We *had* time when we were young, Constance. We don't anymore. I wish it had been right back then. Maybe it never can be."

Constance picked up her phone. After a few seconds, it began playing Bruce Springsteen's "Hungry Heart." And in an instant, Erica wasn't in a bathroom in 2016 anymore.

The first week Erica was at college, the power went out overnight. As Erica arced through a kaleidoscope of flashlights to meet the girl she'd been spending all her free time with lately, even then, her body felt wrong to her. Too tall and angular and bulky. Now, in hindsight, it felt *less* wrong. It had still held possibility inside of it.

Erica recognized the silhouette of Constance before she revealed her face with her flashlight. The faint sounds of "Hungry Heart" carried on the wind from the dorm across the street, a chorus of girls shout-singing it in the late-summer night. Erica neared Constance, reaching up to swat a mosquito from the back of her—

"Erica?" Constance says. Erica looks up to see her ex-wife, holding a phone playing the very same song. "Stay with me. You went somewhere."

"I was remembering." Erica almost starts to cry.

"Let's try something different." Constance sets the phone on the toilet paper holder. "It's the first week at college. I've just moved to South Dakota from Boise, and the only person I know is this girl from my Intro to Theater class."

"I wasn't a—"

"This girl from my theater class. She's taller than she knows what to do with, and she has sandy-blonde hair and the deepest brown eyes I've ever seen. I've never been with another girl, so I don't quite recognize what's happening to me when I start to fall for her." She smiles. "Do you know what her name is?"

"Erica." Erica closes her eyes, letting this new history envelop her.

"I'm scared. I've barely talked to anyone at school. But when I meet Erica, it's like she knows me before she sees me.

"That first week, the power goes out, and I make plans to meet Erica in the dark. I see her before she sees me. She's beautiful, and I feel lucky to know her. We can hear music from nearby. Erica comes up to me and threads her fingers through mine and asks me to dance."

Erica, eyes still closed, feels Constance's fingers thread through hers and briefly fears she's hallucinating. Her body tingles with what she recognizes immediately, without taxonomizing it, as desire.

Fuck dancing, Erica thinks. She pulls Constance into a kiss, pressing her against the wall and sliding her bra strap down over her shoulder. She trails kisses down Constance's neck, and Constance closes her hand over Erica's crotch. Yet even as her erection returns, Constance says, "It's okay. I have you. It's okay."

They do not do much talking after that.

Abigail

Saturday,

October 22

My mom always did this thing when she was getting ready. She sucked on her front teeth a couple times, then rubbed her finger over them. I try doing it while getting ready for this stupid dinner at Caleb's house, just to see if it works. My teeth look only marginally cleaner, but as a bonus, I realize all over again how much I look like my mom.

Jennifer walks in and gives me a side squeeze. She was furious I bailed on dinner with our parents, but she's also glad I'm getting to be a normal teenager for once, so she was a little conflicted. "You look beautiful."

"They're going to devour me whole." I rub my finger over my teeth again, then lean in close to the mirror. Maybe they do look better? I don't know.

"Could you do dinner with Mom and Dad on Wednesday?"

God, Jennifer. Stop talking about this. "Can't they just leave me alone?"

"Abigail . . ." She hunches up her shoulders, then lets out a long breath. "Don't do this."

"I don't want to live with them! That should be that!"

She doesn't say anything. I look in the mirror and rub my teeth again.

"Ugh! Wednesday's fine. But they have to call me Abigail."

"I bargained Mom down to not saying your old name, which she saw as a major concession." Jennifer rolls her eyes. "I tried, Abigail. I really did. She said she doesn't like feeding your delusion. I said I didn't like feeding hers. She loved hearing that."

"Shit, you *are* my sister."

"I'll tell them Wednesday's good. *Please* don't blow this dinner up too." She kisses the top of my head. "And make good choices tonight." She winks.

"Shut the fuck up, Jennifer," I say. But I laugh.

I've been to Caleb's house a bunch of times, but tonight, in the fading light, I can really see how it stands out against the sky. All the lights inside are on, so it looks like the place is swallowing the last drops of the sun. Even if you were lost, it wouldn't be hard to find your way back here.

"Did Caleb tell you the story of this place?" Caleb's dad says as he shows me around, all of us pretending I haven't seen most of this house already. "This old hermit farmer over by Mount Vernon built it and kept adding on to it his whole life. When he died, the realtor cleared it out, and it was full of dead cats."

"My house has a cat-ghost problem too."

He looks at me funny, so I smile. "Good joke." (He doesn't laugh.) "No, no ghosts. We moved it here, all ten miles, and started fixing it up right before the recession. What a bad idea that was!" He mimics something plunging to the ground and makes a whistling noise. But he seems like he's doing well for himself, so it must have been a good idea on some level. He's probably six foot four, and he's got a nice beer belly and square-rimmed glasses. He's a little handsome in that way farmers sometimes are, where it's like they were outside so long they eroded into a better version of themselves.

"Let me show you this, Abigail. You'll love it." He leads me outside onto a little patio. The sunset reflects off Lake Mitchell at the bottom of the hill. You can probably see all the way to Sioux Falls up here. "If Caleb ever gives you guff, we can put him in a wagon and roll him all the way down to the water!" Now, he laughs, so I laugh too to be polite.

I wrap my arms around myself as it gets chilly. Caleb's dad is holding the door to the inside open for me when I hear a gunshot and nearly scream. Caleb's dad shouts down, "You get him?"

A dog bounds up the hill with something in its mouth, dropping it at our feet. It's a rabbit, still twitching, and the dog looks up at Caleb's dad like it wants a gold star. Caleb's dad brushes grass off the rabbit's fur, and then Ruth comes up out of the dark behind, gun over her shoulder. "He's a big one! I caught him chewing on one of the trees."

Caleb's dad whistles sharply, then tosses the rabbit into the shadows. The dog leaps after it, and it slobbers and snarls as it chows down. Caleb's dad digs a twenty-dollar bill out of his wallet, and Ruth takes it. "You're robbing me blind, Ruth." He turns to me. "I pay the kids for every rabbit they kill. Ruth's always been better at it than Caleb."

Caleb steps outside. He's wearing a tie, and I'd make a joke, except I'm wearing my nicest dress (the orange one). "Mom says dinner's ready." Somewhere out there in the dark, I hear the dog snarl as it eats. Caleb looks over in that direction. "Unless you've got stuff going on out here."

"Just rabbit murder!" I say. Nobody laughs.

"You're leaving money on the table, C," Ruth says. She unloads her gun. "I'll be up in a second."

We go back inside, making our way to the dining room, where Caleb's mom stands at the head of the table, hands on the back of a chair. She smiles at me. Honestly, I think she's trying to get me to let my guard down, and honestly, it's working. (Resist, Abigail!) "You look beautiful in that dress," she says. I'm sure I look ridiculous, like I always do when I wear a dress and try to seem elegant. But I also can't detect any lies.

"My friend Erica said I should wear it," I say. Fuck. If she knew I spoke her name in this woman's presence, Erica would explode. Let's not tell her.

"Who's Erica?" Caleb says, shoving a carrot stick in his mouth.

"Someone I know from support group." It's not exactly a lie.

"Abigail goes to trans support group in Sioux Falls most Fridays," Caleb tells his mom. He smiles at me, and even though I'd really rather he not say the t-word, I smile back. "It's why I get so mopey those evenings. I can't see her." He squeezes my hand.

"I didn't know they had a trans group there!" Caleb's mom says.

"They have everything in Sioux Falls now," says Caleb's dad as he reenters from the bathroom. "They have a Texas Roadhouse even."

"This is a little different than *that*," Caleb's mom says.

Ruth comes upstairs, sniffling from the cold. She goes to the kitchen sink to wash her hands. "Come sit by me, Abigail," Caleb says. Their big table is set on all four sides, a fifth place laid out for me. Something in me almost collapses when I imagine all four of them gathering here for every meal.

"Milk or water, Abigail?" Caleb's mom says. She smiles (again! stop!) and shows all her teeth. She's softening me up for the kill, huh?

"Water's fine, Mrs. Daniels," I say.

"Please call me Brooke," she says, as she pours water out of a pitcher into a glass and hands it to Caleb, who hands it to me. "We're all friends here."

"*Are* we?" Everybody *does* laugh at that one.

Ruth sits, and Brooke (what?! she *told* me to call her that!) sticks her hand out toward me. Caleb nudges me. "We're gonna bless the meal," he says, taking my other hand in his. I take Brooke's hand. It's smooth and dry and very cold.

"Father God," says Caleb's dad, "we come before you today to just ask you to place your blessing upon this meal, as you have blessed so many meals before."

He goes on, but I hear something and un-bow my head. Across from me, Ruth stares up at the ceiling. I look to see a moth scuttling along up there. Every so often, I can hear Brooke whisper, "Thank you, Jesus. Thank you," as an accompaniment to this prayer.

Shit, Caleb's dad is saying my name.

"—could join us tonight! We hope we all get to know her better. We thank you, again, oh Lord, for your abundance. In Jesus's name. Amen."

Everybody but me says, "Amen," and then they pass the food around.

"Caleb told me your favorite was lasagna," Brooke says. I don't think I told Caleb that. It's not my favorite food, though I don't bear it any particular ill will. "I took a stab at it. I've never made it before. I hope it's not too bad."

"I'm sure it will be great." I take a piece and a half to prove my faith.

I know she's on her best behavior, and I know I have some mom issues going on right now, but Brooke, honestly, seems like she's doing a good job. She listens to a meandering story Caleb tells about his friends trying to find a duck they shot, and she's *really listening*, even though I tapped out the second he started telling it. She tries to get Ruth to talk about something other than the moth on the ceiling (which she keeps bringing up, to the degree that Caleb's dad went to get a flyswatter to try to knock it down), but she never gets pushy. She laughs a little too hard at Caleb's dad's jokes, and she smiles at me a bunch, and the way her wrinkles crinkle around her eyes makes me feel like I've slipped into some other version of my life. She seems *comfortable*, like she always knew her life was headed to this moment exactly.

They talk around me, not to me, but it's nice, like I'm part of them. The lasagna is overcooked but still good. Brooke apologizes for this five separate times, until every single one of us assures her it's okay. "It was a good first try," Caleb's dad says, and Brooke (still) smiles while also sagging a little, like a puppet whose head is being held up on a string.

"So, Abigail," Ruth says, "how did you know you were trans?"

"Ruth, that's very impolite." Brooke glares.

"Abigail is our guest," Caleb's dad says.

"She'll share that information if she wants to tell us that information," Brooke says.

Okay. What the fuck is going on? Did Caleb's parents read a "what not to say to trans people" article online or something?

"Okay. What's going on?" (See? I censored myself. Polite!)

"You don't have to answer her question," Brooke says. "Ruth likes getting a rise out of people."

"I just think it's weird!" Ruth says. (I guess we're on the same page about this.) "When Caleb told me he was dating a trans girl, I was, like, 'Mom and Dad are going to kill you!'"

"I didn't say I was dating a *trans girl*. I said I was dating Abigail."

"Who's a trans girl!" Ruth says, nodding at me like I should back her up on this.

"Technically, we only started officially dating a few weeks ago," I say. Why not correct the record about something that doesn't even fucking matter?

"Yeah, well, Caleb told me he was super into you in July, so," Ruth says.

I'm going to say, "You did?" but Caleb blushes and looks away, being extremely cute, so I guess he did.

"You could have told me about her earlier," Brooke says.

"I was scared of what you'd say," Caleb says.

"Why?" Brooke leans forward.

"How can you possibly ask me that?"

"We don't support everything Pastor Rose stands for," Caleb's dad says.

"We go to his church," Caleb says, counting off on his fingers. "Mom practically *runs* his campaign. And he sponsors bills meant to keep trans people from just fucking living their lives!"

"Hey," Caleb's dad says. "Language."

"So, *yes*, I thought dating Abigail would be a bigger deal than it apparently is. I wish somebody had told me that dating a trans girl was fine, but that if I dated a guy, I'd be in deep shit."

That's not fair, but when you're me, you get used to people talking about you without realizing you're there, so I stay quiet.

"We're not your enemy, Caleb. And the kinds of people that the bill is meant for aren't trans people," Brooke says. "At least not trans people like Abigail."

Caleb looks mad. From the way everyone is reacting, I realize he has maybe never had a real conversation about this with his parents. *He's hiding himself*, I think, and for just a second, I wonder if everybody here is woodworking just a little bit.

"The bill protects us from deviants!" Brooke continues. "From people who want to hurt us! From men who wear costumes and pretend to be women! Not Abigail!"

"I'm glad you know who wants to hurt you and who doesn't," I say, before I realize I said it.

"I didn't mean it like that. It's clear that you're a trans girl, who struggled with gender dysphoria from a young age. You took steps to remedy it. That bill would have *protected* you." (Brooke apparently knows the term "gender dysphoria." That article she read must have been really good.) "And as I've told Isaiah, that bill was unenforceable. How can you stop people from using the bathroom?"

"Literally everybody at school knows Abigail is trans," Caleb says, and *thank* you, Caleb, and *fuck* you, Caleb. Remind me to tell you all about my plans to completely fucking disappear. "You're telling me that bill wouldn't stop her from using the bathroom at school?"

"Maybe you're right," Brooke says. "That's why we need other solutions to questions like that. But out in public, nobody's going to stop Abigail if she decides to use the restroom. You can't tell she's trans."

"Oh my God." I lean back, trying to claw my eyes out of my head. "You realize I'm here, right?"

"Let's talk about something else," Brooke says.

"There's a woman in my support group," I say, because I know if I don't say these words, I'll just keep listening to them dissect me. "She's probably sixty. Her name is Florence. She tells these elaborate stories about her fiancée from Omaha, and I don't think she actually has a fiancée from Omaha. She makes cookies that are pretty good and really dry, but she just wants us all to be happy. She's not like me. She didn't figure it out when she was sixteen. She wears the same dress every week, and her wig is falling apart, and she isn't like me, and she can't be like me, and she doesn't deserve any of the shit you want to drop on top of her head. And you'd see her and say she was wearing a costume. You're hurting real people. *Real people*. Not fucking hypotheticals."

Nobody says anything. Even Caleb focuses on his plate. I have a dim sense that Caleb's dad is gripping the edge of the table very tightly. Ruth has a dumb smile on her face. Brooke is looking out the big picture window, and then she looks back at me. She reaches out and touches my arm.

"I know," she says. "And I'm sorry."

I think she might say more. Instead, she smiles (a-fucking-gain) and asks who's ready for dessert.

I wander away from the house, down the hill where Ruth shot the rabbit. I need someone to talk to, and Erica is the person I think of first. I try four times before she answers the phone, and she doesn't seem pleased when she answers. "You can't just call me out of the blue anymore," she says.

I only get "Hello" out before I choke up. I wipe my eyes a few times. "I just fucked everything up with Caleb."

There's a long-enough pause that I think I've lost her until, finally, she says, "I'm so sorry, Abigail. Tell me everything."

I tell her about the whole stupid night and how bad I feel about making such a big scene and how weird Brooke was. By the time I'm almost done, my foot hits something, and I stop. Tiny trees, probably planted earlier this year, march along in a little row down here. One has been chewed off by a rabbit. "I don't know why Brooke said, 'I'm sorry.' Does she even know what she's sorry for?"

"Rarely," Erica says. "But she means well."

"Does it matter? Anyway, I left. I said I needed some air. Nobody stopped me, and now I'm looking at some trees."

"Any good ones?"

"Any good *trees*?" I laugh, and Erica laughs too. "You're such a weirdo."

I watch my breath puff out of my mouth, staring up at the tiny sliver of the moon. "I looked really fucking cute in my dress. So there's that," I say.

It's *nice* to know she's out there, hearing me, and I'm hearing her, and we're the same, even if we're not at all like each other. Remember when Ron said that just knowing somebody else was a fan of the Bears was enough to build something real on? Maybe he was righter than I gave him credit for. Fucking Ron.

"And I've gotta have dinner with my parents soon. I keep putting it off." I shiver. Maybe not just because it's cold. "For a long time after I moved out, when I got upset, I would call my mom. I don't even know why."

"Maybe you hoped she'd pick up the phone and be a different person."

"I thought for a second that maybe Brooke was a good mom, but she's just as bad as everybody else. They're all just as bad as everybody else. I just wanna leave here forever."

She's quiet, and I can almost see her biting her lip. "Why don't you come over? Constance and I are watching a movie, and you should join. We'll make popcorn."

"Didn't you just freak the fuck out over me calling you?"

"You're my friend, Abigail. And you're in pain."

"Yeah, I guess I am." Above my head, the stars are everywhere, and I feel so lonely. "Maybe I'll come over. I think I'd like that."

"Can I say something?"

"Sure," I say, but there's a long silence. "Erica?"

"Just because she doesn't love you doesn't mean you're not worthy of love. So many people want good things for you. I don't want you to chase something you've lost into the dark."

“All I do is chase things into the dark.”

“I know. Please don’t get lost there.”

“Abigail?” I hear Caleb’s voice carrying from closer to the house.

I look back, and I imagine how empty this place must have felt before Caleb’s parents moved their home here. I can see what my life would look like if I married Caleb. They’d open the door to let me in, then snap it shut behind me, so no one else could follow. Caleb’s parents would hug and kiss me and Caleb and our kids, then wouldn’t so much as give Erica or Florence table scraps. But would I care if I finally had somewhere to come home to?

Brooke and Mr. Daniels only love the people it’s convenient to love. I hate everything about that except for how I’m one of the people they love. I feel great, and I feel awful, and I pick “great” because somewhere in there, I got tired of caring so much.

“There you are,” Caleb says. I hear footsteps behind me on the hill.

“Thanks for talking to me, girl,” I say to Erica. “I’ll check in tomorrow.”

“You sure you’re—” I hang up before she can say “okay,” and then Caleb’s arms are around me from behind again.

This time, he’s helping me up. This time, he’s dragging me into the light, to a place where everybody will see me with him. I give him a hug, so he knows I’m okay. I follow him back up the hill, leaving behind some little piece of myself still sitting in the dark.

Erica

Sunday,

October 23

As soon as their call ends, it's clear that Abigail isn't coming for movie night. Erica feels embarrassed for ever imagining she would deign to watch *Legally Blonde 2*, the latest film in Constance's "Studies in Elder Millennial Girlhood" series, with her.

Shortly after midnight, Constance gets up to leave, and Erica is just drunk enough to say, "Back to your real life," with a heavy sadness she immediately wishes she could take back.

"You know how complicated this is."

Erica's phone buzzes, and she fumbles to pick it up, only to see a spam email. "Abigail's not coming over," she says.

"She probably has a curfew." Constance rubs Erica's neck, and bile rises in Erica's throat. She remembers riding in the back of her high school friend's car, a six-pack of Smirnoff Ice clinking like wind chimes on the floor.

Her eyes water. "I was never a teenager. Not in a way that mattered."

"Most of us weren't."

"It's not the same when you're queer."

"Erica, please. You think I didn't want to kiss a billion girls in high school and wouldn't let myself? You think I don't wish I could get another shot at figuring things out?"

"It's not the same."

Constance looks like she might snap Erica's neck between her fingers. Instead, she picks up her purse and fishes out her keys. "We'll talk tomorrow, okay? Get some sleep. I love you."

When she's gone, Erica picks up her phone and wills it to display a message from the only person she wants to hear from. She falls asleep well after 1:30 a.m.

At school Monday morning, Abigail seems like an entirely different person. She nestles in the crook of Caleb's arm, her hair (now dyed a glossy honey blonde) neatly brushed, earrings glinting. Her army jacket is nowhere to be seen. She looks like an Abigail who's been patched to remove bugs. It both unnerves Erica and fills her with an immense, embarrassing envy. Imagine changing your whole self to fit in that easily!

Just before she enters her homeroom, Erica notices Megan also watching Abigail. Now that she thinks about it, since Caleb stood up for Abigail to Isaiah, she has slowly turned the boy into her center of gravity. She sits with him at lunch, and she skipped Thursday's Students for Democracy meeting to hang with him. And who did she ditch in both cases? Megan. *We're both jealous*, Erica realizes, and instead of feeling ashamed, she feels vindicated.

"You okay?" she says. *Fuck Caleb!* she tries to psychically project.

Megan jumps when Erica speaks. "I'm fine." She slams her locker shut, and Caleb's cabal looks over, snickering. Abigail doesn't, but she also doesn't look at Megan.

"It'll pass. Young love always does."

"What do *you* know about it?" Megan freezes. "Sorry for snapping. Please don't give me detention?"

Erica sighs and waves her toward her homeroom.

The worse Erica feels about Abigail 2.0, the more she judges herself for feeling that way.

The only class she has Abigail in is American Lit, and Erica cannot imagine that anyone (least of all Abigail) has read “Bartleby, the Scrivener,” so she throws together a pop quiz. (“Keep at ’em, ████. Don’t let those kids get soft!” Hank says when he sees Erica printing out the questions.)

She is aware of her ulterior motivation. Having something to grade lets her focus on something other than her flailing emotions. (One kid scrawls “I WOULD PREFER NOT TO,” across his paper. Erica gives him an A. Why not?)

When she looks up at the end of class, Abigail hovers over her desk. “I assume you stayed at Caleb’s Saturday? How did it go?”

“Sorry for not coming over? We played Scattergories, and you know how it goes with Scattergories. The time just flies.”

Erica flips over the next quiz to grade it.

“I have this dinner with my parents on Wednesday. Which sucks. But . . .” Abigail twists her hands together like she does when she needs something. “I was wondering . . .”

Erica looks up so quickly she nearly gets whiplash. “*Whatever* you need, just ask.”

Abigail steps back. “Could you write me a letter? About how much better I’m doing in school? As, like, a symbol of how I’m a model citizen now?”

“We’ll see how you did on this quiz.” Erica chuckles, but Abigail doesn’t. “Of course I will.”

“Cool.” Abigail leaves without saying anything more.

When Erica grades Abigail’s quiz, there’s just one answer wrong. It only annoys her more.

When she sits down to write her letter, Erica contemplates playing with fire. She considers explaining just how much Abigail means to her. Despite her constant paranoia, she wants to make Abigail’s parents *see* what they have so casually thrown away in the name of their own delusions.

But, she realizes, such a letter would not be for Abigail's parents. It would be for Abigail, a frantic attempt to grab hold of a friendship Erica worries is slipping through her fingers. And it might only make things worse. Maybe, she thinks, Abigail is trying to erase herself from her life before her parents do it for her.

So she writes the blandest, most professional letter she can imagine, one she might write for any student she thought showed promise. She concludes with, "In the time I have known her, Abigail has become one of my strongest students." (She looks over at the almost-perfect pop quiz and realizes that's not really a lie.) "She's a credit to Mitchell High School. You should be proud."

She signs it with her old name and wants to vomit.

Erica hands Abigail the letter at the end of school on Wednesday, right before she leaves for dinner with her parents. She wears a dark-colored dress, and she's done her makeup. She looks like she's going to a funeral.

Abigail reads the letter once, then again more slowly. "You make me sound so . . . good. I hate it."

Erica smiles faintly. "Everything in that letter is true."

Abigail clutches the letter to her chest. "Thanks. Wish me luck. If I'm not here tomorrow, figure out what detransition camp my parents sent me to and break me out." She laughs, like she made a joke, but it's clear she believes she might suffer such a fate.

"I will find you anywhere, okay?" Erica says. Abigail gives her a look, and Erica realizes it was too much. "It's going to be okay. They're going to take one look at you and realize how stupid they are."

Abigail shakes her head. "You don't know them at all." She folds up the letter, turns on her heel, and leaves.

The next morning, Abigail is not in American Lit.

Nor is she there on Friday.

When Erica texts, Abigail doesn't respond. Doris at the front office will only say that Abigail has called in sick. Yet when Erica drives by Abigail's house with her favorite order from Culver's, all the windows are dark.

Erica needs to see other people, other trans people. So, Friday night, she attends support group. When Bernadette asks everyone to share their weekly victories, Erica sobs. "My friend is gone," she says before running off and hiding in the men's room, too embarrassed to even try to be herself.

She emerges to find Bernadette waiting. "Let's go for a coffee," she says.

Outside, an unseasonably hot and muggy day has broken into an increasingly cold rain. Bernadette drives them to the Perkins on 41st, and Erica cries softly on the way.

Inside, Erica tries to tell the full story, beginning with coming out to Abigail six weeks ago. Bernadette has heard this story before, but it now sounds so hollow in Erica's mouth that she jumps to her worst fear: Abigail is gone forever, at least spiritually. Her parents have sealed her away.

She realizes how much she is crying and shakes her head. "I'm sorry. I got so used to feeling nothing, and now I feel *everything*, and I don't know how to talk about it."

Bernadette smiles kindly. "Is it like every emotion you've ever had is trying to get through a tiny door at once?" Erica nods. "Yeah. Happens to a lot of us. The world made it too painful to feel anything, so you stopped feeling altogether."

Erica swallows. "It's awful."

"It's necessary." Bernadette wags a Splenda packet back and forth, chasing the granules to the bottom before ripping open the top and pouring it into her coffee. "More importantly, if you think Abigail's been kidnapped—and I'm aware this would not fit the legal definition of kidnapping, but it's the spirit of the thing—why did you come *here*?"

"I thought maybe she'd come to group. It sounds stupid when I say it out loud."

"Abigail gets a lot out of group, but I do not think she would attend without you to walk in with her, even if someone dropped her off across the street." Bernadette cranes her neck to look around the room. "The service at this place has really turned to shit. I'm starving."

"Aren't you worried?" Erica sniffles.

"Of course I am! If Abigail called me and said, 'I'm being held prisoner at the bottom of the ocean. Can you get a boat?' I would be there in a second. But Abigail hasn't called for a boat. She called in sick to school."

"After dinner with her parents!"

"What if—go with me here—the dinner was so awful that Abigail needed a few days to recuperate, mentally and emotionally? What if she just needs a hermit period?"

The more Bernadette talks, the more ridiculous Erica feels. She stares down into her coffee and says nothing, furious.

"I'm going to give you some good advice that will sound like bad advice: Abigail needs you to look out for her. She does not need you to *save* her."

"But she's my best friend," Erica says. Almost immediately, she wants to crawl under the table.

"Is she? Or is she just the first person who knew your name?"

It finally hits Erica. It isn't just that Abigail supports her; it is that she recognizes her. Abigail sees Erica in a way that extends from the present outward, making the past feel whole again and building promise for the future. Constance, for instance, has gotten very good at reducing the time it takes her to mentally shift from "ex-husband" to "girlfriend" to a split second. Yet that split second still exists. To Abigail, Erica has always been a woman—an annoying English-teacher woman, yes, but a woman nonetheless.

Of course, she doesn't know how to say that, so she settles for, "She's my friend."

"She's seventeen," Bernadette says.

"I'm closer to her in age than I am to you." Erica tears open a sugar packet, eyes blurred with tears. Its contents scatter everywhere. "A lot closer."

"Yes, clearly what I'm doing here is trying to build a deep, abiding friendship with you by criticizing all your life choices. You've cracked my love language."

Erica laughs despite herself. She sweeps the sugar from the table into her hand, then pours it into her coffee. "The weather's getting worse. I'm going to drive home, hunching over my steering wheel to see through the rain. My house will be dark. Constance is out with her fiancé at a Halloween party. Abigail is gone. I'm alone. Like always."

Bernadette places her hand over Erica's. "I'm here." Erica pulls her hand away. "Erica, sweetheart, you wouldn't hate the dark so much if you weren't scared of your own shadow."

"What the fuck does that mean?"

Bernadette makes a sour face. "No need to be crass."

Before Erica can ask her for clarification, a pimply teenage boy arrives to wait on them, and Bernadette orders cherry pie with so many qualifiers that it takes him three separate tries to get everything down. Erica stares at the cars outside hissing past the restaurant. She imagines herself driving each—a harried mom, a teenage girl cutting every lane change a little close, a drunk twentysomething driving her best friends around.

"And you, sir?" the server says to Erica. "Do you know what you want?"

"Sorry, no," Erica says. "Give me a minute."

Abigail

Wednesday,

October 26

The dress was Jennifer's idea. It's stiff and so dark blue it's almost black. It has a white collar, like Jennifer wanted to make sure she skipped past "slut" when dressing me but landed on "great-aunt" instead.

I look at myself in the school bathroom mirror, then claw at the collar to give my neck a little fucking room. That's when Megan walks in and freezes. My interactions with her lately have mostly been of the "replying to a text with 'haha'" variety, but I've had a lot going on. I'm trying to make sure Caleb still likes me! She's still my friend! She knows that!

"Hi!" I say.

"Hi."

"You like my dress?" She doesn't say anything. "Jennifer thinks it will help my parents see I'm respectable." She stays silent. "At our dinner."

"That's happening? I thought you were going to get out of it?"

Did I really not tell her about the dinner? Maybe not? "I say I'm going to get out of lots of things but end up doing them anyway."

"So, the trick for getting you to do things is to get you to say you won't do them? Got it."

"Okay, lay it on me. How'd I fuck up this time?"

"The debate you said you'd help with? I'm planning it all by myself."

"That's over a week away!"

"We can't just *throw it together* the day before." She takes a breath, and her voice wavers. "Helen's fundraiser is Saturday."

"I said I would go to that!" It's like she doesn't listen to me at all.

She shakes her head. "We don't have to pretend. I get it. It's more fun to be Caleb's girlfriend. Nobody notices you, and you don't have to think for yourself."

She's right, and she shouldn't have said it. "That's fucking shitty. But whatever. I deserve it."

"Yeah, you do. A little." She looks me up and down, then closes her eyes, like she's printing an image of me on the inside of her eyelids. "You look very pretty."

"I look like a fucking doll. Look, I'll come over Saturday and help you set up."

"Don't you have to get ready for church with your future in-laws and pray for God to kill all the trans people who aren't you?"

"Fuck you, Megan." I almost tell her she doesn't understand me because she's never had a boyfriend because no one wants to be with her to begin with. I almost tell her she's being an unreasonable bitch. But I'm not sure those things are true.

"Come over Saturday; don't come over Saturday. I don't care. I've had so many friendships fall apart when people found something better to do than hang out with me. I'm used to it."

"You don't *sound* used to it. I'm just nervous about this dinner. After tonight, I'll have time for things other than reflecting Caleb's light back at him."

She does smile at that. "I know I'm a lot. I know you have other stuff going on. Let's just go back to being colleagues in democracy saving." She starts to leave.

"Wait? Are you friend breaking up with me?" I laugh because she's not, right? "Okay, now I *will* come over Saturday. So you have to stare at me."

"Sure." She sounds so tired.

"Megan, can you . . ." I look down at my stupid starchy dress again. "Can you tell me it's going to be okay? You would know."

She stops at the main door and doesn't look back. "You're going to be fine, Abigail. You always are."

Six frames decorate the back wall of my parents' living room, each containing photos of their kids. It's the same setup for all: a big senior picture at the center, smaller photos from kindergarten to junior year orbiting it. Jennifer grows up from a pigtailed girl to a freckly teen wearing a magenta prom dress and Invisalign braces. "Cute!" Ron says when he sees her pictures. She leans against him. She's so nervous.

The frames make growing up seem easy, like a straight line from baby to adult. They're not really pictures of us but pictures of my parents' achievements.

Then there's my frame, which goes from a little girl in a Minnesota Twins T-shirt to a dead-eyed sophomore in flannel and acne. There's no photo in the junior- or senior-year spots. Instead, a photo of me as a baby, in full Western wear (including cowboy boots), sits at the center.

"Dinner's not quite ready yet," Mom says. Her teeth gleam when she smiles. She must have rubbed them extra hard. "Can I get anyone anything?"

I'm going to ask for a Coke when I hear my dad's footsteps. They cross above us, heavy. I hear the squeak on the top stair. If I bolted, I could get to the back door and . . .

Jennifer runs a hand over my back, and I feel how tense I am.

Mom sees Jennifer acting all mom-like, swallows, and goes into the kitchen. "I'll grab your dad a beer quick."

We turn to look when Dad enters. We can't resist. He's taller than any of us, with glasses perched in his shaggy hair. He fastens his sleeve buttons and looks at me. "Hello, son."

"You're not supposed to call her that," Jennifer says. She wraps an arm around me.

"Right, I forgot," Dad says. He sits down in his ancient puke-yellow recliner. He does everything heavily, like gravity likes him too much.

Ron extends a hand. Dad takes it, squeezes once, and drops it. "Nice to meet you, Mr. Hawkes. I'm Ron Howard. Not that one." Dad goes "ha" once. It reminds me of when I text Megan.

(Don't think about Megan! One crisis at a time!)

Mom sweeps in with a Bud Light. "We're all finally here."

Dad cracks open his beer where he sits. The rest of us stand at the edges of the room and wait for someone else to talk first.

The internal count I start gets to fifty-two before Mom breaks the silence. "We want you to come home, hon. We miss you." Her voice cracks.

Dad takes a sip of his beer. His lips make slurping noises. I should say something, but I can't make my mouth move.

"I tried, honey. For you, I really, really tried." Mom wipes a tear. "I went online to do research on your condition. So I can understand how hard this is for you. I'm sorry I wasn't there for you."

"It's okay," somebody who sounds like me says.

Dad runs his thumb over the rim of his beer can and starts rocking his chair.

"Daddy and I have a proposal: Come home. You'll keep going to school in Mitchell, where you can be whoever you want. And at home, be our happy little guy again? Please?"

"Out of the question," Jennifer says. "Show her the letter, Abigail."

The springs in Dad's chair squeak as he rocks. He eyes me like I'm a picture hanging on the wall. He sniffs, then sneezes into his elbow. He seems so loud, like he's wearing a microph—

"Abigail," Jennifer says.

"I had my teacher . . . ," somebody who sounds like me says. That person pulls Erica's letter out of my purse and hands it to Mom, who hands it to Dad. He tilts down his glasses to read it, then hands it back to Mom. He returns to examining me.

"Her grades have improved so much," Jennifer says. "Mr. Skyberg thinks she could go to college."

Mom squints to read the letter. "Mr. Skyberg thinks highly of you. Is all of this true? I find it hard to believe your grades have improved that much!"

"It's absolutely true," Jennifer says. She side squeezes me.

"We went about this all wrong before," Mom says. "So when you come back home, we'll get you a counselor and do this properly."

The door is right there. Run.

"This family isn't known for its belief in seeking help from mental health professionals. As I found out the hard way." Jennifer glares at Mom until Mom looks away. I guess some shit went down when I wasn't paying attention back in the day. Which happens a lot. You know that by now.

"There's a program through a church in Mitchell. With good counselors."

"For fuck's sake, Mom," Jennifer says. "You want them to brainwash her?"

The timer goes off in the kitchen. "Dinner's ready! I need a second to . . ."

"It'll keep," Jennifer says. "We're not done talking."

"Maybe if we all had something to eat—" Ron says.

"It'll keep, *Ron*," Jennifer says.

"I can get it," somebody who sounds like me says. She goes into the kitchen, where the oven mitts are in the same place as always, and she pulls the casserole out of the oven, and she smells it, and she looks outside to where the car she never drove (since she never got her license) sits on the same patch of lawn it did the night she left.

She braces herself on the counter and takes three deep breaths, and I'm me again. For now.

I make my way through the back porch to my old room. It looks the same, down to the boy clothes stuffed in the dresser and the Bible I got for confirmation (and never read) sitting on the bedside table.

It's frozen in time. Like I died.

"You don't know *anything about it*." Mom says loudly enough for me to hear.

I make my way back into the living room. I try to remember everything I see in the house, what's different and what's the same, but I can't. Life's too big. It won't fit in your brain, even though I, a dumbass, keep trying.

"—a *delusion*," Mom says to Jennifer. "We help people with delusions by disabusing them of them! My perfect son wakes up one morning and decides he's a girl, and I don't get to have feelings about that? I can't be worried about my kid without everybody yelling at me?"

"Dinner's ready," I say, trying hard to stay me.

"Sweetheart, don't you see?" Mom turns to me. "You'll be . . . this person at school, and at home, you'll be you. We can see what makes you happier, and that will be that!"

Jennifer laughs. "See what makes her happier? *Look at her*, Mom. Stop looking for someone you made up and look at your fucking daughter."

Dad stands. For a moment, I can't see his face because he's in the shadows of the darkening room. He flips on the overhead lights, and everything gets too bright. "Jennifer Marie, we *will* get the police involved."

This is the part where everybody in my family shuts up and does what Dad says, except Jennifer evidently missed the memo. She digs in her purse without breaking eye contact with him. "Do you really want me talking to them about growing up in this house? What it was like?" (I guess she means the part about him hitting us pretty hard sometimes, but whatever. We usually deserved it.) She hands a pile of papers to Dad. "Read them."

He starts laughing before he's even read half a sheet. "What a crock of shit," he says.

Mom takes the papers from him. Her voice gets squeaky. "Termination of parental rights?"

"Ron and I are going to adopt Abigail," Jennifer says.

"We got married today!" Ron says. He sounds so happy I almost start crying.

"And as a married couple, one of whom is directly related to Abigail, we have a strong case if we sue for custody. Especially if Abigail is part of that suit."

Why didn't anybody tell *me* about this plan? "Why are we talking about this? I'm almost eighteen," I say (somehow). "This shouldn't be a problem. I'm almost eighteen." I say that five or six times, but they're not listening to me.

"This is *absurd*, Jennifer," Mom says.

"I love your daughter more than I can say. I will spend the rest of my life making her happy," Ron says to two parents who aren't here and never existed.

"I won't let you erase my sister," Jennifer says.

The door's—

"Oh, like *you* haven't erased my son?" Mom's almost screaming.

—right there.

"You know what?" Dad says. "Congratulations! Welcome to the family, Ron."

I should—

"Thank you, sir."

—just—

Dad's gaze sweeps across me. "The man of the hour has been awfully quiet. What do *you* want, █████?"

—run.

I haven't ever really thought about what I want. I wanted to be a girl, and then I did that, and a whole bunch of life met me on the other side.

As I run toward the last place any of them will think to look for me—because fuck my parents, obviously, and fuck Jennifer, too, for not telling me about her fucking plan. Why does she think I want to be *adopted*?—I decide to answer Dad's question.

So, here's a list of things I want:

- To be left alone.
- To not have anybody worry about me ever again.
- To not have anybody *think* about me ever again.
- To have an entirely different fucking family.
- To never hear that name again.
- To not have to think about being trans for one second more.
- To be normal, to feel safe, to not be treated like a car accident, to be able to see lights on the horizon in the middle of the night and know, somehow, that it's where I belong, that it's where I'm going and where I've always been, and to go there, and to open the door, and to have somebody say, "Where were you?" and to see them, and to know them, and to love them, and to have everything fall off of me, like a snake shedding its skin, until all that's left is a person who can walk down the street without being known, a person who can wear herself as a disguise like everyfuckingbody else.
- To be left alone, mostly.

I approach my parents' store and slow down to a walk. I took the long way around, so I doubt they'll look for me here. The parking lot is empty.

I let myself in the back door (the code's the same, thank God) and find the phone in my dad's office. Except, fuck, I, like a fucking idiot, don't know anybody's number. *My* phone is in my purse back at my parents' house.

I find a phone book. Practically nobody I know has a phone number that would be listed—except for one. And she always answers her phone.

Brooke pulls into the back alley like I asked. She leans over to open the passenger side door and startles when I jump in. "Go," I say. "Just fucking go."

She doesn't peel out dramatically, but she does drive. "Where am I taking you?"

"Anywhere," I say. "Just go, go, go."

Once we're outside of town, I sob. It's a little embarrassing, but Brooke lets me be. After I quiet down, she says, "Do you have somewhere in mind?"

I shake my head, hiccupping as I try to breathe.

She nods. "Okay. Do you want to stay with us?"

Erica

Saturday,

October 29

Erica pulls up outside the Osborne house for Helen's fundraiser, the short driveway marked by wind-buffeted mylar balloons tied to the mailbox. Cars line both sides of the driveway, and the Osborne sons direct traffic to park on the browning lawn.

The first thing Erica sees when she gets out of her car is Helen herself, who stands just outside the front door listening intently to an older man with a Santa Claus beard. Erica adjusts her tie. Look how perfectly she plays the role of "pillar of the community"! She wants to make things right with Helen, and she had hoped that showing up here in "steady guy" disguise might do the trick. Now that she can *see* Helen, though, she thinks she needs a better plan.

Helen spots her and immediately turns to go inside. Erica adjusts her tie again and enters the Osborne house. She has never been inside before. She has seen it from afar, of course. If you take a boat out on Lake Mitchell, you can't *avoid* seeing its floor-to-ceiling glass windows. Now, seeing through those windows, Erica has the feeling of being placed in a spotlight, which she gathers Troy Osborne probably likes.

People in town whisper about how much money Troy makes. It's better, surely, to flaunt your wealth fixing up a rundown house in the middle of nowhere, like Brooke and Victor did, than to build a house this ostentatious from scratch. Troy quite obviously doesn't care what people think. He's the kind of man Erica found the most intimidating when she was pretending to have a handle on masculinity.

Troy steers Megan around the room, introducing her to his rich and powerful friends. They lean in to talk to her like they are speaking to a child dressed up as a doctor. She smiles despite their condescension and has them laughing a few seconds later.

Helen huddles by the massive windows overlooking the lake and flips through note cards. Erica makes her way over before she loses her nerve. "Good luck out there today." She chuckles uncomfortably.

Irritation floods Helen's eyes, but the lower half of her face spreads into a polite smile. "Mr. Skyberg! Thanks for coming. Make sure you get some snacks. Troy and Viv went all out." She breezes past Erica to find someone else to talk to.

Erica sags. Too often, she fears, the more she tries to fix things, the more she breaks them. Now that she's here, she understands how bad her plan to work things out with Helen here truly was. Today is important to Helen, not to Erica. Not even Helen expects Helen to win, but if she runs strong, it could mark her as someone who might lose a little less badly next time. Simply getting Troy in her corner, who previously said he was done giving the local Democratic Party money because it was "a total shitshow," was huge. Helen is impressing all the right people.

And Erica is also here, pretending to be a man.

Erica hovers near the snack table, pouring herself a healthy glass of wine. Megan steps into the center of the room, hands raised above her head. "Gather around, all, so I can introduce you to Helen Swee." Helen smiles indulgently as Megan introduces her, and Erica feels a dull ache. She fucked things up so badly. She guzzles her wine and bumps into an older woman trying to push past her to the snack table. "Let me squeeze past you, Mr. Skyberg," the woman says.

Erica's stomach turns. The more she hides within the shell of her public self, the less she feels like the hiding is helping.

"I don't know how many of you know me," Megan says, "but this is the first election I can vote in, and it's just ten days away! I'm so excited to exercise my right to vote for a woman for president!" The crowd applauds dutifully. "And I'm even *more* excited that in my first local election, I can vote for Helen Swee."

Erica needs to escape. She spots a staircase leading down, a card table loosely leaned in front of it to provide a barrier. She pulls it aside and then slips downstairs into a beautifully furnished basement where two men nurse beers and gaze upon an enormous TV hung on the wall. They turn, briefly, to look at her, then resume chatting.

A door hangs half open in front of her. She hears the tinny whine of music and, curious, nudges the door open.

Abigail lies on the floor, staring at the ceiling.

Three days' worth of pent-up emotions flood Erica. She wants to slap Abigail, and she wants to hug her, and she wants to sob with relief, and she wants to scream at her. If anyone found them alone in this room together (especially Helen), they would assume the worst, but she doesn't care. She takes a long breath and says, "So you're okay, then?"

Abigail turns her head, her cheek pressed against the floor. "Have they started?"

"Where the fuck have you been?"

"Safe." Abigail pulls herself into a seated position. "The parent thing went badly. I left my phone there, I've been too cowardly to go home to Jennifer's, and the cops might be looking for me." She frowns. "Though you'd think they would have found me by now. A lot of people are worried about me apparently, which is annoying, but I'm fine."

"Isn't it good to have people worry about you?" Erica takes a step inside the room, which is covered in mirrors and rubber padding, a horrifying combination of sex dungeon and dance studio.

"So you've been staying here?"

"Jesus, Mom. No. Megan hates me now. I came to help out, but everything was already done when I got here. She asked me to go away, so I came downstairs. I'm a bad friend. She finally figured that out."

Above them, the crowd applauds, and the muffled sound of Helen saying, "Thank you!" filters down to them. Erica circles the room's perimeter, keeping her distance from Abigail, both scared of making the girl bolt and of anybody seeing them together. "Where *are* you—"

"Fucking *fine*." Abigail folds her knees against her chest and settles her chin on them. "I'm staying with Caleb."

"With *Brooke*?"

"I like the way she treats me like a science fair project she's scared of fucking up. It beats all the . . ." She waves her hand around the room, and Erica's not sure what she means to indicate. "Anyway, are you sure it's safe to be within fifty feet of me when Helen is here? Especially in *this* room? Someone might get *ideas*."

Erica tries to laugh, and it comes out as a choked squawk. She begins her second circuit of the room's perimeter. Abigail exhales, stretching her legs out on the floor.

"Maybe you're right about us being . . . friends. When I was trying to flee my parents, I really wanted to call you, but . . . no phone. That sounds like we're maybe friends, doesn't it?"

"I would have come to get you. And not to immediately contradict myself, but I think we need to stop hanging out. Talking so much. Texting."

"No. Please, don't . . ." Abigail stands but stays put. Erica will bolt if Abigail takes one step closer to her. "This is so stupid, but okay: I like having you around." She winches her eyes shut. "I *need* you around. Just knowing you existed changed my life. I felt less theoretical."

"Thanks. I feel similarly."

"I thought when I finally said how much you mean to me, you'd explode into glitter and sunshine. Didn't expect you to be so formal."

"Fine, how about: You're the best friend I've ever had." For once, Abigail doesn't flinch or roll her eyes. "You're the *only* friend I've ever had. You're also my student."

"And I'm your trans mom, duh! It's all scrambled. We haven't done anything *wrong*."

"It's just how it looks." Above them, everyone laughs at something Helen says. "Half the town thinks we're . . ."

"Fucking?"

"Jesus, Abigail. It's just . . . People see us together, and they don't know what's going on, but they know we're . . . connected. And assume the worst." Her voice cracks.

"You could just tell everybody *why* we have such an intense connection?" Abigail takes a step toward Erica, and she shrinks against the mirror wall. "At least tell Helen! Tell *her* I'm your trans mom. She'll probably be, like, 'Well, that's a novel reason to be a corrupting influence.'"

Erica eyes herself in the mirror opposite. She's been out to herself for two months and has done nothing about it, despite longing to begin her real life. Anytime she thinks about doing so, she remembers the world is cruel to those who are sure of themselves and shuts down. "I've told you, I don't want people knowing I'm trans."

"Well, tough shit. I cannot believe *I'm* saying this, but: You can't hide forever. Take your time coming out to the world, sure. You might lose a lot. But with Helen, you might *gain* a lot. At least do it for me? I'm sick of finding creative ways to not misgender you in front of people." Abigail smiles broadly, but it carries the weight of all she has kept for Erica.

Erica holds Abigail's gaze and sees her almost for the first time. She looks so small in the coat she wears (one of Brooke's, Erica thinks), and she doesn't mean her hair, whatever the shade, not really. She is so loud, and she is so scared, and she is so angry, and she loves too much, and she wants even more, and she is seventeen.

"I'll think about it," Erica says. Above them, the crowd swells with applause.

When Erica goes back upstairs, the house has emptied out. The Osborne boys pick up trash. Megan lets out a happy yelp when she sees Erica. "Mr. Skyberg!" she says. "Wasn't it great?"

Erica offers a wan smile. "It was wonderful."

Helen looks over from where she's profusely thanking Troy. "Did you see any of it? You disappeared." Behind them, Abigail ascends the staircase and quickly slips outside, avoiding Megan entirely. Helen notices. "Ah."

Erica feels Helen placing the last bricks in the wall between them and summons her courage. She needs most of her walls but maybe not this one anymore. "Can we talk?" Helen's eyes are cold, but Erica knows if she doesn't do this now, she never will.

Troy gestures to doors that open onto the deck overlooking the lake. "If you need privacy, you can step outside." Helen glares at him, and he stammers. "Only if you want, of course!"

Helen offers her biggest, fakest smile. "No. Let's talk."

On the deck, Helen wraps her arms around herself, yesterday's heat having given way to the first signs of winter. She looks at Erica with narrowed eyes. "I'm not keeping your secret. Abigail deserves better from me than to cover your ass for fucking a—"

"We're not having sex."

"Well, you're certainly not helping her with schoolwork!"

"We're friends. She's helping me and I'm helping her—"

"I don't care about your midlife crisis. At least have some dignity and fuck a twenty-two-year-old." Helen pushes past her to leave. "I'm talking to Principal DeWaard in the morning."

"Wait," Erica says. Helen turns back. Erica sees her almost for the first time too. She is built like a stick, and her close-cropped hair has grown out into something shaggy. She clutches a too-expensive purse that sprouts endless fraying threads. She is so angry at Erica but out of kindness toward others, a sincere, probably naive, belief that the world does not have to be as it is.

Erica takes a deep breath. She stops. She takes another. She stops. She takes another.

Helen rolls her eyes, and then Erica maybe stops breathing altogether.

Erica will always remember telling Helen as though she were watching from inside the house, looking out toward the conversation on the patio through the enormous windows. It is as if she consciously distances herself from this moment, leaving it sacred and mysterious. As long as she lives, she will have a reverence for it she doesn't dare disturb.

Erica talks for a long time, eyes filling with tears (though that might be the cold). Helen says something. Erica says something. Helen asks a question. Erica answers. They eventually sit down on the patio chairs, and Helen lets Erica talk, occasionally reaching out to squeeze her hand. When they stand, Helen pulls Erica into a hug that Erica feels all through herself, like she is being invited back into her body.

They reenter the house to the sound of a vacuum. Helen says, "I'll text, yeah? I'm happy to know you." Then, she stops. "It's still a bad idea, you know. Not as bad as I feared, but . . . she deserves better."

"I know," Erica says.

"Thank you for trusting me with you." Helen gives Erica another quick hug, and Erica watches her all the way out the door.

At a four-way stop three blocks from Erica's house, a group of children, all in costume, carrying buckets full of candy, cross the street in a long chain linked by held hands. Two girls—one Princess Elsa and one witch—bring up the end of the line. They lean toward each other to talk, barely staying part of the group.

A gust of wind whips down the street, tugging the witch's hat from her head and sending it flying into someone's front yard. She drops her friends' hands and retrieves it, pulling it down more tightly on her head.

When she runs back, the chain reforms effortlessly, as though some greater power is at work.

Erica thinks of Helen, and she thinks of Abigail, and she thinks, even, of Constance. There are always hands waiting to grab hold again.

When Erica gets home, Constance's car sits in her driveway. Her ex-wife-turned-possible-girlfriend-sort-of sits on the stoop.

"I'm cold! Why did you move the key?" Constance says.

"I changed the locks and forgot to get a spare."

"Can I stay tonight?" Constance stands and walks onto the lawn. "John told his entire family about the baby. I told him I didn't want to yet. I mean, it's the first trimester. Everything could still go wrong!" She starts to cry. "He just keeps *telling* people! I shouldn't care, but I do."

Erica pulls her into a hug. "Of course you can stay. You can always stay." She kisses the top of Constance's head, then tilts her chin up to kiss her lips. Only then does she see the truck parked half a block down. The driver's side door opens, and John steps out. He saunters over to them, his face unreadable, like his anger is rushing to catch up to him.

"You told me you were with your friend Erica," John says.

"We can expl—" Constance begins to say, but she is cut off by John lunging and punching Erica in the eye. She topples onto the dried grass. Constance screams at John, and he screams back, and Erica hears it all through a haze. Above her, the streetlights start to turn on, a few flakes of snow suspended in them, not enough to blanket the ground but a promise of the freeze to come.

Erica gets to her feet, rubbing her eye, and looks at John, who falls into a defensive crouch. A dog barks across the street. She laughs, breath hanging in the air, and she realizes what she needs to do.

"Constance is right. She's with Erica. I'm Erica." All tension exits her body. "My name is Erica."

Abigail

Saturday,

October 29

Don't worry. I'm fine. Okay? I'll get you all caught up.

After I spent a couple days at the Danielses' house, I realized they were always *doing* something. There was always a board game or a movie night or a church event, always an excuse to spend time together. I don't remember the last time all my siblings got together, even before I destroyed the family with my inconvenient gender. We maybe saw a movie together once when I was four.

Then again, it's not like my parents were ever there when I was growing up. My dad even kept the store open Christmas morning so people could buy last-second groceries. I tried to explain to Caleb that his family was rich enough to be a family. I don't think he got it.

But you know what? They want me here. They keep a seat open for me, whatever they're doing, and I like that I always have somewhere to sit. I can't decide if they want me to feel welcome or trapped, but every day I'm here, the less I care.

Friday night, Caleb and Ruth "made dinner," by which I mean they ordered pizza for us to eat before all four of them headed into town for the football game. I think they said it's the start of the playoffs. (Caleb's on the basketball team, and I try not to pay attention to sports otherwise.)

As we sat down to eat, Ruth walked in, caked in makeup and wearing a football practice jersey. Everybody stopped eating to look. Usually, if a girl's wearing a guy's jersey, that means they're dating, and Ruth was wearing Jan Blaha's, the Czech exchange student who's the punter or kicker or something. (You don't know about him because you hang out with me, and I don't care. Sorry!)

She saw us all looking. "What?"

"You're dating *Jan*?" Caleb said. "But he's *my age*. You're a freshman!"

"People like me, too, Caleb. Get used to it," Ruth said.

"You're not allowed to date," Mr. Daniels said.

At the same time Brooke said, "We'll have to talk about it." Mr. Daniels shut up, and she added, "A European, no less."

Ruth's nostrils flared. "Abigail basically lives here now! And you won't let me go on a *single date* with someone?"

"Your brother is eighteen, and Abigail is a very important person in his life," Brooke said, "which means she's a very important person in all of our lives."

"She's not important to me," Ruth said matter-of-factly.

"If I had to ask your permission to date someone," Caleb said, "you'd only let me date weird, angry girls who listen to crappy music and are terrible at video games."

Ruth snarled. "Fuck you, Caleb!"

"Hey!" both of Caleb's parents said. Mr. Daniels got to his feet. "Apologize."

Ruth's face was so red. "I'm sorry, Caleb. I just don't get why it's different with Abigail. Is it because he tried to kill himself?"

Caleb let out a burst of air and jumped out of his chair, running down the hall.

Caleb's dad slammed his hand on the table. I jumped. Before he could say anything, Brooke held her hand up to cut him off. "You can be a very cruel person, Ruth."

Ruth turned pale and looked over at me. "You didn't know?" I shook my head. "Fuck," she said. "It just came out. I'm sorry." She started to cry.

The good-girlfriend part of my brain made me stand up to follow Caleb. He was in the office, sitting on the floor in the corner, shirt up around his face, his whole body shaking. "Caleb?" He lowered his shirt, and I saw his red, raw eyes. "It's okay," I said, and I realized it was. Everything made sense suddenly. If your kid who tried to kill himself fell in love, maybe you'd be okay with that, even if he didn't fall for the girl you'd pick for him.

"It was a stupid thing I did last year. I didn't want you to know. My therapist put me on some pills, and they helped." He took a deep breath. "You can break up with me. I deserve it."

I sat down beside him and took his hand. "I've thought about dying too. I don't know if I trust anybody who *hasn't* thought about it. I'm glad you're here."

He sobbed into my shoulder. He kept saying, "I didn't want you to know," and "I love you," one after the other until the last sobs fell out of him. I didn't know what to say to the second thing, so I just let him be.

Brooke cleared her throat from the door, and we both looked up at her. She opened her arms. "Mom," Caleb said. He went to her, and she rocked him back and forth. She seemed the most herself I'd ever seen.

She whispered something I couldn't hear to him, then looked over the top of his head at me. "Thank you, Abigail. Thank you for everything."

Anyway, Caleb stayed home from the game, and we just cuddled, like a real girlfriend comforting her real boyfriend or something. Then today, I went to Helen's fundraiser. See? You're all caught up!

After the fundraiser, I kind of feel like being alone, so I go to bed early. But I can't sleep. I listen to Mitski and remember how shitty it felt when Megan just ignored me as much as possible the whole time I was at her stupid house.

Just after midnight, Caleb texts: *if you're awake come say hey*.

Every single step up to the second floor squeaks, and I'm sure Ruth is going to shoot me to collect the twenty-dollar bounty from her dad. When I get to Caleb's room, he's hunched over a notebook at his desk, a reading lamp softly glowing. "I didn't think you would be awake."

"Well, I was." I lean on the doorframe, trying to be sexy.

Caleb holds up a hand, stopping me from entering the room. "Sorry. The way you look . . ." He scribbles in his notebook. "I want to capture it."

"Jesus, Caleb." He writes in his notebook so long something goes raw in my brain. "I'm more than a character in a story to you, right?"

"This isn't for my book." He sounds offended. "It's for me. I want to remember you like you are right now." He blushes.

"Perv!" I laugh, but God, I want him to say nice things about me.

"You *are* wearing my mom's pajamas, though. I'm trying not to think about that."

I laugh. He comes over and pulls me close, leaning down to kiss me. His hand slides up over my left boob (the larger one).

It's different when other people are here. I thought it would feel sexier or maybe more dangerous, but instead, it feels more real. I'm not a secret he's keeping anymore. I'm a person he fucks discreetly, but everybody knows he fucks me all the same. There's a difference.

We fall asleep for a while, naked, his arms wrapped around me. I wake up at four thirty and sit up, figuring I should probably sneak back to my room. When I stand, Caleb lets out the cutest sigh. His eyes flutter open. "Don't go."

"I'm trying to not get kicked out."

"We could have texted my mom with a play-by-play, and she would still let you stay."

I smile, and he leans up to kiss me long enough that I almost get back in bed. But I have to go. He whispers my name when I get to the door. I think he might say something incredible, but he says, "I wrote my college application essay about you."

"*Why?*"

"It has to be about someone who inspires me." He swallows. "I hope that was okay."

I should be used to Caleb being an idiot about me, but I get a silly grin on my face anyway. "Oh, whatever. Just a bunch of old guys will read it, right? I hope you weren't too horny about me."

He thinks. "I want to write about the Abigail everybody should see but doesn't. Because they're blind. And idiots."

Okay, fine, it's time to say the thing before I lose my nerve. "I love you." Fuck, I mean it, don't I? You probably got there ahead of me again.

He smiles. "I love you too. But you already know that."

I sneak back to the guest room but freeze at the base of the stairs. Brooke is doing a jigsaw puzzle by moonlight at a card table in the corner of the living room. She looks up and I wave. Then she goes back to her puzzle.

The next morning, as they all get ready to go to church, she doesn't once mention seeing me return from so obviously sleeping with her son.

Sunday night, everybody decides to watch game five of the World Series. All sports bore me, but it's sweet when Caleb explains to me how long it's been since the Cubs have been there, so I'll allow it.

Midway through the second inning, Brooke enters, holding a phone. "Call for you, Abigail." I take note of where the door is and try to figure out how far I could get before she adds, "It's your sister."

I step outside onto the patio to talk to her. Outdoor lights snap on, and a rabbit freezes in the middle of nibbling some grass. Uh-oh. Now an owl or coyote or Ruth might see it.

I take a deep breath and lift the phone to my ear. "Congratulations! You found me!"

"Abigail . . ." Jennifer's breath shudders. "Thank God."

"Did Skyberg rat me out?"

"Are you safe?"

"Of course I'm fucking *safe*."

"When you ran away . . ." I can hear her swallow an angrier Jennifer. "There were only so many places you might be. But I also didn't want to look because . . . well, I didn't want you to be in none of them." She swallows again. "I love you, which I know you hate. Come home."

"So you can adopt me without consulting me?"

"We're not going to do anything you don't want to do." She sniffles. "I know I should have told you our plan. I was so scared you might run. Then you did. But I swear it was only ever something to tie Mom and Dad up in court until you turn eighteen."

"Well, you should have fucking told me. You betrayed me."

She sighs. "I'm not going to argue with you about this."

I watch the rabbit. As long as I'm looking at it, I decide, nothing bad can happen.

"I'm safe here." The rabbit hops to the very edge of the light and locks eyes with me. "Would I be safe with you and Ron?"

"I don't know. I don't know how much Mom and Dad know we're bullshitting them, how much they actually want you back, and how much they're sick of the whole thing. But I promise you that if you are under my roof, I will fight tooth and nail to keep you there. Like I've already been doing." She pauses. "Is this actually true of Caleb's family? Or do you just want it to be?"

"Fuck you, Jennifer."

"Don't abuse their hospitality."

"Like I've been abusing yours?"

Her voice gets tight. "That's different. You know that's different."

"Maybe I'll come home after the election," I say. The rabbit hops back into the dark. I imagine it screaming. "Helen will lose, Megan will complete the process of hating me, I'll tank my grades from skipping so much school, and I'll just be Caleb's girlfriend."

"Don't sell yourself short."

"Great advice, Mrs. Ron."

She doesn't say anything.

"Well. Thanks for calling. See you eventually."

She gets out a wobbly, "See you—" before I hang up. I can't see anything where the rabbit had been, not even a close-cropped patch of grass.

When I get inside, hands red from the cold, Brooke is working on her puzzle. She looks up and gestures to the other chair at the card table. "Sit. Help me."

I do sit, rubbing my hands together. "Don't you want to watch the game?"

"There are few things in this world I cannot stand, but one of them is the Chicago Cubs. So I edited Caleb's application essay, and now I'm doing this." She snaps a piece into place and makes a satisfied noise. "His essay is really something. All about a special girl in his life." She smiles at me, teasing. "I'm a little jealous, honestly. Who are you writing about?"

"Oh, I'm not going to college."

"I could see you and Caleb together at Northwestern! You'd be happy there. Unburdened."

For a second, I can see it too—our whole lives ahead of us, living in Chicago, sharing an apartment. I'd get bottom surgery, and nobody would know I was trans, and I'd have a guy I loved at my side. It would be perfect if it weren't completely fucking impossible.

"Brooke. I have terrible grades and no money. Even *if* my parents weren't pretending I no longer exist, *they* don't . . ." I imagine overturning the table, puzzle pieces flying. "Some of us don't get to just solve our problems with money, sorry."

"Yes, I sit here and think, 'Oh! Good! My problems are solved!'" Her laugh dies when she sees the expression on my face. "I want you to know you can escape the person everybody sees in high school, even if, right now, it seems like you can't. You, of all people, deserve to."

"Whatever." My hands are warm enough now that I can rummage through the pieces myself, looking for the eye of the kitten in the center of the puzzle.

For a couple minutes, we work in silence. Then she says, "So you're not going to college. That's fine. If you were, who would you write your essay about?"

I consider this. "Maybe my friend Erica? She's had an interesting life." Brooke seems disappointed. "C'mon. It already wasn't you, and your odds look grimmer by the second."

She keeps looking down. "I didn't want you to . . . Well, I just briefly worried you might want to write about your mother. She doesn't deserve you."

I'm quiet a long time. Brooke watches me assemble this kitten eye. "Maybe I *like* a mom who plays hard to get," I say eventually.

Brooke's smile gets very sad. "You need to leave. Go anywhere else. Maybe college isn't right for you, but I *know* Mitchell isn't right for you either. If you stay here, you'll wait for her to change into the person you need her to be, and when that doesn't happen, you're going to change into someone you don't very much like being."

"Well, joke's on you! I'm already someone I don't like being!"

"Don't say that." I could swear her eye glistens with tears. "You remind me so much of my friend . . . Danielle. She loved to do puzzles with me too."

I remember Caleb telling me about the card from the mysterious Danielle. "I don't make a habit of doing puzzles. Don't draw any conclusions from me needing to pass the time."

Brooke smiles in a way that covers up the face she'd rather be making. "I haven't thought about her in years. But with you here . . ." She blinks twice, and the smile is suddenly genuine, the hint of tears gone. "There. I just needed that piece."

And just like that, Danielle's no longer in the room with us.

Monday is Halloween. I should go back to school, but I just can't yet. Brooke needs help stuffing envelopes for Isaiah Rose (boo! booooooo!), which will give my hands something to do. Later, I'll join Caleb to greet trick-or-treaters. Everything here is easy. I like not having to think so much.

Before Caleb gets home, Brooke leaves to meet with Isaiah. (She doesn't seem to like him much. Don't tell her I said that.) She gives me a big hug and tells me not to burn the house down.

The whole time I've stayed here, someone else has always been home with me, but now, alone for an hour, I feel like this is actually my house. I blast Mitski on the speakers in the screw-around room and take an incredibly long, incredibly hot shower in Brooke's bathroom.

When I get out, wearing Brooke's clothes (like always), Caleb's eating a peanut butter sandwich in the kitchen. He swallows a bite so big his eyes water and gives me a kiss hello. "I mailed off my Northwestern application today."

"Yeah, your mom's super fucking jealous you wrote your essay about me."

He laughs. "Once I decided to write about you, it just flowed."

"Can I read it?"

He tenses. "Why? It's a stupid college essay, not a novel." He kisses my forehead, but I know when people are lying to me.

The part of me that likes burrowing down into this house like a little mouse screams at me to stop pushing, but the part of me that keeps talking to you needs to know what's going on. So I walk into Brooke's office, and I close and lock the door. It takes me just sixty seconds to figure out the password to her computer (his birthday) and another thirty seconds to find his essay.

As soon as I open it, I know why he didn't want me reading it.

Please write an essay—no more than 750 words— on one of the following topics:

- **Someone who has inspired you**

When my girlfriend was born, her name was Justin. It's still the name her mother uses when she tries to make contact. I happened to be over one night, hanging out with my girlfriend, and her mom came into the house. "Justin!" she yelled. "Justin!"

I have never called my girlfriend by her old name. I have always called her by her real name, the name I fell in love with, which is Abigail. When I first met her, it was in English class. "I don't know any Abigails," I said. "Well, you do now," she replied.

Later, some other kids said she was trans and told me her old name. I already knew all of that. It's hard not to hear gossip in a small town. But I was falling for her too. I almost couldn't understand what was happening to me. I even thought I might be gay!

It took me a while to admit that I was in love with her. I thought I had been in love before, but it wasn't like this time. She made me feel like I didn't know anything, and she made me laugh so much. And she's so beautiful. She gets this little look when she's going to say something really mean but funny. Her eyes dart around like she's not sure who's listening, and she leans forward and says what she has to say, just to you. You feel like the most important person in the world.

A couple weeks ago, she did an amazing thing. A local candidate who sponsored a bad bill that would keep trans people from using the bathroom spoke to our group at school. She read him the riot act, then left the room. It was so cool, but the other kids started to laugh.

I got up, and I said, "You're all jerks. That was the bravest thing I've ever seen." I walked into the hallway and found her sitting on the stairs, crying. I held out my hand to her, and she took it. We walked back into the room together, holding hands, so even the worst people I know would see Abigail was *my* girlfriend. It was maybe the most courageous thing I've ever done.

Every time I tell her how I feel about her, I can tell she doesn't totally believe me, but that's why I tell her as often as I can. I want everybody to know how much better my life is because of her! Every time I see her, I remember that it's possible to be brave and kind. She makes me want to be a better person every single day. I hope she never lets go of my hand.

I'm so inspired by Abigail. I would never have the strength or bravery to do what she does every day. She knew there was something wrong with herself, and she did what she had to do to be happy. In her, I see someone whose perseverance and beauty shine through, even when people call her by a name that doesn't fit her, even when those people are her own mother!

So, when you ask me who has most instilled in me the values that I would hope to express as a student at Northwestern, it is my girlfriend. Abigail Hawkes. Because I love her, I've learned so much about courage, about bravery, and about diversity. She's taught me how to model the best behavior for everyone around me, and I hope I've taught her that people can surprise you sometimes.

Those are all qualities I would bring to the Northwestern campus as a freshman, should I be so lucky to attend.

—Caleb Daniels
10/24/2016

I don't know why I read the whole thing. I think I keep expecting him to reveal that it was all a joke or a prank or a dream, so I can say, "Well, that wasn't very nice!" and get on with my life. But I get to the end and read it all again, and it's still the same essay as before.

I unlock the office. He's waiting right outside, and I push past him toward the front door. He grabs my arm, and I spin around so quickly I worry I'll fall over. "Just when you think everybody who could betray you already has . . . ," I say.

He looks guilty, like he knows how fucked-up what he did is, like he's *always* known how fucked-up it is, but he manages to say, "Can we talk about it? I'm open to criticism."

I jerk my arm away. "Get the fuck out of my way."

I have a clear line to the door. Three steps and I'm gone. But he cry-laughs, and he sounds hysterical, and I turn to look back at him. He looks red and raw, and then he steps between me and the door.

"Please let me go. Please." I can't say anything more. If I listen to him too much, if I let him touch me the right way, he'll suck me right back into him again, and I'll forget who he really is.

"Can I at least give you a ride?" His voice breaks. "Please? It's not always safe for me to be alone."

"*I* need to be alone right now, Caleb. I'm sorry but get the fuck out of my way." His lower lip trembles, and his eyes fill with tears. I stomp my foot. "*Now*."

He steps to the side, looking at the floor. "I love you."

"You love a character in a story," I say. He's going to say something else, but I can't let myself hear it. I leave and start the long walk back into town.

It starts getting dark and cold the second I leave Caleb's driveway and begin walking along the highway into town. I realize a quarter mile down the road that I left my stupid army jacket at his house. That gets me to cry, and the tears sting against my face as semis barrel past me, blaring their horns. I think about texting someone, but who? Erica? She's the only person who doesn't totally hate me, and she's made it quite clear we can't hang out anymore.

Brooke's SUV slows next to me, but I keep walking. She pulls onto the shoulder right beside me, then rolls down the passenger window to shout at me.

"Get in, Abigail," she says. "It's not safe out here."

"I'm doing just fine not dying so far."

"I'm sorry," she says. Whatever else she wants to say gets caught in her throat.

"If this is about your clothes, I'll fucking mail them to you."

"I get it," she shouts over the sound of a passing pickup. "I should have made him take your old name out of the essay. It's my fault. I'm sorry."

"You can't *fix* this, Mrs. Daniels. Why do you think . . ." I throw my arms out to my sides. "I'm not your fucking kid! Stop caring about me!"

She keeps looking at me, the car still running exactly parallel to me. So I stop walking and hope she'll keep rolling into town. Instead, she brakes so hard the car jolts, even though she was going maybe two miles per hour. But of course she stopped exactly when I did. She's always *watching* me like *she's* trying to take instructions from *me*.

Then, all at once, it's like I can see *through* her somehow, like she's already told me everything about herself without opening her mouth.

In that moment, some part of me knows. Some part of me has always known.

"Go away!" I say because I don't need this.

"I know Florence and her too-dry cookies. And I know Bernadette. Not as well as I should, but . . . I met her. Once." A sob escapes her, and she squeezes her eyes with her fingers until she sucks it back into herself. "Abigail, if you go . . ."

How do I keep getting into these fucking situations? I open the passenger door to get in. Warm air blasts me. "I guess you should tell me everything," I say.

And she does.

Brooke

1989–

2016

You will always remember the song playing on the radio when the guy gives you your first hormone pills.

You're in the back booth at an awful diner by the United Center. Drunk Bulls fans keep shouting incoherently about Michael Jordan. The song is "American Girl." Tom Petty. You laugh when it plays. The guy asks you what's so funny.

It's 1989. You are sixteen. In six months, you will see your parents and sister for the last time.

"Don't take them all at once," he says. "You might get addicted."

"Where do I get more?" you say.

He laughs. "Find a doctor next time, bud."

"Where?" you say.

He shoves the money you gave him in his pocket. "You'll figure it out."

You take the first pill with the copper-tasting diner water. The waitress will arrive with your food soon, but for now, it's just you and the cars skshing outside on the slushy boulevard and the pills inside your body, already answering a question you still haven't found the words to ask.

You go to the jukebox and play "American Girl" again. It feels right for this moment. Nobody else notices the song repeating.

It's a secret you're telling yourself. You don't dare say you're an American girl, but you know you've been raised on promises.

You barely eat. You know what will happen to your body if you do.

You take after your father more than your mother, and he was a high school linebacker who still lifts cars by their back bumpers to show off. It would be wrong to say your father doesn't know how to talk to you. It would be wrong to say he is disappointed in you. It would be accurate to say he keeps raising a son he doesn't have and assuming he's getting through to you.

Your mother, for her part, notices how scrawny you are getting. She starts watching what you eat. You get creative about eating less. You don't want to starve. You just don't want the body you know you will grow into. You can't even put words to that fear. You look in the mirror and see how skinny you are, how the bones press against your skin.

It's not enough. Something inside of you won't let it be enough.

You know your name is Brooke before you know you are a woman. The first time you hear it is when your sister introduces a girl on the far fringes of her social circle with, "This is *Brooke*," her voice dripping with disgust. But you hear that name, and something inside you says, "Of course."

Your mother finds the page in your notebook covered in your name. She believes Brooke is a girl you have a crush on, but you also know she knows you're lying. Everybody in your family knows you're lying. They just don't know that the lie you're telling looks and talks and moves exactly like you.

There isn't a word for you. Your mother thinks you're gay. *You* think you might be gay.

So you make out with Seth from drama club a couple times. The way he wants to kiss you feels inaccurate, like he's kissing someone who overlaps with you but isn't you. There is a version of you who gets kissed the right way, but it is not this version of you.

The version of you who gets kissed the right way is Brooke. You don't know how you get from you to Brooke, but she has a girl's name, so that seems like the place to start.

You try wearing your mother's clothes. You date a girl who seems like she could be a friend. You are happy to let your sister soak up all the friendship energy in the house, because her friendships give you a contact high. You try wearing your mother's clothes. You look in the mirror at your diminishing body and imagine being erased. You dream every night about a bird whose shadow covers you on the ground far below. You avoid your father. You try wearing your mother's clothes. You hang out with the girl who seemed like she might be your friend and learn she really did want to be a girlfriend. You take home ec and play it off as needing to know how to cook when you're living as a bachelor. You kiss Seth again, and it's still not right. You try wearing your mother's clothes. You learn how to bake a chocolate cake, and it's the class's best, but when the teacher congratulates you, she calls you by a name that already tastes like ash. You cover whole notebooks in the name you know is yours. You try wearing your mother's clothes. You can't tell Seth what it is you need, so he pushes you over and rubs your face into the dirt until you bleed because he doesn't know what he needs either. You start to tell your dad, but he thinks you've been in a fight, and he's proud of you. You try wearing your mother's clothes. You make excuses to talk to your sister and her friends during sleepovers. Your beard starts to come in, and you pay attention as your father teaches you how to shave. You try wearing your mother's clothes. You read about cross-dressing in the newspaper, but it doesn't sound like the word you need. You hear someone in class make fun of someone they saw on TV, a man who thinks he's a woman, and every part of you eavesdrops like you've never eavesdropped before to find out what show it was. You find it in the programming grid. You try wearing your mother's clothes, and you break down in tears, because you finally understand that you don't want her clothes to be her clothes but, instead, a door that will take you to the life you deserved. You cry that night when your parents are out at the movies, and when your sister asks you what's wrong, you tell her that you are a ghost who thinks she is a human. You use the word "she," and your sister nods, like she understands, but you know she doesn't. You try to talk about it, but the words still aren't there. You try again. You try again. You try again. You watch as her face falls because she fundamentally doesn't understand what you are trying to say. You wish someone would call you Brooke and mean it. You lie awake until 2:30 a.m., staring at the ceiling of your bedroom, trying to force yourself to be the person you should be. You clutch your old stuffed bunny, the one your father thinks he put in the attic, and you take long, fluttering breaths. You look over at the clock and see it's almost time. You go downstairs and hunch in front of the TV. You see a reflection of your face in the screen for a moment before the fuzz of static obscures it, and you decide it's as close as you'll get to a self-portrait. You are not a person. You are a signal that has gone missing with no antenna to interpret it.

Her name is Phyllis. She is a lawyer in Texas. She is like you. You are like her. You cry because you finally have words for yourself. You barely catch any of the show you woke up to watch because you are crying so much, still clutching your stuffed rabbit. You can tell Donahue's audience is deeply confused and disgusted by this woman, at the idea she might dare be something she is not. But she is so clearly herself. She feels like the first person you can see.

She takes medicine. She takes medicine that makes her who she is. They have that medicine everywhere. They have had it for decades. Why didn't someone tell you that there is a way to be something other than the blur on the edge of the photograph?

You don't hear your father come downstairs until he's already seen you, holding your rabbit, watching a woman named Phyllis on TV, who is like you (and you like her), and sobbing. He looks at the TV, then back at you, and he says, "Get to bed." He uses the wrong name.

You start making your plan that night. A few weeks later, you find someone who will sell you the pills you need for cheap. You agree to meet him at a diner near the United Center.

You are a promise you make to yourself.

It's called woodworking.

Someday, they will wake up, and you will be gone. To have a future, you cannot have a past. You will have to disappear into the woodwork to finally be seen. If Brooke is to live, then the person she was before must cease to exist. The choice is that simple. That stark.

These options are presented to you by Octavia, a transsexual woman you meet at the diner where you got your first dose of hormones. You could have mistaken her for your mother. She says this is the point. She and her friends have left parents and siblings and wives and sometimes even children. Some of them have run for their lives. They have come to Chicago because they've been able to find the things they need here. They have jobs. They have lives. Some of them even have husbands. (Octavia seems uninterested in hers, but he helps her avoid suspicion. "So I keep him around," she says.)

"Where do I go?" you say. Your hair now trickles down to touch the tops of your ears. Your father will almost certainly demand you cut it soon. You're surprised to realize you wouldn't do it, even if he got out his belt. Something in you is getting strong.

"Darling," Octavia says, "anywhere but here." She slides you a small piece of paper. A phone number is written on it. "My friend Danielle lives in Minneapolis, and she thinks she can help you out. That's her number. You'll have to get there on your own."

Octavia always has a phone number. She gave you the number that helped you find a doctor willing to pretend you were eighteen, after she learned you were buying your hormones from a guy you called after reading a classified ad in the *Chicago Reader*. She calls you things like "sweetie" and "darling." You have no idea how old she is, or where she's from, or who she used to be.

"So I just leave?" you say.

"You have to. Are you doing what I told you? Making them think everything's fine?" You nod. "Good. But if your daddy really did see you watching the Donahue program, your time's coming. Be ready to run."

"I can't just not talk to them ever again," you say, because you can't just not talk to them ever again.

"You'd be surprised," she says. She looks outside at the snow whirling around the parking lot.

It is 1990. You will see your parents and sister for the last time in one month, two weeks, and one day.

You start getting ready.

You steal a duffel bag from the locker room at school and tuck it in the back of your closet. You fill it with clothes and toiletries and other things you'll need to live if you suddenly have to make a break for it. You become incredibly familiar with how to get to the bus terminal that will let you head north to Milwaukee, where you will make a transfer west to Minneapolis. You put the exact amount of money for a ticket in the duffel. You convince someone to give you an extra month's worth of your hormones. Those go in the bag too. You barely take off the new shoes you got for Christmas to break them in. They're running shoes.

You don't let yourself be yourself. You think about it sometimes. You long to buy nail polish or makeup when you are shopping for more practical items to put in your duffel. You think about purchasing them. You never do. You save every penny you have for Minneapolis.

You convince your parents to get you an ATM card. You put every dollar you can into an account you can empty in moments if you need to. It's not your money. It's Brooke's money. She'll need it.

You are being piloted by someone else, who is probably Brooke and might be you but definitely isn't anyone you recognize. Someone else is making your decisions. Someone else is building your future. She smiles and plays nice with your parents. She has half a thought that the two of you might be able to make it to graduation, get the haul from all the relatives you barely think about anymore, and *then* split town. You're going to need some serious cash, and you already know you don't have enough. If you could make it another year, you could have some breathing room.

You don't make it another year.

You come home from school, and your father stands up from the kitchen table. He is mad. He is very mad. Your mother has been crying. When she sees you, she starts crying again.

Your sister comes in behind you, and your father hisses, "Jeannie, get to your room." You will never again remember anyone saying your sister's name with love. You will always hear the propane-leak hiss of his voice. She almost says something, but she sees how mad your father is, and she obeys.

"Is everything okay?" you manage. You drop your voice a little lower when talking to your father. You won't realize you do this until years later, when your own son does it to attempt to fit in with the other guys. When he does it, it's cute. When you do it, it's camouflage.

Your father steps toward you, his whole body tensed, but not to strike. He is going to run right at you. He is going to knock you into the goddamn wall. You see the duffel bag's contents spread across the kitchen table's surface in orderly fashion. Your mother's handiwork, most likely.

"What the fuck is that?" your dad says, one meaty finger pointing at the items on the table. He gets closer to you without moving, oozing like an eclipse.

"Those are my things," you say. They are. Everything in that bag is yours.

"I hadn't seen your good sweater in a while, not even in the wash," your mother says, "and I thought maybe you misplaced it or left it in your closet . . ."

"I was keeping it in the bag," you say. You were. It's the warmest thing you own.

"Why are you keeping money in there?" your dad asks.

"For an emergency," you say. You won't realize it's a terrible excuse until your daughter tries it on you many years later. But she is trying to explain why she needs an extra hundred dollars for summer camp, not why she deserves to live.

"What are you doing?" your mother says. She sobs, violently, out of nowhere. "Are you trying to leave us?"

You are. "No. Of course not."

"What are these?" Your dad holds the bottle in his hand. "The pharmacist said they're a hormone treatment. For women."

"Give me those. They're mine." You reach for them. He jerks them away.

Forget the duffel bag. What do you *need* to go? Your room is upstairs. It's not a good idea to run up there, but you need money, and that's where the ATM card is. The hormones you're currently taking are in your backpack, which is on your back, so that's good. You only have about a week's worth left, but you can ration until you get a new supply. You need more clothes. You need warmer clothes. It was almost springlike today, but it's January. It will be cold again. Soon.

You need money. You need money. You need money. Everything was in the bag. How could you think they wouldn't find it?!

Brooke. Stop. Stop it, Brooke. Slow down. You are going to run past him. You have your good shoes on. The shoes you asked for.

You are going to grab the sweater on the way by the table. It's on top. After that, run upstairs and grab the card. You'll have enough money for a bus ticket and maybe a week of—

The phone number for that woman Octavia knows was in the duffel bag. In the cute little wallet with the money. You need that phone number. You need that phone number. You need—

His fist slams into the wall next to you. He pulls it away and shakes it out. He pulls you close, his breath hot on your face. You can see the fillings in the back of his mouth. He pulls you into a too-tight hug. "I'm so sorry, son. I should have seen."

"Why don't you want to be here?" your mom says. She sobs again, but not because you are leaving. She cries because she now knows she loves a phantom.

Hey, Brooke? It's me, okay? Stay with me, Brooke.

Your father hugs you even tighter. You can breathe, but only if you breathe the way he wants you to. He wants to turn your body into his. He drags you toward the living room, and you have a dull sense he is going to take his belt to you again. (You don't recognize where the "again" comes from, until you realize I only let you remember these things when you can handle them.)

Okay, you feel that thing in his chest pocket? That's probably the wallet. (Or it's his wallet, and that might be better.) The odds are good they didn't find the phone number, even if they took the cash out. I'm going to lay this out one step at a time, all right? You need to cause a distraction, so he'll look away just long enough for you to grab it.

His hands can feel how scrawny you are. "You're built like a sissy. You've been taking those pills, haven't you? You're like those fruitcakes on that program."

Your mother sobs.

The *distraction*, Brooke.

"JEANNIE!" you say. "CALL THE COPS! HE'S TRYING TO KILL ME!"

There's a dreadful pause. You hear Jeannie open her door upstairs and call down. It distracts your dad long enough for you to grab the wallet out of his chest pocket and confirm that, yes, it's yours. From the feel of it, the money is still inside.

Good work, Brooke. You have to punch him now.

You don't want to.

I know you don't want to, Brooke. But you have to. Now. And before he realizes you have the wallet. Then. Run. Sweater. Stairs. Card. Go.

You were never strong to begin with, and you're even weaker now, but your backpack is heavy with textbooks, and it gives you just enough weight to rear back and plow forward. Your fist doesn't do any damage, but it connects perfectly with his jaw. He takes a step back, which means he lets you go, which means it's time to run.

Don't look at Mom. Just look at the sweater. Jeannie's coming downstairs, so you'll have to guess which side she's coming down and hope you're right. She'll slow him down if you can get past her. He's big, Brooke, and you are so tiny. You've got this. He's right behind you, but he can't catch you. He was so happy about how fast you would be in these shoes.

"You fucking little—"

Don't you dare listen to him. He's not a real person anymore. He's just noise. You are a Doppler shift, and he is going to recede behind you.

You grab the sweater. Thank God, you grab the sweater. You know, somehow, that Jeannie is coming down the left side of the staircase, so you dart to the right, and you get past her before your dad comes up behind you. She screams in his face because he must look terrifying. You hear your mother shout the names of everybody who isn't her. She wants someone to undo everything she's just learned. She doesn't want to choose between you and the phantom, because she knows she will choose the phantom. You are fast enough to make her regret that choice.

The cat comes down the stairs to see the commotion, and you stutter step just long enough that your dad gets his hand around your foot. You fall, your chin hitting one of the stairs. Your mouth fills with blood and at least one tooth. He tries to grab hold of you, to pull you back into his jaws. You can see the frantic look on his face, even though you aren't looking at him. Your mother is screaming. Jeannie is screaming. You should be screaming.

Kick him in the fucking face, Brooke, Jesus Christ.

You kick him in the fucking face. You kick him in the fucking face once, twice, three times, and he bellows, but he lets go. You are up the stairs, spitting out the blood in your mouth, and he is calling you every name in the book, because he doesn't have it in him to keep coming, and the only way you can keep living is to keep going. So you go to your room because you still need the ATM card.

Fortunately, you put that inside your sock drawer. Easy to grab, and, hell, grab some socks while you're there. He'll recover and come after you again, in a minute, but remember how you convinced them to put a lock on your door for privacy, because you were such a good kid? I knew that would come in handy.

You lock the door. He'll break it down, but it'll take a second. You grab the card. You grab socks. You grab whatever clothes you see lying around, and you dump everything out of your backpack. You grab the bottle of hormones that was in there, and you shove in everything you can manage. Most of your clothes are dirty, but you'll find a laundromat. You can do anything. You are only now realizing this fact.

The door bulges, but he can't get to you. If he gets inside, he'll try to make you go away, but you aren't going away anymore. He is fighting yesterday's war.

You look around your bedroom to check for anything you might have missed. You open the window. It's a long fall, but there are bushes. You will be okay. You are strong, Brooke. You are so fucking strong. You've got this.

You look at your childhood bedroom one last time. The door splinters and gives way. You grab your stuffed rabbit from the bedside table, because you need the company, and you duck out the window, and you go.

When you were born, when the doctor said, "It's a boy," you were going to escape.

When your mother kissed your scraped knee and put a bandage on it, you were going to escape.

When you invited only girls to your fourth birthday party and your mom insisted you invite at least one boy, you were going to escape.

When he hit you, you were going to escape.

When he hit you with his belt, you were going to escape.

When he put your rabbit in the attic and told you to stop being such a baby, you were going to escape.

When you realized "American Girl" was playing on the jukebox, you were going to escape.

When he got his hand around your foot on the stairs, you were going to escape.

If he had caught you, if he had dragged you back into his maw, if he had locked you up, if he had beaten you bloody until you agreed to be who he wanted you to be, if you had lived a life in his shadow, if you had forced yourself into the shape he wanted you to be in, if you had erased everything about yourself but my voice, if you had locked me inside a safe, if you had thrown that safe into the sea, you still would have escaped.

That is the mistake they made, Brooke. They thought the act of keeping you meant you would always be kept. They forgot that when you build a prison, you also create its escape route, no matter how hard you try to safeguard its walls.

You were always going to escape. They were always going to watch you go. That was the story they set in motion from the moment they first held you.

The window was open. The wind was cold. You jumped. You went. You lived. You don't know what you're going to do next, but you're on a bus to Minneapolis, and you have a little over one hundred dollars in your pocket. Nothing will ever be as hard as what you just did. Nothing.

It is 1992. You just turned nineteen. You have been on hormones for twenty-nine months. Your legal name is Brooke Morgan.

You work in a hamburger joint named the Lion's Tap in Eden Prairie. You are saving up for a vaginoplasty, which you can get down the road in Rochester. You should have the money by mid-1994, if you do your best. A few months ago, you finally made enough money to move out of Danielle's basement. She told you not to be a stranger. You're sure she meant not to be a stranger to her, but some part of you thinks she also meant not to be a stranger to yourself. Good luck, you think.

The money at the restaurant isn't great, but the tips are better. The customers like you. You're starting to trust that you might be a little pretty. Nobody at the restaurant knows. Nobody in the city but Danielle and the doctor who prescribes your hormones knows. You are starting to realize nobody needs to know.

You are a normal girl. You are a normal, pretty girl who walks home with her friends late at night, a little drunk. You are a normal girl who gets better tips when she smiles a little too long at the older, richer guys who drift through the restaurant after church on a Sunday. You are drunk not on being young or on being beautiful but on being normal. You feel like you're letting the other girls down, but when one of those old guys calls you "sweetheart," you could just about cry.

You remember the moment the shift happened. One of the regulars had left some of the girls Twins tickets as a tip, and they asked you if you wanted to go. The game was a snooze, and you all left after the seventh-inning stretch. Walking back to the car through the endless Metrodome parking lot, tipsy, swinging your purse, belting out "We're Gonna Win Twins" with the other girls, you caught yourself thinking of them as the "other" girls, which implied a singular girl who was not them but was also here, which implied you. You started hanging out with them a lot more after that. They didn't know. Nobody knows.

There is a blank space in your memory where your home should be. You wonder if you abandoned your sister to hell, so you send her a birthday card one year to her school. You have no idea if she got it, but it felt good to tell her your name is Brooke.

You don't know about school. You don't know about a career. You don't know about love or romance or any of that. You kiss a couple guys, and the way they want you, like you are *necessary*, finally feels right to you. But it never goes beyond that. You don't dare risk doing anything sexual right now, maybe not even after you have your surgery. The chances of you picking the wrong guy are high. If he doesn't kill you, he might expose you, and you'd have to go right back. You dream about that bird in the sky, still. You dream about him grabbing you in his talons and carrying you off somewhere you don't want to go.

You are careful. You are cautious. You are smart. You are beautiful. You are a beam of goddamn sunlight. You are so, so, *so* good.

And you don't ever listen to me.

You meet Victor Daniels on your thirty-month anniversary of taking hormones. An hour before close, he walks into the Lion's Tap, drenched from the rain. You are the only waitress working, and he is about to be the only customer here after an old couple three booths down gets their change.

He stands by the "please seat yourself" sign, clutching his coat against his body, wiping the fog off his glasses with a soggy handkerchief he pulls from his pocket. "Wherever you'd like," you say, gesturing to the empty place.

He makes a puzzled face, then reads the sign and laughs. "Sorry. Saw it. Didn't read it." He's dressed like he's visiting, which means he's wearing a big belt buckle, a checkered button-up shirt, Wrangler jeans, and brand-new Nike sneakers. He seats himself at the far end of the restaurant, and he doesn't even look at a menu before ordering a cheeseburger, fries, and a Coke. He comes here every year on his way back from the farm show (he tells you), and he always orders the same thing.

You put his order in with the chef, then grab a handful of clean dish towels and carry them over to his booth. "You look like you could use these." You don't know how cute your smile is. (I do, but you don't give a shit what I think.)

He mops himself off, paying particular attention to his arms. "My mom told me to bring an umbrella." He runs a towel over his face. "See what I get for being rebellious."

When you look at him, you're reminded of a cartoon you once saw where a big, vicious dog was undone by a cute little kitten. You don't fall for Victor because he's the dog but because he's the kitten. "I never listened to my mother, and look where I ended up," you say. You gesture to your glamorous place of business.

"This is my favorite restaurant in the whole world," he says. It's like he's already echoing the hundreds of times he will tell the story of how he met you. "I'd say it's a good place to end up."

You leave him your phone number.

Victor is twenty-seven. He's the oldest son of a farming family from Mitchell, South Dakota, a town you had never heard of until he started calling you on the phone almost every night. He doesn't love farming, but he does love not having to worry about money.

He's had two girlfriends, and he thought he was going to marry both. The first one cried after they slept together on prom night. The second one left him for a guy he thought was his friend. He dates, but it's hard to find a girl who wants to live down on the farm. It's so far from anything. You really have to want to be lonely, he says. You have to want to get a little bit lost.

Uh-huh, you think.

Victor is not especially handsome. He has a certain charm, but his face looks like Silly Putty into which someone pressed symmetrical indentations. His hands, though, know exactly how to make sense of you. When they run over you, the few times he makes it over to the Cities for a long weekend, you discover yourself. You see yourself in the mirror every day, so you don't know how much you've changed. But when Victor touches you, you can feel how little of the old you is left. (Still, you don't let him so much as undress you.)

You don't honestly know if you fall for him because you fall for him or because falling for him gets you one state farther away from Chicago, gets you into a family with all the money you'd ever need, gets you that much closer to erasing your old self from existence. You sometimes think you took all the parts of yourself that might lead you to do something stupid, all the parts of you that could be reckless or carefree or even just silly, and locked them away, so all you had left were a handful of brute calculations that counted your value as a human being against building a life where *he* could never again break open the door and drag you down the stairs and into that living room.

(For the record, I can assure you that you *did*, indeed, lock away all those parts of yourself.)

Above all else, Victor is kind. He never asks you to do something you don't want to do. He seems scared of you, and you realize with a start one night as you cuddle in his hotel bed that he is terrified you will realize who he is.

But you already have, is the thing.

"Brooke," Danielle says, looking up from her menu, "I told you not to be a stranger!" She's laughing, but not enough to indicate that she's goofing around.

"Danielle! What a nice surprise!" (You speak Minnesota nice now. You speak it with the fucking best.)

"I'll just have a hamburger and a Diet Coke," she says. "Can you take a break? It's been a second." You would like to say you can't, but you were already headed for lunch.

Every time you see Danielle is like the first time you saw Danielle. She got you at the bus depot and drove you home and made you a bowl of alphabet soup and called you Brooke as many times as she could. When you had to set your rabbit down so you could eat, she put him in a chair next to you and said he seemed like a good friend, which made you burst into tears.

You don't know how Octavia got Danielle's number, because whatever Danielle is doing is the opposite of woodworking. She passes. She looks like any other sixty-something Midwestern woman, but she spends so much time telling the world—through advocacy groups and community outreach and other things that sound exhausting—that she's a transsexual. She was even in the *Star Trib* in 1989. She has the article framed and hanging up in the house she shares with her wife. (Danielle and her wife stayed married even after Danielle told her wife her secret, a thing that blows your mind.)

They let you stay in that house for as long as you needed. They helped you find a doctor. They helped you find support. They helped you find your job. You owe them everything, which might be why you haven't talked to them since you moved out five months ago.

"You've been busy?" Danielle says.

"I have. Working extra hours to save up for my procedure."

Danielle huffs with laughter when you call it a "procedure," then folds her hands together, looking over the table. "Brooke, what are you doing?"

"I told you."

"You're trying to disappear."

"I'm right here," you say.

She takes a long slurp from her Diet Coke. "That's not what I mean. You've stopped coming to group."

Ah. Group. "I don't need it anymore," you say. "I'm doing okay."

"Of course you are. You're a twenty-year-old blonde girl. I'm sure you're having the time of your fucking life." You don't say anything, but you also look away in a manner that is incredibly guilty. "I see. Who's the guy?"

"Victor," you say.

"Does he know?"

You shake your head, then look down at your hands. "I think he might be okay with it."

"Okay. Say he is," she says. "Say you convince him not to run away when he learns the truth. What about his family? His friends?"

"Why do they have to know?"

"They don't. None of them do. Your life is your life to do with as you please. But *he* deserves to know. You owe him that, especially if the question of kids comes up. Nobody else *has* to know." She frowns. "But would you invite Evelyn and me to the wedding and introduce us to everybody there?"

Of course you wouldn't. Both of you know that. "What do you care?"

She laughs. "The world missed a true natural when it didn't make you a teenage girl the first time around. I care because if you stay with this guy, you're going to shove yourself into a new kind of closet."

You're silent, and Danielle gnaws on her burger, taking small bites to avoid overeating. "Is it the worst thing for me to marry a guy I love?"

"No. But if you're only honest about yourself with one person, Brooke, and if you need to lie to everybody else to be with him, you're going to start lying to yourself too. You can't hide this part of yourself. You'll get lost inside."

"He loves me."

"I'm sure he does. He must think, every day, how lucky he is to know you. And he is. He is lucky." She reaches across the table and puts her hand over yours. "Come back to group."

That's the last time you see Danielle.

Hi, Brooke.

It's 2015, and the girl's name is Abigail. You first hear her name at church. Well, you don't really hear her "name" so much as you hear the word "transgendered," and you eavesdrop as hard as you've ever eavesdropped before, and somewhere deep inside you, I start to wake up.

It's 2015, and the girl's name is Abigail. She had to leave her family, and she wound up in Mitchell, South Dakota, too. Your son says she "seems mean." Some part of you knows you might have seemed mean, too, if you hadn't been trying so hard to disappear. When you finally see her, leaning against the wall in her army jacket at a basketball game, you feel a thrill at how normal she looks. The white-blonde hair doesn't really suit her, and her scowl seems permanently etched into her face. But she's real.

It's 2015, and the girl's name is Abigail. When you introduce yourself, insisting the Christian thing to do is welcome her with open arms, you tell her who you are without bursting into tears. She seems confused as to why you're saying hello, so you say you're Caleb's mom, and she seems more confused. But you shake her hand. Good for you, Brooke.

It's 2015, and the girl's name is Abigail. You go home that night and look at Victor brushing his teeth in the bathroom, and you feel something inside you, beating its wings against your rib cage. He looks over at you and frowns. "What?" he says, and you say, "Nothing," because how could you begin to explain it to him? You don't talk about this. Ever. It's the price you've paid to never have to think about yourself anymore.

But it's 2015, and the girl's name is Abigail.

How long has it been, Brooke? How long has it been since you saw another woman like you? No, I don't mean when your kids made fun of that woman working the register at the gas station in Orlando, and I don't mean when you saw that actress being interviewed on TV. You didn't know those people.

I don't even mean those women at the group in Sioux Falls you talked yourself into attending once. All that happened there was you said, "I transitioned a long time ago. I think it was a dream," and after a long silence, Bernadette, the nice woman in charge, said, "Choosing to be ourselves is a constant process, isn't it?" and you got up and left. To this day, you remember the name of every person who was there. But you don't *know* them.

The last time you *saw* someone like you, where she knew you and you knew her, was Danielle.

I've been counting, Brooke. It's been twenty-two years, nine months, and twenty-two days between when you last saw Danielle on November 1, 1992, and when you first met Abigail on August 23, 2015. You threw away the cards Danielle sent you over the years. I fucking watched.

You left the Lion's Tap that day, and you called Victor, and you told him the truth, because you weren't sure whose bluff you were calling. He was silent a long time, and you didn't dare say anything, because you knew he would hang up. But you wanted him to hang up. You didn't want him to throw you a lifeline because you knew you would take it.

"Well," he said, "we'll fix it."

He had so much money. He could get more from his parents. He paid for the operation himself, in cash. He counted the bills out in front of you, one by one, on the hotel-room bed. You stood and watched him, towel wrapped around yourself, hair dripping on the pebbly carpet. He didn't look up the whole time. Neither of you wanted to acknowledge you as you.

This is a price you've paid every day since you left Danielle behind, Brooke. When Octavia (remember Octavia?) mentioned "woodworking" to you, you thought she was presenting you with a solution, but now you know she was trying to warn you. Whose number did Octavia give you? Danielle's. And Danielle wasn't woodworking. She was out there, every day, fighting. Octavia didn't see herself in you, Brooke. She saw Danielle. You could have been different. You should have been different.

Instead, you invented a burden you could never bear. Victor never asked you to consider it a burden. He merely asked you to love him unconditionally. But you also knew that "unconditionally" meant loving the parts of him that could only see you as the person you pretended to be, the person who made his life easier. You adopted his favorite foods and his hobbies and his faith and his politics and his family and his empire. You got used to the way his hand felt holding yours as you prayed. You learned how to be the person he needed you to be, and you forgot how to be yourself.

In return for your devotion, he never told anyone. He introduced you to his family as his girlfriend. When you got engaged, he told his parents about the childhood accident that left you unable to get pregnant. When you got married, he explained that your parents were dead and you had no siblings. All you had to do was be the wife he expected you to be. He didn't even ask. You could hear the request before it was spoken.

You once watched a show about ghosts, up late at night, feeding Ruth. You started to cry at the thought of being trapped in a house that was not really yours, trying to get someone to listen to you. I'd say the metaphor was a little obvious, but you told yourself you didn't know why you were crying.

"Well, at least he can't get her pregnant," Victor says, laughing. Your son is fucking Abigail Hawkes. You wish you could tell Caleb how funny this is.

"That's not funny." Victor looks at you, surprised to hear you even the slightest bit cross. (Hi, Victor.) "I don't think it's funny."

"Oh," he says. He walks across the bedroom and pulls you into a hug, which is to say he leans you against himself like a board, because every part of you is locked up. "I'm sorry. I didn't think about that. I don't think of you as . . . I didn't think of that."

"She's like me," you say into his shoulder. He rocks you back and forth. Neither of you speaks. You cry. He holds you.

"I should invite her to dinner," you say.

"Don't you think that's a bad idea? With the campaign. Given Isaiah's stance on—"

"I should invite her to dinner," you say again, and you realize how much of you aches for a chance to get to know her a little bit better.

"Well, I'll put on my good jeans," he says. He's a good husband. You're not just saying that to assure yourself you didn't make a mistake. I'm saying that, and I wish I could hate the motherfucker. He is kind and considerate, and even though he assumes that a space is his just because he's occupying it, he'll leave that space if you ask. That's more than most men will do—certainly more than your father. (Right. We're not thinking about him. Sorry.)

He knows how much you need this, Brooke. He knows there were maybe two years in Minneapolis when you weren't actively trying to erase yourself, but he also doesn't know how to say he's sorry.

"Maybe I'll make her lasagna," you say.

"Do you even know how to make lasagna?" he says, and you laugh, and he laughs, and he gives you a kiss, and just like that, you are again playing a woman who looks a lot like you but isn't you.

The first time you held your son, some other part of you came to life. I don't know who she is, Brooke. She lives somewhere else. I've never met her. She seems neat. She's a really good mom, and you seem to like being her. But you've concluded that it's impossible for her and me to occupy the same space. Maybe you're right.

So I hang out in the subbasement of yourself, stored away on a shelf somewhere like Christmas decorations, and I wait and wait and wait for you to notice me. Sometimes, you hear your pastor (that smug fuck) talk about how women like you defy God's plan. You nod your head and look solemn and pretend I'm not throwing myself against the door down here.

I don't even know what I want.

That's a lie. I know exactly what I want. The first time you saw Caleb, I looked through your eyes into his wide brown eyes. I could feel the warmth of his body in our hands as we hugged him. I could sense how fragile he was. I felt the way he laughed when your hair tickled over his face. I didn't hear it. I felt it. Like thunder that doesn't know it's a sound yet.

I want to be the one holding him, Brooke. It really sucks that I'm not.

"I found her!" Caleb says as he reenters the house. Abigail follows, grass stains all over her orange dress. She looks cold and tearstained. She is so beautiful. The dinner, so far, has gone poorly. Your fault, mostly.

"Abigail!" Victor says. "We're about to play Scattergories! You in?"

Abigail half nods, then runs her hands over her arms. Everybody looks at her like they think she's going to go back to being Caleb's pliant girlfriend. But you know that look. She'll bolt if you say the wrong thing.

"Why don't you wash your hands in warm water, Abigail? You look really cold." You lead her down the hall, pushing open the door to the bathroom and tugging on the faucet until water steams up from the sink. She closes the door most of the way. She takes her time, and you think she might be crying again. Maybe don't hover outside the bathroom like this, Brooke.

"Jesus Christ," she says. She's done washing her hands, and she's seen you lurking.

"Sorry, I just . . . I wanted to make sure you didn't need anything more."

"To wash my hands?"

You laugh. She's funny. "No, not that." You put your hands on your hips. Her face turns toward you, but her entire body angles back toward the main room and the board game about to begin. "I'm sorry."

"It's fine."

"No, it's not," you say. You should tell her, Brooke. Fuck it, you know? Just tell her.

"Thank you but I really don't need you to, like, be my ally."

"I meant what I said. About not agreeing with everything Isaiah preaches. He's clumsy sometimes. Like a bull. I try to get through to him."

"You're clearly doing a fantastic job," she says.

You smile. You hope it's disarming. She spins to go back, and you want to reach out and touch her, to feel that she's real.

"You are always, always, always welcome here, Abigail. With or without Caleb. This is your home too. If you ever need somewhere to go. Or, you know, you just want to hang out."

Jesus Christ, Brooke.

"Jesus Christ, Brooke," Abigail says. "Can I just accept your apology or what?"

You look at your feet. "Sorry. Again. Caleb's had a lot of girlfriends. You're the first one I've liked."

"You have weird taste, but thanks."

The truth hovers just inside your teeth like a hummingbird. You swallow it. "I just want you to know that I get it. I really do."

Abigail gives you a long look. For a moment, I think she can see me, but instead, she puts a hand on your arm. You could cry. "I appreciate that you think you get it, but you don't. You can't." She drops the hand. You could cry. "While your husband was praying, I looked over at you, because I could hear you saying, 'Thank you, Jesus.' And I think it's a lot easier to be thankful when you live here."

"It is," you say. It's the one time you don't lie to her.

Several years ago, you decided to look up Jeannie on Facebook. You thought it would be hard to find her. She might have gotten married. But searching for her by the high school you both attended eventually revealed her.

She had gotten even farther away than you had, winding up in Boston. She had two little boys. You looked at Jeannie's family photos for a few minutes, memorizing every element. Then you closed the browser and filed everything you knew about her down here with me, where the inconvenient things about yourself are left to rot.

A few months ago, you searched for her again. Her Facebook was locked down tight this time, but on a whim, you asked to follow her on Instagram, and she accepted. She has no idea that you—SoDakBrooke—are her sister. You don't look like the person she saw all those years ago, if she can even remember that face. There's a photo of her at Boston's Pride parade. So she's an activist. Good for her. (You might be one too if you let yourself think about your politics for five seconds. But you can't. You need Victor like a drowning woman needs driftwood, and Victor is a Republican. So you are too.)

You stared at Jeannie's feed for what felt like hours, searching for something important (beyond your long-lost sister's face). And then you found it. You scrolled past several photos of her family until one from the summer stopped you in your tracks.

Jeannie and her husband stand behind their kids on the shore of a lake somewhere. They have the tired look of people who have realized they are on vacation just in time to discover that vacation is about to end. Jeannie has a weak smile. Her husband's eyes are squinted closed. Her son makes a face at the camera, because he's still a little boy. Her daughter, nearly a teenager from the looks of it, gazes off camera, as if seeking an excuse to run.

Brooke.

It took you a second. But then you scrolled and scrolled, and you started to cry. There are no photos of Jeannie with two sons. Not here. The account stretches back four years, and in every one of them, she has an older daughter (Emma) and a younger son (Gabriel). You lean in close to the screen, and you feel that flutter in your chest again, and you look at your niece's face.

You don't know, but you know. You might have been wrong about Jeannie having two little boys all those years ago. You get things wrong.

But you're pretty sure you didn't get this wrong.

As you drive home Halloween night, you see your house glittering atop the hill. The first time you saw it lit up like this, you breathed an involuntary prayer of gratefulness. Your whole life, you had wanted a place like this. You invited Abigail to stay here because you needed to believe you would treat her better than you were treated. But you must know, Brooke, that you built the place you always wished you could go, then closed the door behind you. Your house is not a haven. Your house is a fortress, meant to keep out monsters you barely acknowledge anymore.

You think about that scared girl in that diner in Chicago. You imagine her realizing the dim wash of headlights in the slushy streets outside would eventually reveal itself to be a place like this. You ache for her because you know you aren't really her.

You are close enough to make out the big windows in the dining room. You see Victor setting the table. He gives you a wave. When you get inside, you'll find that he's started a frozen pizza because he thought you needed the night off. He's better than I give him credit for.

You have a moment. You step onto the lawn and look up to where the moon fades into view, like it has been superimposed on the sky in a camera trick. You look back at your house. It is a promise you kept to yourself. Think about how lucky you are, Brooke. Think about how few people like you find a life like this.

Inside that house, your husband licks his fingers after pulling the pizza from the oven without a mitt. Your daughter sits in the same room as your son, doing her homework, because she is so scared to lose him. Your son lies in bed and cries, but he looks over every so often to remind himself that your daughter is still there. Down the road, your son's girlfriend flips off a reckless driver as she walks through the freezing cold back to her home. Half a city away, the man who asked you to advise on his campaign masturbates to incredibly boring pornography. A few blocks away from there, the woman challenging him for his seat makes canned soup for her mother, who's fallen asleep in front of the TV. Just down the street, one of the few people you consider a close friend helps her ex-wife move her things into the house they used to share. Her ex-wife takes a moment to look back out at the street before closing the door, a sigh dying in her throat. Somewhere in Minneapolis, Danielle (who is still alive) stares blankly at a wall in the eldercare facility where she lives. She has forgotten everything about herself but not that her name is Danielle. Farther off in suburban Chicago, your parents (who are dead) rest in their graves. And half a continent away, there's a twelve-year-old girl finally agreeing to go downstairs for dinner, after her mom called and called and called. She's your niece, Brooke, and if you could talk to her, you might have so much to tell each other.

You could have that life, Brooke. You could speak it into existence. You could say who you are. You have a gift for reinvention, love. We both do.

We also both know you won't do this. The cruelest thing about what you did is that you robbed yourself of definition. You only behaved rationally in the face of everything you had to face. But to disappear into the woodwork in the name of safety is still to disappear.

I know you'll stop listening to me again. Maybe the next time we meet, we'll find a way to be a little better to each other. Until then, let me stay a little longer as you walk through the cold grass, back to your house. I don't blame you, Brooke. I don't blame you.

You step inside, and you kick off your shoes, and you wash your hands in hot water. In the kitchen, Victor makes clean slices through the pizza, then gives you a soft, sad smile, and you know it will be bad news. "You should talk to Caleb," he says. "I think something happened with Abigail."

November

Erica

Tuesday,

November 1

Constance tosses and turns all night, occasionally sitting up to angrily fluff a pillow or tug her blankets up around her chin. *It's okay*, Erica thinks. *She lives here again.*

At dawn, Erica gets out of bed. In the living room, she collides with one of several boxes Constance moved out of John's house two days ago and has yet to unpack. She winces at her stubbed toe, then smiles. Against all odds, things have worked out.

For too much of her life, Erica has been lost in her past. Since she self-accepted, she has been clawing frantically at the present, trying to build a home for herself there. Now that Constance is back, however, the *future* has a shape too. It is not just something Erica avoids looking at. She has herself, and she has the woman she loves, and she has a job she tolerates. What more does a girl need?

Of late, she has allowed herself a fantasy of that future. She imagines her and Constance owning a Victorian out in the country near Sioux Falls. Erica would draw up lesson plans for her wonderfully inspiring students. Constance would teach acting lessons or something. They would have a daughter (no way could she imagine her and Constance having a *son*), and a cat. Probably a dog too. And they would be happy, their marriage put together correctly at last.

As easy as this future is to picture, Erica finds it all but impossible to imagine herself as a woman within it. Even in this vision, she is still hiding, still wearing her man costume. To come out is to lose her job and possibly most everything else. It's hard to imagine buying a Victorian out in the country on a teacher's salary, yes, but it's impossible to imagine doing so with no income whatsoever.

And now John knows her secret. There is a hidden countdown clock somewhere.

So maybe there will be no future at all.

"You don't need to wear the tie," Helen says. "I don't want to make you feel . . ."

"I'm getting into character." Erica thrusts her chest forward, like she might thump it and start caterwauling. Her necktie hangs slightly too short, like Isaiah's always does.

She is playing the part of the reverend at Helen's debate preparation. She's not sure she's doing a great job, but in the last few days, the wall she's always felt between her and the women she wanted to be friends with has started to crumble between her and Helen. It's like she fell forward, then kept falling. It's intoxicating.

Helen laughs. "You look like someone's respectable lesbian aunt. That's a compliment."

Erica shuffles through the note cards Helen handed her earlier. They're covered in block capitals and say things like "WHY EVEN HAVE AN ENVIRONMENT?" and "SAY SOMETHING NICE ABOUT GOD." They've been at this two hours already, and Helen is crushing it.

"From what I know of Isaiah, he only gets animated when he's talking about abortion or making trans people miserable."

"Well, if he leans into the trans stuff, I can say, 'One of my best friends is trans!'" Erica's face twitches, the part of her thrilled at the use of "best friends" colliding with her ever-present paranoia. Helen winces. "Shit. Sorry. I'd never do that! Are you still worried about John?"

Erica fingers the suddenly alien necktie. "I think he puts seeming like a nice guy ahead of everything else, but I don't imagine he'll keep my secret forever. A few weeks? Maybe."

"Why not come out before he can out you? Save yourself the worry." Helen holds her hands up flat, as if to show she's not carrying weapons. "It should be on your terms. Obviously. I just don't like seeing you worry this much about something you can't control."

Erica holds the tie out from her body so she can see it. She usually wears it to the school's annual awards dinner. The thought of not wearing it is now terrifying. The paradox is that the closer she gets to the moment she might be out in public as herself, the further away it seems.

"I don't want to wear this." Erica takes the tie off and wads it up in a ball, dropping it.

Helen's eyes remain fixed on the tie. "What's the worst that would happen if you came out? Absolute worst-case scenario?"

"I'd lose my job," Erica says. "Guaranteed. Constance would leave me again because I'd have no money coming in. People would misconstrue my relationship with Abigail, and I would end up in jail."

"Okay. Best-case scenario?"

Erica rolls her eyes. Helen sees the world as a broad series of possible outcomes. She considers every angle, then works her way inward to a conclusion that is the most good and least bad. It makes her a pretty good politician and an irritating best-friend-in-training.

"I have a good job, a woman I love, and some new friends. I'd say I'm living it."

"If I'm part of your best-case scenario, you can absolutely do better."

"Only one of us gets to hate herself at a time, and I've got squatter's rights." Erica shuffles through the note cards again. "Okay, so what if he says something like, 'My opponent wants to raise taxes'?"

Helen scoffs. "I *do* want to raise taxes. You don't need your money. I should get to have it. Roar, roar, roar, I'm an evil monster." She takes the cards from Erica and tucks them in her purse. "Can we keep talking about this?" Erica mutely nods. "Okay. Say you do lose your job? Do you even *want* to be a teacher?"

"I want to be with Constance, and I want to raise our kid, and I want to keep directing plays. I teach to barely afford those dreams. And I want this one big thing—to be a woman. After that, it feels a little presumptuous to want anything more."

"Then it's worth fighting for. On your terms."

"I'll lose. Is the thing."

Helen squeezes Erica's hand, getting her to look back at her. "Some fights are worth losing," She picks up the necktie from the floor and twirls it around her fingers. "You're looking at the poster girl."

Brooke isn't there when Erica and Constance show up for rehearsal. She didn't show up yesterday either, texting Erica a quick *Emergency. Please run acts two and three*, ten minutes after rehearsal started.

Before Erica can wonder what the fuck is up, however, she hears the sounds of drilling and hammering fill the auditorium. *John doubled down*, she thinks. She had expected him to abandon building the set, but of *course* he would insist on finishing—possibly out of spite, possibly because the work was nearly complete and John, if nothing else, was proud of a job well done.

Some part of Erica—okay, the part that has always avoided thinking too intently about the way her actions might hurt other people—assumed John would simply disappear from her life after he caught her and Constance together. But every time she hears the zap of a power screwdriver, she is reminded that she has done something Wrong. John loved Constance, and Erica blew that up. Having to be herself means having to feel the weight of her sins. Guilt throbs in the back of her mouth.

John steps onstage through one of the doors in the set. "We're done back here, ████. We'll get out of your way."

John now uses Erica's old name like a bullet. (On some level, Erica feels she deserves to be hurt.) "Oh, thanks," she says.

John turns to check a door for squeaky hinges. His smile broadens, genuine, at his craftsmanship. "Would you look at that, ████? I saw how often Brooke had blocked scenes so people were exiting backstage, and I figured an extra exit would be helpful."

"You know more about stagecraft than I expected." Erica feels like she is floating, full of helium.

"I'm not some dumb asshole, ████! I was really involved in the theater program back at the U." He unplugs the center stage ghost light, looping the cord loosely around the lamp, then lifting it in one hand like a walking stick or weapon. "I got into it because of a girl, ████. Didn't work out, but I learned to appreciate stagecraft anyway."

Erica swallows.

"That's how I met Connie, actually," John says. "She tell you that?" Erica shakes her head. "I went and saw that *Christmas Carol* you put on a couple years ago. Thought the girl who played Christmas Past was brilliant, and I wanted to meet her. Found out she was married and backed off. For a while. But it turned out she was married to the right man all along. So no hard feelings, ████."

"Sure," Erica says.

Constance coughs, and John looks at her, as if remembering she's there. "When's your next ultrasound?"

Constance looks around, like another person here might be pregnant. "Friday in Sioux Falls."

"I'll be there. When do we find out the gender?"

"Soon," Constance says. "It's not necessary for you to come. I—"

"I'll be there," Erica says.

"—can do it by myself," Constance says at the same time.

"And baby makes four." John grins, clearly pleased with his joke.

"Thanks for all your hard work," Erica can't stop herself from saying.

"You're welcome, ████!" John sounds pleased. He sets down the lamp and beckons for Erica to approach the stage, where he drops into a crouch. "I just want to say again that your secret's safe with me. I don't have a prejudiced bone in my body."

Erica smiles queasily. "You've always been kind to me, John."

"I know I have. Makes it hurt even more what you did." He stands again. "It's too bad. I'd love to hear all about your life and how you decided to change. But when I see you, I want to punch you."

"You wouldn't hit a lady, right?" Erica doesn't realize she has said it out loud.

John laughs once, darkly. "Like I said, I'm a good guy. Your secret's safe with me. Can't guarantee anybody else will keep it though."

"I thought you said—"

"People find things out, ████. They always do."

Heavy boots tromp in from offstage, and Ollie clears his throat. "C'mon. I wanna watch the Cubbies." He nods to Erica, a strange smile crossing his face. "Night, Constance. Night, ████." Erica can feel a smile she cannot see. She'll never prove it, but from how Ollie says her old name, slow and deliberate, he so obviously knows. And he wants her to know he knows.

The back doors of the theater open with a loud bang. Erica cannot believe how relieved she is to see Brooke Daniels, who, weirdly, is beaming.

"I always thought you two would work it out," Brooke says during break. "When she told you she was pregnant before John, that's when I thought, aha, this is headed in a particular direction. She trusts you. More than anyone."

Erica stares at Brooke, convinced she's been replaced by a clone. "Thanks, I guess?"

Yet Erica has asked herself the same question many times of late: Why did Constance tell her first? Their relationship rekindling seemed so tied to the honesty inherent in Erica coming out, but the pregnancy reveal has never quite sat right with her.

You know why she told you, dummy, says the voice in her head that sounds like Abigail.

No, I don't, Erica replies.

She doesn't want to have this fucking baby. She knew you would know that. She wanted you to remind her who she was.

"Don't forget to remind the cast there's no rehearsal on Monday because of the debate," Brooke says, interrupting Erica's personal revelation. Before she can respond, Brooke adds, "By the way, what are you doing tomorrow night? I thought you, Abigail, and I could meet for dinner. Maybe at Crossroads in Huron?"

Brooke's completely bizarre invitation takes a moment to register. When it does, she feels faint. "What? Why?"

"Abigail thought I should talk to her friend Erica, so she gave me her number. When I plugged it into my phone, I saw I already had it." Brooke smiles. "I can't wait to talk."

Erica laughs suddenly, wildly, then squeaks out, "Oh, fuck." She stands and nearly topples over, before speed-walking out of the theater and into the men's room, where she immediately throws up.

Abigail

Wednesday,

November 2

"Listen. When I said you should imagine Brooke was a tranny when you tried making friends with her, I didn't *actually think*—"

"Abigail, don't."

"Just trying to lighten the mood," I say. Erica glares at me, uninterested in mood-lightening, then turns to watch the door. We're sitting in the pool area of a hotel in Huron, an hour north of Mitchell. Brooke insisted we all meet here—in case she's being spied on, I guess. She said this was a great "quiet" place for us to "get to know each other." Perfect. She's yet another person I would rather not know is trans, but it's not like I can unknow it. So here we are, waiting for what should be a super wonderful, not stressful dinner.

(Also, that she did a little IRL woodworking and turned into trans Darth Vader is not lost on me.)

An old man is swimming laps in the pool, barely taking a breath. I find myself holding my breath too, either because I'm susceptible to peer pressure or because I can tell Erica is mega-pissed at me. Maybe both.

"You can talk to me," I say. "Please talk to me. This is all very weird, and I'm tired of being the only one acknowledging how weird it is."

Erica almost says something, then returns to watching the door. The man swimming laps reaches the wall and calls out, "Twenty!"

to nobody before heading back the other way. He came down here carrying a briefcase and no towel, which raises an obvious question: Is he keeping his towel in the briefcase? If Brooke doesn't show up soon, we might get to find out.

"Are you sure she's fine with you outing her?" Erica says. "Because I never gave *my* okay."

"I didn't *out* you. Brooke vomited this whole fucking bananas story to me, and I wanted her to stop, because I'm tired of adults thinking I'm their trans identity receptacle, so I thought, *You know who needs more friends . . .*"

"You gave her my number and outed me."

"I made a fucking mistake! She's not going to tell anyone, Erica. I promise."

"Twenty-one!" shouts briefcase swimming pool possible-spy man.

"After what you told me about Caleb's essay, yes, I'm sure she won't divulge anything about a fellow trans person if it'll help her gain some minor advantage."

"This is different." I can hear how unconvincing I sound. "Let's just leave. She's a half hour late, and the restaurant closes soon. She's not coming. Or we can wait until we get an answer to the briefcase-towel mystery."

"The what?"

Right. I never shared that observation with her. But just as I'm about to explain what I mean, Brooke glides in. "Thank you, both of you, for meeting me here. Apologies for my lateness. I can't wait to discuss Abigail's scholarship application. Join me in the restaurant, please." She heads for the restaurant without another word.

"Twenty-two!" the old-man swimmer says. I would rather stay here and see how that turns out, but I follow Brooke instead.

"My treat," Brooke says as we sit down at the table, Erica and I across from her. I know what she really means by this: *I'm rich as fuck, and yes, you can have the steak. Still, you should probably order the chicken sandwich.*

"The chicken sandwich looks good," I say, shutting my menu.

Brooke focuses on unwrapping a straw, then slowly shreds the paper piece by piece. "What has Abigail told you, Erica?" she says.

"Grew up in Chicago, transitioned as a teen, deep stealth, nobody knows except Victor. And us. Did I miss anything?"

"My doctor also knows, but he's in Minneapolis." Brooke turns to me. "When I found out Caleb was dating you, I thought it was quite funny." She smiles.

"Yeah," I say. I don't laugh.

"I'm happy keeping your secret, but I don't know what else you expect from me," Erica says. I nod emphatically. I accidentally outed Erica to Brooke and couldn't think about anything else most of today.

"What a lovely bunch!" the waitress says in a sneak attack. "I see she has your hair, Mom, and your nose, Dad!"

It takes me a second, but I burst out laughing. "We're not her parents," Brooke says. "We're merely discussing her scholarship application." She hands her menu to the waitress. "The chicken sandwich, please." I'm still laughing, so Brooke adds, "And another chicken sandwich for my 'daughter.'" She winks. I wish I wasn't so mad at her. This version of Brooke is kind of fun.

Erica goes off-book to order a cheeseburger, and then Brooke leans forward and whispers, "I want to talk to some other—" She gestures to us, to convey generalized transness. "I've been alone a long time."

"That sucks," Erica says. She doesn't sound particularly sympathetic.

"You should go to support group again. Make some new friends," I say. If it minorly helped me, it'll sure as shit help her.

"Oh, I can't do that. No, I don't think that I can do that. Too much risk."

"We could smuggle you in in a box if you want," I say.

Brooke shakes her head. "I thought maybe the three of us could meet every so often instead?"

"You're really going to keep this secret forever?" Erica says. "Even from your kids?"

What a stupid thing to say! Clearly Brooke can keep this secret forever! "I've made it over twenty-five years," Brooke says. "What are twenty-five more?" She coughs.

There's a roar from the bar area, where a bunch of Cubs fans are watching the last game of the World Series. "You a fan?" Erica says. "Given Chicago and all?"

"Twins," Brooke says. "If the Cubs win, I hope my father's dead, so he can't appreciate it."

The waitress delivers our food. I take a bite, and the chicken squeaks between my teeth, the bread too dry. I don't want to eat the rest of it, but then again, I don't even want to be here. I glare at Brooke. "What are we even doing?" I say. "Why are we here?"

"Maybe this was a bad idea," Brooke says. She wads up a napkin and dabs at her eyes. I fold my arms across my chest. "I guess I wanted you to see I'm not who you think I am."

"Oh! So you *didn't* let Caleb put my dead name in his college-application essay? Some other person edited it and neglected to tell him, 'Hey, maybe don't do that'?"

"Abigail . . . ," Erica says.

"Come now. At most, five or six people will read that essay. They wouldn't know you from Eve, and . . ."

"And if *I* hadn't, I would have kept showing up at your house, eating your food, watching your TV, fucking him in his bed?" She focuses very intently on pulling the chicken breast out of her sandwich. "He would have gotten into Northwestern, and you would have always known it was because he threw me under the bus. And you wouldn't have ever told me?"

"I'm very good at pretending things didn't happen," she says quietly. The fans cheer again, and she looks toward the noise, away from us.

"Fuck off, you fucking fascist cunt." It makes no sense, but it feels good to say.

"*Abigail*," Erica says.

"I *loved* him. I loved all of you. And all any of you saw was a prop in a story you were telling about how good and kind and giving you were." I laugh, so I don't sob. "Erica annoys the shit out of me, but at least she tries to know me as I am."

Brooke's hands shake as she pours a pepper packet over her chicken patty. "I really didn't think you would read the essay."

Erica puts a hand on my arm and squeezes tightly. "I understand why Abigail is frustrated. She has a right to be. I would love to keep talking to you, Brooke, but the clandestine secret keeping? I'm not cut out for that. It's unfair to do to someone." Erica flashes me a look that's supposed to mean "I'm sorry," I guess. "You can't outrun yourself forever."

Brooke stabs her chicken with her fork. "I'm doing a fucking fantastic job so far."

"And Isaiah," I say. "What the fuck?"

Her eyes are very red. "I don't know. He's not . . ." She takes another bite.

"He's making life harder for all three of us, yet somehow you're in his corner," Erica says, part statement, part question.

"You need to understand. When I escaped, it was all different." She puts a single fry into her mouth and blinks back tears. "This was a bad idea."

"We have one thing in common, Brooke." I hold up a finger for emphasis. "One. That's not enough to overcome everything else. This was *absolutely* a bad idea."

"I'm sure it hurt to go through all that," Erica says. "We can keep talking. I just hope you can—"

"No," Brooke says. Something shifts behind her eyes. Whoever we were just talking to is gone, and somebody else is here now. "I'm so glad we all had this evening together, and I dearly appreciate your candor. But maybe you're right. Maybe I'm exactly who you think I am."

As we exit, swimming man is gone, as is his briefcase. I guess that will forever remain a mystery.

Neither Erica nor I say anything until we're halfway back to Mitchell.

I use the long silence to scroll through endless apology texts from Caleb and a handful of *Are you okay??*'s from Megan. (I haven't been back to school in a week.) I scroll up to a few weeks ago, when we were texting all the time about Helen's "movement in the polls" (which was only ever Megan seeing marginally more Helen Swee yard signs). I guess that's another thing I've fucked up.

"You were a little hard on Brooke," Erica says. I almost forgot she was here.

"*I* was hard on *her*?"

"Trauma leaves scars. Hurt people hurt people." Erica nods, impressed with herself, like she's the first person to have ever said this.

"*I've* been through a lot. *You've* been through a lot. We're not ride or die for Isaiah Rose."

"People deserve to be seen for more than the worst things they do, Abigail. We're all complicated." She sighs. "Sometimes, you aren't very careful with people's hearts."

"For fuck's sake! If a bear is eating me, I don't stop to get to know it better. I stab the bear!"

"That's a good metaphor. I'm impressed."

"Fuck you, Erica." I should leave it there, but I can't. "What do you mean 'careful'?"

"You don't always think through the emotional ramifications of what you do, about how you might hurt other people."

"Is this about me giving fucking Brooke your fucking number? *Again*? That was *dumb*, not *cruel*."

"You were so desperate to stop listening to her life story that you didn't think through the consequences of what you were doing!"

"I didn't want to keep her story inside me! Do you get that?" I press my hand against an air vent spewing heat, so something hurts more than the inside of my head. "I didn't want to keep your story inside me either. I did, because you're my friend, but it was too big for just me, and the one time I screw up—the one time I made a mistake by telling another *trans* woman about you!—you lecture me about how I'm careless with people's hearts? You're such a dumb bitch!"

She shakes her head. "I suppose it's just being seventeen . . ."

"Motherfucker, don't put up the 'I'm an adult' shield. You broke up your ex's relationship with the father of her baby. You're just as much a careless, shitty teenager as me."

Erica swallows and stares at the road. "I knew what I was doing. I knew the risks."

"Did you? Because all you ever told me about her fiancé was that he liked Trump, and I was like, 'Seems bad,' and you were like, 'I know!' You're so eager to see Brooke's 'humanity' or whatever, but his doesn't matter?"

"Let's table this discussion," she says.

"You know what I learned tonight? I learned the world is made of walls, but all the doors are being held closed. We need some fucking hammers."

"Easy for you to say, 'Let's tear everything down!' You're seventeen."

"And that makes me an idiot?"

"It makes you seventeen." She takes a shuddering breath. "Maybe you're right. This should be the last time we hang out like this. I'm happy to help you with schoolwork, but this relationship was inappropriate to begin with, and it's only gotten more so."

"Fine by me." My voice cracks. "Except . . ."

I don't know what. Except I lose things, and I can't lose her? Except I seem to have broken every relationship in my life much more quickly than I built them, and I can't break this one too? Except we're teammates or at least fellow Chicago Bears fans? Except.

"Except you're my best friend," I finally say. "You're the only person I trust."

"You have lots of friends."

"Not anymore. Caleb only ever saw me as a character. Megan liked me, maybe, but only because I might help her achieve her goals. You cared. You listened. You understood."

She looks over at me. She looks like she might cry. "But Abigail," she says, "I haven't been very careful with your heart."

That's when I see the flash of fur and scream, "Erica, what the fuck!" and that's when she screams, "Oh, shit!" and that's when she hits the deer.

The deer is obliterated, a trail of blood on the road. Something was alive, and now it isn't. I can't stop crying about it the whole way home in the back seat of Constance's car after she picks Erica and me up.

Neither Erica nor Constance quite know what to do with the suddenly catatonic girl, so they leave me outside my house with promises to check in tomorrow. (I wonder how Erica will ask me how I'm doing after witnessing her murder a deer in a manner befitting an appropriate teacher-student relationship.) It's late enough that everybody might just be asleep, so I can cry in peace.

But when I get inside, the TV is on. Ron, Jennifer, and a bunch of Ron's friends sit in front of it, watching baseball guys spread a tarp over the field. "A fucking rain delay!" Ron says.

"Just prolonging the inevitable," says a depressed guy.

"It's not over yet! Cubbies can still pull this out," Ron says. "I just don't want to stay up late. Work tomorrow. Hey, Abigail!" His cheery tone drops when he sees me. "Uh. Welcome home."

Everybody else turns to me. From the way they look at me, I can tell I look like hell. "My friend hit a deer," I say. They relax. A girl crying because she was present for a deer dying? *That* they can properly file in their emotion boxes.

Jennifer stands from where she sits by Ron and guides me to the bathroom, wetting a washcloth. "You have blood all over you," she says. "Did you *punch* the deer?" I give her a tenth of a smile as she raises the washcloth to wipe me down.

"It happened so fast. And I tried to move the deer off the hood, but it was just dead. Which made it heavier. And I got blood all over me, and . . ."

"Was Caleb driving?"

"In case all the crying and me sleeping here the last two nights didn't indicate, that's not really happening anymore."

"Oh. I'm sorry." She shakes her head sadly.

"My friend Erica was driving."

"Ah, the mysterious Erica," she says with a smile. "Support-group Erica who isn't ready to meet anybody as herself yet. Will you tell her I'd love to meet her? Buy her something nice? I'm sure she's even more shaken up than you."

"She's really wonderful," I say. That's when I start crying about what I'm really sad about. "I fucked everything up, Jennifer. I fucked everything up, and I don't get it back."

She washes a smudge of blood from my cheek, then presses her hand against it before pulling me into a hug. "I don't believe that."

"I did. I had a whole life, and then . . ." I make an explosion noise. "Atomic bomb Abigail."

"Abigail." She hugs me more tightly, and I remember the first time she said that name into my ear, breath sticky with wine cooler, and I sob again. "Abigail, Abigail, Abigail. Shh, shh, shh." She rocks me back and forth, then almost carries me to my bed, where she lies down beside me and wraps her arms around me.

Erica

Friday,

November 4

"Come around here, Dad. I want you to see too." The obstetrician motions for Erica to stand behind Constance. Erica places a hand on her shoulder, and Constance's hand covers Erica's. The whole drive over to Sioux Falls, Constance stared out the window, talking rarely, and Erica tried to think of a way to casually interject, "By the way, you don't have to have this baby." But every time she started to say those words, they felt like a lie.

The wum wum wum wum sounds of muscles that will become a heart fill the room. In the pale white of the ultrasound, the fetus doesn't yet look like a person, but it's easy to imagine the shape of one if someone tells you where to look, like in a photo of a supposed ghost. Someday, Erica imagines, this ghost will be a person, and she will be its . . . parent. She tries to feel happy about this thought but fails. Guilt sidles in.

"It looks like a storm," Constance says quietly.

"A little bit," the obstetrician says. "But I see a healthy baby there."

"It does look vaguely mammalian," Erica says.

"Like a bush baby," Constance says.

The obstetrician laughs. "You two are a good couple. I see lots of laughter in Baby's future."

Constance closes her eyes and breathes deeply as the doctor takes more measurements. He jams the ultrasound device right up against the lower fold of where her small belly curves over her pelvis, and it must be terribly uncomfortable. Erica squeezes her shoulder again.

"What do you think, Dad? Are we going to have a little boy to play catch with?"

Erica, who cannot imagine she would have played catch with a son even as a cis man, chuckles in gender dysphoria. "We'll just be happy with a healthy baby."

"We're just past eleven weeks, Mom. We need to do bloodwork to check for genetic conditions, things that could go wrong. That bloodwork can tell us baby's gender too. Only if you want to."

"That sounds great," Erica says simultaneous to Constance saying, "No thanks." Constance adds, "And it's only what we *think* the baby's gender would be."

"Right. Yes," Erica says.

"The test is very accurate," the obstetrician says. "It will tell you the little one's gender."

"We're fine," Constance says. "But hold on. I need to take a picture to send to . . . family." Last night, she was in the bedroom for over an hour talking to John on the phone, finally emerging with the promise that he would not be there, so long as she took "lots of pictures."

Erica lets her mind go blank.

The room falls silent, save for the rhythmic throb of a heart-to-be and the occasional sound of a shutter from Constance's phone. Erica waits, and she squeezes Constance's shoulder again, and she wonders how much the being onscreen has changed in the handful of minutes she has been watching it.

"We could partition out some space in the living room for the nursery," Erica says. Constance, who is driving, has her lips in a thin line, her blinker signaling her intent to turn left. She's fourth in line, and the car at the front has yet to even cheat out. "We could buy some screens? It's not an ideal solution, I know."

"Fuck this," Constance says, throwing her right blinker on before swerving to cut off a car racing to beat a yellow light. She blasts through the light as it turns red, her car shuddering as it bottoms out upon entering the parking lot on the other side.

"Careful," Erica says.

Constance slams on the brakes to avoid hitting a car backing out of a parking spot. "Look where you're going, asshole!" She doesn't even look over at Erica before saying, "I'm being fucking careful, Erica. I am. We'll cut through the parking lot, and . . ." As with so many things Constance has said since they left the ultrasound, the sentence is left unfinished.

A couple walks through the parking lot. A man built like a frozen can of pop tucks a small TV under one arm and fishes for his keys in his pocket. A gaunt woman wearing a pink headscarf follows him and coughs into her hand. When he hears her, he sets the TV on the ground and goes back to her, putting his arms on either side of her.

Erica feels an ancient pang of guilt. She failed at being that man for Constance.

"We'd have to move the TV and buy some new curtains too," Erica says. Constance looks confused, so she adds, "We'll want the baby in the far corner of the living room where the TV is."

"We need groceries, right? Should we go to Hy-Vee?" Constance eases to a stop and waves her hand to signal that a family should cross in front of her. The father (carrying a bag) raises a single hand in thanks, as a little girl dressed in a bedraggled Princess Elsa costume races ahead, arms outstretched in the universal symbol of "I'm flying now."

"What time's your support group anyway?"

"Seven," Erica says. "And yeah, maybe groceries."

Before Constance can lay off the brake, a couple incredibly attractive teenagers dash out in front of her, fingers barely intertwined. The guy (letterman's jacket, single pop bottle in hand) grabs the girl's wrist, to pull her into a kiss.

"I see these couples, and I realize they look at us and think we're another boring straight couple like them," Erica says.

"Mmm," Constance says. "Which we aren't. Of course."

"Right." Erica tries to imagine her and Constance in a year, leaving a store together, both dressed in their late-autumn finest, one of them pushing a stroller. She tries to picture anyone other than the version of herself who looks like a boring male English teacher, but it still feels too difficult.

"We should stop at Michaels to see about screens for the nursery."

"Erica, I cannot tell you how little I want to talk about this right now," Constance says as she enters another long line of people trying and failing to turn left.

Erica extends her arm to the back of the shelf, fingers closing around the last bag of cheesy popcorn available in the whole of the enormous Hy-Vee they've stopped at. "This might be the last bag in the entire state. I'm going to ration it so that it lasts until the baby's born. I'll drop three kernels into your mouth each night before bed."

"My hero," Constance says. "-Ine. My heroine."

Being in the grocery store seems to have lightened Constance's mood. In college, Constance would sometimes call Erica at three in the morning to ask if she wanted to wander around the twenty-four-hour supermarket. They would buy packs of store-baked cookies, then drive out beyond the edge of Brookings and wait for the sun to rise. In none of Erica's memories do these adventures culminate in anything more than kissing. Sometimes, she thinks that what Constance needed more than anything back then was a friend.

Constance sways down the aisle, slowly placing one foot in front of the other. Somewhere in the last few days, the hitch in her step has returned, but she doesn't seem bothered. She spins on her heel to face Erica, who pushes the cart. "Who's going to carry the groceries?"

"Me, probably. Seeing as you're pregnant."

"I'm pregnant, not helpless. What I mean is: Who will carry the groceries, after you . . . you know?" Constance clears her throat in a way that keys Erica into the fact they are talking about the possibility (no, the *likelihood*) of her public-facing transition. "You used to carry the heavy things when we'd go to the store. In the future, when you're less strong . . . will you still carry the heavy things? Is that offensive? Don't worry, I know you're still you, blah, blah, blah."

These last few days, Constance has tried to press Erica not on the grand sweep of her gender identity but on the smaller, more practical elements, trying to make the enormous and theoretical into something plausible and even mundane. (Then again, Erica thinks, she's doing just that with the baby.) "I think I get it," she says. "I know how to be your husband, even though I'm not great at it." Erica nods to a passing mother and daughter. "I don't know how to do . . . other things."

Even in this early stage, when Erica has come out to so few people, when her secret is still relatively (if poorly) contained, she has begun to feel the fuzzy darkness that lies on the other side of the words, "I'm a woman." To say "I'm a woman" is simply to lump yourself in with another four billion or so people. It's another thing altogether to figure out who *you* are, and that is where Erica keeps getting tripped up.

The thing she has said every time she has come out is, "I'm still me, just more myself." But the version of herself that everybody knows is someone who takes up as little space as possible. She has scrupulously spent her adulthood asking other people to set her preferences, boundaries, and desires for her. In so doing, she has asked the world to construct a chalk outline of herself that she can lay within to attract as little attention as possible. To be more herself, however, is to stick a toe over the edge of the outline, then a finger, then a whole arm, until she's left it behind. To be more oneself, she realizes now, can be seen as a great violence by anyone who thinks they understand how the world works. Or how you work.

Constance forces the issue as she peruses the coffee section. "So, when are you planning on starting? Becoming less strong? Don't you need meds and stuff? Don't you *want* them?"

Erica knows she doesn't need to take hormones to be trans, nor does she need to be out publicly to be herself. But she doesn't really *believe* either of those statements. Abigail has been wrong about several things but not this one: The Erica who never comes out to everyone then lives her life as a woman *is* deeply annoying. How many people would she force to keep her secret and ask to call her one thing in private and another in public?

"I'll make an appointment someday—just not anytime soon. I'm taking it slow for now." She sees Constance's expression. "So I can keep my job. So we can save up for the kid. I'm not any less me if I'm only myself to a few people for a few years."

"Glad you've got it all figured out," Constance says. She strides to the end of the aisle and disappears into the next. Erica chases after her, one of the shopping cart's wheels juddering.

"I'm not saying I'll *never* do it," she says when she catches up to Constance. "I'm saying there are a lot of other things on my plate right now."

"Is one of the people you're going to ask to keep your secret a three-year-old?" Constance says, voice bitter. "Or are you going to let them call you Dad and roll with it until the world has been made safe enough for you to be the last trans person to ever come out?"

Erica feels the familiar panic rising again. "Can you maybe not talk so loudly?"

Constance whispers, "Fuck you," before walking away at a steady clip.

"This is my decision!" Erica says when she catches up again, out of breath. "You don't get to make it for me."

"No, I don't. But the decision you make traps me inside of it because I was stupid enough to fall in love with you." She drops four packages of ice cream sandwiches in the cart. "Twice."

"I'm not trapping you! I just want to take my time!"

Constance holds up her phone, a photo of the ultrasound on it. "No part of you looks at me and this baby and thinks, *Oh, good, the perfect disguise*? You're using me and you're using *it* to *hide*."

"I'll carry the fucking groceries forever if that's what you want!"

"Fucking fantastic! So glad I get one thing!" Constance says so loudly it carries over the Christmas music overhead. Her eyes scan the store, seeing the other shoppers as if for the first time. She sags and slides her phone back into her back pocket, then places her hand atop Erica's where it holds the cart. "I'm sorry. Pregnancy hormones."

"My *goodness*," Bernadette says, handing the phone back to Constance. "They already look like a little fighter, just like their mothers. Now, *where* is our *waiter*?" No matter where Bernadette goes, she believes the service has gone to shit.

After Constance blurted out she was pregnant in the middle of support group, horrified as the other attendees shared their congratulations ("Thank you!" she'd said, voice pinched. "Somebody else talk!"), Bernadette insisted they celebrate by going out for pie. Then she had given Erica a raised eyebrow that Erica had no idea how to interpret.

"We're excited." Erica drapes an arm over the back of the booth behind Constance, then removes it because it feels too possessive and masculine. She senses Constance's tightness next to her and adds, "More or less."

"Wonderful," Bernadette says. "More or less."

"Thank you," Constance says. Her voice sounds very far away. "Your support means a lot. To both of us." Bernadette smiles warmly at Constance, then folds her hands and looks at Erica.

"So. If you're having a baby, that gives you one hell of a ticking clock, my girl. Better start thinking about how you're going to come out!"

"Not yet," Erica says. Constance scoffs.

"Some decisions make themselves for us," Bernadette says. "I don't think children are well-served by parents living half-lives. Mine sure as shit weren't. Give your little one all of yourself. It's what you owe them."

Erica looks at the cream swirling in her coffee. "I don't like not being in control. I don't want to lose everything. I like my life." Constance scoffs again.

"The soon-to-be mother says she hates not being in control? Good luck with that!" Bernadette smiles. "Understand this: The world tells us we will lose everything, but look right next to you. The person you love most is still here. So already you haven't lost everything. But you will lose *something*. All of us do. But we have no idea what it will be. I know how terrifying that is."

"Wasn't this an argument to get me to come out?"

"I lost my wife. I lost all three of my kids. I lost my siblings. I lost my job. But then I found new work I loved more. Bex came back to me, then my other two. My brother and I are going to grab lunch over Christmas."

Bernadette reaches over to take Erica's hand. Constance stares intently at her water glass. "Transitioning is like running a long series of tests on the old proverb about loving something and setting it free. I opened my rib cage, and a whole mess of birds flew out of it. Some came back bearing olive branches. Those that didn't? Oh well! Their loss!"

Erica looks outside to where a light snow falls. "I'll definitely lose my job. I'll lose . . ." She trails off at the endless list of potential losses. She looks to Constance for moral support, but Constance is looking at the sonogram on her phone.

"Girl, I was a *minister* in my old life. Don't tell me about being scared to lose your job!" Erica, deeply embarrassed at having never bothered to ask Bernadette about her past, says nothing, so

Bernadette plows ahead. "Do you know how many deathbeds I sat at all those years? And do you know what those dying people regretted most? All the lives they never led because they thought they might regret them. I realized God gave me one life, and he expected me to use it well. Fuck anybody who says otherwise."

Erica tries to laugh, but she can't. She realizes how tightly her hand grips Constance's knee, and she thinks, briefly, about how Brooke partially fossilized herself to support the weight of her own secrets. "You make it sound so *easy*."

"It will seem easy once you've done it and impossible until you have. But you *can* do it. Your imagination simply isn't big enough yet. You'll see."

The pie arrives, and Constance squeezes Erica's hand lightly. "Can I get out? I need to use the bathroom."

It's only once Constance is halfway to the restroom that Bernadette says, "I think she's crying."

Constance calling the being on the ultrasound a storm cloud.

Constance rewriting history to give Erica the gift of herself.

Constance leaning out on the steps of a tractor, then calling Erica beautiful.

Constance telling Erica she is pregnant.

Constance talking to Erica as a friend, not a spouse, the night they separated.

Constance never wanting kids (and believing Erica always wanted them).

Constance using her index fingers to wipe tears from her eyes after they saw *Cabaret* on their honeymoon.

Constance painting Erica's nails.

Constance wandering around a supermarket at 3:00 a.m. freshman year, carrying a coconut under her arm and saying she will figure out what to do with it when she gets home. (She never does.)

Constance sitting beside Erica on the first day of Intro to Theater.

The Constance before that is a phantom to Erica, but she ran from the home she grew up in. Erica has always imagined this happening at dawn, Constance sneaking out and getting into the shitty car she drove all through college, a handful of boxes inside, driving east from Boise until she found another space lonely enough in which to get lost.

Imagine that girl, Erica thinks. *Imagine all those women. Place them on a continuum. Try to make them turn into the one who has spent all day quietly breaking down. Then try to turn them into a woman who slides neatly into the role of mother and wife, who hides inside the life she landed in. You can't*, Erica thinks. *That woman is a chalk outline*.

Erica imagines the future again. No matter how many times she tries to picture her and Constance with a child, she imagines herself as a man. Of course she does. She knows that Constance, mother Constance, is living a deep and fundamental lie, so Erica must make her imagined self a lie too. To at long last move forward, then, maybe Erica must also remind Constance that her life and her choices are her own.

To love someone, she thinks, *means being able to set them free, yes. But not just from you. From your expectations too.* She pushes into the women's restroom where Constance waits.

The faucet runs as Constance stares into the mirror. Her eyes are red. When Erica enters, she smiles weakly. "I do love you," Constance says. "More than anything."

"I know," Erica says.

"I don't like talking about it because I don't like thinking about it. When I try, it starts to feel too big." Constance leans over the counter, her heels lifting from the ground. "Too many people know about the pregnancy. Once those people know the baby's never coming, then they'll never see *me* again, just the thing I did. But that's the fucking thing. If I have this baby, all people will see is *them*. I'm not me anymore, no matter what I do."

"Okay. Who are you? What do you want?"

"I wish I knew. I was my parents' daughter and then your wife and then John's . . ." Constance closes her eyes. "Planned Parenthood in Minneapolis is open tomorrow. I told myself when this faucet shut off, I would get my keys and drive up there. And then I thought about how unfair it would be to strand you here, and I thought about how excited you are about being a mom and buying screens and rearranging the living room, and I thought about how nobody would ever look at me the same way again." She swallows. "And then the faucet wouldn't turn off."

"Try taking two steps back."

Constance takes two steps back and collides with Erica, who wraps her arms around her waist. "I don't want to have this baby." Constance starts to cry again.

"I know." Erica digs in her pocket where she placed Constance's keys when she left the table. "Here. Go. I'll come with you. If you want."

The faucet finally shuts off. "I need to do this alone, so I don't lose my nerve," Constance says.

"Then I'll be fine here," Erica says. She feels something in Constance release. "I'll crash with Bernadette, and Helen can pick me up in the morning."

Constance gives Erica a small kiss. "I don't care if I lose everyone else because I know I'll have you."

"Same," Erica says. "Now go."

Constance hits the door to the bathroom at a run. Erica takes two steps forward, and the faucet turns on again. The irony is that after all of that, she ended up in the same place. She always used to tell Constance she didn't want to have kids as much as she wanted to be with her, and now, finally, she knows that to be true.

A toilet flushes in one of the stalls, and a tall woman exits and glares at her. "Happy Friday!" Erica says, and the woman hisses, "This is the *ladies* room," and scurries out.

Helen picks Erica up just before seven the next morning, already two cups of coffee into her day. "I'm only bailing your ass out because you're a good girlfriend, E. But you need to make fifteen campaign stops with me before I'm bringing you home. Sorry. Those are the rules."

"I'm just E now?"

"When I've had this much coffee, you are."

Erica takes a sip from the cup Helen brought her and thinks about all the people she's been waiting to meet but kept herself from finding by being so scared of what she might lose. She has held so many people back beyond just herself.

"I'll help," she says. "But I need your help too. I'm going to do something very stupid."

Abigail

Friday,

November 4

I dare myself to answer the phone. It's the eighth time Mom has called this week, the second today. If I answer, she'll just say the wrong name, and I'll have to hang up. I should block her, again, but some part of me still wants her to magically not suck. That part hovers her finger over the answer button.

I drop my phone and flop back on my bed. I'm alone. Jennifer and Ron, concerned about my overall mood, insisted I go to school again after missing the last six days. They watched me go, then I waited for them to leave for work and doubled back. Then I slept until two because the seventh day is when you rest.

I'm getting tired of staying here all by myself with my worst thoughts, to be honest, but if I went to school, I might be tempted to patch things up with Megan or Erica. I might even get back together with Caleb. And I can't do that.

The only problem that me and everyone I know has *is* me. If I hadn't been trans, or if I had just sucked it up and tried not to be, or if I hadn't moved in with Jennifer, or if I hadn't let Megan get the wrong idea about us being best friends, or if I hadn't let Caleb think he could take whatever he wanted from me, or if I hadn't let Erica come to rely on me so much, everyone would have been better off. Deep down, all I ever want is to help people, and all I ever do is fuck them over.

So I'm going to solve everybody's problems for them. If there's no Abigail around to worry about, then they can get on with their lives.

No, not that. Jesus. Who do you think I am?

I'm going to run away tonight. I'm going to woodwork until I can't woodwork anymore. If fucking Brooke Daniels can be so good at it, I can be a world champion. I told you I would do this, and you only have yourself to blame if you didn't believe me.

About ten minutes after four, someone hammers at our door. "Abigail?" Caleb says. "I know you're in there."

I peek through the window. He paces back and forth on the front stoop, then knocks again. "Abigail? All I want to do is talk. I'm worried about you."

I throw the door open. "Well, don't be. I'm fine. Go away."

He looks at me. I've worn these pajamas three straight days, save my brief "going to school" disguise I put on for Jennifer this morning. My hair is greasy, and my skin is greasier, and I'm sure I smell. "Yeah, you look fine."

"I'm *fine*."

"Okay. But . . ." He pulls a messy and rumpled sheet of notebook paper out of his pocket. "Can I read you something?"

The wind hits him, and he hunches his shoulders against it. He's still so hot, which is annoying. "You might as well come in." I show him into the living room. He sits on the couch. I don't. "Well?"

He unfolds the paper. "Dear Abigail—"

"If this is a letter, shouldn't *I* read it?"

"I would rather . . ." He clears his throat and continues. "When I was born, I also had a different name. I love my life, but I want to know that name."

"Okay, first of all, that's a totally different situation and—"

"I am aware now," he reads, raising his voice, "that these are very different situations. My mistake was in thinking you wanted a past as much as I do."

It's not an awful start, so I sit down on the other end of the couch. Our eyes lock briefly. He looks back down.

"You had a past, and it was awful. You long only for your future. You told me that a million times, and I didn't listen. I was wrong not to. I fucked up, Abigail. I'm sorry. I do not expect you to take me back, but I hope we can remain friends. I will spend every day of my life making this up to you. Love, Caleb."

I want this to be okay. I want him to hold me for so long that he shoves all the parts of me that he stole back into my heart. All I would have to do is reach out and touch his hand. But the same piece of me that won't answer my mom's calls stops me.

"Making what up to me, exactly?"

"I deadnamed you in my essay. It was a fucked-up thing to do. I'm sorry." That sounded rehearsed, but maybe he wanted to make sure he said exactly the right thing? Except he keeps going. "Maybe I was jealous you knew all your names? And I thought it would only be read by five or six people. And I thought . . . it would be clever."

Clever? Fucking writers.

I need him to go. I need him to go, so I can leave town. That means I need to be a fucking bitch. It's what I do.

"Northwestern's your dream school, right?"

"Yeah! So, I got stupid."

"I'd hate to see you not achieve your dreams." I stand and stretch out my arms. "Hug?"

He pulls me close. It's so warm and calming. My heart slows to the same rhythm as his, and his lips press against the top of my head. I could kiss him. Maybe I *should* kiss him, call this whole stupid plan off.

But he will swallow me whole again if I let him.

"I knew you'd understand it was a mistake," he says.

I look up at him. I feel dizzy. "I hope you get in." He smiles, and I can feel him floating to the ceiling. "And I hope every second you spend on that campus, you think about how you betrayed me to get there." He gasps like I stabbed him and releases the hug. "I hope you never enjoy your dream school because I'm haunting you the whole time. Good luck."

He gulps for air. "Nobody ever saw me like you did. I never *let* anybody see me like . . ."

"Telling everybody my parents forced me to be a boy isn't *seeing* me, Caleb."

"I get it!" he says. "I get it now! I get it, I get it! But only five or—"

I point to the door. "*Go*. Before I make up some weird rumor about your dick."

He looks at me, eyes filled with tears. It's all I can do not to cry myself, but he finally turns on his heel and leaves. He drops his letter on the welcome mat.

That night, Jennifer and Ron disappear into their bedroom and talk for a long time. Then Ron goes into the bathroom and turns on the shower. I put my ear to the door and hear him talking to someone, probably his dad, probably because they haven't hired a lawyer yet and they'll need money to.

All because of me.

"Can I sleep over at Megan's tonight?" I ask Jennifer.

She stops cutting the plastic wrap off a frozen pizza. "Aren't you two fighting?"

"We made up."

She hasn't smiled much since I got back from Caleb's, but she smiles now. "Of course."

"Great. We're meeting at the movies, so I'd better get going."

"Have fun!"

There's a bus to Denver leaving from a local gas station just before 11:30 p.m. I grab a couple hundreds out of Ron's underwear drawer, where he thinks his little wad of cash is completely hidden. Just enough to hold me until I can get a job out there.

I've done the bare minimum of research on bus travel, so I don't know if I need an ID to get on the bus. If I do, the only one I have is for a former occupant of this body. I dig into the back of my closet and find the boy clothes I wore when I moved in with Jennifer. I pull them on, then drag my hair back into a ponytail. One of Ron's Chicago Bears caps completes my disguise.

I don't look like a boy at all. I look like a girl running away from home. But it doesn't matter. People will see a boy the second I tell them I am one. Gender is a magic trick, and I'm amazing at performing it.

I wait until Jennifer disappears back into the bedroom again to call out, "Bye!" and I go before I think about how leaving here means leaving Jennifer, who has been pretty okay to me, all things considered.

My shaky breath mists in the air outside. The walk to the gas station is just over two miles, but I have hours to kill. I take my time. I don't want to remember Mitchell, but I don't want to *not* remember it either. I put Mitski on my headphones and try to remember things not as they are but as they could have been.

Turns out I have way more time than I need, so I decide to see a movie after all. It's a superhero thing about a guy who can make orange circles in the air. I don't like it much, but it's long enough to get me closer to my ultimate escape and distracting enough to quiet any objections in my mind.

When I leave, it's nine thirty. The streets have gotten quiet, and the only places with any people in them are bars. Without really thinking about it, I start to walk home, then remember what I'm doing and resume walking to the gas station. When I walk past the World's Only Corn Palace—it's a building decorated with corn; it's not *that* cool—I realize the lights are on in the theater across the street, the one Erica spends half her life at.

Megan's car is parked out front.

The theater door opens, and she emerges from it, struggling with an enormous American flag. She gets it outside, and the door swings shut behind her. She tries the door, but it won't open. So she leans her head back and screams, "*FUCK!*" then looks all around (probably because she thinks she might get arrested for shouting) and sees me.

I look at the clock on my phone. Almost ten. Plenty of time still. Maybe Megan will even give me a ride. So I wave.

"Am I hallucinating you?" she says.

"Yes. Do you need help?"

She looks like she's going to say something angry, and I would probably just go if she did. Instead, she holds out a ring of keys. "Can you re-unlock the theater for me? I brought five different American flags and four South Dakota flags. I'm mixing and matching to find just the right ones."

I'm going to say I can do that. But what comes out, for some reason, is, "I've missed you."

She rolls her eyes. "Just hold the door, okay?"

Once we get her supplies inside, I see what a mess she's already made. A couple podiums turned on their sides lie in the shadows of the fake buildings that cover the stage. (I hope Megan didn't build an entire, way-too-elaborate set for this thing.) Red, white, and blue ribbons decorate half the front of the stage, but they taper off, as though Megan gave up on that project and turned to operation flag.

"I wanted to try to finish setting everything up tonight. All by myself." She smiles tightly, like this is how she always wanted it to be. "You haven't been in school. Like, at all." She looks over my very bad boy disguise. "Are you dressed as the Zodiac Killer?"

"Shouldn't the rest of the club help you with this?"

"The club is just me now. Most members were only there for Caleb. And he was only there for you. Courtney and I tried to make a go of it for a couple sessions, but after we established democracy was great, we didn't have much left to discuss. Even Mr. Skyberg lost interest. Another failed experiment for Megan Osborne."

"Sorry I stopped going. Like you said, I've barely been in school."

"You stopped going after you ripped Isaiah Rose a new one and turned yourself into a Caleb accessory."

I stopped going that long ago? I guess I did. Huh.

"When something makes you feel uncomfortable, you stop doing it," she says. "I should have realized that would apply to me eventually."

"It . . ." I can't finish the sentence. She might be right.

"Whatever. Help me move these podiums."

The podiums are heavy, and after we have them set up, we're sweaty and gross. She fans herself with her shirt. Then we finish hanging the ribbons and positioning the flags. We're about to start hand-painting signs that read "NO APPLAUSE, PLEASE" when I check my phone. It's 10:45 p.m. Now or never.

"I'm sorry," I say. "For forgetting about you. For making Caleb my personality." I swallow. "He and I broke up anyway."

"So I'm enough for you again?"

"It's not like that."

"Sure feels like that. I thought we were friends, and then you just ditched me, which . . . whatever. Your prerogative."

"No," I say, but I can't figure out how to fix it. So instead, I admit it. "I'm running away from home. The bus leaves at eleven thirty."

She wobbles and grabs the podium. "Well, don't do *that*."

"If I had left town without getting to tell you I was sorry . . . well, you were the *only* one I wanted to say that to." (Is that true? I guess it's true? Can you fact-check me on this?) "I know I fucked you over. But that's what I do."

"You didn't fuck me over. We had a *fight*. Friends have fights."

"Now you're contradicting yourself from two seconds ago, but whatever. I *do* fuck everybody over. I made my sister basically destroy her entire life and marry a guy fifteen years older than her so she could keep me safe, and it didn't even work. That's just exhibit A."

"*You* didn't do that. *She* did that."

"Well, it was really fucking stupid! If I'm not here, people won't jump in front of the Abigail train and get run over."

Megan leans against the podium again. "Don't go," she says so quietly I almost don't hear her.

"I can't miss the bus." I pick up my backpack. "Why shouldn't I go?"

"Because I don't want you to?" She laughs, like she thinks it's a bad answer, but it's not. "We had a fight, and if you leave, that fight lasts forever. And I'll say, 'Oh, I once had this amazing friend named Abigail,' and it will always be 'had,' past tense, and I won't know if you're alive or dead, and I need to know if you're alive or dead." She gulps. "You're my best friend. So don't go?"

"Be friends with Courtney! As established, I'm a crushing disappointment."

"Oh my *God*," she says. "People *love you*, Abigail. *I* love you. I realize that's inconvenient for you to hear, but it's true. My life is better with you in it. You listen to me when I have a problem, and you don't just expect me to pay for everything, and you make me laugh. These last two weeks when we've barely talked have been the shittiest of my life. So don't fucking go."

"But what do I do if I don't go? I don't want to *be here*, Megan. So tell me what to do!"

She swallows. "Here's what you should do: Help me finish painting these signs. That's all that needs to be done right now. And then we'll go sleep somewhere and wake up in the morning and come back to do the rest. And we'll do it together. Okay?" Her voice wavers. "If I know you at all, you don't even have a ticket yet."

I drop my bag. "Twist my arm."

She turns to the other podium, and she looks so small. There's an enormous American flag behind her. I don't understand how she doesn't let the world swallow her up. Before I know what I'm doing, I hug her from behind, tightly as I can. She puts her hand on my arm and gives a single little squeeze, and then we get to work.

Ron and Jennifer don't know about my near-runaway status, but Megan still insists we surprise them with breakfast foods just in case. So when Jennifer opens the door and says, "Megan! What a nice surprise!" I'm carrying donuts and coffee from Casey's.

After breakfast, Jennifer clears her throat. "We think things are going to be okay."

"We won't have to go to court, and your parents won't get the cops involved," Ron says.

My heart pounds. "How?"

"They were playing chicken," Jennifer says. "They're not going to risk the scandal of having the cops forcibly return you to them. Can't have the store's sales suffer."

"*And* cops are lazy," Ron says. "My brother's first rule of lawyering."

"Plus, Mom and Dad had about as much money to hire a lawyer as we did, so when Ron and I started getting serious about doing so . . ."

"You realize my dad's a lawyer, right?" Megan says. "Not family law, obviously, but he could sign scary letters and stuff."

"It won't come to that," Jennifer says. "I called Mom last night, and we made a deal. I'll keep her up to date on your grades, and she wants you to call once a week. She won't say your name—I know—but she promises to at least not say the old one." She grimaces. "And we're all going to spend Christmas together."

"Gross."

"But Ron and I will be there, and we'll leave the second you ask. Okay? Then, come January, you're an adult, and none of this matters. So keep your nose clean. Go to school Monday. Don't give Mom any reasons to doubt my maternal instincts, and it's going to be fine."

"Mom will have some other fucking scheme. She always does."

"Probably, but the three of us—" Jennifer nods to Megan "—the four of us . . . can handle it."

I let out a breath I've been holding for two years and then notice I'm still wearing an ancient Nickelback T-shirt I inherited from one of my older brothers.

"I need to change," I say.

"I was going to say." Jennifer smiles and pops a final donut into her mouth.

Monday morning, Megan picks me up for school. For a second, I think she's going to have to wheel me in on a cart, but she finally coaxes me inside. She vibrates with nerves about the debate tonight and the election tomorrow, but I manage to calm her down a little bit. (I'll figure out this "best friend" thing yet.)

All I have to do is make it to January, I think. *I have this life, crummy as it can be, and maybe it doesn't have to be a prison.* Before I can contemplate that too much more, I'm interrupted by Erica marching down the hallway. She gives me a single nod and says, "It's good to see you back." She leans in like she might give me a hug, changes the movement to an awkward handshake, then disappears into Mr. DeWaard's office, the door slamming behind her.

Megan gives me a "the fuck was that?" look. A few students laugh at Erica's weird and unusual display of emotion.

My phone buzzes with a text from Helen, of all people. *Hey, look out for Erica today, okay? She's going to blow up her life.* And another. *Which is impressive!!!!!!*

And I know just what that dumb bitch is going to do.

Erica

Monday,

November 7

Erica barely slept last night. Constance had been unable to schedule an appointment until this morning, which left Erica alone all weekend, knowing what she had to do come Monday morning and preparing for the worst. The lack of sleep gives Hank's cheery office the quality of a bad dream. Sun filters in through the windows, hitting a lonely cutout of a smiling turkey in a pilgrim's hat hung on the wall.

Hank enters, whistling "Hail to the Chief" in an accidental minor key. He sees Erica and smiles. "Mr. Skyberg! Need something?"

"I was hoping we could talk," she says. "I have some personal news."

"Lucky you, I'm free all morning," Hank says.

A headache spreads behind Erica's eyes. She is here to commit career suicide and hope she will get points for technique.

She finds herself thinking about Bernadette's dream about the flood. She thinks about watching the waters rise and realizing they are coming for *you*. Erica hasn't gotten that far. She has been stuck, always, in neutral, just far enough away from herself to watch the waters carry her away.

Hank settles behind his large desk, which is covered in perfectly aligned stacks of paper. It sits in the exact center of the room. (Erica would not be surprised if tape measures were involved.) "So what's this personal news? I heard you and Constance got back together. Good for you! Didn't I tell you God always has a plan?"

"This has nothing to do with Constance, actually."

Hank frowns and folds his hands together, eyebrows knitting in worry. "Are you sick?"

Erica shakes her head. She hears the door open and someone barge in. Abigail stands in the room, eyes wide, breath ragged.

"Um. Uh. Skyberg, Megan and I need you. It's a . . . Students for Democracy emergency."

"Abigail," Hank says, sounding, as always, like he's been told he must call her Abigail.

"If you come with me, we can save democracy!"

Abigail catches Erica's eye and gives an almost-imperceptible nod toward the hallway. The light hits Abigail's face just so, and Erica realizes how much she has missed her these last few days. Their friendship has always been transitory, yes, and Erica, greedy, tried to squeeze too much out of it. But that doesn't mean their friendship isn't *real*.

She knows what Abigail is trying to tell her. Erica imagines her saying, "You don't have to do this, you dumb bitch." She imagines standing. She imagines telling Hank that she was hoping to ask for some time off to work on her relationship, maybe in the new year. She imagines going out into the hall. She imagines keeping her job this year, another year, another year, another year. She imagines clutching her life in her fist until blood runs over her hand. She imagines seeing Abigail every couple years at Christmas and being glad the girl got on with her life. She imagines the safety in knowing every moment of her life before it happens.

She smiles at Abigail, and she realizes how close she is to crying.

"I'm transgender," Erica says, still looking at Abigail, who now steps fully inside the room and closes the door behind her. Erica turns back to Hank. "I intend to start hormone treatments soon."

Hank shifts in his seat and clears his throat.

"I don't expect anything from the district but a change in my name and pronouns. Ms. Skyberg instead of Mr. Skyberg. That sort of thing."

"What . . . sort of . . . name . . . were you thinking?" As a first question from Hank, it isn't great, but it isn't a disaster either. It at least has an answer.

"Erica. My name is Erica." Abigail, the first person she ever told that name to, is watching, but Erica doesn't dare look at her. It's enough to know she has a witness to whatever happens next.

"Abigail," Hank says, "maybe you should go."

"No. I'm here for Erica," Abigail says, putting a hand on her shoulder. Hank rolls his eyes.

Erica, still nominally in control of the conversation, plows ahead. "The district's health plan covers hormone treatments and bottom surgery—"

"The sex-change operation?" Hank says.

"We don't call it that," Erica says, and Abigail snorts just loudly enough to draw Hank's eyes in her direction. "These treatments are already covered by our insurance, so you don't have to worry about me getting special dispensation."

Hank leans back in his chair. "How long have you been thinking about . . . this sort of thing?"

"To be honest, there are three answers. I finally admitted it to myself in August. I realized I was probably trans in 2008. I've known my whole life. All three are right. It's just a question of how much I was lying to myself."

"What does Constance make of all this?"

"Constance supports me. She loves me and wants me to be happy."

"Huh." Hank shakes his head. "And what makes you think you're not just deluded?"

Erica takes a long sip of coffee, hearing the dull wash of it inside her mouth. "Because I know I'm not. I could point you to scientific research or philosophical treatises. But the best proof is that until a few minutes ago, you still thought I was smart and capable."

"I didn't have all the information a few minutes ago," Hank says.

Erica can hear it now, the roar of water over the horizon, the trees ripped from the ground. She is standing here all alone. Except she isn't. Abigail's hand is still on her shoulder.

"Erica isn't deluded," Abigail says. "I'm not deluded."

"But you are," Hank says.

Erica expected him to yell. She expected him to throw her out of his office. She hadn't expected this cruel calm. She thinks about tsunamis, about the people who say that before the wave hits the shore, everything goes deathly quiet—no birds, no animals, no wind, just long, echoing silence ahead of the flood. She is in that silence right now. Whoever she is preemptively begins kicking as the waters rise.

"Tell you what," Hank says. "Don't do it. Don't do it, and I'll pretend this conversation never happened. Abigail here will graduate and go off to college, and you can keep working, no problem." Kick. Kick. Kick. Kick. Something's coming. "You'll get therapy to learn how to deal with this problem. I can recommend a good counselor. My church sponsors a program, even. If you want to join my prayer group, I think it would really benefit you."

"I can't do that," Erica says. Abigail's hand squeezes her shoulder, and she grips it a few seconds before releasing it.

The day after she self-accepted, Erica sat down and did the math. She had lied to herself for thirty-five years, eight months, one week, and three days. She has lived two months, three weeks, and one day as herself. Except she has been lying a little to herself all that time, too, treating what she is doing as something theoretical instead of something real. "Erica" isn't something she can control if need be. Erica is *her*. She almost cries again with relief as she realizes it. She has waited so long to simply occupy her own body, and now, finally, on the verge of losing so much, she is *here*. *Swim, girl*, she thinks. *Swim*.

"Well," Hank says. "You'd better take the rest of the week off while we figure this out."

And for the first time, I can see the flood.

Being myself feels a little like being high. Hank explains the ways the district handles paid leave—"at least until we get this sorted out"—and I can't stop staring at my hand on my pant leg. That's *my* hand. Why didn't I paint my nails today? That would have really freaked him out.

Even though I'm not officially fired, Hank acts like it's a foregone conclusion, enlisting his secretary to watch me gather my things and make sure I leave the premises. He tells her I'm dealing with a "family matter." He thinks he's dealing with this in a "compassionate" manner, but he can't keep this quiet forever. I won't let him.

Abigail meets me near the exit as I tote my box out to the car. "I'm really good at biting," she says. "Want me to bite him?"

"You should go," I say. "I'm fine, okay? And I meant it: It's good to see you back in school. Go live your life. Don't worry about me."

"Why would I start worrying about you now?" Abigail says, but her eyes say something else.

I set the box down on the floor and give her a hug. It feels good, real, solid. I imagine a world where we are the same age, both seventeen or thirty-five. I can almost see the contours of it. I don't know if we are friends in that life. We never really had that much in common but this one thing.

But this one thing is a pretty big fucking thing.

"You're a good kid, Abigail. Don't forget that." I pick up the box again.

"I lied," she says. "I do worry about you. Sometimes, I think I worry about everyone."

"I know. Like I said: You're a good kid." I back into the door to the parking lot, stepping into the sunlight, and I leave Mitchell High School for what's almost certainly the last time.

"Good evening, and welcome to the District Twenty state senate debate," the moderator says from the stage. Just offstage, where she doesn't think anybody can see her, Megan mouths the introduction along with the moderator. Abigail stands just behind her, occasionally nudging Megan and grinning, as if to say, "Look at this. You did this." When they made up, I don't know, but I'm glad they did. Constance, sitting beside me, stops looking at polling data for the presidential race and puts her phone back in her purse.

The woman sitting on the other side of me clears her throat. She looks familiar in the way a long-lost relative looks familiar. She's surprisingly tall, with round cheeks that suggest she's lost a lot of weight recently, and she has spiky hair fringing toward silver. Her husband glares toward the stage, mechanically chewing something. He folds his arms over his beer belly, only disturbing them to furiously clap when Isaiah tosses some red meat to the crowd.

The spotlights trained on Helen and Isaiah leave John's enormous, impractical set in menacing silhouette behind them, like it might rise from its perch and snatch them in its talons.

Helen stands at her podium and sorts through her notes. When Isaiah answers yet another question ("Should the state impose a new half-cent sales tax?") by talking about abortion, she once again misses an opening she could capitalize on. I know she doesn't think she can win the election, but she does think she can win this debate. And she's losing. She keeps getting dragged down to the ground he wants to play on, and she's obviously furious about that.

"Isn't he good at this?" the woman sitting next to me says. I nod because Isaiah is indeed very good at whatever this is.

And then it happens.

"It gets worse than that, Ms. Swee," Isaiah says. (I've lost track of the question he's answering.) "I can see why we all might sympathize with students who have been misled by the world. But it's not just students. I've been told by someone I trust in the school system that one of the English teachers in one of our local high schools believes they are transgender, so soon they're going to pee in the same place as your daughters. An adult man using the same restroom as your precious girls!"

A ripple of emotion washes through the room. A man up front loudly guffaws. The woman next to me sucks in her breath sharply, clicking her tongue. Every inch of Constance tenses, as though she's ready to spring to her feet. I want to hide. I want to vomit. I want to charge the stage and tackle him. I want Helen to pull out the gun she must have brought and shoot him. But what would it matter?

The thing about a man like Isaiah is that you don't have to know his particulars to know him. He is the same man everywhere. To try to understand him is to try to understand a sinkhole. He is sure of himself, and he likes feeling sure of himself, because he has built a world in which he can always be sure of himself. He is a feedback loop that exists only to perpetuate himself. I could tell you every word he said, and you could try to find meaning in it, and you would learn the meaning was always right there on the surface. He doesn't need subtext because text is built to encompass him.

"You know what, Isaiah? Shut up." Helen says before blinking quickly, as if quietly thinking, *Shit!* to herself. "By which I mean: You're so hyperfocused on trans people, a group of people that is *at most* one percent of the population, because you know it feels great to be a bully, and you hope your voters will enjoy that taste of cruel self-righteousness too. Do you honestly think—honestly!—a genuine sexual predator is going to go to the lengths involved in creating a believable trans identity because the symbol on a bathroom door contains some kind of ancient, mystical power? Again: Shut up, shut up, shut up."

She takes a deep breath. "Sorry." And another deep breath. "No. Not sorry. I can't even pretend to take you seriously. I sincerely used to believe that even if I disagreed, it was worth listening to men like you, about your deeply held moral convictions. And then . . ."

Her eyes search the darkness beyond the spotlight. I wonder for a moment if she's looking for me in the crowd, and then she smiles the smile of someone setting their life on fire. "And then I had an abortion in college. Statistically speaking, a lot of women in this room have had the same experience. It's, what? One in four?" She shields her eyes and looks out at the audience. "Anybody out there want to go out on a limb with me?"

Not a single hand goes up, but several people scan the crowd. One of them is Brooke, in the front row, all but craning herself around to see. Constance holds my hand tightly. She starts to raise her other hand, then shrinks back when the woman next to me looks over.

"Well, maybe not in *this* room," Helen says, and that gets a little laugh. "But you know what? My freshman year of college, I was at a party with a guy, and we got super drunk, and he had sex with me, and I don't like to call it rape, but it was, and then I was pregnant. I thought about telling him, but I knew he would try to talk me into keeping it and I didn't want to see him again. I called my friend Marcy, and she held my hand all the way to the clinic. It was a sunny day. I left the clinic, and there were people outside protesting, and I didn't know how to tell them that it was just another Wednesday, that the world wasn't over, like I half feared it would be."

"The world was over for that poor child," Isaiah says, tears in his eyes.

"I knew you would say that," Helen says. "That's the thing about these guys. Everything they say you could write in a script. 'You shouldn't have gotten drunk.' 'You shouldn't have been alone with that man.' 'Quit blaming other people for your problems.' He doesn't need to think of what to say, because there is no world in which he can't just say something and get people to act like he's said something very serious. Even if they disagree with him! I did it for years! But he's said nothing. Do you get that? He's said *nothing*. He's just said, 'The world works pretty well as is for me.' And yes. Agreed. It does. It works beautifully for Isaiah Rose.

"I could quote you facts and figures and data and statistics, but me doing that wouldn't convince anyone who isn't already convinced. What you pretend to offer, Isaiah, because you're a man of God, is moral clarity, but everything you say is bankrupt, warped by money and power and privilege. And I know I won't win, and I know, like, four people in this room are going to vote for me anyway, but I want everybody here to understand one thing: There are so many people in this room for whom the world doesn't work beautifully. Somebody else here *has* had an abortion. Somebody here is trying to figure out a way to put food on the table. Somebody here is down to her last three dollars. And, yes, Isaiah, maybe somebody here is trans and terrified at the way you keep turning them into a punching bag. Some of these people are folks I've met campaigning. Some just found out who I am. Some are dear friends. And we all want the world to work for more people, Isaiah. That's all."

I want to clap. I don't. A few people do, and I recognize Megan's lonely cheer.

"And I want the world to *exist* for poor children like your own," he says.

The room bursts into applause.

After the debate, Helen found me in the crowd and gave me a long hug, apologizing over and over no matter how much I reassured her it was okay. Then she dragged me across the street to empty her stomach. Now, she's leaning against the brick exterior wall of the Corn Palace, vomit pooled at her feet. Megan awkwardly stands nearby, feet rooted, body leaning toward Helen, unsure of what to do. She must know I'm the teacher Isaiah singled out tonight, but she hasn't said anything.

"Fuck," Helen says, and then she adds, for emphasis, "FUUUUUUCK." I run a hand over her back. "I fucked it all up."

"No, you were great," Megan says. It's at least the fifteenth time she has repeated this basic statement. Her hands hover halfway between her and Helen, never making contact.

"You can go, Megan," Helen says eventually. She rubs her eyes with her sleeve, mascara going everywhere. "I'll be fine."

Megan waits, mouth open, trying to find words. "I thought you were great," she says one more time. She shoves her hands in her pockets and disappears around the corner of the building.

"I don't know what I was thinking," Helen says. "Maybe I thought I could get on YouTube if I did something sufficiently viral?"

"Maybe you said the thing somebody needed to hear in that moment."

"So, it's worth it to reach just one person?"

"I like to think so."

"Really not how democracy works, but okay." I start to laugh, and then she starts to laugh. She stands up and leans against me, wiping her eyes. "Was that motherfucker talking about you?"

"Probably. I came out to Hank this morning, and they're thick as thieves."

"Fuck. So I guess you're out of here?"

"Almost certainly. If you win the election and need a chief of staff . . ."

"Girl, I am not winning this election. Even the 'Will Helen lose by slightly less than Democrats in Mitchell usually do?' ship has sailed. Make alternate plans."

I've been turning the idea of what I might do next over in my brain. I've only started to find the edges of the answer, but they feel solid enough. "I might go back to school. I always wanted to be the kind of college theater professor who stages productions of *Twelfth Night* set during the fall of Saigon or something. When I was younger, I had planned to get my master's at Minnesota or Wisconsin, and then I just . . . didn't. Inertia."

"In Madison?" Helen says. I nod. "I have a job offer there. Working for a labor union. I'm going to lose, and when I do . . . well, there aren't many jobs for people with a poli-sci master's here, and Mom wants me to be fulfilled. I want something new, E. I don't know how to find it, but I want to try looking. So if you go to

Madison, maybe you and Constance will want a roommate?" Her face falls. "Did I just make it weird?"

"Everything in my life lately has been very weird. I promise." Headlights round the corner, revealing Constance's car. "If you want to see if Constance and I can make it work as first-time lesbians . . ."

"E, you've always been the *most* lesbian. You just had to believe in yourself."

I laugh and walk toward the car, then turn back. "You gonna be okay?"

She nods. "Let's have lunch soon?"

"The people who needed to hear you tonight will hear you," I say. "It just might take a bit."

"Well, none of them can vote for me, the pieces of shit."

"Skyberg," says a voice, ragged, out of breath. Megan rounds the corner again and leans against the wall, panting. "Please. Help me. It's Abigail. It's bad."

I motion for Constance to follow in the car and run after Megan to where a commotion rises from the lot behind the performing arts center. A woman calls out, "Help! Please help my son!"

Megan points. "They're trying to take her back."

I see Abigail, hanging limply from the arms of a tall, stocky man with his hands locked across her chest. He drags her toward a minivan with its doors open. A sticker on the vehicle's back bumper has been scratched off, leaving the words "D FOR OIL." Caleb is in a crouch, looking like he might leap forward and tackle the man. A few onlookers have gathered to watch.

The woman calling for help is the same woman who sat next to me at the debate. I realize all at once why she looked so familiar to me.

She looks exactly like Abigail.

Abigail

Monday,

November 7

When my dad said my old name and then grabbed me by the shoulder, something inside me snapped. I guess I floated up into the sky or something, because I'm there right now, watching everything that's happening on a five-second delay, tied to my body like a balloon. It's more comfortable up here than down there, but I'm struggling to keep up, so I might not be the most reliable narrator for a bit. I apologize. I tried my best. I swear.

After I left my body, it sagged, and Dad barely caught me. The weight made him stagger backward before he got his feet under him. "What do I do now?" he asked Mom. "He's catatonic."

"Get him in the van. Maybe he'll come to." Mom pinched the bridge of her nose. "I just wanted to talk to him. That's all." She sounded like she was trying to convince herself.

"No," my body said. "No, no, no." It moaned.

"He's awake, Jess," Dad said.

Mom got down in my face and said the wrong name and snapped her fingers a couple times. "We just want to talk, honey. You've been shutting us out. Okay? That's all. Just talk." My body gave her a glassy-eyed stare, so she put a hand on my cheek. "We're worried about what they're teaching you at this school."

Dad started tugging me toward the van. She opened the door to help him get me in.

Caleb came around the corner into the parking lot, headed for his truck. He stopped when he saw the three of us. "What are you doing to her?" He sounded panicked.

Mom and Dad looked at him, as if realizing them holding my seemingly unconscious form like that made it look like they were about to seal it up in a body bag. Caleb tucked his keys in his pocket and took a step toward them. With every step, it was like I could see his whole life stretching out from him like roots in the earth, the person he was and the person he is and the person he might become.

"Who are you? What's your relationship to my son?" Dad said.

"She's my . . ." Caleb shook his head. "Abigail's my ex-girlfriend."

"Oh, son," Dad said, looking at Caleb, voice full of pity.

"Oh, son," Mom said, looking at me, sounding like she might sob.

"Caleb, help," my body said.

Caleb leaned back, then threw a punch at Dad, but he's not really a fighter and he had to avoid my dumb body. His fist hit the fleshy part of Dad's side. Dad made the tiniest little "oof" noise. "I'm warning you, son. Stay out of my family's business."

"Too late," Caleb said, and it was probably supposed to sound brave and cool. (It didn't. Sorry, Caleb.)

Mom looked around and realized what this might look like to anybody passing by, so she played the "concerned parent" card. "Help! Please help my son!" Mom said. (This could work, fuck.)

Somewhere in here, from up above, I could *feel* Megan's low-level anxiety before I could see her. She stopped across the street where nobody but me would notice her. (My body tried to say, "Megan," but Dad was holding on too tight.) Someone tall was with her, and it was weird then, the way I could see Erica as the person she is and not the person everybody perceives. Helen ran up a couple steps behind her.

"Let her go," Caleb said, jumping forward again. Dad took a sidestep to avoid him and nearly dropped my body. (Please drop it.

I can deal with the skinned knees later. I just need to *get away from you now right now please let me get*—) An older married couple had stopped to watch the show.

A car's headlights flooded the parking lot, and my eyes made out Constance's car before being temporarily blinded. Constance laid on the horn, probably to scare Dad, but it was so loud that anybody who happened to pass would stop and look.

Caleb successfully landed a punch on Dad's shoulder, which must have hurt more than the last because Dad briefly let my body slump a few inches. "Let her go, and I won't hurt you!" Caleb said.

Dad started laughing. "Really, kid?" He regained hold of my body and dragged it closer to the car, like he decided that if he had to kidnap me to prove a point, he would fucking kidnap me. (Also, even I know that if he and Mom forcibly take me back home before I'm eighteen, it wouldn't really be kidnapping, especially not in a backwards-ass state like South Dakota.)

Erica—who had crossed the street at some point, apparently—put a hand on Dad's shoulder, trying to seem masc, even though anybody could tell she's the least masc person ever. "Sir, I'm one of Abigail's teachers. Is everything okay?"

"Mr. Skyberg," Caleb said, nearly sobbing, "they're taking her away. Please stop them."

"You're Abigail's parents?" Erica said.

My mom corrected Erica by saying my old name.

"Her name is Abigail," Erica said.

Something shifted in Dad's eyes. "You're the teacher Isaiah talked about, aren't you? You're the pervert making my son think he's a girl." A couple other people had joined the others, and Dad turned to face them. "Isaiah told us about this freak!"

Erica took two steps backward. "I think you have the wrong—"

"Someone call the police!" Mom said, playing her momness to the hilt.

Helen turned to the small but growing crowd, trying to get their attention, even though this was Isaiah Rose country. "Hey, let's take a second before we needlessly escalate—"

"Shut the fuck up!" someone shouted.

Caleb threw another punch while Dad looked up to see who had said that, which made Caleb totally miss, tripping over his own clumsy feet. He fell onto the pavement hard.

Dad grunted and dragged my body a few more steps toward the van. Mom climbed inside so she could help him lift me up into it when he got there. He was so close.

But standing between him and the van was Erica. "I don't think Abigail wants to go with you, sir. Please let her go."

"Or what?" Dad said, looking back at her over his shoulder. "You'll stop me from taking my son home and deprogramming him of—"

An unearthly shriek filled the parking lot. Megan leapt through the air and wrapped her arms around Dad's neck, hanging on, even as he thrashed to throw her off. She raised a single fist to punch him wherever she could, even though she was mostly flailing. "LET. HER. GO."

He dropped me, and I felt the sharp pain of skin colliding with pavement. Caleb crawled forward, wrapping his arms around my body, trying to help it stand.

Dad threw an elbow, and it connected with Megan's face, crack, right across the nose. Blood gushed everywhere, and she fell backward onto the ground, where she wailed loudly. "She's not *yours*," Megan said. "She was never *yours*."

The sound of police sirens rose from a few blocks away.

Megan spat blood and staggered to her feet, glaring at Dad.

Dad, who had always taught the child he believed to be his youngest son there was nothing worse than hitting a defenseless girl (though he'd often hit that youngest child who was, in fact, a girl), held his hands up in the air. "I didn't mean to do that," he said.

"We need to *go*," Erica said.

Caleb helped my body up to its feet. "Can you walk?" he said.

My body nodded. "The car," it said. Constance's car still sat in the entry to the parking lot.

"I didn't mean to do that," Dad said again.

Helen put a hand on Erica's shoulder as my body hobbled past. "I can handle the cops. Just get the kids somewhere safe."

Erica threw open the back doors to Constance's car, and Caleb helped my body inside. Megan hopped in the other side, pressing one hand to her nose, trying to stop the bleeding.

Erica got in front. Constance said, "Where are we going?"

Erica shook her head. "Just drive."

My body's hand found Megan's and squeezed it. She squeezed back. "We're safe," my body said, even though I don't think it will ever feel safe.

Caleb stretched a protective arm across the back seat. The sirens drew closer but not close enough. Constance squealed out of the lot and drove off into the darkness as fast as she dared go.

My body moaned, its head in Caleb's lap. Constance had given up on traveling in any specific direction and instead drove around the countryside while she and Erica argued about the best place to go where nobody would give us too much shit.

"I think we should go to the hospital," Constance said. "She seems like she's in a bad way. I'm not taking her back home to just sleep it off or something."

"We're not taking her anywhere her parents might find her," Erica said.

They squabbled about where it would be safest, where my parents couldn't get to my body. (They can't get to *me* because I'm hanging out up here with you.) It was too much to listen to, but I didn't have anything else to do, so I kept one ear on it. I tried to think about places nobody would try to find me, places you could hide so long as you stopped being yourself and became the place. Only one came to mind. (You must know which one.)

It was a lot of work forcing open my body's mouth and making its tongue move. It really didn't want to do the job, but it does still (sort of) belong to me, so I made it happen. "Please," my body said.

They were talking too loudly to hear me, but Caleb held up a hand. "She said something."

"Please," I puppeteered my body into saying again. "I know where we can go."

Nobody liked my suggestion, but in the end, they knew I was right.

Brooke panicked when she saw Erica at her door. She stepped out into the frosty night and put a hand on Erica's arm. "I don't know how he knew," she said. "I'm so sorry." Erica winced.

"Who knew what, Mom?" Caleb said.

Brooke looked past Erica to see Caleb and Megan supporting my body, Constance just behind them. "Abigail needs our help," Erica said.

Brooke walked across the lawn to place a hand on my body's forehead. She saw the bruising spreading up the body's arms, the scraped skin on the knees, the black eye beginning to bloom. But most of all, she must have seen the way the eyes were empty. Whoever piloted that body wasn't inside of it. She softly ran a hand over the cheek.

Brooke nodded to Caleb. "Get her inside. We need to figure out how to get her back."

"How do you know—"

"Get her inside, Caleb," Brooke said. "*Now*."

Caleb and Megan helped my body into the house. Erica and Constance waited by the door, standing guard. Erica put her arm around Constance, but neither of them seemed invested in anything but what was happening to my body.

Ruth sat at the puzzle table. She blinked in surprise as the group entered. "Ruth, honey," Brooke said, "I need a bowl with ice water in it and some bath towels." Ruth looked like she might say something, but Brooke threw her a look, and, instead, she headed straight into the kitchen. The ice dispenser whirred. Mr. Daniels appeared at the entry to the hall, and Brooke shut up whatever he was going to say with a shake of her head. "Vic? Get the first aid kit and some warm washcloths for Megan, please."

Megan and Caleb deposited my body in a puffy recliner. Brooke sat on her haunches and extended her hands, palms facing up, so the only possible action my body could take was to place its hands in hers. It felt like a ritual she had performed many times in the past but had gotten rusty at. Her hands felt small and wrinkly and slightly soapy. She had been washing dishes. She had come directly home from the debate and started washing dishes. Something about that felt so sad, but that feeling belonged to nobody in particular. It just existed in the temperature of the room.

Then Brooke's hands squeezed my body's hands, and her eyes looked into mine. "Abigail?" she said. "Hi, Abigail."

"Abigail," my body said. Christ, what a stupid body.

Brooke released my body's hands when Ruth approached, carrying the bowl of ice water. It was one of those big metal bowls you eat popcorn out of, and it must have been so cold, but Brooke didn't flinch. The water sloshed as she lowered it in front of my face. Some spattered over the edge and onto my body's leg. My body whimpered.

"Abigail, I need you to put your face in this water, okay?" Brooke said. "Whatever happened, it was bad, but it's over, and I need you here with me right now, Abigail. We've got to jolt your system to do that."

She jostled the bowl again, the ice water rotating in it. "But—" my body managed.

"I'm here, Abigail," Brooke said. "I'm not going to let you drown, okay? Nobody is getting you here. Not if I have anything to say about it. Okay, Abigail?"

(Every time she says Abigail, something in me tries to turn over, like a car on a cold morning.)

From up here, a girl really can see everything. Caleb stands just off to his mother's side. Ruth paces down the hallway, then back, disappearing into the dark, reemerging into the light. Victor kneels beside Megan at the table, gently washing away the blood on her face. Megan keeps asking what is happening with Abigail. And still by the door, still in their coats, Erica kisses the top of Constance's head, while she mutters, "I'll kill the asshole."

A dog barks outside. I wonder if I can keep floating up, to see the dog, the rabbits chewing the trees, the yard lights in the distance, the whole town. I think about seeing how high I can go, about rising out of that room and into the sky, off into nothing, and seeing if somebody else wants to rent my body for a while. Since I don't know how to figure out the problem of knowing my parents will never love me as me and desperately wanting that love anyway, I figure somebody else might want to take a crack at it. Why not?

Down below again, Brooke says, "Abigail," and it sounds like someone calling you home in the dark.

So I look at her, because my mom might never say my name, but Brooke is a mom, and *she* said my fucking name, like it was the easiest thing in the world, like she always has, and I hear her jostle the bowl of ice water again, and I dunk my head forward, and it is cold, so cold, and I scream into the water, and then I pull my head back, my hair sending water droplets flying, and I am suddenly back inside myself, in an armchair, in this room, watching everyone look at me.

"Okay," I say, "what the *fuck* is going on?"

After that, all I want to do is sleep until it's over (whatever "it" is). Brooke gets me settled in the guest room again. A glass I was using for water when I stayed here last time still sits on the nightstand. That Abigail feels like she lived a million years ago.

I wake up three times in the night, and somebody is always watching over me.

The first time, Ruth sits in a big armchair they dragged in here while I was out. I know Brooke must be making her do this, but I feel thankful anyway. She plays a game on her phone, and it lights her face in a way that makes her look so beautiful. I think about telling her this, but I fall asleep again before she even notices I was awake.

The second time, Constance sits in the chair, reading by the light of a desk lamp.

"What time is it?" I say.

She folds a corner and closes her book. "Just after midnight. Sorry I woke you."

I shake my head and grab the glass. "Can I have some water?"

She catches me staring at the funny hitch in her walk when she returns. "You want to know why I walk like this? I'll tell you, but it's a sad story." I look away but nod. "I was trying to protect my little brother, and my dad hit me 'accidentally.' I fell down the stairs and broke my leg. It never healed right."

"My dad's an asshole too." Some of the water dribbles down onto the sheets from my lips.

"Erica doesn't know that story. People who had adequate-to-great parents hate hearing about those of us who didn't. They don't get it. They can't. And, like . . . I still miss my dad sometimes. Which is fucked."

"It is, and it isn't."

"Exactly." She wipes water off my chin with her sleeve. "You should sleep more."

I'm out again before I can tell her I'd like to talk about having a bad dad sometime with someone who might get it.

When I wake up the last time, it's Caleb asleep in the chair, lit by the moon. As if he felt my eyes open, he sits up. He smiles tiredly. "Go back to sleep."

"Thank you for stopping them," I say. "I'm sorry I broke up with you."

He stands and kisses my forehead. "Go to sleep, please." He tugs the covers up around me, and I'm out.

When the morning sun becomes unbearable, I open my eyes to see the foggy outline of a stuffed rabbit sitting opposite me on the bed.

"Mrs. Daniels left it," Megan says from the armchair. "She said you might like to wake up to a friendly face."

I roll over to look at her. "You're a friendly face, though?"

Dark circles surround her eyes, and a bandage covers her nose. I flinch. "I think she worried you would do exactly that."

I stand. Everything hurts, but I need to hug her. Once I do, she says, "Ow," quietly, then pats my back.

"Go get cleaned up. You look like shit. I'll call Ms. Skyberg to—" She stops herself. "Shit. I just outed her. Shit, shit, shit. I'm *so* bad at this!"

"I know about Erica. I've known for a while."

"Oh." Six or seven or a hundred pennies drop behind her eyes. "That explains a lot. Anyway, she insisted on giving us a ride home. Something about closure?"

I limp to the bathroom. I let the faucet run and examine myself in the mirror. My face is smudged with dirt, and it has a big bruise along the cheek. I grab a washcloth, and the cleaner my face gets, the emptier I feel. I brace against the counter and let something old and painful flow out of me in a moan, again and again. When I'm done, I'm really fucking hungry.

I hear Brooke singing in the kitchen before I see her. When she speaks, her voice is careful, modulated. Yet her singing voice is unguarded, nasal, and creaky, snapping in half on the high notes. I wait a moment outside the kitchen. She probably doesn't let many people hear her like this, and I don't want to take it from her.

"I know I leave wounds behind me," she sings, "but I won't let tomorrow find me—" She sees me and snaps to, rigid, both herself and not. "Good morning. Oatmeal?"

"Please. With brown sugar. And don't stop singing because of me."

"My voice is awful. I don't want to torture you." She turns down the music playing in the background, then dishes oatmeal into a bowl, fishing brown sugar out of a cabinet. She's so fluid moving around her kitchen like this I almost forget to look for the places where the seams show, the places where "Brooke Daniels" ends and the terrified but much freer version of herself peeks through.

"Should you even be here? Don't you have an election to win?"

"What Isaiah said about Erica really, really . . . really made me mad. So I quit his campaign. Said I won't be giving him money in the future."

"Oh. That's good. I guess. Thank you for the symbolic gesture."

She slides the bowl to me. I take a bite and nearly moan again. It shouldn't taste this good, but in this moment, with my former temp mom, it's exactly what I need.

"Don't joke, Abigail. Quitting was hard. Really hard. When I . . . began my journey . . . you had to hide in plain sight. If I stood in Isaiah's shadow . . . I'm sure Danielle would shake her head at what a disappointment I've become," she says. "I wanted to be for you what she was for me, but I messed everything up. I wanted to let you shine, but I only know how to snuff things out. As the song goes."

I can tell she's waiting for me to say something like, "Aw, shucks, Brooke, you're not a disappointment!" But I won't. She did disappoint me.

So she goes to her purse on the kitchen table. "I wanted to give you something, as this is likely the last time we'll talk in any real depth." She must see my skeptical look. "When you get as old as me, you get a feel for how things end." She digs a check out of the purse. "Here."

It's from a bank in Minneapolis, in the name Brooke Morgan. It's made out to me. And it's for $25,000.

"I can't take this," I say. I shove it back toward her.

"You can. You should. When I was a little older than you, I was saving up for surgery. But Victor paid for it, so that money has been sitting in an account, gathering dust and interest all this time. I've always wondered who I could have been if I'd paid for it myself, if I hadn't made myself dependent on . . ." She shakes her head. "Time moves in one direction, Abigail."

Brooke slides the check back to me, and I take it. (What? It's a lot of money!) "Do whatever you want with it. No strings attached. It's too late for me."

I swallow hard. "I don't think it's too late for you."

She gives me a sad smile, and then the doorbell rings, and the real Brooke disappears again, back behind the woman she pretends to be. Just like that, the last conversation I will ever have with Brooke Daniels (by her estimation) ends. Megan comes in, followed by Erica, who gives me a hug equal parts enormous and gentle.

Brooke becomes her most hostessest self, offering Erica and Megan food, something to drink, cream with their coffee. In some other universe, Brooke might have loved having breakfast with two other transes and Mitchell's number one Hillary Clinton stan. But we live in this universe, where Brooke is forever an outsider in the house she made her husband build for her.

The whole way to Megan's house, she chatters excitedly about the morning's polls, about the first woman president, about history being made. When we get there, she pats Erica on her arm and says, "*Remember*: This is *your* history too."

"Thanks, Megan," Erica says. She manages to keep from laughing until we've turned out of the Osborne driveway, which sets me off too.

"I can't believe my best friend is such a *normie*," I say.

Erica smiles and turns down the NPR station Megan made us listen to.

"Hey, you didn't vomit when I said someone other than you was my best friend. The electroshock therapy is working!"

She doesn't say anything. We sit at a traffic light a beat too long, so the person behind us beeps their horn. I try to see what she was distracted by, but it might have just been a tree in the Coborn's parking lot.

"I made an appointment to see a doctor about starting HRT," she says out of nowhere.

"Aw. My little girl is growing up." I ruffle Erica's hair. "I'm proud of you."

"You're going to say, 'Fuck you, you would have figured it out on your own,' but I couldn't have done this without you."

"Fuck you, Erica. You would have figured it out on your own."

"Abigail. Seriously. Do you know you're one of the most important people I've ever known? Do you have *any* idea . . ." She shakes her head. "I told you who I was, what? Almost two months ago? If I hadn't, I would have kept hiding from myself. I would have gotten older and sadder and more exhausted. Instead, I talked to you. You complained the whole time, but you helped me figure out how to be myself."

"I just bought you nail polish! Jesus."

"More than I could do." We come to another stoplight, where two guys hang Christmas decorations between light poles. One of the guys notices us and nudges the other guy, pointing. The other guy says something, and they laugh. "Small-town gossip," Erica says.

I roll down my window and lean out. "Fucking *assholes*!" I flip both the guys off, and they only laugh more. The light changes, and Erica hits the gas a little too hard. "Sorry," I say. "With all the . . . stuff . . . I kinda forgot Isaiah outed you."

"Only implicitly, but . . ." She fishes out her phone and opens her texts, handing it to me. It's an endless scroll of the worst shit I've ever seen. "Nobody else fits the description he gave. I wasn't going to keep my job anyway, but with a bunch of angry parents yelling in the board's ear . . . well, I always wanted to go back to grad school."

"Fuck that. I'll write a million letters about what a good teacher you are, and how you—I don't know—saved my life? That will sound good, right?" My voice ripples. "Right?"

I remember what Brooke said about knowing when a thing was ending. Suddenly, the nearly two months I've known Erica Skyberg as herself don't feel like enough.

"Constance and I are leaving. Probably to Madison. I'll try to get into the theater program at UW." She can't look at me. "It's long past time. This place takes and takes and takes, and I'm not sure it knows how to give back."

"So I just won't ever see you again?"

"Abigail, it's Wisconsin, not *the moon*." She smiles at me, and I start to breathe so fast I hiccup. "Hey? Hey, it's okay! Will I have had a minor transition milestone if I don't immediately send you five annoying texts about it?"

"We can fix this. *I* can fix this. Or Megan can, and I'll be charming in a supporting role."

"It wouldn't be your job to fix this even if it could be fixed." She pulls to a stop, and I realize we're right outside my house. "The world is fucked, and things can't always be saved. But you're good at helping people, Abigail. You should do more of it."

"Fuck. You."

"You need to find your place, Abigail. You need to find your people. I don't think that's going to happen here."

"Oh, God, don't give me that. What? The world deserves Abigail?"

"Yes," she says. "But Abigail also deserves the world."

I hug her then, tackling her across the center console. I do a really good job of not crying because I try so hard to memorize how this feels because Wisconsin's not the moon, but it's still Wisconsin, and I don't go there very often.

"You changed my life, too, you stupid bitch," I say, and I sniffle.

"Nah." But she grins in a way where I know she knows.

Then I remember something. "Look: My sister is already probably pissed at me for taking my sweet time getting home after my very shitty day yesterday, but she'll be super, mega-pissed at me if I never introduce her to my friend Erica, who I bring up all the time. So . . ."

Her eyes get wide, and the terror quicksand almost sucks her in. But then she turns off the car and gets out. "Okay."

I go up the walk a few steps ahead of her. I hope I was better to her than Brooke was to me. I don't know. But I think I did pretty good.

Jennifer steps out onto the lawn, still in her pajamas. She sags with relief when she sees me, then looks up at Erica and beams. "Thank you, Mr. Skyberg. For everything."

"Can I . . ." I take a moment. I want to get it just right. "Can I introduce you to a friend of mine?"

December

Brooke

Thursday,

December 8

Hi, Brooke.

I'm still here, which surprises me. You're not listening to me, not quite, but sometimes, like when you told Isaiah what a piece of shit he was and quit his campaign, or when you opened a private browser tab to find information about the support group in Sioux Falls, I'd almost think you were aware of me. I don't want to get my hopes up, but you and I might have something here, kid.

That's for the future. Tonight, it's opening night for *Our Town*, the theater is packed, and Constance is crushing it. It might be the best performance you've ever seen—and not just by Mitchell's standards. (*I* wouldn't go quite that far, but she is good.)

In this scene, Constance's character, Emily, is dead, and she stops at the edge of the door separating the dead from the living, as if daring herself to walk through. "I can't. I can't go on." She's whispering where the script says she should be shouting, and she's facing away from the audience, but somehow, all of it is reading perfectly. Sometimes, you just let an actor go for it. "It goes so fast. We don't have time to look at one another."

"She's *good*," Victor says on one side of you. On the other side, Erica beams.

You start to cry. You have always loved this scene. This time around, it reminds you of when Victor took you to New York to celebrate your tenth anniversary. You found yourself headed in the wrong direction on an express line. As the train whipped past the many stations it wouldn't stop at, you had the dim sense of a film projector displaying lives you would never live. Another train pulled alongside yours and ran parallel for a few seconds. Through the window, you saw a woman who looked just like you, but with hair cut short, dyed black. "Jeannie?" you said, and then the train bore her away, and you became aware of how lonely you have always been.

Erica sees you crying. She grips your arm for a second, and you look at her with tearstained eyes. "Can I come with you on Friday?" you say, a low whisper. "To group?"

When she nods, you let yourself feel relief.

When you start to speak at group, when all those faces turn to look at you, your story feels too big to leave your body, like if you say it out loud to this many people, the costume you wear will deflate and leave me in its stead, a scrawny teenager who used to be you, trying to figure out what the fuck to do.

So you say, "I have been hiding a long time." You fall silent, then add, "It hurt. A lot." You fall silent, then add, "I miss my sister. So much."

"You should try to find her," says Bernadette, who told everyone at the start to offer support and not advice, then proceeded to give everybody advice. "It's almost Christmas. This time of year . . . she might be so happy to hear from you."

Jeannie won't be happy. She won't. Too much water under the bridge, and you in the current. But you nod anyway, eyes watery. Why not? You know?

It's almost 4:00 a.m. Outside, snowflakes somersault down from the sky, casting shadows in the yard light. The play's final performance ended several hours ago, and when you got home, you were so high on it you decided to write to Jeannie. Now, your message to her sits half-finished on the family computer screen. You need to send it tonight, or you know you will strike the set on this chapter and put your life back into a box.

You've circled the kitchen island nine times. You are thinking about giving up.

From this far away, without your glasses on, the monitor blurs into a hazy white. Victor mostly uses the nearly decade-old machine to check farm prices and the weather. But sometimes, when you can't sleep (when I won't let you sleep), you use an incognito browser to examine Jeannie's minuscule digital footprint in the hopes she will have posted something to indicate she misses you too. She never does. Maybe that's how it would be if the situation were reversed. At a certain point, you must give someone up for dead. It's cleaner that way.

You pause at the top of the island, and you ball up your fists, bundling the cuffs of Victor's too-long DWU sweatshirt into your fingers and marching over to the screen.

Dear Jeannie,

Merry Christmas! It's been a long time.

That's all you have. "It's been a long time." To be fair, it *has* been a long time. You don't know what to say next. You can't bring yourself to say you were her brother, nor her sibling. The word you want to say—"sister"—feels wrong too. You suspect she knows you were her sister. But you also can't imagine her describing you to anyone as such. You are a brother ghost blurring in her peripheral vision.

You hit the backspace key thirty-nine times until all you have left is "Dear Jeannie." You're about to delete that, too, and give up on this whole foolhardy plan when you hear footsteps behind you. You turn and see Caleb, hair messed, eyes red. Normally, he'd never let you see the aftermath of his crying. Then again, it's four in the morning. The last thing he'd expect to see is his mother standing over the family computer.

"Mom?" He rubs his eyes, as if trying to confirm you're really here.

"I couldn't sleep, sweetheart, so I thought I'd browse the net."

He smiles skeptically, then turns toward the fridge. "Maybe I should warm up some milk for us." You are hit with a piercing memory of your own mother, heating milk on the stovetop while you sat at the kitchen table, watching her. She never looked at you, only at the spoon she used to trace circles through the white liquid.

You pick up your glasses from beside the keyboard and slide them over your eyes. Caleb snaps into focus as he puts a mug full of milk into the microwave. You interrupt before he can begin to heat it up. "You should do that on the stovetop," you say.

Before you know you're doing it, you've taken the glass from him and poured it into a saucepan over medium-low heat. As you stir with a wooden spoon, you feel connected to your mother, which makes you feel angry, disgusted, lonely. You don't let Caleb see any of these things. As always, I'm the only one who looks at them.

The computer switches to a screen saver, the words "DANIELS FARMS" bouncing around the screen. Caleb leans against the fridge and watches them ricochet. "What *are* you doing up?"

"Writing a letter."

"To who?" You're not sure how long you don't speak. Long enough to make him say, bitterly, "Right. I forgot. You never answer simple questions."

You trace patterns in the milk. What became of the house you grew up in? You've been tempted to look it up now and then, but you can never bring yourself to type in the address. In your mind's eye, it sits empty, a canker in the middle of a lovely city block. You imagine it turning gangrenous, the ground reclaiming it. You imagine it burying your parents beneath its weight and bearing them down into the dirt. Your father always called it his dream house. Some dream.

How easy would it have been for your parents to make that house feel like a place worthy of two daughters? How much harder did they have to work to send both you and Jeannie spattering away, patternless? What if you heating this milk for your son felt like part of a continuum, instead of an animatronic recreation of a real thing nobody quite remembers?

"I'm writing to my sister," you say, and Caleb's head snaps up. "I have a sister." You watch the spoon twist. "I haven't spoken to her in many years. Not since long before you were born. And I thought . . . since it's Christmas and all . . ."

"Whoa, whoa, whoa, Mom . . . Does Dad know about this?" He sounds like a little boy again.

"Yes." You dip a finger into the milk. Not quite.

He stands at the living room's edge, clearly wanting to walk to the computer and turn off the screen saver. All he would see are the words "Dear Jeannie," but then the dam would break. You would tell him everything.

Why *not* tell him everything, Brooke? What will he remember when he thinks of this house, of you?

"Her name is Jeannie," you say. "I haven't seen her since I ran away from home at sixteen."

He watches you, like you might stop speaking if he looks away. "You're full of shit."

You shake your head.

He approaches you warily. "What's your real name?"

You laugh. "My real name is Brooke."

"I thought maybe you adopted a new identity or something?"

"This isn't a spy novel, sweetie." You dip a finger in the milk again. Just right. You pour it into a mug in a languorous drizzle.

"Why did you run away?"

You realize the question he's asked you has the same answer as the one he keeps asking himself. "Why did Abigail break up with you?" He looks away, immediately embarrassed, which makes him look even sadder. "If you're still this upset about it, you must know it was your fault."

"She didn't like my essay," he says. "C'mon. Answer my question."

"And why do you think she didn't like your essay?"

"I called her the wrong name! But that's your fault too!" He scrunches his eyes closed. "I originally wanted to write about my birth mom, how much I love her, even though I'll never know her name. But I knew that would make you sad." (It would have.) "So I wrote about Abigail instead. And you told me it was really good!"

You did say that, Brooke. Worse, you really thought it was, even though you knew how Abigail would feel if she read it. And yet . . .

You imagine everyone learning your secrets. Yes, there would be devastation but also, eventually, relief. You want everyone to know, deep down, or at least you want someone to know.

You give him the mug of warm milk, and his face sours at its taste.

"When I was thirteen or so, I realized I couldn't be the person my parents wanted me to be. It made me very anxious, then very angry, then very sad. They would never understand me for who I was, so I had to leave. If I could have taken Jeannie . . ." You couldn't have taken Jeannie. You didn't even realize that you *wanted* to take her until this very moment.

"What did your parents want you to be?"

You pour what's left in the saucepan into a mug and lift it to your lips, blowing on it. Outside, the snow falls, thick. The Christmas lights Victor worked so hard to hang all over the farm cut through the gloom, an icy glimmer.

"A son," you say.

You watch his face, but it doesn't change. Instead, he scans the room, possibly looking for hidden cameras. He and his sister laugh themselves silly at prank videos on YouTube. Maybe he thinks that's what's happening right now. You wait until those beautiful, brilliant, compassionate eyes settle back on you. "But," he says. It's all he has.

"You tried to make Abigail's story into your own," you say. "I wish I had said something, but I have spent a lot of time running from my own story. That made it too easy for me to think her story was fair game, so long as you didn't see mine. When you were . . . very stupid—" you wave your hand to vaguely indicate suicidal depression "—I worried that maybe I had trapped you in my secret too. And then you got better, and I stopped worrying. Prematurely. I'm sorry."

"Holy shit." He sets the mug down. "Holy shit. You're trans. That's why you told Isaiah off for outing Ms. Skyberg. That's why you had to adopt. That's why . . ."

"I wanted to be a mom, and I didn't have many options."

A gust of wind slams against the house, and he jumps. "You should have told me!"

Remember the first time you held him, Brooke? He seemed so angry then too. You wanted nothing more than to take him home and soothe him. What if you spent all these years anesthetizing him instead?

"It wasn't something you needed to know. I'm telling you now, because I trust you, and I love you, and I want you to know. But you never *needed* to know. It doesn't change that I'm your mother." You swallow. "I miss you every day, even though you're right here. That's all motherhood is."

He's deathly pale, and his eyes fill with tears. He looks like he might go to his room and never come back downstairs. "Mama?" he says.

You put a hand over his. He almost jerks away, then stops. Your fingers overlap. He looks out the window. Sometimes, you can almost see in him the woman who gave birth to him. Neither of you have a past, Brooke. But you sacrificed yours to survive, then stole his by never talking about it. You have always tried to do unto others as you would have them do unto you, but that doesn't work when you want to obliterate yourself.

He swallows. "Does Dad know?"

You laugh. "It's come up."

"You should have told me." Already the fight is leaking out of him.

"The day I left home, my father found out I was on estrogen. He was going to beat the shit out of me. Somehow, I got out. I kept running and eventually ran out of places to run to. One day I woke up here, in a life that looked like mine but wasn't." You frown. You're listening to me, and you're out of the habit. "I wanted to tell you. But I feared what would happen. Then when you . . . when *we* hurt Abigail . . ."

"Does she know?"

You hesitate, but in for a penny, Brooke. You nod.

"Fuck," he says. "Is that why you . . . were so *invested* in her?"

"She needed a mom. I proved . . . unworthy of that title. Most women would."

After a long silence, he says, "Where did you grow up?"

"Chicago."

He mutters, "Ruth," under his breath. "She guessed you were from there. I guessed New York."

"You have a smart sister," you say with a smile, then dump what's left in your mug down the sink and begin rinsing out the saucepan. "I'll tell her too. Soon. But I wanted you to know now because . . . well, because. I'm making this up as I go."

He looks up at the ceiling, then back at you. "You should have told me."

"I just did," you say.

After you've given him a hug and sent him back to bed, unsure he will keep your secret but certain he will all the same, you sit down at the computer again.

I can feel you holding open the door for me, just a bit, Brooke. It is *so good* to see through your eyes again. You know nobody else can write this letter for you, and I'm so honored you've asked. "Dear Jeannie" is a good start. I'll take it from here.

You put your fingers on the keyboard. In a few hours, the house will stir with activity, and in a few days, you'll gather around the tree to open presents, and over the next few months, you'll start to tell other people you love, starting with Ruth. But for right now, we have a letter to write. *I'm so sorry it's taken this long for me to write*, I type, using our hands, *but I never knew what to say. Now, I do. I'm your sister Brooke.*

You could send just this, Brooke. It would be enough. *You* will be enough. You're going to see her again. I'll make sure of it.

But I also want to say so much more.

Behind us, the coffeepot whirs. Outside, the wind turns the Christmas lights into a kaleidoscope. I start to type again.

Erica

Tuesday,

December 13

THE OLD WOMAN WRAPS long-nailed fingers around Constance's wrist. She wears a fake fur over a polka-dot sweater, and she tilts her head back and cackles loudly whenever Constance says something. She's the fourth person to stop Constance today to talk about *Our Town*.

Other shoppers in the Walmart produce section turn to find the source of this throaty cackle. Their eyes inevitably fall on me, tall, ungainly, wearing a women's sweater (under my zipped-up coat) and pink nail polish. Some know me from the gossip mill and look askance. A couple spot the nail polish and raise an eyebrow. Most look right past me, an anonymity I know I will miss as I slough off a life I drag behind me.

I check my phone. In a half hour, my prescription for spironolactone (to block the production of testosterone) and estradiol (to encourage the production of estrogen) will be ready at the pharmacy counter. It still doesn't seem real. Getting the pills involved jumping through more hoops than I had anticipated, but I was intent on getting them before I left for Madison, so (with Bernadette's help) I speed-ran the therapy sessions, the physician's consult, the freezing of sperm.

Constance came to every appointment and sat in the waiting room, headphones in, ignoring the news of the incoming White

House administration dominating the TV. Having her there felt like we were a couple at long last, fighting together against overwhelming odds.

It also felt like she was packing my bags to send me off to sea.

Since her abortion, since John called her every name in the book and threatened to sue, especially since *Our Town* opened and she seemed the most herself she has in years, I've been waiting for Constance to say she won't be moving to Madison with me. She hasn't yet, but the shoe will drop soon enough. She has never gotten to have a life where she is just Constance, defined by nobody else. And I know she longs for that.

I plan to leave for Madison today, while she plans to visit college friends in Chicago. I wonder how extended the visit will become.

"I think what you're doing is *so brave*," the old woman says. I had no idea she had noticed me. "And your nails are darling. Good for you."

"Erica codirected *Our Town*," Constance says, looping an arm through mine.

"Oh, marvelous! It was the best show I've seen here in years."

As the woman peppers Constance with questions about whether she's ever thought about acting professionally, my phone buzzes with a text from Helen, who is already in Madison. *He appointed MR. FOSSIL FUEL the HEAD of the EPA. THIS. FUCKING. GUY. I. SWEAR. TO. GOD.*

His name's literally Mr. Fossil Fuel??

Yeah. Which made it hard to find a job in other fields, I guess. He was, like, gotta be evil lol.

The old woman theatrically air kisses both of Constance's cheeks, then gives her a hug.

You get your girl drugs? You on your way? You get in tonight?

In order: Not yet, soon, very late. Lunch tomorrow?

Hell yeah.

"Sorry about that," Constance says. "My adoring public." She laughs self-deprecatingly.

"People loved you in that show. I hope you're proud of what you did."

She shrugs. "It's Mitchell Community Theater. Big deal."

We walk deeper into the store together. "So can we talk about it?" I say.

"The thing we're avoiding?"

"Yes. As best friends, not . . . ex-wives turned girlfriends?"

She smiles. "Well. As your best friend, I wanted to say how happy I am you froze your sperm." She winces. "Sorry. Your *genetic material*."

I blink. "That's not what we're not talking about."

"It's not? Usually, when we're not talking about a thing, we're not talking about how, all things considered, if you want to be a mom, you should be a mom. You'd be fantastic at it. Did I miss a memo? Don't tell me you froze your jizz because you wanted a souvenir?"

"No! I banked sperm . . . just in case. To be safe. What I want is to be with you, and I know 'let's never have kids' is the buy-in."

She takes my hands and stretches up on tiptoes to kiss the corner of my mouth. "Haven't you bent yourself into the person you think I want enough times by now?"

My heart hops over a beat or three. "This is different. I couldn't go the rest of my life not being a woman. I'm not intrinsically a mom. Not in the same way."

"Abigail would surely beg to differ."

"She'd also tell you to shut the fuck up and go away and God, who needs a mom, etc., etc."

We laugh. She disappears into the women's clothing section, running her fingers along the hanging garments. All those years I imagined transforming into a woman somehow tangentially connected to her did not prepare me for becoming a woman who loves her and is loved in return, which is so much better than I could have imagined and so much worse because it is transient. When I was younger, I thought our love made time slow around us, but of late, time passes terribly fast. I only have so long with her, and I have so many things to tell her.

"Okay, *this* one is *very* 'grad student making a good first impression,'" she says, holding up a long-sleeved red sweater that might just fit me. It's beautiful.

"*If* I get into the program, I won't start until next September. I'd sweat my balls off."

"All the more reason to get it, then!" She tosses it in her basket. "My treat."

I watch her riffle through the racks. She is buying me outfits for a time when she might not be there to give them to me because she will be elsewhere. I don't know if she realizes that.

I swallow. "Are you thinking about staying in Chicago?"

"Why would I do that?" She doesn't wait for my answer. "Yes, some part of me wants to give acting another shot, but I'm thirty-five. We just figured our shit out as a couple, and my savings would run out quickly, and how would I even get auditions, and . . ."

"And you might never forgive yourself if you don't give it another try?"

She looks at me, something inscrutable on her face, and then she turns away and holds a dress up against herself in the mirror.

"Excuse me. Were you in the play last week?" a woman says, tapping Constance on the shoulder. She's accompanied by a girl, probably about nine, who wears a cast on her arm. "We just *loved* you."

Constance leans down to talk to the girl. Every day, it gets a little easier to picture the life we were meant to lead together. To lose that now . . .

But a person's life is their own. Few sins are greater than trying to squeeze someone else into the shape you require them to be.

The alarm on my phone goes off, and I make my way to the pharmacy counter. The pharmacist rattles off a list of potential side effects from the hormones, side-eying me the whole time, but I hardly notice as I watch Constance stoop to sign the girl's cast.

In my car, I tuck the first estrogen tablet under my tongue, so it can dissolve, something the pharmacist told me might take up to fifteen minutes. It's the placebo effect, almost certainly, but I already feel calmer, secure in myself for possibly the first time ever. All these years running away from this, and now I'm finally doing it. In the back seat sit the four boxes I am bringing to Madison. Everything else I own has been sold or donated.

"What if I did stay?" she says. "In Chicago, I mean. At least for a little while."

"I'd come visit. It's not that far."

"Damn, I was hoping you'd have to keep your mouth closed so none of the estrogen escapes. I didn't want this to be an *actual* conversation."

I clamp my lips firmly shut and gesture for her to go ahead.

"I think I need to try acting one more time. I don't know if I'm good enough, or . . . No, I know I'm good enough. I don't know if anybody but me will ever see that, but I have to try." She turns up the heat in my car. "What does that do to us?"

"Do we have to decide right now?"

"Maybe we can get married again, after a suitable courtship period. Maybe we have world-shattering sex every few months. Maybe I'm your kids' cool aunt."

"I'm not having any . . ."

She smiles sadly. "Erica."

"I know." I reach over and touch her cheek.

"But *if* we need to define it, then . . . I'm Constance, and you're Erica, and when everything got dark, you found me, and I found you. That's good enough for me. You?"

I nod, but I don't say anything. The still-dissolving estrogen makes a convenient excuse.

Instead, I drive us to the little house we bought as a young couple, a good starter home for two people who didn't know where to start. A "FOR SALE" sign sits in the front yard. I pull up next to her car in the driveway.

We get out and face each other, neither wanting to speak first. Finally, she reaches up to hug me, and her body collapses against mine. I wonder how different it will feel as the years pass, as my body changes, as both of us age.

I know I will get to find out.

I drive east.

Somewhere in Minnesota, the sky darkens as night falls. A cold rain sputters. I stop in Albert Lea and eat dinner in an Applebee's, one of only a few people here this late. I feel the bottle of estrogen in my coat pocket, and I thrill at having a secret self only I can see just now. Slowly but surely, I am changing. If I come here again, they might not recognize me.

In the car, I pop another tablet under my tongue to dissolve. I turn up the radio. The windshield wipers flick away rain becoming sleet. Somewhere ahead of me lies the Mississippi River and, once I'm across that, the state I'm about to call home. Someday, sooner than I think, there will be people who have only ever known me as Erica.

The stories I used to read where men transformed into women suggested a kind of instantaneous loss—a sudden vacuum where their manhood had once been, both literally and figuratively. But what has happened to me has actually been a slow blossoming, a colonization of myself with myself. The estrogen dissolving under my tongue will enter my bloodstream and slowly disseminate throughout my body, just as the other pills I am taking will shut down production of testosterone in other parts of my body. Sooner or later, my cells will realize that estrogen is now my dominant hormone and begin to soften my skin, to grow my breasts, to thicken my hair.

We are, none of us, a single set of destinies set by the accident of our birth. We can change and be changed. Our bodies know the language they must speak to make us the people we must become.

Up ahead, the bridge across the river looms, my wheels hissing through the rainy night. At the far end, I can see a sign that I know will say "Welcome to Wisconsin," but I cannot quite make it out yet. I don't need to see it to know what it is. It will all make sense in time.

Abigail

Friday,
December 16

THE PARTY'S TOO LOUD, too crowded, too sweaty. I can't find Megan, and if she thought closing me up in a shoebox of a house with dozens of sweaty U of M students would be the way to convince me to go with her to college . . . she wasn't *wrong*. Mostly, though, I want to sleep, and we're staying with her cousin. I would feel weird going back by myself.

An email from Erica with notes on my scholarship-application essay (shut up) pops in on my phone, and I step out onto the back porch to read it. Here, the music muffles like in a YouTube video where you're listening to music while standing outside a party. (I'm a *little* high.)

Abigail, this is a wonderful essay. I have a few notes . . . blah, blah, blah *so proud* of me.

A tall, thin person with a fuzz of hair atop their head leans against the railing, lifting a joint to their lips. They wear a black leather coat that fits them so well they look like a gap in reality. They extend the joint toward me, and that's when I recognize them. It's Bex, Bernadette's kid, the *fucking hot* one.

I take a hit. They grin. "Oh shit. You're Abigail! My mom won't shut up about you. You drive her fucking nuts."

I curtsey wobblily. "My reputation precedes—" My feet give out underneath me slightly, and I grab for the railing, the joint flying out of my hand and landing in the snow.

Bex hops down the stairs and picks it up, trying to dry it out against their coat. "You thinking about U of M?" they ask.

"I don't know if college is the right call when the world is about to fucking end," I say, but there's a thing I've been thinking about lately that I haven't said to anyone out loud. Why not Bex? "But I like helping people. I think I'd like to be a therapist. That feels like a thing you go to college for."

Bex snaps open a lighter, and the joint fizzles. "If the world ends, I don't think anyone will check your diploma out in the wastes. You can just say you're a therapist."

"I need professional training, so I can give the mutants and scavengers strong guidance."

They laugh, and this time, the joint catches the lighter's flame. "There are worse places to watch the world end than here. You can almost imagine there's a future." They take a hit. "There's a good support group on campus too. If you're into that. Or you can blend in. Get a little lost. Be just another one of the girls."

"Why not both?" I say, then add, "Dot GIF." (Okay, I am *really* high.)

"World's your oyster, Abigail." They offer me the joint again, but I shake my head.

"I should find my friend before she accidentally gets married or something."

They lean against the railing—*God*, do they lean!—then smile. "Cool. See you around?" When I nod, I realize that, yeah, they probably will.

The next day, I drag myself down Nicollet behind Megan, still feeling a little high. Fucking Megan, whose ass moseyed into the apartment at 5:00 a.m., wants to throw her hat in the air.

Two questions and a comment:

1. When did Megan get a hat?
2. Why?
3. I can't believe I'm the one keeping us on schedule. I'm even tapping the imaginary watch on my wrist.

"Relax," Megan says. "You'll have plenty of time to do your thing."

She drags me toward a statue of a woman throwing her hat in the air. Horrible gusts of wind crash into us, but there are lights everywhere, and people have rosy cheeks. It's nice if you can ignore how you need to shove your hands in your pockets because you forgot your gloves. I take six pictures of Megan throwing her hat before it's enough al-fucking-ready.

Seeing Megan without the trappings of our lives in Mitchell around her is like seeing Megan for the first time, like she was half-assing being the most annoying girl in South Dakota and now she can let it rip. She asked our tour guide a billion questions yesterday, and I'm pretty sure she consciously flirted with a girl at last night's party (but by talking about how our options as a species are socialism or barbarism, so we *must* choose socialism, so *extremely Megan flirting*), and she spent over a hundred dollars on "RESIST" merchandise. Soon, she'll be the most annoying girl in Minnesota and also my roommate. Thank God. I love her so much. Don't tell her, okay? We don't want her thinking I've gotten weak. (Also, I tell her all the time.)

Megan tugs me toward a department store. "Gloves. Before you cease to be able to function."

"What's gotten into you?" I say as we shop. "You're chipper even by your standards."

She leans over a display counter and whispers, "I made out with that girl last night." She twists her hands together, a too-expensive pair of leather gloves caught between them. "We almost had sex. Then we didn't."

"Oh shit," I say. "How . . . was that for you?"

"Great!" She laughs. "Might be gay. Might be bi. Might be pan. So many options. She's a *Marxist*, who's in a *punk band* that plays *Taylor Swift covers*, and she *played some for me*, and her name is *Libby*, like the *pumpkins*."

"I'm sure she's never heard that one."

"Oh God, I texted her the pumpkins thing. You must think I'm ridiculous. *I* think I'm ridiculous."

"I think you get to be a little ridiculous. Pumpkin pie's delicious." I hold up a pair of stretchy cloth gloves. She gives me a thumbs-up. "But seriously. Thank you for trusting me with you."

She basically levitates. "What did you do?"

"Talked about the end of the world with a hot enby. Told them all my future plans." Her eyebrow raises. "Yes! I have them! Sort of! I would hate for you to be all alone up here until you inevitably shack up with the heir to the Libby's pumpkin fortune. Maybe you could use a roommate, and maybe I should come here, because maybe I want to be a therapist someday."

I expect her to laugh in my face, but she points at me. "Yes." She turns away to check out, then turns back. "*Yes*. Perfect. Absolutely. You will be *so good* at that." For once, I don't say anything. Having a future's weird like that.

Before I can get to that future, though, I gotta do one more thing.

I've barely caught the end of visiting hours. The orderly hands me a clipboard and a form to fill out. I write down that my name is Abigail Hawkes and that I want to see Danielle Washington.

It wasn't hard to find her. I don't know how many trans women named Danielle lived in the Twin Cities in the 1990s, but only one kept popping up in the newspaper. She really fought the good fight, even trying court cases and writing op-eds up until ten years ago. But so far as I can tell, she's been in this assisted living place for the past few years.

The orderly looks at the clipboard, then at me. He pulls out an enormous book filled with names and flips through it. The air smells too clean, and the lights are too bright, except when they're not turned on at all. Christmas music plays in one of the common rooms. It seems like a nice facility, as these things go, though I'm sure Brooke could get her something better. If she really wanted to. Which she clearly doesn't.

"Abigail, you're not on Ms. Washington's list of approved visitors. I'm sorry. We can ask if she'll see you, but if she says no, there's nothing we can do."

I rehearsed for this. "To be honest, she might not know I even exist. Can you see if there's a Brooke Morgan on the list? I'm her daughter. Hawkes is her married name."

The orderly reads the (short) list again, and his eyebrows raise. A few minutes later, he leads me to her room.

Danielle huddles under a blanket in a wheelchair, staring out at the gray sky. A few strands of multicolored lights line her window, and a Santa Claus is taped to her door. What hair she still has is combed over the top of her scalp. She looks tiny, about half of herself. Thin fingers clutch the blanket tightly around her neck. The nails are perfectly manicured, tapered, bright pink. Everything's rosy.

"Hi," I say. "I'm Abigail Hawkes. I know your daughter. Well, I know Brooke. I shouldn't assume anything about how you thought about her. I know how disappointing daughters can be." She looks over her shoulder at me, frowning. "That was a joke. Sorry."

"Brooke," Danielle says.

"I usually say her name with that tone of irritation too."

She huffs and turns back to look out the window.

"I don't want to stay long because I'm sure you're tired and don't have time for my nonsense. But I wanted you to know that Brooke is okay. Physically okay. She's in peak physical condition. I'm aware she has a lot of psychological baggage to unpack. But she's well cared for, and she has a husband and kids she loves, and when I—" Something catches in my throat, and I clear it. "And when I needed somebody to be there for me, she was the only person who knew how to call me back into myself. Something tells me you taught her how to do that, so I guess that kind of makes me your granddaughter. Don't ask me to do that math. I just wanted you to know that even though she's a piece of shit, she was there when it counted."

Danielle's shoulders go up and down in a little sigh.

"Look: We have a lot of things in common, you and I, and if you wanted me to come by every so often to hang out, I would like that. I'm going to school at U of M in the fall. Probably. I haven't been accepted just yet, but I have powerful people on my side. That was a joke, but also *not* a joke? I could stop by and read to you or . . . I hear you like to do puzzles?"

She laughs. "You talk a lot."

I laugh, too, then swallow. "I totally get if you don't want some random teenage tran popping into your life to talk at you on a regular basis, but I keep trying to make everything fit in my head, and the best I can figure is: We're all we've got. You know? We have to take care of each other. I know how sad you were that Brooke forgot that, and I don't want to. We all lose something when we go on """our transition journeys.""" (Yes, I do six air quotes, because oh my God, I can't believe I said the words "our transition journeys.") "But maybe we gain things too. Like I spent the last few months learning that just because one life collapses doesn't mean you don't get to have another one that's maybe even better. The point is: I am a *world champion* jigsaw puzzle solver, and I'd love to give you the gift of observing my skills."

"Come here, please," she says.

I walk over to her, and she turns her wheelchair just enough to face me. I stoop beside her, and she smiles when she sees my face. She shivers and extends her hands to me, each palm turned upward, waiting for other hands to fill them. Her grip is still strong. She runs her thumbs over my hands. We sit like that for a long time.

Someone knocks on the door, and a different orderly clears her throat. "Sorry, Danielle. Time for your bath. Your friend here will have to take off. Maybe she can visit another time."

"Maybe," I say. I squeeze her hands again and stand to leave.

"You can visit." She nods. "You should visit. I do love puzzles."

"Cool." I give her the world's most awkward thumbs-up before I go.

"Abigail?" she says. I turn back at the door. "You look just like her."

Megan stops at Walmart on the way home because she wants to buy Libby a Christmas present. She tries to figure out how much to spend and how serious to pretend this thing is. (I don't have the heart to tell her, "Not that serious." She deserves gay chaos.) I finally bail when I answer her question of "Do socks say, 'Thinking of you?'" in the affirmative, then realize she was asking herself. I leave her and wander through the store.

I'm in town, but I gotta help Megan buy a present for a pumpkin girl, I text Jennifer.

Cannot wait to hear what any of this means, she replies.

I'm typing out a response when I see her.

There's a trans girl handing out fliers at the Mitchell, South Dakota, Walmart Supercenter. Her name tag reads "ZOE." If she's on hormones, it's early days, and even from over here, I can hear that her voice is deep. A couple teenage boys snicker, and I see her face fall. I want to tell her teenage boys always snicker, but instead, I watch as an old lady says, "Don't you look darling!" Zoe's smile returns to her face, recognizing the Midwestern politeness for what it is.

Zoe keeps handing out her fliers. It's a week before Christmas, and people keep streaming in. Most are cool or breeze right past her, but I know too well how easy it is to only see the handful of people who treat you like shit. A few more teenage boys laugh at her. Some men sneer at her. It clearly takes a toll.

A big guy walks right up to Zoe and takes a flier. He looks down at the little boy walking alongside him and says, "I'd better never catch you showing up here looking like *him*." He tears up the flier and drops the pieces at Zoe's feet.

Zoe stoops to pick up the scraps, fighting not to cry. I imagine Brooke coming here and breezing right past her, maybe offering a halting, "Merry Christmas," because she's so scared of her shadow. And I think about Danielle in her prime, walking straight up to that guy and shouting, "Fuck you." And I think about me and who I want to be and that poem about two roads diverging in a wood or whatever. (Erica made us memorize it. Tell me this surprises you.)

Fuck it. I walk over. "That guy was a real dick," I say.

"Guys like him always are," she says shakily. "Asshole."

"They're just jealous of how good we look." We look down the long aisle where his red cap bobs above the heads of other customers.

She read me the second I walked up to her, and I can tell she's embarrassed about it. But I don't care. Until there are generations of trans kids who grow up with the care they need, so that they're so indistinguishable from any other kid that even I, Abigail Hawkes, who accidentally sorta clocked Brooke fucking Daniels when she was *buried* in the closet, can't pick them out of a lineup, the rest of us need to send up signal flares to each other. *You're safe. I've got you. Especially here. Especially now.*

"I like your hair," I say. "Did you dye?"

"It's my natural color," she says, coming back to earth.

"Lucky," I say, then point to my hair, which is currently a neon-orange monstrosity. "Dye job."

She laughs. "I should get back to work."

"Don't let the assholes get you down, Zoe." She blossoms when I say her name. I give her a little shoulder squeeze and walk away.

She turns back to her work, and I watch her from a distance. A couple people, here and there, see her, and with every one, I see her become more herself. Somewhere in this store is someone who has seen her and realized that she, too, could be herself.

That's all we are, maybe—people who pick each other out in a crowd and realize that the face of someone you've just met can feel like home.

I wait until I'm sure she might be okay, and then I go to the nail polish aisle, for old time's sake.

Author's Note

I began writing *Woodworking* in the fall of 2020. I set it during the election of 2016. As I did my best to re-create what it was like to be a trans woman in 2016, I realized all over again how much worse things had gotten for trans people in the four years since.

In 2016, our existence was treated as a political cudgel from time to time, yes, but the worst policies aimed at us were the sorts of bathroom bills Isaiah Rose proposes in this book. Those bathroom bills were disgusting pieces of legislation, yet few passed. Those that did in states like North Carolina tended to result in massive blowback from both individual citizens and corporate interests.

By 2020, much of the global right had gone all in on limiting our rights to exist as ourselves and pursue lives we found meaningful. Yet a rather sound defeat for the Republican party in that year's elections made me hopeful that the days of trans people being at the center of the American culture war were ending.

That hope of mine was dangerously naive. In the years since 2020, despite several electoral setbacks for those who run on anti-trans platforms, the number of bills aimed at curtailing the rights of trans people—especially trans kids like Abigail—has skyrocketed. Many have passed, including several that limit our access to the medication and health care we need to live our lives.

What has been most disappointing about this setback has not been the Isaiah Roses of the world—I grew up around men like him, and I know what to expect from them. No, it has been the many, many well-meaning, left-of-center people and publications who see the global right tearing trans lives apart and don't leap to defend our right to live as ourselves. Instead, too many of these folks see the frothing rage being kicked up against trans people and assume that cruelty must have a valid point buried somewhere inside of it.

Even though we know how often access to medical care is used by reactionary movements to punish minority groups, too many assume that what is happening to trans health care is driven by a sober need to modulate a growing epidemic of trans kids who will later experience massive waves of regret in adulthood. Despite the lack of anything more than anecdotal evidence for either the growing epidemic or the massive waves of regret, the belief that something must be done to protect trans kids from themselves persists.

Here, I could drop data. (Where the regret rate for trans surgeries is less than 1 percent, the average rate of regret for *all surgeries* is 14.4 percent.) I could point out the fallacies in popular arguments. (Young children are not having gender-affirming surgeries because gender-affirming surgeries can only be performed on physically mature bodies. What's more, gender-affirming surgeries—particularly breast enhancements and reductions—are performed on cis teenagers *all the time*.) I could even point out the bone-deep misogyny and sexism that drives these beliefs.

But if you wanted all of that, you are probably reading the wrong book. (You should, however, check out Evan Urquhart's essential website Assigned Media. He and his team have done the research.) Despite setting my book during an election, I really did not want to write a political treatise. I wanted to write about trans solidarity and unlikely friendship and the ways in which women build shadow communities amid oppressive power structures. Alas, the state of the world is such that my book will be interpreted as a political one whether I like it or not.

Over the last few years, I have come to realize that most cis people support trans people once they get to know us. And I've also come to realize that most of the concern around trans kids is driven by an understandable anxiety. Our society and culture too often make it seem as though being trans is one of the worst fates imaginable, a regrettable reality some of us are made to endure.

Nothing could be further from the truth. Our lives are as beautiful, as wonderful, as vital as anyone else's. You could erase every trans person living on the planet right now, whether through coercion or death, and you could not erase trans people as a population because we are a naturally occurring human variance. What makes being trans such a terrible fate has nothing to do with transness and everything to do with a society filled with too many who cannot imagine a life outside the one in their own head. That society too often sees human variance as something to fear, rather than something to greet with curiosity and compassion.

At base level, what is so radically threatening about trans identities to those who would oppress just about anyone is that our very existence argues that no one's body is an obligation they are duty bound to suffer but, instead, a gift they can reinvent and remake as they see fit. Your body is your own. Your life is your life. Doubt anyone who would tell you—or anybody else—otherwise.

They say the single greatest determinant of whether someone will support and affirm trans people is if they know a trans person. Erica, Abigail, and Brooke are fictional characters, sure, but they are all based on women I have known. So, you know them now. I hope you carry them in your heart going forward, every time someone who is not trans tries to explain to you in grave and serious tones who we are.

—Emily St. James,
March 2024

Acknowledgments

Writing acknowledgments for one's first novel is a deeply intimidating process, so let me open this by saying: I want to thank everyone I've ever met or interacted with across my entire life, even the people I didn't like much. You're all in here somewhere!

But let's get a little more specific.

Victoria Marini is the agent of my dreams. She loved *Woodworking* so much when it was still a messy little bundle of scraps that she told me she didn't think she was the right agent to sell it. I'm so glad she changed her mind. This book isn't this book without her involvement.

Lindsay Ribar worked with me on what was essentially the very first draft of the book, helping me see what worked and what I could let go. She also convinced me the title was *Woodworking* by trying to get me to change it. At Zando, Caolinn Douglas asked thoughtful, probing questions about all the characters and helped me find ways to tease inner lives out of two protagonists who didn't want to share them.

My friend Lily Osler read almost every draft of this book multiple times. (One day, I briefly forgot Megan's last name, and Lily immediately said, "You mean, *Osborne?*") Beyond Lily, a *whole bunch* of other folks read this book. A huge thanks to Julia Bicknell, Eliza Clark, Chris Dole, Jude Doyle, Ari Drennen, Andrew Farke, Laura Khoo, Cassie LaBelle, Laura Stratford, Saoirse Sullivan, Megan Wegenke, Eliza Wheeler, Libby Woodbridge, Amy Wren, Coraline Wren, and Amanda Yang. Apologies to anyone I forgot.

The entire team at Zando and Crooked Reads made me feel wonderfully cared for. Everybody I've interacted with at both companies has believed in this book, believed in telling complicated trans stories, and (most importantly) believed in Abigail being kind of a shithead. My colleagues at *Yellowjackets* taught me so much about storytelling, and my former colleagues at The A.V. Club and Vox (especially the incomparable Jen Trolio) taught me so much about writing in general.

I owe an immense debt to the writing of Charlie Jane Anders, Gretchen Felker-Martin, Torrey Peters, Hazel Jane Plante, Casey Plett, Alison Rumfitt, Jeanne Thornton, and Emily Zhou. As far as I'm concerned, all trans feminine authors are standing on the shoulders of Imogen Binnie, whose *Nevada* is one of the great American novels.

The stories of Erica, Abigail, Brooke, and even Bernadette are heavily influenced by the lives of trans women I have known, and I owe everyone who shared their story with me an immense debt of gratitude. That goes triply for deep-stealth trans women who trusted me enough to tell me their life stories as I was trying to figure out Brooke's whole deal. The episode of *Donahue* that Brooke watches is real, as is the woman featured in it. Her name is Phyllis Randolph Frye, and the ground she broke for all trans people provided the soil this book grew out of.

Like Erica, my coming-out process was a tortured, nonlinear one. The first person I told who didn't run away screaming was my high school friend Allison, who gave me so much of Megan and Abigail's ride-or-die friendship. The second person was my adult friend Amy, who gave me "Thank you so much for trusting me with you," which, like, five hundred characters say in this book.

I would not be alive without my therapist, Melissa Wasserman.

I have an abundance of family, scattered across time zones, some of whom learned I existed as I wrote this novel. My sister Jill always had my back when we were growing up, and she and her husband, Trent, have always had my back as an adult. My biological siblings Arielle, Brittany, Erik, and Maaike have opened their lives and hearts to me, even though we met and became family as adults. It often feels like they've always been in my life.

Over the course of writing this book, my biological mother, Tamara, and her husband, Dwight, gave me love, guidance, and free babysitting and reminded me that family isn't simply an obligation but something one can choose to practice.

My daughter was born while I was writing this book, and every day, she reveals new wonders to me.

My wife and screenwriting partner, Libby Hill, read every draft of this book, told me when a line of dialogue was all wrong, and gave me thousands of great suggestions on how to explain South Dakota to people who'd never been there. She and I have been together through a dozen iterations of our relationship. I hope we're together through a dozen more.

Finally, the seeds of this book were planted when a glamourous middle-aged woman walked into the trans support group at the Los Angeles LGBT Center and proceeded to have a breakdown over having come out as a teenager in the 1980s, transitioning in secret, then hiding her transness from everyone she had met for over thirty years. She was as desperate for community as I was, a few months into my transition, yet I never saw her again. I hope in some small way, she can feel like a part of this book.

About the Author

Emily St. James is a writer and cultural critic. This is her first novel. Her journalism and criticism have appeared in the *New York Times*, Vox, and The A.V. Club, and her writing for television has been featured on the Emmy-nominated series *Yellowjackets*. She lives in Los Angeles with her family.

Reading Group Guide

1. The novel's title references the act of severing oneself completely from one's past in a bid to create a better future. How do Erica and Abigail's attitudes towards woodworking differ? What does this novel suggest about the pain, as well as the joy, of woodworking successfully?

2. The author employs a black box whenever Erica's dead name is said. Why do you think she chose to do this?

3. The novel is set in 2016, during both a state and federal election. How does the relationship between Isaiah and Helen help us with understanding the broader politics at the heart of the novel?

4. *Woodworking* is a multi-perspective novel. How did the author's use of first-person narration for Abigail and third-person narration for Erica broaden the novel's observations on the stages of transition?

5. We learn about Brooke's story in two of the novel's chapters. How do you feel her perspective added to the author's message? Why do you think she chose to include her voice at all?

6. Brooke, Erica, and Constance are part of a community theatre production of Thomas Wilder's *Our Town*. What parallels can be drawn between the themes of the play and the themes of this novel at large?

7. *Woodworking* was praised for its balanced execution of uplifting and deeply complex, sometimes traumatic, moments. Which parts of the novel do you feel really achieved this?

8. Towards the end of the book, Brooke says that she tried to be a mom for Abigail. Constance says that Erica tried to do the same,

all while Abigail calls herself Erica's "trans mom." How do these women model motherhood for each other?

9. The novel is set in Mitchell, South Dakota, which becomes a character in and of itself. How does the author's choice to set the narrative in this small pocket of Midwest America impact its commentary on identity?

10. Of all the supporting characters in this novel, whose story would you like to learn more about? What do you think they would have to say?

11. In the concluding author's note, the author says that the political landscape for trans people has become far harsher since 2016. What are some of the ways you have noticed this?

12. If you could ask the author one question about this book, what would it be?